De

Welcome to Twilight. No, not *that* Twilight. This is darker, sexier—part thriller, part fantasy, and part fairy tale. It's the realm of In Between, where the land of Death crosses over into the world of the living.

I first read *Shadow Bound* in a writers' contest, and the haunting opening immediately made me sit up and take notice. I knew right away this was a special book. Who was this mysterious Shadowman, so protective and so dangerous all at the same time? How in the world could any woman survive being hunted by a horde of soul-sucking wraiths? What will it take to end the existence of a brother who has now become a twisted monster? Erin Kellison's vivid imagination guarantees that you never know what will happen next.

With ghosts, the fae of the Otherworld, and a little *Sleeping Beauty* thrown in for fun, *Shadow Bound* is a one-of-a-kind debut that takes romance in fantastically new directions.

In fact, we feel so sure that you will fall in love with this book, we're willing to pay a full refund to anyone who doesn't find it everything they want in a paranormal novel. See the back of the book for details on our Publisher's Pledge program.

And now, let's slip

All best,
Leah Hultenschmidt
Editor

WELCOME TO SHADOW

Talia heard Adam's intake of breath as she wrapped the veil around them, the day falling from sunny blue to a dreamy murk. They stood in layered fog, the veils of shadow sensuously lapping at their bodies. The trees, the meadow beyond, the hulk of The Segue Institute were all there, yet somehow appeared transient. As if one good gust of wind might carry it all away.

Adam's hand warmed in hers. He filled her with his wonder, which was better than all the rest. Made her realize how beautiful shadow was, too.

"A little more," he said.

Talia reached, and the day darkened to dusk, the orb of the sun shifting from blazing yellow to deep violet. The world turned to myriad purples and shades of blue and black. Sounds stretched so that the birds' twitters and crickets' chirps became high, eerie notes warped by darkness. Shadow settled on her shoulders and slid deliciously against her skin in welcome.

Adam's wonder turned to awe and building excitement.

Talia glanced at him to see how much of what he felt could be read on his face.

He looked down at her, about to say something, but instead he stopped and stared. That sensation was back, a trickle in the sense of his discovery, then a flood blotting it out. Desire.

ERIN KELLISON

SHADOW BOUND

LEISURE BOOKS NEW YORK CITY

A LEISURE BOOK®

July 2010

Published by

Dorchester Publishing Co., Inc.
200 Madison Avenue
New York, NY 10016

ISBN 10: 0-505-52829-0
ISBN 13: 978-0-505-52829-2
E-ISBN: 978-1-4285-0890-3

Visit us online at www.dorchesterpub.com.

To Matt
all my heart
ox

ACKNOWLEDGMENTS

Tremendous thanks to Leah Hultenschmidt, my editor, for her support and enthusiasm. To Alicia Condon, who made that incredible call one January morning. And to Jessica Faust, my agent, for her expert counsel and a whirlwind week I'll never forget. Thank you to my husband, Matt, for kicking all obstacles out of the way and reading every word of every version so carefully. To Mom and Dad for love and support, to my awesome sister Deborah, with whom I learned to write, and to the rest of my family for their encouragement and excellent humor. Thanks to Brian Anderson, for his detailed information on weapons and tactical situations. Any mistakes are mine. And of course, to my GNO girls, Jill, Jen, and Jeni. And finally, to my critique partners and the wonderful writers of WriteSpot: Julie Ellis, Jo Gregory, Kathleen Grieve, Tes Hilaire, jj Keller, KC Klein, Lynnette Labelle, Theresa Sallach, Jenn Thor, and Dee Ann Williamson, and to my fantastic beta readers, Kris Tualla and Nora Needham.

SHADOW BOUND

PROLOGUE

A light in deepest Shadow.

The fae lord pulled his cloak around his face to dampen the intensity of the glow. *Futile.* The woman was still there, in his mind, shining like molten gold. The heat of her soul-fire penetrated the veils between the mortal world and Twilight and slid across his skin in a caress. She, the sun, powerful enough to quicken even him.

From his dark vantage, he peered into her room. Her bed was made, pillow undented. He'd come too early to ride the rough waves of her dreams, to mellow her sharp knocks of pain and worry so that she could rest. He'd done as much since she was a child. It pleased him that the detritus of the sickroom huddled in a corner, unused. Oxygen in a tank. Machines dozing, their cords wrapped and waiting.

She sat on a stool in front of her easel, brush in hand, facing into a deep triangle of darkness cut away by the fall of light from the bedside lamp. She gazed into his Shadow world, just as he marveled at hers. On the canvas before her, she painted a fairy-tale landscape: lush hills lit by star shine, a border of black forest, and the wide gray sea beyond.

Her heart hitched, and the veils between them thinned as her time drew near. He both welcomed and braced against the sudden ache of her pain as it echoed through him—something of *her* to feel.

She paused for breath, hands falling to her knees. The tip of the brush made a drop of green on the skirt of her dress. He wondered at her strength of will as she gritted her teeth and forced her body back into a steady rhythm. Strange how she clung so fiercely to life, yet bent her skill to an image of Twilight.

He crept closer, into the variegated grays of her room, until he could just catch the scent of her—the bright smells that danced on her skin and clung to her hair, the musk of the paint on her fingers that never quite washed away, and something denser, darker, that was woman and mortal.

He sensed her grim resolve, tainted by desperation, in a concentration of spirit that kept her young heart beating, commanding its exercise long enough for her to embrace life, to make something that would last, a legacy of herself to the world. Though her emotion coursed over him like a wild river, he could not unravel her structured thoughts, the building blocks of her intellect, of motivation and creation as she changed her world in ways both subtle and great. Such was the beauty and power of mortality. If she only knew.

She mastered herself. Picked up her brush, put tip to canvas, then paused, head tilting.

"Are you there?" she called, her voice barely above a whisper.

Her sister was in a room beyond, out of earshot, staring into a silver window of moving lights and laughter.

"I know you're there," she said, though she regarded her painting. Her brush resumed its stroke. "You might as well come out and talk to me for once."

So. She seeks me. It's come to that at last, and yet, still too soon. A small flame sparked to life in his chest, but he forced himself to pull back into Shadow, drawing his cloak around his shoulders.

She sighed. "I didn't mean to scare you."

She paused again to scan the room, her gaze touching on this corner and that empty chair, glancing off him, only to peer more keenly into the deepening grays to her other side.

She laughed, short and full of irony. "Fancy *you* being afraid of *me*. That's got to be a first."

Indeed. Most cowered from the very idea of him. Not her.

"And after all this time we've spent together. Well, not exactly *together*, but you know what I mean. I wish we could talk for once. But then, I suppose it won't be long before we meet. There will be more than enough time after."

Not true. She would pass through Twilight but briefly before moving on to the next world. Twilight was merely the boundary. She could not bide there long, no matter how he tried to delay her passage. And he would. He could not let her pass by him like a guttering candle at the end of its wick. Not his Bright Light.

Darkness lay heavy on his back, and he itched to cast his cloak away. Already she was aware of him. And her painting was proof that her view of Twilight was nigh unobstructed.

What harm could come of it, really? If he could not keep her long in Twilight, perhaps he might steal a moment here. *Now.*

Rending a thin layer of veil, the last remaining before her crossing, he stepped out of Twilight and into the half shadows of her room. Scents of the mortal world crowded around him, too many to discern individually. Except for her. She filled him with a single breath.

Her gaze darted to him. The brush fell to the floor. Her skin, already pale, washed white. Her eyes blinked like butterfly wings, blue-ringed indigo and fringed with curling black.

"Hush," he said, reaching out a down-turned hand to calm the sudden shock and surprise that stopped her breath.

Her eyes filled with tears as she took in his presence, her

mind working its mortal power to shape his form according to her soul's deepest conception of what he would be. It did not change his essence; now and forever he would be the Final Courier. The Ultimate Host. Captain of the small boat that would carry her from the mortal world, across the waters of Twilight, and release her on the shore beyond.

But the *form* he took—that was in her keeping. If mortals only knew the power they wielded, they could reshape the three worlds with a thought. Perhaps one day they would.

What did she see when she looked at him at last? A nightmare concocted of fear, aged beyond reckoning and grotesque? It happened like that quite often. Those whose dread of the dark passage created a terror out of the ether, shaping him with their minds into a being bent on horror.

No. She did not fear time or Death. She did not tremble as he advanced closer to her. As he stepped forward to view her painting.

She'd gotten some things wrong: The black forest was darker, dark as pitch, and as inky as abject fear. She'd missed, too, the pillar of smoke that rose in the center from the fire of rage. But *he* was there, crouched in the foreground, a figure wrapped in gray wind. Storm wind. The kind that harries or hinders, a force unto itself. She'd caught *that* exactly, but she did not depict his face.

What did she see? The question pricked him.

"Is it a good likeness?" Anxiety pitched her voice high.

He shifted his gaze to her. "Yes."

She inhaled deeply, tamping down her emotion. "What is beyond the sea?"

He contemplated that often himself. "I don't know. I can't go there."

"But I will."

It wasn't a question, but he nodded a confirmation anyway. She brushed her tears away with a wrist. Then she held a slightly trembling hand to him. "I'm Kathleen O'Brien. Nice to finally meet you in person."

Ah, a friend, then. A companion. That was good. He did not know if he could bear it if she feared him. If she saw him as a monster.

He knew the custom, had witnessed it for a millennia or more, but still he wondered as he reached out his own hand and grasped hers in a slow slide of Twilight and mortal skin. She was warm, soft, and for all her frailty, as strong as the tide. Her heartbeat reached to the end of her fingertips and stirred something alien in him. *Curious.*

She drew a careful breath. "And what's yours?"

He'd been called many things over the years, but all those he rejected. He would not have *those* names formed by her lips. "I don't have one."

"Everyone has a name."

"Then I've forgotten it. Pick another for me. I swear I won't forget again." He laid himself open to her, waiting for the word that would name his soul, the sound of her claim on him.

A slow smile bloomed across her face, delight washing away the last of her unease. For that alone, trespassing the boundary had been worth it, come what may.

"I've been calling you Shadowman for, well . . . forever."

"Then I am Shadowman forever."

She kept his hand. He did not release hers. They were anchored together yet adrift. Kindred spirits from different worlds.

The light in her spirit darkened. "Is it time?"

"No. Not now." He skimmed his mind along the shimmering veil. The membrane was thin, but still impenetrable for a mortal. "Not today, I think."

Creases formed between her brows as she frowned. "I'm not sure that I am ready to go, but I am tired of waiting."

He smiled slightly. Impatience was a universal trait for mortals. For them everything had a beginning and an end, like fixed points in a landscape of life, and that knowledge incited a persistent expectation of what was to come. Not so in Twilight, where everything stretched in-between and time was something Twilight folk wove into their midnight music.

"Do you know when?"

"I don't. No one can know that. Would you really want to?"

Her gaze darted up, forehead tight.

"No. And yes. I want to know—or, or understand *something*. I've been sick my whole life. What is the point of being alive if I never get to live? I want—" Her words choked off. She took another steadying breath. "I guess I just want a reason."

Riding through her body, down her arm, across her fingertips and into his hand—frustration and loneliness. Almost unbearable. Certainly unacceptable.

"There is no reason for beauty. It just is." Scant comfort, he knew. "Perhaps you will find a better answer in the next world." He raised his hand to the horizon line on her painting. "In the world beyond the sea."

"And you can't go there?"

"Just you. The faerie are forbidden."

"So this is it." She turned back, eyes shimmering with fresh pain. "This is all the time I get?"

He inclined his head in answer, but slightly, carefully. He did not know precisely what she meant, so he could not agree in totality. Not with that strange light shining in her eyes. Not with the alien intent that coursed out of her and into him, the velvety longing that gathered in his gut.

"Touch me," she said, suddenly. "I mean—will you?"

Then, not a friend. Or, not only a friend. *What did she see?*

She stood, her body a breath before his. "I want to feel something real while I can. You've been there all my life, waiting. Just out of sight. I'd hoped that we were . . . that you and I . . ." She dropped her gaze, shaking her head in frustration.

You and I. Yes. Nothing else was necessary; she'd captured the truth in a marriage of words that had power on any side of the veil.

He felt her will harden inside her, and she slowly raised her head to meet his gaze. "Please touch me."

No. Being in this room, speaking thus, already broke the laws of Twilight. There would be repercussions as it was. But her heart pounded in his head, pushing out all thought. Heat rose in his chest. He searched blindly with his mind for the coolness of Shadow. He should not have come here; the laws of Twilight existed for a reason. He understood that now.

"Shadowman."

The sound of his name stopped him short.

She released his hand, reached up to his face, and dipped into his dark hood. Finding his cheek, she drew back just enough to skim her fingertips over his lips.

"I cannot do this," he said. He should remove himself from her reach at once and draw the fae shadows tightly round his shoulders. Never come here again. He'd meet her in Twilight, perhaps soon, and that would have to be enough.

Yet he turned his face into her palm, her soft skin burning away the last of his resolve. Her mortal will was stronger than any he could marshal.

He could not pinpoint the moment he fell—perhaps when he first stepped out of Shadow. Or in that breath drawn to shape the sound of his first word, *hush.* Or years before when he came to watch her from his dim vantage when he had no call to do so.

"Shadowman?"

But he was lost now, bending his head, tasting her lips for

the first time. The dark, wet wine of her mouth, sweeter than anything on any world or in-between. One taste, one deep drink, and then he'd go.

Her heart beat strongly, thudding over the bridge that they'd created. Hardly weak. Perhaps if he touched her like this she might live forever.

He pulled away and the loss of her hollowed him out. "There are laws that even you must know, deep inside, should not be broken."

"I don't care. I've been *careful* too damn long."

Only a mortal could be so brave. They know an end will come and so, too, a new beginning. But for an immortal, the repercussions were simple and never finite. She had no idea.

"You said it yourself," she insisted. "It will not be today. Maybe tomorrow or the day after, but I have *right now*. Can you understand?"

"Kathleen . . ." His argument died on his lips. He'd never said her name before.

"You've been there all my life making the worst better, the most frightening moments easier. Why? You have to love me."

"I do." *Beyond reason.*

She stilled, her breath suppressed, waiting for a flicker of hope from him. For *him*. Incomprehensible.

How did mortals bear it? In the space of a single lift and fall of her lashes, he was done with waiting. To lie down with her, Kathleen, to be able to pierce the darkness with light just once, he would dare anything. There was no penalty that could mitigate the need. No retribution that he had not already paid in the dark corners of her room, waiting.

If the tightness that gathered in his gut, complaining to touch her, to meld his body to hers, if that was what men called passion, then he could do this thing. Pour himself inside her. Give and take a moment of that beauty.

And *yes!*—he understood it now—time *was* short. Her impatience was a catching thing. He'd been here but moments and already a nagging current of it tainted his blood, itching under his fingertips.

He brought a hand to the cotton of her skirt just below her waist. The fabric was coarse to his touch, nothing like the silks on his side of the boundary that poorly mimicked the fall and function of mortal cloth. This had weight—the strange magic of mass. Slight though it was, the cloth required physical effort to draw it upward in a miracle of movement that stirred the air and carried a sweet, dark scent off her skin. Without this form, this gift of a body, he could not have done it.

Kathleen. Her power was formidable, indeed. Dangerously so. *Bid me come, and here I am. Shape my being, and for a short time I can move mortal air in and out of my chest. Ask me to love you, Bright Light, and you make real a dream-giver's deepest desire.*

She quivered when he lifted her dress, but she raised her arms to let it pass easily over her head. The skin beneath was pure white. It had seen so little sun. He dismissed his dark cloak, which lifted like smoke off his body. For the first time, his dusky skin born of Twilight was revealed entirely.

Her lips parted, but the thought that sparked in her mind never took structured form.

What did she see? Did she fear him at last?

He glanced down, following her line of sight.

She'd made him a man. Strong and well formed, aroused and wanting, if such a thing were possible. How much was her desire and how much his, he did not know. He did not care. All that mattered was that some mortal magic had conspired to enable him to love her.

"You're beautiful," she said, her color pinked.

A smile twitched at his mouth. She should know; she'd shaped him from her own fantasies.

His hand moved up the long line of her arm to the bend in her elbow, the secret tuck of sensitive skin. A rainbow of sensation spread through her and echoed through him. No one had touched her like this before. Just him. Just this once.

"My sister . . ." she began.

". . . is asleep and will remain so for the rest of the night."

She bit her bottom lip; it flooded with color. Red, intoxicating. Taking his hands, she pulled him to the bed. She shed the rest of her clothes and shifted her hips onto the side.

For all her daring, her trembling redoubled. The last thing he wanted was fear between them. His existence was influenced too much by that already. He wanted only light. Only Kathleen. He covered her body with his, bracing his elbows on either side of her head. He wiped away the tears that quickly gathered and fell off her cheeks with his thumbs. Wet and wonderful.

"Hush, now," he said again.

A curl of fear whipped up inside of her to sting him. "Can you show me how to go? I don't know . . ."

He grinned. "I don't know either."

"So we just . . ." she began.

". . . love each other, I think." Before her fear could grow, he bent his head to kiss her again. He did not know the niceties of the act, but that seemed insignificant. He reveled in her mouth, warm and lush. Given to him freely.

Her fingers laced into the hair at his nape, her courage rising.

She lifted her chin to his kiss and wrapped a leg around his body to stroke him in a long caress that reached from his hip to his calf. He shuddered. She laughed low and throaty against his mouth. Alive.

He settled himself in the sweet valley of her body, hands molding her, setting each nerve singing. He took the cherry of her nipple in his mouth and suckled like a babe. Born to her, to himself, to this world at last. Her hands gripped his hair by the roots, holding him in place.

Not necessary. He couldn't move if he wanted to. *Well, perhaps to attend the other one.* And the hollow at her neck, and then down again to the smooth plane of her belly. Below that his thoughts fragmented into senseless feeling. Her hands tangled loosely in his hair, fluttering at his crown while he bowed to hers.

One moment they arched, pelvis to pelvis, the next moment he was inside her. There was pain on both sides, his an echo of hers, but soon forgotten in a welling of intense pleasure, of suffused senses weeping in carnal delight.

A drum set up in his chest, then fell lower into a mindless place. A place that was all dark, hot sensation. Greedy to give. The drum beat an old rhythm, older than even he, underscoring the melody of her sighs. Her desire set the pace for his, led it and drove it until his body answered hers beat for beat.

He moved like the ocean, pushed by forces within and without, by the moon and stars and deep black of space, by some nameless power men somehow knew, but he, for all his aged wisdom, did not.

He explored the subtle rise and dip of her hips, the swell of her breasts. He poured himself over her body like a flood just bursting its dam. Water rushing to fill, to leave no dark place unquickened.

It was the kind of water that gave, and when the storm was over, he knew he left some small part of himself inside her. Yet he remained undiminished. If anything, he was augmented, bearing a knowledge that was hot and sweet, a single incandescent thought burned into being: Kathleen.

He cradled her close with his back to the bed; she curled into his side, leg carelessly draped over his. The scent of mingled waters hung in the air.

From the dark corners of the room, Shadow seeped out to grasp him, to bind him, to carry him back across. No wonder this world made him a monster. The deepening shadows—his place of power—seemed a menace to *him* now.

A lick of frigid blackness slid around his ankle. With his mind, he pushed the Shadow away with vehemence. It held firm and scrolled up his leg.

They had little time left together, he and his beloved, floating softly on an echo of pleasure.

Except they weren't alone. Something else had sparked into being and glimmered in his mind's eye. He reached between them to find the source.

There. An unsettled spark.

"Something is happening," he said, touching her lower abdomen.

Her eyes rounded. She lifted her head to check her naked belly, then shifted her gaze to his face. "What do you mean?"

"I don't know. A life maybe. I don't know much about that." A lash of darkness twisted up his other leg. He could feel himself beginning to come apart. It was near impossible to hold his form long in mortality. "Be still while I try to stop it. I don't have much time left."

"No," she breathed, her hand drawn protectively to the spot. "No." She pulled away from him, sliding off the bed to stand at the brink of threatening blackness.

He reached out to her. "I don't know what it is. What it

will be." A spark could turn into a fire, and a fire can become a changing force of nature. When her resolve didn't falter, he added, "I don't know if it *should* be."

"If it shouldn't, then why is it happening?"

"I broke a law to be here. And more to be with you like this. I've lost count how many, and I don't care. But this . . . this could be the beginning of the repercussions." The thought had him by the throat: It was one thing for him to endure the effects of his trespass, but for her to bear them, his lovely Kathleen, alone, that was intolerable. He had to end it.

"No," she said.

Grasping darkness inked up his body. No *time*. "Kathleen, you can't know what it is. Or what it will cost."

"I don't care. It's ours. Yours and mine together," she answered. She met his outstretched hand and flattened it on her pelvis.

He could quash the spark now, be done with it. But her heart stuttered, stopping him. Her eyes filled with new hope, a world's worth of hope, her smile struggling with a painful joy.

"You don't understand," he said. And he did not have the time to convince her. Something terrible would come of this. Her happiness had to come at a price. A darkness born to match that glimmering spark. He should not have come, yet could not regret it either.

"I do, too. More than you." She pressed the back of his hand. "We're making something. Something of us."

The spirit in her eyes never burned brighter. He could not bring himself to diminish it. He tried another tack. "You may not have the time to see it through as it is."

"I will."

Her conviction staggered him. "Kathleen, even now your heart falters."

She met his eyes while taking a deep, controlled breath. "I only need nine months. Nine months is nothing. They've been telling me that I only have six for years."

"Kathleen. Love," he said, his voice rough, near breaking. He gathered her to him, speaking into her eyes. "Neither of us knows what time you have. Better to end it now. I may be back for you with the sun."

"You won't."

"I have no power over this, Kathleen." And no power to fight what must surely accompany the life she prized. He caressed the length of her arm for the last time.

"You defied the laws. Now watch me do it."

"Kathleen . . ." He could not stop saying her name. He didn't want to, not as he felt himself unraveling into the icy darkness. His substance dissolved into the chiaroscuro of Twilight, while his Shadow-bred senses reached toward mortality.

The spark. Her joy blooming within her.

And, yes, in a weak film clinging to the corners of the room: a smudge of black spit on the world, to grow and thrive, a horror to match her miracle.

Kathleen! Something terrible, indeed.

ONE

Aᴅᴀᴍ Thorne took the graveyard shift at Jacob's cell.

He was wired with jet lag anyway, his circadian rhythms lagging somewhere over the Atlantic. He'd be right as rain in Korea, where he'd spent the last three weeks following up on a lead with the mystics on Mount Inwangsan. But in the Appalachian Mountains of West Virginia, in a concrete hole under The Segue Institute, his body did not know if it was night, day, or some strange time zone in between.

Scrubbing a hand over his face, he tried to focus on the keypad next to the outer security door. Hot lightning burned across the whites of his eyes, and his face had roughened behind twenty-four hours of growth. A bottle of pills promised to take him out for eight hours, but the sleep would be poor at best if he didn't check in with Jacob first. Do his own time, albeit on the other side of the prison door.

Adam coded into the security room. A slight smell of rot hit him as the steel-reinforced door slid open. He frowned and braced inwardly. With a jerk of his head, he dismissed the guard, wondering how the man withstood the constant funk up his nose.

Signing on to the master security console, Adam caught a glimpse of Jacob in the video monitor: he lay on his side, arms wrapped around his naked belly as if to ward off cold or in an expression of acute modesty. He'd once chaired the board of

Thorne Industries. Now he was cornered like a lab animal in a sterile white box. Overly thin and pale, Jacob was frightening only in the sense that no human being should ever be caged and starved like he'd been for the last six years. But then, Adam didn't think Jacob was human anymore.

Adam dropped four inches of files on the console before him. Might as well get some work in before he crashed.

It always amazed him how so little progress could generate so much work. He picked up the first file and opened the manila folder. A detailed spreadsheet of numbers blurred before his eyes. *Budget can wait.* He closed the file again and exchanged it for another. Inside was a stack of papers so thick as to require a rubber band to hold them together. A Post-it was stuck to the top.

I thought this might interest you. ~C.

Celia Eubanks was a research fellow at Johns Hopkins and an old family friend. He focused on the text of the document, titled, *An examination of common motifs described in near-death experiences,* by Talia Kathleen O'Brien.

Near-death. *That* wouldn't do him any good.

A shuffle hissed out of the speakers in the console. Jacob was moving in there.

"Ho, Adam. Good to have you back." The voice was nonchalant and familiar at the same time, coming in crystal clear over the monitor.

Adam ignored Jacob. Early on they'd attempted to test how he knew who was beyond his cell walls, each a foot-thick plane of reinforced steel, to determine which of his senses exceeded human parameters and by how much, but Jacob had caught on and started messing with their data.

Adam scanned the 316 pages of Ms. Talia O'Brien's dissertation. Dense text filled the pages, broken up by a chart or two. Deep reading. She could have chosen a larger point size for the font. He'd be blind before the end.

"You could answer me. Our mother taught you better manners than that," Jacob said in his usual condescending tone.

Mom would be weeping for both of us.

Adam forced his concentration away from Jacob and into chapter one, the section where Ms. O'Brien laid out her theory and her method of analysis. He liked the way her mind worked, her odd angle of inquiry. She did not assume near-death experiences were real, but neither did she suggest they were false. She positioned herself outside the stories and looked for common threads. She noted patterns between them to analyze how the living conceived of death, and not death itself. Death as a concept, an idea entertained by a subconscious grappling with mortality.

"Adam, it's just that I am so hungry, I can't even think. I may be ready to try some soup. Or a sandwich. What do you think? Just a little bite to give me something to go on."

You don't want a sandwich, Jacob. You don't even remember what to do with one. You just want the person who brings it to you, even if it is your own brother.

But any kind of dialogue with the thing that had his older brother's face and memories would be pointless. Whatever came out of his mouth since his *change* was a manipulation of the truth, contrived to keep Adam in hell. Nothing to learn there.

Adam focused on the study. Chapter two related the author's interactions with her sources. She'd managed to get a wide age range, which was laudable. Selected experiences had been transcribed and included in an appendix. Real work went into this.

Life after death.

Adam frowned. He hadn't pursued this approach; perhaps it was time he did. And this—he flipped to the front—*Talia O'Brien* came at the subject from a neatly objective point of view. He'd have to check her out. See if she was safe to come on staff at Segue.

"God, Adam, I don't know why you have to be such a shit about this. All I want is a sandwich. You could at least answer me. Answer me, goddamn it!"

Adam flipped through the dissertation, past her analysis, to her conclusions. Something caught his eye, made his stomach tighten. He skimmed back again. *There.* On the bottom of page sixty-nine. Footnote 3b. A source claimed to have met an individual named Shadowman.

A memory stirred, a long-ago rant from a gleeful Jacob, his eyes bright and wild, voice shrill. "*Shadowman* can't reach me!"

Jacob's face had been bloody, their father limp on the floor at his feet.

Adam braced against the flood of pain the recollection triggered and stuffed the vision back in the small box in his head. Shut it. Tight.

He blinked hard to restore his normal sight, shook off the heat that had suddenly slicked his skin, and forced a cleansing breath.

In the intervening years, he'd searched the name Shadowman exhaustively, attempted to question (and goad) Jacob further, but had come up with nothing. Nothing.

Until now.

Adam's heart hit his throat. *Shadowman.* Ms. O'Brien's source had conversed with him, and Shadowman had returned her from death back to mortal life.

I'll be damned. The Shadowman.

A strange sensation welled up in him, pushing at his chest, buzzing in his mind.

Near-death experiences. He should have thought of it before. Incredible lapse of imagination on his part. Here he'd been consulting wiccans, shamans, and holy men.

Adam pulled his mobile phone from his pocket. "Custo.

Track down Ms. Talia O'Brien. PhD student. No—she's probably been awarded her doctorate by now, out of—" he turned to the title page—"University of Maryland. I expect she's got an offer and is teaching somewhere. Her field—damn, she's covered just about everything—but try sociology, anthropology, psychiatry perhaps. Find out what you can about her. Use whatever resources you deem necessary."

"I'll get right on it. Any particular reason you're interested?"

"For starters, her work is outstanding. You've got to read her dissertation. Tonight, if possible. I'll leave a copy on your desk. Let me know when you've located her." Adam had to get to the plane. Frantic energy coursed through his veins.

"Must be good. You haven't sounded this excited since . . . well, in years."

"You will be, too. Read all the footnotes, and you'll see." Adam ended the call and stooped to pick up his files. Budget would just have to come with him.

"Talia O'Brien." Jacob drew the name out. "Sounds uptight to me, Bro. More my type than yours."

Adam glanced into the monitor. Jacob was on his feet, face belligerently in the camera.

"I know what to do with her," Jacob said with a grin. He licked his teeth in a gross parody of lust or hunger. Probably both.

"But I found her first," Adam murmured, turning away. He buzzed for the guard.

Behind him the room shuddered. Adam knew the sound: Jacob kicking at the cell door. Pray to God the reinforced steel held. An unearthly screech followed. Six years and it still raised the hair at Adam's nape. No bullet or blade could stop that monster.

Talia O'Brien.

Maybe she could help him kill his brother.

TWO

THE silk of Talia's interview blouse slid beneath her fingers in a sigh of delight, but she didn't have time to linger. Her gaze flicked to her bedside alarm clock. 4:12 P.M. Her flight left in a little under three hours, and she'd only marked off half the items on her pretrip list.

White blouse, check.

Warped male laughter filtered through her bedroom wall from the apartment next door. Tuesday night. Right about now, the guys would be getting high for band practice. On cue, a bass guitar bellowed an accusatory, *boo, dop, boo, dop-dow.* Made the framed painting of one of her mother's fairy-tale landscapes buzz. Made her teeth buzz, too.

Well, she wouldn't have to put up with it for much longer.

Talia glided the blouse over her interview suit to latch at the hanger clip of a brand-new suitcase. Just looking at the clothes made her heartbeat skip. Including shoes, panty hose, slip, and two coordinated blouses, the ensemble cost her nearly a month's rent. On sale. But she didn't begrudge the expense a bit, not if she got the assistant professor position at UC–Berkeley.

Please, God, let me get this job. Talia's silent prayer had been going around in her mind and accelerating her heart to near bursting since she'd received the invitation to visit

Berkeley for in-person interviews. *Please, pretty please, God. Just this one little favor . . .*

"Knock knock."

Talia turned to find her roommate Melanie at her door.

Oh hell. What now? The last thing Talia needed was a fight right before she had to leave. Tension climbed the ladder of her spine while the electric guitar next door squealed a chaos of rapid notes.

From her sleek, side-swept coif to her pointy heels, Melanie managed an urban sophistication on a student budget. She already had job offers, and she still had a semester to go on her advanced business degree. A perfectly plucked eyebrow arched as she brought up a hand holding a thick gold bar of Godiva hazelnut chocolate. Sweet heaven and rich, delicious sin wrapped in gold foil.

"Peace offering," Melanie yelled over the band's noise.

"Thanks." Talia took the bar, careful not to touch Melanie skin to skin and be flooded with her negative emotional backwash. Talia forced a smile. She hoped the smile looked more natural than it felt. Melanie had been bitchy from the moment Talia moved in eight months ago. But the rent and location had been too good to move again.

"It's for after the interview, to celebrate," Melanie clarified. "I should have congratulated you when you defended your dissertation. It was shitty of me not to, so I'm sorry. I really wish you the best of luck. So . . . congratulations Dr. O'Brien."

The music cut off at *congratulations*. The shouted *Dr.* that followed did wonders for Talia's mood. Suddenly she could forgive anything. All her work was going to pay off. Not with money—not in the more esoteric social sciences. But soon—*please, God*—soon she'd have a great job at a reputable university.

Papers, publishing, grants. Oh, my.

Then her own apartment, though rent was astronomical near the Berkeley campus. No roommates, Melanie's sudden goodwill notwithstanding, but maybe friends. Who knows? If she were very, very good she might get a real life. She might even pass for *normal.* Okay, that was stretching the fantasy a bit. She'd settle for inconspicuous.

"Why don't we break it open and make the declaration of peace official?" Talia said. Just one square would go a long way toward calming her nerves.

"No. It's for after the interview." Melanie waved away the bar and stepped back over the threshold.

Okay, then. Girl bonding over. But this was nice. Ending on a good note.

Talia tucked the chocolate into her carry-on. No way on earth that delicious bar would survive the wait in the airport, much less until tomorrow evening when the Berkeley interviews, student panel, and campus tour were finally finished.

A new pounding bounced through the apartment. Talia frowned. The persistent thudding did not come from the band next door. It wasn't quite obnoxious enough, but close.

"It's the front door," Melanie said. "I'll get it. You finish packing."

"Thanks again. This was really sweet." But she was already gone. Probably the last time they'd talk, what with the semester winding down to graduation.

Talia turned back to her list. *White blouse, check. Camisole . . .*

Broken words filtered down the hallway. An unfamiliar woman's voice dominated, but a low rumble suggested a man was there, too. Talia tilted her head and listened.

"Who did you say you were?" Melanie's tone hardened with irritation. She was good at that.

Talia stepped forward and peeked down the hall. Melanie gripped the doorknob and was trying to shut the door in their faces, which was rude in the extreme, even from her. Her body rigid with attention, she planted her foot to block the door from opening more.

Something was wrong.

"Well, she's not here. She studies at the library on Tuesday nights to get away from the band noise, but I'll tell her you stopped by."

Talia kept back, waiting a beat. No point in spoiling the lie. Whoever it was should be on their way shortly.

The woman spoke again, but was cut off by a sudden rise in distorted music. Talia strained, but she couldn't make out any words. The band stopped just as abruptly, the drums dribbling down to a halfhearted *smack-rat-tap*.

"No, you can't come in," Melanie snapped. "I said she's not here."

A loud crack from the front of the apartment jerked Talia's heart in her chest. She dropped her notepad and darted down the hall.

The front door stood gaping. Melanie lay twisted on the floor in the center of the room, pushing herself up to a pained crawl. The man and woman were just stepping inside the apartment. He kicked the door closed and then leaned up against it, while she scanned the room, lips pressed into an unfriendly smile.

Talia went cold.

Melanie looked up at her from the floor. "They want to see Talia."

"She's not here," Talia echoed. The wide, frightened look in Melanie's usually confident eyes made Talia both enormously grateful and nauseated. Her roommate could have just as easily pointed a finger and been done with this. But then again, Melanie didn't let anyone bully her.

Melanie stood, eyes narrowing as her spine straightened again.

Talia caught the question in her roommate's expression— *You know them?*—and returned a shallow shake, *No.*

Talia had no idea who these people were. They were young, probably midtwenties. The woman was tall and sleek, with rich, dark hair and ample breasts, but an unfortunate lantern jaw. The guy, leaning against the door, was short and square, his shape accentuated by pleated dress slacks and a tucked polo. He sported an outdated side part like a news anchor from the eighties. The two were incongruous, unlikely partners, but for the similar flatness of their eyes and unforgiving lines of their mouths.

"We can wait," the woman said, seeming at her leisure in their apartment.

Goose bumps spread across Talia's scalp and pricked down her spine. She swallowed. "Why do you want her anyway?"

"We're her ride. She has a date tonight," she said.

Talia had no dates. Not now, not ever. Guys picked up on her weirdness instantly and kept away. And the thought of getting physical, of letting someone touch her . . . *No.* Her only companionship was books.

The tall, slick woman stepped closer, leaning into her to closely inspect Talia's features before moving away. The smell coming from her was beyond foul. The assessment in the woman's eyes was calculating, cruel, and searching.

Instinctively, Talia backed into the shadows. The grays slipped around her body like silk veils, cold but always comforting. The room darkened. Others might have passed it off as a trick of light or a dimming bulb, but she knew better. Enough to try to control her fear and push the gathering shadows back. It had been a long time since she'd lost control. With effort, she shrugged off the dark again.

The best place to hide was always in plain sight.

"I think you have the wrong person," Melanie said. "I'm her roommate, and I know for a fact that she is not dating anyone right now."

"Talia O'Brien, age twenty-six. PhD in anthropology. Her mother was Kathleen O'Brien, died at Talia's birth from complications due to a congenital heart defect. Raised by her aunt Margaret, also deceased," the tall man recited.

Guilt and regret stirred to life within Talia over her mother, mixing with the loss of Aunt Maggie. Aunt Maggie who had died in the car accident while Talia crept unwillingly back to life and health, alone in the world at fifteen.

The band's noise spiraled up again to deafening.

For the memory of Aunt Maggie, Talia swallowed her fear and forced her voice over the music. "Is this a joke? 'Cause it's not funny."

The tall woman smiled over her shoulder. "No joke." She lifted a plucked brow. "You know, you have very unusual eyes."

Talia felt speared like an insect under examination. She hated when people remarked on her appearance, her eyes in particular. *Exotic*, Aunt Maggie had said once. But *exotic* was too generous. *Strange* would be more accurate. They tipped up a little too much at the outside. And the color had a habit of shifting with her moods. Right now they'd be as dark as her shadow.

The woman gave her a raking once-over. "What did you say your name was?"

I didn't.

In her peripheral vision, Talia saw Mel reach down to the phone. "I've had enough of this," she bit out loudly. "If this *is* some kind of shitty practical joke . . ."

Talia knew it wasn't. This was her deepest fear realized. These horrible people knew she was different, and they were going to ruin everything. She would never find a place to belong. Not at a university. Not anywhere. Not even when all she wanted to do was bury her nose in books and bother no one.

Talia saw Melanie's finger press *9-1-1*. Help seemed ridiculous. No screaming sirens could reach them in time. Anything beyond the apartment door was worlds too far away.

In a single blink, the square man was at Mel's side. He knocked the phone out of her hand, caught the receiver, and replaced it on the cradle. He twitched his other hand out and caught Melanie around her neck.

His mouth formed the words, "None of that," though his voice was buried in noise.

Melanie kicked out and thrashed with her arms as her face reddened.

Oh, no. Oh, please . . . Talia started forward, pushing against the rise in the band's rock.

"Let her go. I'm Talia O'Brien," she yelled, clasping the man's wrist to pull it away from Melanie's throat. Sickness inundated her, intense and thick, as if her belly were filling up with hot tar. He felt rank, malevolent, and vicious.

Talia craned her head back to the man's partner. "Tell him to stop."

The woman smiled with edged condescension. "Ms. O'Brien. It's my honor to serve you. My master sends his regards and looks forward to meeting you in person." She turned to her companion. "Finish that one quickly, Grady. We need to get going."

Grady lifted Melanie off the floor.

"Stop it!" The room was getting darker, but Talia couldn't help it. "Put her down!" Melanie was almost purple. "Please let her go. I'll do whatever you want."

"You'll do that anyway," the woman answered. "And Grady's hungry. If he doesn't eat now, he'll be pestering me all the way back to stop for a little human takeout. And I can't have that."

Melanie's eyes flickered back in her head like some kind of waking REM.

Talia looped her arms over Grady's outstretched one and put her weight into pulling them both down. He would not budge. He smiled at her efforts. She kicked at him. He seemed flesh enough, but he reacted like stone.

The woman grabbed Talia's shoulder and pulled her away with such unexpected strength that Talia stumbled backward.

"You can't hurt him," the woman said, "it's useless to try."

Talia swiped at the tears of frustration blurring her vision. *Please let this be a nightmare.*

Then Grady opened his mouth. Opened and opened beyond anything human. He bared his teeth, all sharply pointed and strangely extended, and pulled Melanie toward him. Mouth clamped over mouth.

Talia froze midbreath in horror. She felt a tug in her gut. A tug from a well of life and soul. Not hers, still seated snugly in her body. But an echo of Melanie's *self* being ripped out, fed upon in a desecration of spirit that scored Talia's mind and heart.

Utter blackness fell as Talia screamed.

The dark didn't hide anything from her. It never had. Shadows only deepened color, and textures took on added dimension. Total darkness revealed a realm of sensation as seductive and terrifying as any fertile imagination could conjure.

So she witnessed it all.

Her scream was edged with a strange power, burning up her throat to rend the world. It ripped the dark shadows of her shelter, shredding the layers of her protection into wisps of smoke that quivered as if harried by turbulent, angry wind. The shape that came out of the wind, emerging from the center of the hell storm, was darkness incarnate, monstrous eyes glowing with purpose. He could only be Death, the heartless devil who'd taken both her mother and her aunt. He was shaped like a man, wrapped in an absence of light, and therefore readily visible to her. He grasped a glittering arched blade. Already twisting in the air, the scythe came down.

The blade did not discriminate. The metal met no resistance as it cut through the couple locked in a gruesome mockery of a French kiss. Grady dropped like dry, boneless matter. A husk. Melanie fell with greater weight. She hit her knees, eyes open and surprised, then toppled sideways with a rough exhalation.

Talia staggered back, her scream redoubling.

The next swing of the scythe took the woman across her belly. She toppled like an old scarecrow. The immediate stench of decay that lifted from the bodies cramped Talia's stomach with nausea, as if they'd both been long dead already.

Death finally turned on her. Cloaked in blackness, its body swirled in a century of stormy shadow. The blade angled out to the side and caught light where there was none to be had. Death reached toward her. His dark hand caressed the plane of her cheek.

Talia's scream strangled in her throat. Choked. Vanished into a suffocated whimper.

And so did the cloaked nightmare.

Talia hugged herself, her fear drenching the room in blackness, but she could not stop shaking. They were earthquake-level shakes, rippling up from a tectonic shift at her core. She struggled to remain standing, bracing a hand on a wall as the heavy metal insanity from next door echoed the white noise of her inner confusion.

The door to the apartment cracked. Help at last? Help too late?

The silhouette of a man pushed the door open and met resistance at one of the fallen bodies. He shoved harder, and when the door wouldn't budge, he trip-stepped over the obstacle. "Robin? Grady?"

So, not help.

Talia let no air escape her and drew none to sustain her. Had to be another one of *them*. The monsters with bear-trap teeth.

He felt along the wall for the light. A lamp was already on, but Talia kept the dark battened down, hard. Bit her lips, too.

No matter what happened, she would not scream. Not ever again. Not allow that . . . that other devil into the world.

The man, tall, with swarthy skin and long black hair, moved deeper into the room.

"Robin?" He left the door open.

Talia spotted her purse on a chair across the room, out of reach. It held money, ID, her plane ticket. Not that she'd be going to Berkeley. That dream had died with Melanie.

Instead, she made for the door and silently slid out of the apartment. Then she flew down the concrete walkway that led to the apartment building's outer stairs.

"Son of a bitch!" The shout exploded behind her, from inside the apartment.

She had taken the darkness with her. The man had just seen . . . everything.

She ran, leaping down the stairs to the parking lot by twos and threes, a billowing cloud of blackness seething on her skin.

A dark SUV idled next to the building, driver waiting.

She turned away from it, tucking herself behind a low wall that marked the perimeter of the building's parking lot.

The stairs rang low and metallic as rapid footsteps descended.

Had to be him. She quieted her thudding heartbeat by holding her breath.

An automatic window hissed nearby.

"You see the girl?" a man demanded, not six feet from where she crouched.

"No. Nobody," another man answered, drawling and lazy.

"Fucking carnage up there. Grady and Robin are dead." Anger and disbelief roughened his voice.

Talia hunkered in her concrete corner. Her head pounded in time with the blood in her veins, and a residual whine from a memory of the band's music set her teeth on edge.

"That's not possible."

"They were *dead*," the man insisted.

"But He promised . . ."

"I know what *He* promised, and I know what I saw." His words tumbled over each other in his urgency. "They're dead and the girl's gone. I swear she was there when I went in, but I couldn't see worth shit. She's got to be hiding here somewhere."

"If Grady and Robin are dead, I don't want any part of her. I signed on to *live*."

"You dickhead. What happened to them up there is nothing compared to what He will do if we come back empty-handed. Get out of the fucking car and help me look. She's just a girl, and we're not going back without her."

Campus life hummed through the apartment building at Talia's back, students building bright futures and making lasting connections. Heart hollow with loneliness, her hand lingered on the brick for a moment, and then she fled alone into the trees.

* * *

Shadowman fights the lashes of darkness that harry him unwilling back to Twilight. The fae veils of Shadow ruthlessly bind him, silence him, rob him of any power that would permit another trespass across their boundary. Even as little as a word of warning.

He roars into the storm, but Twilight is cold to his pleas.

His daughter.

The deathless ones have found her.

The punishment for his transgression with her mother: to witness the hunt, perchance his daughter's destruction, and in so doing, learn never to break the laws of Twilight again. So the sins of the father are visited upon the child.

In his mind's eye, he can see her. She clings to Shadow for cover, the proof of her fae heritage. Skimming the farthest reaches of the Otherworld she flees, but she cannot cross to safety. Her mother's mortality will not allow it. Thus, she is doomed to Between.

Run, child, run. And when the deathless find you again, scream, and I will come.

Then blood will tell.

THREE

"NOT now," Adam said. He pitched his voice low for Custo's ears only.

They crossed the lobby of the FBI's Phoenix field office, signed out with the guard on post, and exited into the blast of record heat. At 117 degrees, the city baked in a concrete-and-clay oven seasoned with sprigs of cactus and palm trees. Adam held a hand up to shield his face from the glare of the sun as the light seared across red-tiled rooftops. They strode to their rental car. Custo took the driver's seat.

Adam opened the passenger door, burning his fingertips on the handle—*damn hot*—and slid in, adjusting the a/c controls to blow near arctic. Custo glanced over, green eyes transparent in the filtered light, his short dark blond hair spiked from his own drying sweat.

"How'd it go?" Adam asked, snagging a water bottle from the six-pack at his feet. While Adam had been interrogating their latest source, Custo had the unenviable job of bringing the locals up to speed on wraith capture and holding strategies.

"Local feds are skeptical, but informed." Custo pulled away from the lot. "Apparently, Homeland Security has released a report on the wraith phenomena, though detailed accounts are lacking. The Phoenix branch is running a search on area crime with the parameters I provided from Segue. Anything on your end?"

Adam shrugged his frustration. "The kid claims he knows a woman matching Talia's description. Says she runs with the university street crowd, possibly an addict and a prostitute."

Custo scowled. "Another dead end, then?"

"I don't know. The kid said the woman always has a book, used to hang out in the university library until they kicked her out. Says she talks smart and can pass for one of the students." Adam shifted in his seat. In spite of the heat, excess stress and tension had him edgy, his body complaining for a hard run. He contained the energy with grim determination. First things first.

"He was sure it was her, just a strung-out version of her." Adam stared out the window. The deep blue of the sky paled to white overhead as the sun fell farther to the west. Night coming on. Another day lost.

Two months had passed since Talia O'Brien and her roommate, Melanie Prader, disappeared. The Prader family had peppered the University of Maryland campus with a picture of her face and had even managed a TV news spot, the girl's mother pleading over a bold caption that read: *Have you seen Melanie?*

For all his resources, Adam had done little better. He reached beyond the campus to a statewide and then national missing-persons search for both Talia and Melanie. He looked at government institutions, cults, organized crime, calling in favors and motivating the flow of information with the flow of cash. He'd covered the Internet as well, his people insinuating themselves onto message boards, friendship lists, as well as public and private forums. Disturbing forums.

And he'd been inundated with hits:

"Hooked up with the hot one with the short hair in a bar in Chicago . . ."

"The woman with the long hair looks exactly like my sister's kid's preschool teacher . . ."

"The blonde chick lives in the basement of a campus library. Fifty bucks, and I'll tell you which one . . ."

Another dead end? Not acceptable. Talia O'Brien was the only person in his six years of searching to use the name Shadowman in any kind of context that would help his brother. If she still lived, he was going to find her.

Adam forced himself to speak in the present tense. "Talia O'Brien is dependable, steady, and reliable. Predictable. She's been in school all her life. I'll bet she feels most comfortable near a campus. If one kid has seen her, others will have, too. I want to ask around."

"I get why she'd choose Arizona in the winter when it's warm, but why the summer when it's hot as hell?" Custo merged the car onto a freeway marked 101. Traffic ran fast and free down lanes burned almost white and radiating heat in upward waves.

"If she's here, she has a reason."

Adam *knew* Talia, had studied her the way she had studied her academic subjects. One of the first things he did was contact the university to get his hands on her work. Her papers were creative, twisting logic, but she supported her conclusions with an abundance of data. Her life was ordered and planned with study time and classes blocked out in her planner for the semester she had never completed. Her books were even tabbed with color-coded stickies, a system it had taken him two frustrating days to decode. Talia O'Brien liked control. He doubted very much she was a strung-out prostitute. It was simply not in her nature to succumb to that degree of chaos.

They exited the freeway at University Drive and trolled

a palm tree–lined street along the outer perimeter of campus. Two kids lounged in a boxy shadow made by the setting sun ducking behind a building.

Custo slowed to a stop. Adam hopped out, Talia's picture in hand. The heat outside immediately leeched fluid from his body, drying him from the inside out.

One kid shook his head. The other's gaze flicked up at the photo and back down to his iPhone. "Haven't seen her."

Four blocks later, a thicker group gathered in the parking lot of an old 7-Eleven. Dark, short men, brims of baseball caps pulled down over their eyes.

"*No la vi.*" Haven't seen her.

Another group—older teens mixed with university bums this time—swelled in a parking lot in front of an old strip mall. Their attention was trained on a young man, a Caucasian with dreadlocks, holding court from a tall concrete wall that separated the parking lot from the adjacent business.

Adam tried a kid first, maybe fifteen. He held out Talia's picture.

"Nah. Haven't seen her." The kid popped his skateboard. His shirt was salt-stained from perspiration.

Adam's own charcoal-green polo had dampened on his back. He held up a twenty-dollar bill. "Can you tell me where she might hang out?"

"You her old man?" Gaze appraising, the boy spoke with a cynical maturity beyond his years.

"Brother," Adam corrected. *Brother* was the most important relationship in his life. It did him good to remind himself of the bond every chance he got.

The kid snatched the twenty. "She might hang out under the overpass at Dobson and Granite Reef, but I doubt she'd be there now. Night's coming on."

"Oi!" shouted the man with dreadlocks from the wall.

Adam ignored him, addressing the crowd. "All I want is

to take my sister home. Get her the help that she needs. I am willing to pay *anything* to get her back."

The boy slid his gaze over to Dreadlocks, waiting.

"Do you know how much *anything* is?" Adam pressed. "Enough to buy a comfortable life for each one of you."

Come on, give me something.

The group hesitated on the edge of interest. Even to Adam's ears, a big cash outlay sounded like a false promise, but he meant every word. Whoever helped him find Talia O'Brien would be set for life. Based on appearances, these kids had nothing to lose.

Dreadlocks jumped off the concrete wall and sauntered over to Adam. Dirty jeans. Limp black T-shirt. Flip-flops. Braided hemp cord knotted around his thin wrist.

He glanced at the picture. "Yeah, I've seen her."

"Where? I'm going to need specific information." Adam didn't have time to waste here. Police might have a better handle on university sublife. Local hangouts. Ideal abandoned buildings.

Dreadlocks looked over at the sun, now dipping below the tree line, and frowned. "Come back tomorrow. Sun sets and the beasties come out. I got to get my people inside."

Adam's attention arrested. "The beasties?"

"Demons. It's the end of the world, man, but no one can see it except us. End of the world." He gestured to the blaze growing on the horizon. "Sun sets fast here and the beasties come out. You ever heard of Sweet Drink?"

"No."

"It's a band, man. Their music tells how it's gonna be. How it is. End of the world. End of death. It's coming with the setting sun. Listen up: *Demons walk and demons feed. Take away all human need. Join the army. Break the curse. The human race to crush Death first.*"

"I don't understand," Adam said, but the lyrics still sent

chills across his hot back and reminded him somehow of Jacob.

Dreadlocks cocked his head. "You musta inherited that money then, 'cause I'm saying it as plain as I can, and you just don't get it. I'm saying the sun is setting, and if your sister has any brains at all she is going inside somewhere or she will be the demons' feed."

"Where inside?" Adam pulled out a hundred, held it up.

Dreadlocks waved the bill away with a grimace of disdain. "End of the world, man. What the fuck is that paper going to do for me? For any of us?"

"It'll get you off the street." *Just tell me where.*

"*I* can get me off the street. I'm here by *choice*. I'm here because *here* is *real*. It's you and your fancy shirt that are shit, man. You live in the dark; you just don't know it."

Adam kept his voice calm, his expression controlled even though he wanted to grab the punk by the throat. "I want to see, too. Help me see so I can find her."

"If she's here, she's inside. Or she should be. Tally likes to live dangerously. Doesn't trust anybody. I offered her a place in my family, but she refused. Where she's got to now, I don't know."

Adam's chest burned, an emotion he couldn't name breaching containment. He glanced down at the photograph in his hand. "I never said her name."

"Well, I told you I'd seen her. You didn't believe me?" Dreadlocks grinned, spreading his arms wide to invite a laugh at Adam's expense from his crew. The group tittered on cue.

Adam didn't care as long as he got information.

"Well then, maybe now you'll believe me about the demon night," Dreadlocks said.

Adam already believed. "Where inside?" *Please.*

Dreadlocks sighed. "Try Priest, man. North of Santa Maria. Mountainside."

"Priest?" Adam controlled himself through a long inhalation, though his heart pumped to act. He kept a choke hold on his hope.

"They're roads, man. You know what a road is?"

Only Jacob ever talked down to him, but Adam was too grateful to be irritated.

"I get that you don't want my money." Adam stopped and corrected himself. "Don't *choose* my money. But it's all I have to give. That and my thanks." He pulled out his wallet, took every bill in the leather sheath, thumbed a couple of business cards—the personal ones with his direct mobile number—and held them out. When Dreadlocks didn't lift a hand, Adam dropped the lot on the ground.

"Call me if you ever need anything. If you want to tell me more. If you are in trouble." He lifted his gaze to the crowd of kids. "Goes for all of you. If your demons are what I call wraiths, you're going to need my help. Now get inside."

Adam jogged back to the car, his body humming with anticipation. He glanced over his shoulder toward the bonfire glow of the setting sun, and then faced Custo.

Custo must have read the excitement on his face. "She's alive," he concluded.

"Calls herself Tally." Adam could barely speak over the buzzing in his ears.

"Where?"

"Priest and Santa Maria."

"A church?" Custo typed rapidly into the rental car's GPS.

"Roads, man."

Black spots swam in Talia's vision. If she twitched her eyes left, the spots skated left. If she twitched them right, the spots skated right. No matter how hard she tried, she could never examine one of the spots dead-on. Bothersome game. Like keep-away from childhood, but more frustrating because the pastime—and that's all it was good for, *passing time*—made the intense pounding behind her eyes worse. Nauseatingly so.

She gave up for the moment and focused down the alley on the soul-sucking monster at its entrance. Talia was trapped at the other end in a belly made of concrete wall and pavement. The hulking brute blocked the exit of the garbage lane to her apartment complex to stand sentry, to watch for her as he'd done when he caught up with her in Denver, then Las Vegas.

This time she had spotted him first and turned down an unfamiliar alley rather than ducking through the gate to the complex's square of scraggly lawn where a couple of teenage girls had set out chairs to sun themselves. Stupid to ruin their skin and cost her an escape route. But she couldn't very well lead the monster to vibrant young lives. Not after Melanie. Therefore, the alley.

She'd been here a day and a half and smelled just as bad as the garbage. Good thing her shadowy shield obscured more than light or the monster would have discovered her that first day. The dark cloak dampened most sensory perception of her; sight, smell, and sound all concealed under its folds. With the exception of her pulse, she was a shrouded ghost.

Talia worked her thick and uncooperative tongue on the roof of her mouth to swallow. Frustrating reflex—nothing but glue to work with, and the motion made her lungs burn.

A day and a half. Sooner or later something would have to give.

Talia crept forward, palms and knees on blazing pavement, around the side of a sagging yellow mattress that inclined against the back wall of the alley. The small movement set her heart beating wildly, and the throb in her head intensified. But it was worth it. From this position, the cast of her strange shadows matched the trajectory of the sun's waning light, affording her the chance to rest against the musty but soft mattress.

As soon as her head dropped back against the pillowed surface, the world upended, vision blanked, sound roared in her ears as unconsciousness tried to swallow her. She fought back. Blinked hard. Shook her head. Forced the world back into focus. Her gaze darted to the monster.

He had pushed away from the wall and turned to face down the length of the alley, nose in the air, sniffing. Gaze searching.

Talia grabbed at her shadows, eyes wide and dry, fixated on the monster that had scented her. She gathered the darkness tightly to her so her shield would not slip off again.

No resting. Head stays up.

The monster strode the alley's length, pausing at the gated walkway leading to the apartment commons to sniff, then moved deeper into her corner. He pulled the mattress off the concrete wall, swaying over her position. His pant leg brushed her cheek.

She held her breath. If she were going to die, she wouldn't need oxygen anyway. Breathe and die. Don't breathe, maybe die. Every decision was much simpler when reduced to an exercise in logic.

The mattress toppled sideways, twitched aside as the monster strode by her, back to his position at the end of her alley.

Talia held herself upright, the black spots in her vision growing, obscuring sight. Her head full of static fuzz, she was going to throw up.

Okay, now breathe. In. Out. Again.

No way she could remain upright. Gravity, inertia, and

the last dregs of the flamingo sunset all conspired to lower her to the ground. But she kept her eyes open.

Just a little longer. Breathe.

Adam and Custo pulled up to a busy intersection. Cars rushed by with bright headlights, windows down, music blaring. The desert deepened with twilight as night-blooming flowers filtered dusky-sweet fragrance over exhaust. Custo parked along the street. Adam jumped out of the car while Custo listened to his mobile phone, face drawn in concentration as he waited for a detailed crime report for the neighborhood.

Adam took in the layout of the intersection. All the day's untapped energy, anxiety, and tension transmuted into a certainty that lit a fire in his chest. She was here somewhere.

To the north, small single-story houses butted against tall cinder block walls. The houses broke off abruptly at what appeared to be an old strip of stores. A dirty gas station occupied another corner. To the east, an office building of four or five stories. And behind him stood an apartment complex. Large lettering on the side of the building read MOUNTAINSIDE.

It's an apartment complex, man. Dreadlocks was one cocky son of a bitch.

Adam waved Custo toward the entrance. "You find the super."

Custo nodded and jogged down the broken sidewalk to the main entrance of the building.

Adam turned down a rear access road for a quick canvass of the area before the day's light was completely gone. The single large building turned into four, arranged around a yellowing square of grass at the center. A long stretch of his legs took him down its length. The busy street hummed to his left, cars speeding though the intersection without slowing.

To his right, beyond a rusted, squealing gate, lay a black hole of an alley.

"Anyone there?" His breath suspended for thick moments, the sound of his own heartbeat dominating the pressure in his head. Nothing. He had to check it out in person, but he wished he'd brought a piece. The talk of demon feed made him edgy.

Adam moved into the press of blackness. "Hello?"

"Shhhh," a voice hissed.

Adam's eyes adjusted; the darkness thinned to heavy gray. In the litter of the alleyway, a young, filthy woman lay collapsed on the pavement. All eyes in a narrow white face.

Two months of searching, of studying her face in photographs so that he could be prepared for the moment of recognition. He knew every contour by heart. There was no mistaking the angled tilt of her glassy eyes. The curve of her jaw. The straight, thin line of her nose. Talia O'Brien.

The monster glided forward, closing the distance between him and his prey, a man ducking down the alley to help her.

The Good Samaritan was going to die. Talia had witnessed it many times since Melanie: The inhuman strength, the vicious teeth, the kiss. Then the dark, sick pull as the vital essence was ripped from a person.

She couldn't let it happen, especially now at the end of everything.

A part of Talia stretched, not her lethargic body, but something deeper. The last bit of herself extended a lifeline to curl around the man's form and mask his presence from the oncoming monster. To share the shelter of her cloak.

Her shadows enveloped then inundated him, his features snapping into focus. Dark hair, clipped short. Pale, intent eyes in an angular face. Vital body, tall and strong. Trim waist, belted slacks. His polo was a perfect fit over a strong chest and shoulders.

And still more. This deep into her veils, her sight penetrated the surface of the man. He was lit inside with a blazing column of purpose and will. Light permeated every cell of his body with vibrant life and intelligent power.

Spirit. Awe bloomed within Talia and clogged her throat. So beautiful. Too beautiful to be consumed by the oncoming horror.

Talia swallowed hard and tried again. *"Please* be quiet."

"Talia O'Brien?"

Frustration closed her lungs. She couldn't save him if he wouldn't cooperate. Her shadows weren't going to be enough.

Talia concentrated on her body. Flattened her palm on the hard concrete, pushed herself upright. Her head swam; the world rocked hard on its axis. She pulled a foot under her, took a deep, shuddering breath, and propelled herself forward.

Adam tried again. "Talia?"

He stepped forward and held his arms slightly to the side, palms open in the universal posture of peace and friendship. He didn't want to scare her.

Talia darted forward out of her crouch and put a hot hand over his mouth before he could take a full breath of surprise.

"You've got to be quiet now." Her voice was rough, barely audible. Urgent.

The darkness swallowed the alleyway again. He blinked hard, but his eyes wouldn't clear. Wouldn't focus. His senses were suddenly muted, except for the press of her hand at his mouth.

She pushed against him, and he allowed her to back him up. He tripped over alley debris underfoot, and a metallic sound rang out, oddly distorted. Then he hit a hard plane—the wall of a building. He raised his chin to disengage her softly, without force. But she held fast, hand clamped over his mouth.

Footfalls shuffle-stepped on the pavement nearby. One or two people approached, no more. Another step, heavy with echo. Just one, then. Probably male.

Adam's arm circled Talia's waist. He kept his touch light and easy on her back. She was short and much too thin. Her body heat burned through her clothes as if he were holding on to a bolt of lightning. She smelled sharply rank but feminine. Probably hadn't seen a shower in days.

He didn't draw her in, but kept his hold possessive enough to let the other man know she was with him. Now that he had found her, there was no way he was letting her go.

"Here, kitty-kitty." The man's singsong voice doubled up and bounced off the buildings, menace lacing his words.

Adam's gut twisted with understanding: Talia had been trying to warn him. The man was a wraith. A hungry hunter.

He needed a damn gun.

Cold hatred hardened into resolution, blocking all extraneous emotion. No room for fear or panic. Just action.

He yanked Talia hard against him and secured her body with a tight arm around her waist. With his other hand, he found her wrist and forced her hand away from his face.

She resisted, but it took little strength to bend her arm down to her side.

He put his mouth to her ear. "Stay behind me. I can't protect you if you run."

Couldn't protect her in the dark very well either. Why didn't the wraith attack? The dark wouldn't have stopped Jacob for a moment.

"He's a monster." Her words exhaled across his jaw like a soft caress.

"I know," he murmured. "I won't let him touch you. We just have to get to my car."

Adam shifted her weight and turned so that she pressed against the wall, safe behind his body. He faced the darkness, Talia at his back.

Glass crunched into the pavement. Close.

Adam slowly crouched down until he felt rough concrete under his fingertips. He felt around with his palm until his fingers hit smooth metal. He drew his hand along its hot length, identifying a riveted pipe.

"Kitty cat," the wraith called. "There's no way out."

Adam stood, pipe gripped in his hand. He couldn't stop the wraith for long. Not alone. Where the hell was Custo when he needed him? Didn't matter. Adam was not about to fail now. Not when he was so close to finding his answers.

"He can't see you. Use the dark," Talia whispered from behind.

Her suggestion didn't make sense. Not unless this wraith was somehow defective. Wraith senses far exceeded human ones. The woman didn't know what she was dealing with.

Adam steeled himself. All he had to do was get past the wraith to the street. It would not attack in public and risk exposure. Street and light. Custo and the car. Safety.

He reached back to Talia with his free hand and found hers. He gripped it in a silent signal. *Stay with me.* As he stepped to the side, he pulled her with him, but her weight stayed at the wall.

Not a good time for her to resist. Force then. Adam traded her hand for her waist. He'd drag her if he had to.

Then the alley abruptly lightened as her body sagged into him, unconscious.

The wraith stood ten feet from them, broadly built and aggressive with an exaggerated grace. He was pale and fair, his expression ecstatic, as if caught in a moment of rapture, anticipating a feed.

Adam let Talia fall in a heap on the ground and brought the pipe up.

The wraith whirled toward him and screeched loud and high like an ancient bird. Then he lunged.

Adam swung. Connected with a hard thump.

But too low. The pipe struck the wraith at his jaw. The impact stunned, but didn't disable.

The wraith lashed out his arm. Knocked Adam in the chest.

Adam flew back and hit the building over Talia's limp form. His lungs screamed as all the air suddenly burst out of his body, heart arresting for a moment of agony. He fell on top of her body, rolled, and sprang to the balls of his feet. He clenched the bar. Swung again. Slammed the pipe against the bridge of the wraith's nose with a crack, then staggered back to shield Talia.

The wraith's face was broken and bloodied, eyes sunken and turned, without vision until he could heal.

Keep moving, Adam commanded himself. He dropped to all fours, pipe grasped in both hands, his body tabled over Talia.

The wraith lanced out blindly and hit the building where Adam had been standing, raining stucco plaster down on his back.

Adam tightened his grip on the pipe, throwing his weight and twisting to spear the wraith in the gut. The metal pierced with a sickening slide and stuck in the wraith's ribs.

The monster screeched again. He caught Adam at the belt and shirt collar and heaved him off Talia. The shirt ripped with Adam's weight, the cloth searing against his throat as it gave. The belt held fast and the wraith sent him spinning cockeyed back into the wall, headfirst.

Blinding pain bolted down Adam's neck and through his jaw. His ears roared and salty blood coated his mouth. But the pile he landed on was soft. Talia, again.

Adam braced against the building and kicked back with his leg. Knocked the wraith off balance.

Two loud shots echoed out into the night.

Custo. Finally.

Physically subduing a wraith was absurd. They were too strong, regenerated too quickly to kill. Adam had learned that the hard way with Jacob a long time ago. At least the bullets would stun him momentarily, though.

The wraith crashed back into two tall plastic garbage bins. He flailed, ripped a lid off, and sent the cover flying against the building in a warped ricochet.

"I'll take her to the car," Adam called. His head pounded. Thick, warm moisture dripped into his right eye.

Custo responded by plugging the wraith with two more shots. The monster still twitched.

Adam cradled Talia to his chest and rounded the bend of the building. A motley group of people stared into the mouth of the alley. More than one held a phone open. To call for help or catch the fight on video?

Adam couldn't think about the implications of the widespread panic that would follow wraith exposure now. The only thing that mattered was Talia.

The car waited down the street, beyond the gawkers. Adam shouldered his way through and limped toward the vehicle. He shifted her weight to open the back door, then gently laid her inside.

"Stay out of the alley," Custo shouted to the gathering crowd. He burst through the group as Adam crawled in the back over Talia—*careful, now*—and yanked the door shut.

Custo got in the driver's seat, jammed the key in the ignition, and sped away from the intersection.

"How bad is she?" Custo asked.

Adam wiped the blood from his forehead with his shirt-sleeve. Stung, but he didn't care. "I don't know. Wraith didn't touch her, but she's burning up. She's got heatstroke at the very least."

"Hospital?"

Adam found the flutter of Talia's pulse at her neck. He regarded her blonde hair, matted to stringy dun, and her overly thin face, smudged with grime. She'd obviously been through hell and hadn't trusted her troubles to law enforcement. She'd have had a reason. The woman was nothing if not ruled by reason.

Two months missing. Two months hunted, more likely.

In the rearview mirror, red and blue police lights skated across Custo's face.

Much better—safer—to get her back to Segue. A gamble, of course, but she'd survived this long already, she'd just have to hold out a little longer.

"Airport," Adam decided. "We'll see what we can do for her there before takeoff. But we can't take too long. That wraith won't be alone."

FOUR

TALIA woke to a blinding brightness. Unforgiving hands pushed her down into a cruel bathtub of water filled with invisible icy knives. She fought, but the hands would not release her, and the blades speared ever deeper into her muscles.

Shivers racked her body in mean waves, and her heart galloped like a runaway horse, tripping on her chest and beating her deeper into the water.

A face leaned over, the overhead light shining like a solar halo around his head.

"Dr. O'Brien," a low, male voice said. "You have heatstroke. We're trying to bring your body temperature down."

Heatstroke? That was a lie. She was freezing.

She cowered back and squeezed her eyes shut, intensifying the throb in her skull. *They can't find you in the dark.* She gritted her teeth, but they still rattled in her head. *Please don't let them find me.*

Her body knotted, clenching in her calves and at the small of her back. Her clothes, heavy and twisted, seemed glued to her skin. A sound echoed out. A cry building to a scream. She bit her lips—no screams, no dark devil—and grasped at the arms that held her.

"Patty says she'll be cramping up pretty bad. She says we need to massage her legs and calves," another said.

"Then get in here and hold her, so that I can," the first answered.

The shape of a man crept low next to her.

Her stomach spasmed; she choked, felt herself abruptly lifted, and then she vomited over the side of the tub.

"Damn," the second man said under his breath.

They settled her back in the water. A hard bar of an arm fell across her chest while merciless hands stroked deep into the muscles of her calves. Hurt. Bruised. The hands moved up to her thighs.

Strange hands on her body. *No!* She kicked again. A backlash of water swamped her.

"Settle down, Dr. O'Brien. You're going to be okay. You need to drink a little. Can you do that for me?" The first voice again.

Something skimmed her lips. A straw. Her tongue felt too big to work it right. A splash of sour, sweet fluid hit her mouth and mingled with the acid of her vomit. Made her choke and cough.

"That's it. Just a little more."

She tried, but her shakes were too bad.

"More," the voice commanded, losing its kindness.

She wanted to cry, but she did as she was told. Took in a deep drink.

"Watch her temperature," the other man said. "We don't want it to drop too low too fast. That's supposed to be bad."

A hand pressed on her forehead. Lingered there long enough for her to sense a well of great strength within its bearer. Then it was gone. "Still feels hot to me, but the ice water screwed with my hands. Did Patty say how long to keep her in the tub?"

"Until her temp comes down."

Another hand touched to her head, too light and brief for her to sense anything. "I think she's better."

"Okay. Let's get her up and her clothes off. Go get me something to wrap around her. Nothing heavy. Pull the sheet off the bed."

The first man took hold under her arms and hauled her out of the water to stand dripping on the floor. In her clothes. *Strange.* He knelt before her, working the button on her cut-off jeans, peeling them downward, and shifting her weight so she could step out. He paused at her panties, but then stripped those down, too.

Mortifying, but she shook too much to do anything about it. She glanced away from his ministrations and got a brief impression of a small bedroom, spare and utilitarian. Smelled like a garage.

"Scissors," the man stripping her called.

A sudden sob escaped her. Her weight swayed forward and she dropped her hands to the man's shoulders.

A warm arm went up around her waist to steady her. His hand, hot on her waist, branded her with a sense of his strength and purpose. Cued a sensory memory of that very same arm turning her in darkness so that her body was sandwiched—shielded—by his and the wall of a building. The monster not three paces away . . .

Scissors started up her shirt. They parted her bra, too, which didn't make any sense because the clasp was in the back. Then he shrugged the sodden fabric off her shoulders like a jacket.

A deep freeze wafted over her shoulders as a white sheet billowed open and swaddled her. The man lifted her off her feet and gently placed her on a hard chair.

"Drink," he said.

She complied. The sour fluid made her stomach roll.

"Did you ever find a thermometer?" he asked over his shoulder.

"No. Not part of the first-aid kit."

The hand went heavy on her forehead again. "Is the plane ready?"

"Should be, yes," the other answered. "The doctor will be a few more minutes."

Plane? The straw hit her upper lip.

"Drink," the man commanded, again.

She pulled some fluid into her mouth.

"What is this?" Her throat felt raw, voice scratchy. Speaking took too much effort.

The man crouched down near her feet. His eyes were gray-blue, like the ocean, but steady and intent under dark brows drawn together in concentration. An angry abrasion pebbled with scabs crossed his forehead below a short crop of dark hair. He had tan skin, lined slightly at the outer edges of his eyes, but not with laughter. It was a serious face, handsome in its symmetry and lines, but tight with care, disquiet, and trouble.

"It's just water and sugar." His voice was back to kind, its low timbre soothing and warm.

"Lime Gatorade," the other one amended.

"Talia, I'm Adam Thorne. This is my friend, Custo Santovari. We've been looking for you for a long time."

A million questions seeped through her confusion. They hurt almost as much as her body. But one superseded them all and was worth the energy it cost to form the words.

"Am I crazy?"

He smiled. "No. The world's gone crazy, but you're just fine. It took an amazing amount of courage to elude the wraiths for so long. You're safe now. I won't let anything touch you."

Adam stooped and lifted her. Her body pressed against his chest, an arm pinned uncomfortably tight between them. He smelled good—a hint of citrus coming off his jaw, darkened by the labor of the day.

At her hip, wetness spread as the dry sheet absorbed water from his clothes.

Down a narrow hallway. Concrete floors. Long, fluorescent tubes running overhead. Then out into the night across a tarmac to a small plane, white stairs folded down as if awaiting the president or vacationers from an island getaway.

Adam didn't pause at the stairs, but powered up them, his heart drumming against her side with the extra work of her weight. He maneuvered her inside, passed the bulk of a wall and through a door to tuck her into a buttery leather seat.

She was hot, sweat prickling at her scalp, and she couldn't quite seem to catch her breath. He reclined the seat to engage a footrest. A drink appeared at her side from an attendant she had not noticed on boarding. The cabin both spun and tilted at the same time.

Adam brought the glass to her lips. "Easy now."

Cool fluid filled her mouth, splashed her throat, and dripped down her chin. The cabin lost its color and dimmed. Her darkness rolled over her. Claimed her again.

"Where's the goddamned doctor?" Adam shouted.

She reached out blindly for something to hold on to, desperate to keep from drowning. She found Adam, his strength an anchor in the storm of shadows shuddering around her. And beyond their deep, layered depths: Glowing red eyes. Black wind. The devil lurking in the darkness.

Adam watched as Talia descended into a series of tremors, black irises swallowed by dilating pupils.

He dropped the glass he held to her lips and found it again when his knee crushed the broken shards as he knelt to restrain her hands, striking out in clumsy defense at imagined attackers. The cabin went black, lights dimming as the sound of the engine distorted to a hiss, then roared back to life.

Shit. One emergency at a time, please.

Adam fought through the dark to grip Talia's wrists so that she didn't harm herself. The lights flickered back on. Good.

He peered down into her eyes, willing her condition to stabilize. "Help's coming. You're going to be all right. Stay with me, Talia. Just hold on."

Her trembling abated, breath ragged, pulse wild under his fingers. Skin burning again.

Behind him, the plane's door thumped closed as the handlebar engaged to lock for flight. Adam glanced over his shoulder. Custo accompanied a short Asian man bearing two large satchels marked with a red cross and a middle-aged woman holding another.

"She just had some sort of a seizure," Adam informed them.

Talia shuddered again under his arms, but he held fast. He caught the moment her lids closed over the whites of her eyes. And—*damn it*—the lights of the airplane flickered into darkness as the engine whined again.

"Doctor!" Adam barked, then said more quietly, "It's okay, Talia. Hold on. Help is here."

But help didn't arrive. The cabin of the plane remained blackened while Talia trembled uncontrollably on the seat. Adam's heart thudded as he tried in vain to control and comfort her simultaneously.

"Custo!" No answer. Adam couldn't see a damn thing in the darkness. Where the hell was the doctor? Where the hell was Custo?

Securing a new plane, Adam hoped. This one was obviously not fit for flight.

Talia's tremors subsided until only her chest hitched in shallow hiccups. Adam found her hot cheek and brushed away the twisted strands of hair that covered her face. Her chin quivered under his fingertips as she wept without tears.

Adam understood. Between the constant terror of the wraith's pursuit and her current physical condition, Talia would need considerable time and care to return to health.

"You're safe with me, Talia. Just rest. Everything is going to be fine." *I hope.*

Adam's eyes slowly adjusted to the dark until he could just make out the shape of her face condensing into solid form. Her skin gleamed against the backdrop of shadows. Downright ghostly. Disturbingly so. Her gaze sought his, the set of her eyes unusually slanted, and she seemed to relax. The cabin lightened further.

Her features and coloring were a study in contrasts. He found the combination interesting. Strangely so. She reminded him of Jacob, perfect in some otherworldly way and yet, not. But it was the simultaneous lightening and darkening of the surroundings with her seizures that jarred him. Coincidence?

The nurse and doctor rushed forward and dropped their bags on the floor. Adam drew back, knees smarting from glass, to allow room for them to work.

No. The concurrent return of Talia's lucidity and the shift in their environment from mute darkness to light could not be denied. The same damn thing had happened with her in the alley when darkness had blotted out the stars, the light from the street, even the glow from the apartment windows above. The wraith approached, and what had she said? *Use the dark.*

The wraith had not attacked until Talia had passed out, when the darkness receded.

Talia's gaze sought Adam, her oddly tipped eyes looking to him for assurance. He forced himself to smile and nod: *You're going to be okay, now.*

As Adam glanced out the window, he was surprised to find the plane had taken off during the blackout without incident. Adam lowered into a seat across the aisle from Talia and her doctor, his mind blazing through the implications.

Talia hadn't altered the environment, only his perception of the environment. Altered the wraith's perceptions in the alley, too.

Handy, that. No wonder the wraiths were so determined to find her.

Whatever had happened, the event was localized to her immediate area. The plane and its captain were unaffected, taking off, business as usual.

"Did that scare the shit out of you, too?" Custo put a hand to the back of his neck.

"I think we'll be okay," Adam said. "Talia's doing it."

"You can't be serious." Custo dropped into the seat opposite Adam.

Adam continued his thoughts aloud. "The dark. The strange sounds. She's doing it somehow. I figured the wraiths were after her because of the Shadowman mention in her paper, but maybe it's something more. She's not normal."

"Wraith?" Custo's gaze shifted to Talia's supine body.

Adam took in her white face, the deep circles under her eyes.

"No. She's seems to be having a typical response to the extreme heat. Frankly, I don't know what she is. We may have stumbled onto something here that will finally give us some leverage against the wraiths."

The idea made him both cautious and excited, as if he had just found a rare butterfly in an urban jungle. He dropped his gaze to the floor. He needed time to think events through. To disregard all his conclusions and open himself up to new ones.

He took a deep, steeling breath. "But let's not get ahead of ourselves. I want all the information there is on her. I want friends, professors, neighbors questioned. I want birth records, medical records, report cards. Anything and everything."

"We have a good start already from our missing-persons search. I'll go back further, dig deeper," Custo answered. "And for chrissake, when the doctor is done with Talia, make sure to have him take a look at you. You look like hell."

Gray. The perfect color. A little darkness, a little light. Talia was comfortable here.

The wind whispered a nonsense of soft, punctuated *s*'s. ". . . she's stable. Sleeping soundly . . ."

Talia opened her eyes. She lay in an unfamiliar twin bed, covers folded across her chest and tucked under her arms. The walls beyond were painted a soft yellow, unadorned. A bare table stood at the foot of the bed. No windows.

She glanced down at the shape of her body. It seemed foreign to her, a long and shallow mound under a light blanket. A clear tube tethered her to a bag of fluid in her peripheral vision.

Beep. Her eyes flicked over. *Beep.* A monitor of sorts displayed a line dancing with sharp peaks and valleys. *Beep.*

Heartbeat. That was something, at least.

She tried her legs, twitching her feet and pulling a knee up. Her joints ached, and a prickling told her she had to pee.

She shifted her hips.

Something was already between her legs. Burned, that.

Her stomach tightening, she slid a hand under the covers to investigate.

No panties. Narrow tube. *Oh, God.*

"Hello?" she called. "Somebody?"

She held her breath, listening. Then tried again. "Hello?"

Abruptly, the door opened. A woman in a lab coat entered, smiling brightly. She was fiftyish, short, a little heavy, with sensible short brown hair. "Well, hello to you, too, Talia. I'm Dr. Riggs. Patty."

Dr. Riggs lifted the covers at the bottom of the bed and raised a plastic bag half filled with pale yellow fluid. "Good girl."

Her eyes rested on the heart-monitoring machine, then met Talia's gaze. "Excellent. You're doing much better. How do you feel?"

"Um . . . confused?"

Dr. Riggs's smile broadened. "No kidding. You've had rather acute hyperthermia. Heatstroke. It can be very dangerous. Renal failure. Heart attack. You were in pretty bad shape when I got you, but you're making excellent progress now. You'll probably experience some lingering effects like confusion and temperature sensitivity. We'll work on the confusion. Are you too hot or cold?"

"No . . ." Talia had much more pressing worries. "Where am I?"

"The Segue Institute. It's a research facility."

"What am I doing here?"

"You're here for research. Adam will explain it better. Let me call him, and then I'll take care of that catheter for you." Dr. Riggs flashed her bright smile again and exited the room.

Talia froze. She was here for research. So someone could prick her and prod her until they discovered how she worked.

Put me in a maze like a rat. Might as well have left in me in that alley. At least those rats were free.

The door thumped, banged, then reopened. Dr. Riggs pushed in a metal cart and parked it at the side of the bed. "Adam will be right over. Let's remove the catheter and get you comfortable. I'm sure you will have a lot to talk about."

Dr. Riggs flipped up the sheet from the bottom and crouched embarrassingly low. "Can you bring your legs up? A little more?"

Did she have an alternative?

"This might be uncomfortable, but it will pass quickly." Dr. Riggs wore gloves so Talia couldn't gauge her intentions or personality by her touch. Frustrating.

Talia held her breath. A burning sting shot inside her.

"There, now," Dr. Riggs said, standing. "You'll have the IV until the rest of that bag empties, but let's get you out of bed and moving."

Talia nodded. The floor was icy on her feet, all the little bones painfully brittle, but she pulled herself up—Dr. Riggs at her elbow—and shuffled toward the door. The hospital gown gaped at the back, but she lacked a third arm to hold it shut. A cold shiver spiraled up beneath.

Dr. Riggs reached down to a lower shelf on the cart and grabbed a robe that Talia had not noticed. She helped her with the right sleeve. "We'll just wrap this around your left side until you get the IV out."

Talia hobbled out the door into . . . a large, comfortable lab. Of sorts. To one side, it seemed a typical research environment: Stainless-steel counters lined the wall and were placed at parallel and right angles in the middle of the room. Machines of several varieties vied for space. Smaller apparatus, microscope, and computers all had their corners.

The other side of the room was dominated by a flowery sofa set, tufted and pillowed with a matching chair. A colorful rug in an indistinct pattern of blues and reds covered the floor, over which a large coffee table hulked with elaborate rolled legs. A picture of a little white dog sat framed on its surface, next to an empty coffee cup, plate with crumbs, and some strange printout filled with rows of almost-microscopic numbers.

"The chair," Dr. Riggs directed.

Talia was soon tucked in softness. Dr. Riggs reached down and assisted Talia to put her feet up on the table.

"You okay?" Dr. Riggs asked.

"I'm *more* confused." Talia's gaze wandered the room for emphasis.

Dr. Riggs chuckled. "This is my personal lab. We all have our own work space, what we need for work, and enough creature comforts to tailor Segue to our personalities and needs."

Dr. Riggs gestured to the photo of the dog as she took a seat on the sofa. "Handsome is in my apartment upstairs. He used to play with me in the lab, but after a little mishap two months ago, he's been banished."

Apartment upstairs?

Across the lab, two doors slid open and Adam entered, striding in as if he knew his way around. He wore dark slacks and a blue button-down shirt, open at the collar. He was taller than Talia remembered, and he'd shaved, though a scabby rash still smeared across his forehead to his temple. But the eyes were the same. Stormy ocean eyes.

Talia tried to sit up. Without him, she'd have lost herself.

He waved her back. "Dr. O'Brien, relax. Please."

She let herself ease into the cushions, but inwardly she remained upright.

"I'll be just outside," Dr. Riggs said, meeting Adam's gaze in a silent signal. Their communication set Talia's heart beating faster.

Adam took a seat on the sofa and leaned back, arm propped on a pillow. The pose seemed relaxed, but carefully restrained energy hummed just below the surface. His gaze was cool, level, and appraising, belying the ease of his posture. Something about the man told Talia that he was rarely one to be still.

"How are you feeling?" he asked.

That's not important. "Where am I?"

"You're at The Segue Institute. I founded it a little over six years ago to research the wraith phenomenon."

Wraith. "Is that what was in the alley? A wraith?" The word felt strange in her mouth, but solid. Grounding. It was good to finally attach a name to the soul-suckers that had been following her for—she didn't know how long. Another thing to thank Adam for.

"Yes. That was a wraith. He was once a normal person, but something—and we don't know what—happened to augment his physical strength, senses, and regenerative capacity to the point of immortality."

"And what they do . . . ?" An image of Grady's sick kiss, Melanie flailing, came unbidden to Talia's mind.

Adam's eyes darkened. "They feed on human life energy."

Talia shook her head, remembering the echo of Melanie's self as it was ripped from its moorings. "They feed on more than that." She was certain they fed on something more distinct and individual than "human energy."

Adam frowned, seeming to draw inside himself. "Perhaps. As far as we can tell, feeding does not sustain them physically. We think the act grounds them. Gives them a grip on humanity."

Talia swallowed, hard. "And me?"

He smiled, although the expression didn't reach his eyes. "And you wrote a very interesting dissertation. It was posted online by your anthropology department on April twenty-sixth, two days after you defended your doctorate."

That wasn't what she meant by her question—she'd meant, *What do you plan to do with me?*—but she let him continue. "So?"

"You had some provocative . . . suppositions about the boundary between life and death. I was ready to offer you a position here based on your work, but you'd disappeared."

"I don't understand. What does my diss have to do with wraiths?"

"The Segue Institute exists for the express purpose of

discovering how to kill a wraith. We are trying to learn some other things along the way as well, but only as they support our first goal. We have on-staff physicians, academics, para-psychologists . . . and now I am hoping to get an expert on near-death experiences."

Me. "But why all the fuss? There are others more knowledgeable on the subject. You didn't have to track me down to an alley . . ." Or put your body in front of mine during an attack.

Adam held up a hand to stop her. "I've done my research and out of the handful of people dedicated to near-death, only you retain an objective point of view. Most of the others are dedicated to confirming life after death. Segue does not have any spiritual or religious agenda. Instead, I want to learn about the laws or forces that dictate what happens at the brink of death, and any ideas you might have on the exceptions to the rules."

Still . . . There had to be a more specific reason he had selected her. Others were capable of unbiased research.

"Why me?"

Adam shifted into a more intent posture, leaning toward her, his shirt stretching with the breadth of his shoulders, elbows on knees. His fingers laced together, swollen and bruised across one set of knuckles.

His gaze locked on hers, watching. Evaluating. "One of your sources mentioned Shadowman, an individual I would very much like to learn more about."

Panic flared, and she fought to keep her composure.

Shadowman. Her father. The dark and beautiful man she'd met once, right after the car accident when she was fifteen. The near-death experience that inspired her work. Her father, the enigma of her life, had come to greet her on her passing. She'd seen the tilt of his eyes and known with shattering clarity that she was like him, whatever he was. And she didn't care what that was, as long as she wasn't alone with her strangeness anymore. Then he'd been ripped away when she was zapped back to life by paramedics.

Now, of course, she'd have questions for her father. He'd know why the wraiths wanted her. He'd be able to tell her why she could do strange things no one else could. And he could protect her from the devil that came out of her scream.

She'd voice none of that to Adam. She owed him thanks, not herself. All Adam's talk about her dissertation and near-death research was just that, talk. If Adam wanted to study Shadowman, who was not in this world, his only alternative was to study her. She might be "researching" near-death here, but she'd still be a little white rat.

"I have all your materials ready, your books and data. Not knowing if we would ever find you, we went through it."

You would have gone through it anyway. Pressure grew in her chest, her heartbeat quickening though she sat stone still.

"And although you have detailed records, releases, and transcripts from all of your other sources, there is nothing that references Shadowman." His gaze fixed on her face. "Who is the source?"

Talia kept silent, staring right back at him and concentrating on moving air in and out of her lungs. If he knew so much already, she certainly wasn't going to tell him more.

He dropped his head for a moment, then raised it again with strain tugging at his eyes. "Okay, let's set that question aside for the moment. Give you a chance to get set up in your own lab and look over your research. There's something else, too. I'd wait until you were fully on your feet to discuss this with you, but I am a big fan of putting all the cards on the table. Your lab tests came back with some interesting results, off the wall, but strangely consistent with similar tests taken—and disregarded—after the near-fatal car accident you were in ten years ago."

Lab tests. Of course. Lab tests wouldn't lie. Lab tests would reveal abnormalities. Hadn't Aunt Maggie warned her about doctors years ago?

"And you've got a reflex, I think linked to fear, that affects the immediate environment, as a chameleon blends into the bark of a tree, but opposite." He smiled, tilting his head. As if any of this warranted levity. "The flight from Arizona was especially exciting. I'm guessing your gift played a significant part in eluding the wraiths for so long." He paused again, then speared her with his gaze. "What are you?"

If he wanted an answer, he wasn't going to get one. He was peeling away her skin to expose her quivering core to the frigid room.

He sighed heavily; his intensity dropped. "Dr. O'Brien, I've been at this a while now. I've seen some unusual things. I mean you no harm. You saved me in that alley just as much as I saved you. I think we could make good partners, if you'd allow it."

Good partners. Who was he kidding? He wanted to get inside her head. Study *her*.

"The offer of a position here at Segue is open. You'd get your own offices, whatever you require. There are three apartments upstairs you can choose from. West wing is haunted, so if you value your sleep, perhaps stick to the ones in the east wing, although they overlook the parking lot."

Haunted?

"I'd like to say the staff here is friendly—Dr. Riggs is certainly a sweetheart—but the subject matter we research tends to draw an interesting crowd. Don't take anything personally until you get to know them, and even then . . ." He raised his hands in a shrug, then pushed himself to standing.

"Dr. Riggs will discharge you from her care, eh, probably later this afternoon."

And then what?

"I'll drop back by to answer your questions, give you a tour, and help you select that apartment. Until then, get some rest."

Adam stared down at her for a moment, waiting. "See you later then," he said, turning back to the door.

He'd crossed the room before a good question finally burned through Talia's consciousness.

"Wait," she called.

He turned back, expectant.

"What if I don't want to stay? What if I'd rather take my chances with the wraiths?" If that snooping bastard was going to "put all his cards on the table," he had damn well better flip that last one over.

He held her gaze. "I don't think that would be in either of our best interests."

FIVE

THAT went well.

Take a traumatized and ill woman, tell her you know she's a freak, invite her to come on staff, and then insinuate that she has no choice. Excellent work.

Bracing himself on the corridor wall outside Patty's lab, Adam brought a hand up to pinch the bridge of his nose. Idiotic, more like.

He pictured Talia, IV stringing from her arm, wrapped in a clumsy robe, her pale, shocked face draining of color with every word he uttered. There was so little color to her in the first place, what with her white-blonde hair and black eyes. Only her lips retained a hint of pink.

To stay and work at Segue made much better sense on all fronts. For such an intelligent woman, that conclusion shouldn't be difficult to reach. Unless, of course, you're sick and scared to begin with.

"Have you slept?"

Patty. Adam dropped his arms and turned in the direction of her voice.

Patty stood just outside the door to her lab, hands on her hips, penny loafer tapping, mouth pinched in motherly concern. Her gray roots contrasted sharply with her fading brown hair, which he knew she hated, but couldn't be helped. Her every-eight-weeks trip to Middleton's only beauty salon had to wait until Talia was stable and settled. Not that Patty had asked.

"Yes, thanks." At some point in his life he had slept. He didn't need her on his back about it right now. The day was already halfway to hell.

"She looked beat," he said, angling his head toward Patty's lab and changing the subject.

"She should be dead. She isn't going to bounce back as quickly as we—or she—would like. The extent of the effects of heatstroke can take some time to manifest, and with her unusual physiology, I simply don't know what to expect."

"She's concerned that she's not free to leave," he said, warning Patty to be prepared for a difficult patient.

"Frankly, I'm concerned about that as well. I don't like deceiving her, Adam. I don't like it at all." Patty shook her head, eyebrows lifting as if to ask, *What are you going to do about her?*

"I can't very well let her go off to be killed when the answers we need—that the world needs—could be right there inside her. Look, I originally set out to bring her on staff, and that's exactly what I'm going to do. I still believe her work with near-death could challenge us all. She doesn't need to know that we're studying her, specifically."

Patty was already shaking her head again, getting her steam up.

Adam raised a hand for her to let him finish. "I know it's only a half-truth, but that's all she's going to get. That woman eluded the wraiths for two months. A wraith war is coming, and if we don't take advantage of every scrap of knowledge, we'll have nothing to fight with. We're already running out of time."

"It's not right." Patty's gaze met his, as if an accusation of wrongdoing would deter him from his path.

"What part of this whole situation is, Patty? Just run your

tests. You needed to take them because of her hyperthermia anyway."

"Not all of them," she corrected, "and the others I took in order for her get well, not to study her. It's her *consent*, Adam, that bothers me. It should bother you."

Adam's head ached. "Give me an alternative. I can see what's coming. I know you can, too. How do we fight an army of wraiths?"

"It's still not right." She shrugged helplessly.

"Are you going to run your tests or not?" Adam had no time or patience for stalling.

"If I say no?"

Adam put a hand on her shoulder and gentled his voice. "I'll find someone else to do it. I can find someone else, regardless. I can't have you breaking down on me, not now."

She shifted her weight forward. "No, I'll do it. Anyone else won't stand up to you. Won't stand up for her. I won't see her made a prisoner, though. I can tell you that much."

"Look, Talia's a little overwhelmed right now. Perhaps her wanting to leave won't become an issue. I'll be back this afternoon to show her around. I'll convince her to stay with as much truth as I think she can handle." He hadn't remotely considered Talia's leaving a possibility, not after the hell she'd been through, or he'd have been prepared for her question. Smoothed it over a bit.

Adam gripped the back of his neck with one hand to loosen the corded muscles that seemed to grip his skull.

But as long as he was making women mad at him . . . "I want to start testing the extent of Jacob's rapid healing again."

Patty's eyes glittered. "Don't push me, son. No matter what that poor man has become, I won't be part of any purposeful harm. *No harm.* I draw the line there." Patty drew an emphatic imaginary line between them.

"He's a cold-blooded killer and you know very well what the aim of this institution is."

Patty's face flushed. "I was at Jacob's christening. I saw him graduate from Harvard. Your mother borrowed my handkerchief. I will not purposely cause pain until the moment we can euthanize him. Even then, *my* aim is to see that he goes as peacefully as possible."

The argument went back six years to the family "intervention" in Jacob's disturbing new lifestyle. Dr. Patricia Riggs, Mom's childhood friend and the Thorne family doctor, was on hand for discreet support. No one doubted she'd keep her evaluation of Jacob's condition within the Thorne family. Mental illness? Drug addiction? They should be so lucky.

Patty was in the room when Jacob "kissed" Mom, witnessing the extent of Jacob's transformation. She saw what came after, as well. Adam wasn't proud of that. Now she still honored the friendship regardless of the risk to herself.

Ah, hell. She deserved a little honor back, not him snapping at her.

Adam exhaled his frustration and dampened his tone. "You're a softy, Aunt Pat. Always have been."

The *Aunt Pat* had Patty's nose reddening, eyes rapidly blinking against tears. Pat with no family of her own, no family but the fucked-up Thorne brothers.

"I need to get back. Get Dr. O'Brien back in bed," she said, voice high and broken.

"Okay. I'll be around, say two o'clock?"

"That'll be fine. Try to keep the tour short. She's bound to get tired quickly."

Adam nodded and rounded the corner from Patty's lab to his own office. He coded himself inside. A glance at the monitor told him that over the past hour Jacob had migrated to the far corner of his cell to recline, head lolling with boredom. Which was just fine.

Then he got a good look at his desk. The files dedicated to leads on Talia O'Brien's whereabouts could safely be shredded. Security reports had to be seen to. Budget. Correspondence to a half dozen field researchers. And the updated global wraith watch needed reviewing so that he was current on areas of wraith growth, movement, the establishment of supply chains and wealth.

The wraiths were organizing. They even had a friendly and innocuous-sounding name. The Collective.

Budget could wait. The Collective could not. Adam tapped the console on his desk. A three-dimensional image of the world sprang up on a cutting-edge monitor hung from the ceiling beyond his desk. Like blood trails, wraith movements spotted across the United States in red drips of varying concentrations, coagulating in big cities where feeding could be masked by the concentration of crime.

Adam ran a program to track the rate of growth. The computer produced alarming streaks of rapid development that had Adam's chest constricting. Within—what?—a *year* The Collective would have a sizable force in every major U.S. city. Nothing short of war would eradicate them.

Adam sat back in his chair. Willing or not, there was no way he could allow Dr. O'Brien to leave.

"Haunted with a view or peaceful without?" Adam asked as he pushed Talia's wheelchair out of Patty's office.

Talia had been sullen and silent upon his arrival, dressed in khakis, pink blouse with a wavy-looking collar, and slippers. Considering the clothes' conservative and matronly cut, Adam deduced that they were both Patty's selections and taste, ordered and overnighted while Talia recovered. The shoes must not have fit, but Adam wasn't about to ask and stir up trouble between the women. Only Patty could have talked Talia into the wheelchair, ready to go at two o'clock on the spot with mutiny written all over her.

"You can't be serious," Talia returned.

"In your line of study, surely you've considered the existence of ghosts." He stopped at an elevator at the end of the hallway. The silver doors parted to reveal the vestiges of an antique iron cage, a throwback to the building's origins. If Talia thought the ironwork odd, she didn't voice it.

"That's not what I meant," she said. "You can't imagine that I would actually select my own prison cell and give you any kind of false support for your keeping me here against my will. This whole 'tour' is a farce."

"You're not a prisoner; you're a staff member."

"I resign," she said.

"I'll consider your resignation when you can walk on your own two feet without turning green." The lie sounded smooth and reasonable, even friendly, but then Adam was well practiced.

They stopped one floor up, exiting into a marble-tiled atrium over which an enormous crystal chandelier sparkled like a suspended falling star against a background of rich mahogany.

He halted there while he coded them out a set of French doors and onto a sweep of white terrace that stretched around the east side of the building.

Unkempt, overgrown lawns rambled away from the building into the tree line. The natural, rolling green collided with a dense forest of spruce and, farther east, white pine spiking along Knob Ridge. The air outside, thick with moisture and sticky heat, clung to Adam's skin and clothes.

Talia twisted her head to look over her shoulder. Adam followed her line of sight. Segue walls climbed brick and stone, multistoried, with extended wings and terraces jutting symmetrically off at each side. Pretentious front steps led to the white-columned main entrance below them, and to the left.

"Okay, so, one more time: where are we?" Talia asked at last.

Adam grinned. "Segue operates out of what used to be the Fulton Holiday Hotel, a kind of turn-of-the-century West Virginian mountain resort for the upper crust."

Her gaze dropped from the building to him. "The kind of place they profile on the Travel Channel? Ladies in white dresses, croquet on the lawn?"

"Something like that. Or at least until the Spanish flu epidemic of 1918. The hotel was on the brink financially. Apparently, the nearby system of caves was not as much a lure as Theodore Fulton thought they'd be. When the flu hit the hotel, Fulton fell ill himself and died soon after. His sons ran out on the place. It changed hands a couple of times until it came to my family."

Talia pushed herself out of her chair and walked slowly to the edge of the terrace. Adam followed, watchful.

He continued, "I tried to restore what little bits of the hotel I could without impinging on Segue's needs. Found the chandelier from the foyer in a storage cellar, overlooked by the looters and vandals who stripped the place in the years after it was abandoned. Took a little doing, but this is pretty close to how it would have been."

"It's very—" she began.

He stepped to the edge and glanced at Talia's profile. Her white skin glowed against the backdrop of green, the afternoon sun warming her complexion from ash to soft pink and gold marble. Stray twists of blonde tugged away from her shoulder to stream across her cheek, to lift and quiver on the light breeze.

"—remote," Talia finished.

Lovely in profile.

She turned her black-cat eyes on him, meeting his gaze. Disconcerting head-on.

Time to get down to it. Adam took a deep breath. "I've done my near-death research based on the substantial bibliography at the end of your paper."

She turned away again and leaned up on the banister, all curiosity and interest suddenly shuttered behind a hard expression.

"From what I've read, near-death experiences often include a meeting with already-departed family, sometimes friends, but always someone in close connection with the person undergoing the experience."

Talia didn't answer. Kept her gaze off in the distance.

He tensed, watching her every movement for reaction. "What I can't figure is how Shadowman fits into the near-death scenario, unless that's a code name for someone who knows how the wraith threat began." He kept his voice light, tone neutral, as he suggested his theory. "A ghost, maybe, like those that populate Segue?"

Her expression remained impassive.

Adam pushed harder. "It wouldn't be so hard to believe. Jim Remy, our resident parapsychologist, is half in love with Segue's Lady Amunsdale. Been tracking her obsessively since he caught sight of the beauty. Is Shadowman a ghost? Someone who has already passed but might have our answers?"

If that were the case, protocols would have to shift dramatically to the occult. What he needed was a confirmation, a clue, something to point him in the right direction.

The muscles in Talia's face tensed, but she remained composed. "I'm not going to answer your questions. Thank you for saving me in the alley and for the medical attention you've provided. When possible, I'd like a ride into the nearest town, and I'll go from there."

"That's not going to happen," Adam said. He only had to close his eyes to see the computer-generated wraith projections again. The reality was, Talia didn't have the luxury of debating the issue. Time was short. He needed information on Shadowman now.

Her head whipped toward him. "Let's just get this straight—I *am* a prisoner here."

No, prisoners he kept in the basement. Maybe it was time she learned the difference. Her new lodgings could wait, he had an altogether-different destination in mind now.

She's not ready, an internal voice warned.

None of us are, a harder self returned.

"I want you to meet someone. I think he'll be very influential." Adam gestured to the wheelchair.

She took her seat coldly, folding her arms for emphasis, and he pushed her back inside to the elevator. He coded it open, backed her within, and selected Sublevel J. For Jacob.

The elevator hissed downward, doors opening into the outer atrium to Jacob's cell. Two guards stood sentry at the cell entrance, Ben and Thomas. Both had powerful, broad shoulders, thick necks, and muscular legs in command of quick reflexes. Except for their facial features and their coloring, one black and the other olive, they could have come from the same gene pool.

Takes two smart, strong, and trained men working in concert to bring down a wraith.

"I don't want to be here. I want you to know that this is against my will." Talia's voice shook and she gripped the arms of the wheelchair.

While second nature to Adam, the security had to be overwhelming from Talia's perspective. Adam had personally selected the guards, pored over the blueprint to Jacob's cell, and debugged the security program that ran the system. These guards and the coded, locked doors weren't just security, they were the wraith reality. The sooner she got used to it, the better.

"I don't want to be here either." Jacob made Adam's skin crawl and his chest ache, but the time for reservations was over. If he asked it of her, he could give her no less himself.

Adam nodded to the guards and coded the outer door to Jacob's cell open. He angled Talia's wheelchair inside and up to the main console, a white arc of work space fitted with security monitors, control panel, computer oversight, and speakers.

Adam tapped on a screen, set front and center. "That's Jacob." He swallowed hard. "My brother."

Jacob lifted bonelessly to his feet, his movement a subtle and graceful contradiction of nature. White and clean, his junk waggling between his legs, he stepped up to his favorite camera.

"D'you bring me a treat, Adam?"

Talia recoiled from the console. She pushed out of her chair and backed to the wall.

Adam didn't blame her. He didn't even try to keep up a pretense of Jacob's humanity anymore.

"He's a wraith," she said.

The room darkened perceptibly. Talia dissolved into a mottled haze of shadow. Jacob's smiling face was in the monitor, seemingly unperturbed or unaware of the darkness falling on this side of the cell wall.

The guard's hand went to his weapon, but Adam waved him down. "Just stay put and do nothing until I say otherwise."

Adam knew this drill. The flight from Arizona had made him a quick study.

"Smells like a woman, Adam. You finally get yourself a girl?"

"Talia. Dr. O'Brien. Jacob can't get out. You're safe." Adam kept his voice calm and sure. "You saw my security measures. Each has a minimum of three redundant systems. I haven't overlooked anything. I swear it to you."

"You can live and work here? With *that* in your basement?" Her voice was breathy and uneven.

"You will, too." He moved slowly forward.

The trick was to approach without confrontation. To reach her skin to skin. Then bring her out.

"Adam," Jacob sang, making things worse. "Give her to me. I know just how to handle her. I have something very particular in mind."

Adam took her by the shoulders and turned her body toward him. He slid his hands over her collar to her neck, then higher to cup her face, his hands on her bare skin.

His vision grew sharper, his senses more acute. Her skin was taut silk, the contrast of her bright hair and pale skin against half shadow, otherworldly.

He peered into her dark eyes and made damn sure that his were in her own line of sight, capturing her full attention. He didn't expect the pull of physical connection that made him want to draw her closer. To cover her soft form with his body. To protect her.

She was so weak already. If he could have spared her all of this, he would have. But he had no choice.

She was already shaking her head. "Please let me go. I don't want to feel . . ."

"Afraid? It's natural to be afraid. Just don't let yourself be overtaken by it."

Talia's gaze hardened. "My fear has kept me alive."

"No. Your fear just prolonged the inevitable." A hard truth. "You would've died in that alley." A couple more hours in the heat would've done it, even if she'd managed to stay hidden from the wraith.

"So what? Now I owe you my life?" Her pulse raced under his fingertips. Patty was going to kill him.

He kept his voice steady, full of calm reason. He knew of all things she responded to reason. "I want you to hear me out. Come out of your fear and get a good look at what you're afraid of."

"Oh, come on, Adam." Jacob leered into the camera. "You forgot my birthday. Just one little cupcake?"

"Take a good look, Talia. He is trapped in there. Starved for years and mad with it. And with your help, we are going to find a way to undo him."

"She'd have to *do* me first, eh?" Jacob jeered.

"Talia, there's no other place to go. Wraiths cover the country from coast to coast. I don't know where you think you could hide. Here at least you could study them . . ."

". . . like you want to study me?"

The accusation hit home, smart woman, but he knew that to confirm her suspicions was to lose her.

Talia shuddered under Adam's hands. "I don't know what you think I can do."

"Near-death, Talia. And Shadowman." He stroked her check again with his thumb. Had to. Would have drawn her into his arms if she'd let him.

Jacob screeched, high and shrill. He *thamp-thumped* on the cell wall.

Adam's heart lurched at the sound, but he controlled himself. The cell would hold. It'd been designed to hold against anything. "You see, Talia? My brother fears one thing, and one thing only. All I have to do is say the name to terrorize him. The first time I tried to kill him—" the horrible memory slipped from the strongbox in Adam's mind "—he said, no, *taunted*, that Shadowman couldn't get him." There'd been a lot of blood that day. And the smell—Adam packed the memory away and concentrated on how it felt to hold Talia. Concentrated on hope to replace the misery. "Who is the source who met Shadowman?"

Jacob keened, high-pitched and pitiful.

Talia sobbed. "I don't want to be part of this."

"I'll keep you safe. I swear it," Adam pleaded. "Just tell me what you know so we can find out how to kill the wraiths."

"I saw what that one did to Melanie."

"And I saw what Jacob did to my parents." The memory came anyway. The pain of their loss and the burgeoning horror of what Jacob had become.

"Please, I don't want to feel this," Talia said. She groaned and twisted to disengage him, but he would not let go. He had to make her understand.

"Jacob got to my . . ." Adam broke off. Pain sucked the air from his lungs. He took a deep breath. In and out, forcing himself to do what should be automatic. Just like the old days.

Adam tried again. "He got to my mom first. Killed her before we even knew what was happening. When Jacob went after my dad, I grabbed the fireplace poker. I was too late."

Talia whimpered.

"But when he came after me, I hit him across the eyes. I was lucky. Wraiths still need their eyes to see. Once I blinded him, I trapped him in a concrete cellar on our property. Then I shot him."

The gut-twisting, almost hysterical, fear of the time washed over Adam. The first time he'd turned the gun on his brother, the abrupt report, the smoking hole just left of center in Jacob's forehead. If Adam'd had darkness to hide in, he would've very likely stayed there, too.

"I can still hear Jacob, *Shadowman can't get me.* He killed our parents and made a game of it."

"Must have been horrible. You loved them," she said, her

face lined with grief. She'd stopped fighting and instead bowed her head, her forehead just grazing his chin. "The pain of their loss never goes away, does it? It's always there, behind what you do. You keep going for them."

So she did understand. "I have to. I can't let go until this is over. Until Jacob is dead."

"But it's not my fight."

She wanted the truth. He was going to let her have it. "It's everyone's fight, now. The world's. Most just don't know it yet. Besides, a researcher looks for answers, and if this isn't the most practical application of your field of study, I don't know what is."

He dropped his arms in frustration. She leaned back onto the wall and faded into shadow.

"Why aren't you afraid of me?" she asked. "I could be just as horrible as Jacob in there."

Ah, a latent fear. She was just as afraid of herself as she was of Jacob. That alone took her out of the threat category. In contrast, Jacob embraced his inner monster and relished it.

Adam sighed. "I doubt it. You are as set against wraiths as I am. You tried to save my life in the alley. You were nice to Patty even though you were mad at me. And here we are in my personal hell, and you hate it as much as I do. I think you're safe. Further, I think we have a lot in common."

"I don't know what you think I can possibly do to help you."

"Let's find Shadowman," Adam pressed. "He's got answers for both of us."

Jacob shrieked; Adam filled with hope. The key was right here, at last.

He reached out to her in the dark. Found the slope of her neck, the curve of her jaw, just where he had left it. The shadows bled away from his vision. Tears streaked down

Talia's flushed cheeks. He needed to get her back in bed, and soon.

"Listen to him, Talia. Listen to Jacob."

His brother whined in rocking rhythm, a small, scared sound.

"We can stop the wraiths together. My brother first. Come out of your shadows. Face him."

"I don't want this. Any of it."

"Neither do I. When it's all over, we'll go on a nice, long vacation. Anywhere in the world."

Her black eyes filled with tears. A moment passed.

"I'd like to live to see the pyramids," she said, voice clogged with helpless fatigue.

"Egypt it is."

"Maybe the Great Wall." A fat drop slid down her cheek.

Adam laughed, wiping it away. "And China."

"The Eiffel Tower?" An edge of her mouth tipped up, streaking more tears down her cheeks.

"Paris. At New Year's, when the whole city is lit," he promised. "Come out, Talia."

The darkness dissipated. Jacob's keens took on volume. Talia's gaze was trained on the monitor, staring as Jacob bared inhuman jaws better suited to a shark or a piranha or a multifanged snake.

The guard gripped the counter for dear life, sweat running off the side of his face.

Talia trembled, dark eyes huge in a ghost face. "Where do we start?"

SIX

TALIA went with the west-wing apartment, haunted with a view. She had managed two months on the run from wraiths. She could handle this.

She shut herself into her new place, anticipation of some kind of woo-woo event crawling over her skin like creepy spiders. Waiting, breath-bated and twitching at every noise (damn vent rattled every time the a/c came on) was agony until she succumbed to exhaustion.

The bedroom light overhead glared when she woke in the morning. Perspiration pricked at her forehead and dampened her neck under hot, heavy hair in need of a ponytail elastic. She disentangled herself from her twisted sheets and blindly padded out of the bedroom.

Mid-bleary-step, a *Ha!* exploded into her consciousness. Ghosts, indeed. The man clearly spent too much time with his brother. At the meeting scheduled that afternoon to introduce her to the other staff members, she'd let him know. The thought sent a thrill of satisfaction through her.

The living room looked much friendlier dominated by the growing light of day. A deep red square sofa faced a large flat-screen TV mounted on the wall over a working fireplace. Two chunks of wood lay in a woven basket on the floor, as if she weren't hot enough. Tall bookcases flanked each side, mostly empty, though somebody had the dark humor to leave

The Shining to keep her company on her first night in a haunted hotel. Yeah, real funny.

A buzz sounded at the front door.

Talia ran a hand through the tangles of her hair and straightened the tee to the sweats she'd slept in, wishing she'd gone to the bathroom first thing. Too late now.

She peered through the front door's peephole. A woman's face warped into view.

Talia opened the door, crossing her arms to cover her lack of a bra.

"Good morning," the woman said. "I'm Gillian Powell. I'm one of the doctors on staff." She held a bundle of clothes in blues and purples, a flash of look-at-me pink, topped with athletic shoes.

Dread pooled in Talia's empty stomach. *Those better not be for me.*

"Nice to meet you," she said. "I'm Talia O'Brien."

"I know. I'm so glad you're here," Gillian said. "It's such a boys' club at Segue. We've got Vera in the lab and Priya in research and, of course, Mama Pat, but that's it."

Gillian appeared to be in her middle forties and fighting each year. She was compact and overly busty, and wore enough foundation to disguise her true complexion, makeup applied with amazing and enviable precision.

Gillian stepped around Talia to dump the clothes on the sofa. "Anyway, Adam asked me to outfit you this morning for Wraith Defense." She made a sour face. "Goody for you."

Yeah. Goody. Talia had hoped she'd have the morning to herself before the big introduction that afternoon. No such luck.

"I think I've got everything you'll need." Gillian glanced at Talia's comparatively diminutive chest. "Sizing should be okay . . . mostly."

Talia stalled. "Um. So what exactly is Wraith Defense?"

"Just the basics of how to defend yourself. Every month we are all required to drill, but we make a pretty lousy show of it. Most of us belong indoors, in a lab coat."

Talia's stomach growled. "What about breakfast? I haven't had a chance to stock my kitchen."

"Don't bother. Marcie, Segue's cook, is awesome. Just tell her what you like and she'll get it. And that way, you don't have to do dishes. I'll show you on the way down."

"Are you drilling today, too?" Talia reached for the clothes. The hot pink would *not* be going on her body.

"No. You, lucky girl, get a ménage à trois with Adam and Spencer."

Great. Her puddle of dread deepened. "I'll go change."

Adam and another man, presumably Spencer, were sparring when Gillian led her outside to a stretch of fragrant grass near the buzzing, overgrown garden. The air was clingy, the sun still filtered by the trees.

Talia stopped short. Adam couldn't possibly expect her to fight like *that*.

Slim black padding protected the men's knuckles. Each wore a molded helmet. Adam, his dark crop of hair jutting out the back of his gear, wore black sweatpants and a T-shirt. His arm muscles strained the short sleeves, the material subtly stretched over a hard, fit chest to taper to a trim waist. The pants were cut somewhat loosely, the soft fall of the fabric belying the conditioned body within. Talia's gaze lingered in momentary surprise and appreciation, before sudden self-awareness shifted her body from chill to rapid, embarrassed heat again.

The other man, Spencer, pivoted and kicked Adam in the stomach. He, too, was dressed in black, though diagonal silver stripes accented the shirt's ribbing and marked the breadth of his thighs on his pants.

Adam caught the outstretched leg, twisted, and sent Spencer spinning to the ground. Spencer landed on his back, coiled, and sprang to his feet. Only to be sent down again by a side strike from Adam.

Beautiful. They both had to be black belts at whatever they were doing. Gillian hooted approval.

"Enough," Adam called, breathlessly waving Spencer down. Adam unlatched the clasp under his chin and pulled the headgear off his sweaty head. Face flushed, chest heaving, he was the most potent man Talia had ever seen. The sight of him, coupled with what she knew of his character, was enough to confirm the obvious: Adam was a dangerous man.

She wanted an icy-cold bucket over her head. She couldn't very well make a show of fanning herself like Gillian was. Talia looked at the trees, the garden, and her borrowed sneakers. Anything but Adam.

Spencer stood and removed his headgear as well, uncovering a shock of dark blond. When he grinned, one side curled a little higher than the other, making him appear a little naughty.

Adam approached, forehead creasing as he gave Talia a once-over. His close proximity was disconcerting on several levels. Even the dark smell of his sweat was distracting, but not unpleasantly so. On the contrary, the sheen at his neck had her wondering what it tasted li—

"Did you sleep well?" Adam asked. "Any disturbances?"

"Not a one," Talia answered, regrouping. "By the way, I appreciate the reading material you provided."

Adam frowned; then a grin split his face. Made her heart jump.

"The Stephen King," he said, laughing. "You can thank Jim Remy. He charged sixty copies to me and put one in each room. All part of the Segue welcome package. How do you feel today?"

Talia shrugged. "Okay. A little hot and cold."

His gaze turned analytical. Probing. When he looked at her like that, he saw too much. "Pat warned us about that. You'll take some time to recover completely. Let me know if you are uncomfortable."

"I'm fine." She tried for a bright smile, the kind that bounced off further questions, protecting the twisting nerves in her belly.

"Okay, then," Adam said. "I'd like to introduce you to Spencer Benedict, our liaison with the Strategic Preternatural Coalition Initiative, a division under the U.S. Department of Defense. He is here to coordinate and facilitate communication between Segue and SPCI." He pronounced it *speecee*.

Talia had wanted a cold bucket of water, now she got one.

The government? If there were as many wraiths out there as Adam claimed, government cooperation made sense. Mutual aid suggested a shared objective, to discover the origin of wraiths and learn how to cure or destroy them. Intellectually, she accepted that, but anxiety still crawled over her skin. What did SPCI think of her?

Talia approached and held out her hand like any normal person would. It was important to look normal. "Nice to meet you."

Her gaze flicked to Adam in question. *Does he know?*

Adam shook his head shallowly.

Spencer took her hand and squeezed. "Likewise."

Talia caught a quick rush of curiosity mingled with fading resentment and sharp competitiveness. If she had to make a guess, she didn't think Spencer liked losing to Adam, especially in front of female witnesses.

Adam's intensity retreated. "Okay, then. First up, Wraith Defense 101. Spencer, I think we're done here. Thanks for the workout; I needed it."

"Don't you need someone to play wraith?" Spencer winked

at Talia. It was a good cover, but Talia knew better. Spencer wanted another chance to show off.

"We're not doing much today. Dr. O'Brien isn't fully recovered yet."

"You sure? I could stick around . . ." Spencer looked more closely at Talia. Made her retreat a step.

"We'll be fine. Thanks." Adam's tone was decisive.

"You could go get that fifty you still owe me from last week's poker game," Gillian said to Spencer. Her tone was sarcastic, but she'd made a seductive S out of her body. Wasn't hard with those curves. Talia felt awkward and gangly in comparison.

"Why would I want to do that?" Spencer asked, hanging a sweaty arm over Gillian's shoulders. "Then you'd stop bugging me about it."

"Because I'll have to kick your ass if I don't get it," Gillian said.

"Promises, promises," Spencer returned. The two started back to Segue, taking their time to cross the grass.

"Spencer got in this morning," Adam said when the others had reached the building. "He doesn't know anything about you beyond your dissertation and the mention of Shadowman. But he's smart, so watch yourself around him. If he found out about your abilities, he'd feel obligated to inform his superiors."

Talia swallowed. Her knees felt suddenly weak. Now that she was recovered, she could run. Hide. She wouldn't make the same mistakes she'd made before. She could go to . . .

"Talia," Adam said, "if and when your abilities become known to Spencer, I give you my word that I'll be there every moment to see no harm comes to you. I make a good ally. You can trust me to stand by you."

Conviction underscored Adam's words, and Talia knew he was well-meaning. But she'd felt just how close he was to the edge when he showed her Jacob. He was asking her to trust him to take care of her, but she knew the man was at his limit. He couldn't do everything, be everywhere. He was only human.

"Walk with me," he said, and they headed for the trees. As they crossed the shin-deep grasses, Adam began, his tone losing its intimacy and taking on authority. "Every employee of Segue is trained in the basics of wraith defense. Most of it, you already know. You can't kill a wraith; you can only subdue him for as long as he takes to regenerate. A wraith's speed and strength will always outmatch yours several times over, so do not attempt a direct attack. Hiding is—with your exception—impossible; wraith senses far exceed ours."

So run like hell. Long grass stalks whipped at her ankles, stinging and biting. Talia stayed behind Adam to avoid any accidental touches. She couldn't think straight when bits of his emotions buffeted her own. She was barely hanging on as it was.

"The easiest way to subdue a wraith is with firearms. Because wraiths don't react to pain and have superior endurance, shots to the head are much more likely to slow them down than shots to the body," Adam continued. "You will be trained in the use of firearms. A firing range is set up on the other side of the building. There are occasions, however, when you may not have access to a gun."

Talia glanced at Adam's face and regarded the yellow bruises on his temple. He'd had no firearm in the alley and barely escaped with his life.

"Counterintuitive though it may seem, head for large groups of people. The wraiths have thus far retreated from public exposure." Adam held a large tree branch out of the way and gestured for Talia to join the cool company of the trees.

"But then why not expose them? Push the wraiths out in

the open? Put them on the defensive." Make them hide in the shadows for a change.

Adam scowled. The branch slapped back behind him. "And cause widespread public panic? A wraith free-for-all buffet as our focus shifts from learning all we can about them to rescue and containment."

"Still. Public awareness—"

"—would only complicate an already untenable situation. Not an option at this time. This is far enough." Adam stopped in a wide circle of tall trees. Fragrant pine boughs, heavy with needles, overshadowed the spot.

Talia halted and folded her arms, nails biting into her skin at her elbows. Pinched, but the discomfort was distracting her from yelling at the insanity of his position. The man wouldn't even discuss forewarning the public when preemptive action could save lives.

"I won't press you physically today," Adam said, "but we need to explore the possibilities and range of your fear reflex. We should be out of sight of Segue here. I'd have worked with you in the training rooms inside, but they can be monitored discreetly, and with Spencer in residence, I want to play it very safe."

Safe would be getting far, far away from here. Away from Spencer, away from Jacob, and away from Adam and his unnerving way of getting under her skin.

"Let's start with your fear reflex. How your fear—"

Something snapped inside her. "Can you quit calling it that? My *fear*? What the hell is that? Makes me sound pathetic, which I *am*, but you don't have rub it in every chance you get." Talia glanced over her shoulder. Nobody there, the white block of Segue cut into shining ribbons by the trunks of the trees. Nobody was close enough to hear. "And, furthermore, the word is not accurate: It's not a reflex and it's not made of fear. Just because you've witnessed my ability when I've been afraid, does not mean my fear creates it. You're implying a causal relationship where none exists. Bad logic, really."

Adam lips twitched, one moment his demeanor hard, the next he strained for composure and gravity. As if this were funny.

He should save himself the effort.

"If not fear, then what is it? How does it work?"

"I don't know," Talia said. The darkness did not come from inside her like emotion. She reached for the thin, silky layers. Or—or moved into them, but without taking a step. *In between* one place and another, a place wraiths couldn't reach.

But that made no sense. It would be ridiculous to articulate it.

"Well, how do you alter your environment? What is your range?" Adam stepped forward and grazed her jaw with the back of his fingers. "How is it that when I touch you in the midst of it, my perceptions change as well?"

Adam's touch was so quick and unexpected, Talia didn't have time to dodge it or brace for what filled her. His stroke carried an electric current of interest, all his considerable intensity focused on her. It had been there in Jacob's cell, a strange thread of intimate curiosity in the midst of painful revelations. But now, alone with him under the sky, the sensation had an edge of intent, and most disturbing of all, desire.

Talia retreated. She couldn't get her feelings straight when he stood so close. When his emotions tangled with her own. Did he have to crowd her space? Did he have to ask so many questions? Couldn't he just give her a little room to breathe?

"Can you do it at will?" He dropped his hand.

His questions needed answers. She'd had a peek inside him. Now it was her turn. Aunt Maggs would be horrified that she was about to break her childhood promise to never, ever tell anyone about what she could do. Sorry, Maggs— the worst had already happened. She'd been discovered, and now she had to learn how to save herself.

"I—" Damn it. She'd never talked about this before. She remembered what Adam had been through, took a terrifying inward leap, and started again. "For me, shadows have texture and . . . and substance. I can feel them. Even now, I can feel them."

They were all around her—in the dark patches under the trees, the filtered light through the leaves, the cast of her and Adam's body on the ground. If she wanted, she could reach for the darkness, tuck herself under its umbrella to look out at life from a safe refuge.

"How does it feel?" Adam's tone softened.

Talia sighed. "Safe. And cold." And lonely.

"Can we try it together? You've been in distress each time I've experienced it. I'd like to . . . take a look around." He held out a hand. His expression was neutral, almost businesslike, so she didn't trust it.

Talia looked at his outstretched palm, then at his face. She didn't want to touch him. Feel him inside her again.

"Come on." He wiggled his fingers. "We've done this before. Let's just take it nice and slow. Go easy."

But she'd been afraid for so long. It was past time to try something new. Talia braced for the worst and grasped his hand.

Sensations inundated her. His relief. Amazing control. Curiosity with, yes, a distinct sexual undercurrent that sent eddies of arousal to burn and buzz through her blood to her belly. Talia swallowed hard and tamped down on her reaction, fighting to think. *She* couldn't be turning him on, that was for sure. Could be the anticipation of her trick with shadow that gave him a charge. Or fighting Spencer. Anything but her.

Only when she shoved that feeling away did she notice something darker, uncomfortable, even toxic within him that she couldn't name and didn't want to try.

"When you're ready," Adam said.

This was insane. She was certain she'd regret it later. Anxiety constricted her breathing, tightened her skin, but she pulled on shadow, softly.

She heard Adam's intake of breath as she wrapped the veil around them, the day falling from sunny blue to a dreamy murk. They stood in layered fog, the veils of shadow sensuously lapping at their bodies. The trees, the meadow beyond, the hulk of Segue were all there, yet somehow appeared transient. As if one good gust of wind might carry it all away.

Adam's hand warmed in hers. He filled her with his wonder, which was better than all the rest. Made her realize how beautiful shadow was, too.

"A little more," he said.

Talia reached, and the day darkened to dusk, the orb of the sun shifting from blazing yellow to deep violet. The world turned to myriad purples and shades of blue and black. Sounds stretched so that the birds' twitters and crickets' chirps became high, eerie notes warped by darkness. Shadow settled on her shoulders and slid deliciously against her skin in welcome.

Adam's wonder turned to awe and building excitement.

Talia glanced at him to see how much of what he felt could be read on his face.

He looked down at her, about to say something, but instead he stopped and stared. That sensation was back, a trickle in the sense of his discovery, then a flood blotting it out. Desire.

So he did want her.

She'd have torn herself away, but his gaze held her. His eyes lowered to her mouth, then forcibly lifted again.

She trembled, tension coiling in her deepest core, and Adam's grip tightened. Tugged her toward him. She stumbled, but allowed him to enfold her, turning her in the circle of his arms so that her back was trembling against the wall of his chest, yet still holding her hand. He felt so good she let herself stay, and be, quivering in anticipation of what he'd do next.

"Do you have a name for this place?" His voice was a low caress at her ear, his breath in her hair.

Swamped sensations muddled her head. "Segue?"

"This isn't Segue, not anymore. This is . . ."

Oh. "Between. Shadow."

His mouth grazed her neck, temptation roaring across their connection. She could've easily lost herself to it. Wanted to lose herself. To feel everything his touch promised.

He shifted slightly behind her, lifting his head, surveying the valley again. She turned her face to catch the warmth coming off his body—so much better than the chill of her darkness.

But she caught a hint of that bad feeling again, bleeding insidiously into the desire.

"What would happen if . . ." his words cut off in a surge of longing.

"Yes?" her own longing answered.

". . . if someone were to die here? Do you know?"

Talia tensed. Tried to pull out of his hold. "I don't know what you mean."

He held on tightly. "Jacob. If I killed him here, would he stay dead?"

The dark emotion grew dominant, pooling inside her. Viscous, lethal, like a poison, transforming his other feelings. She knew what it was now.

"Let me go." She yanked harder.

Adam wouldn't release her. "We've barely begun . . ."

The sickness leeched through his being, turning his strength and emotions to suit its own ends.

". . . but we're still done," Talia said. She twisted her wrist and broke his grasp. She took the darkness with her as she ran back through the trees, leaving Adam to his demon, Rage.

Adam escorted a silent Talia toward the conference room. He stole a glance at her. She'd changed back into Patty's clothes and looked composed, the epitome of professionalism, but the way she clutched her notebook to her chest told him that she was angry. Even with her expression set, she was lovely, enticing, making him seriously reconsider his "do not fraternize with employees" policy. And Talia in her shadows? A goddess. Too bad she seemed determined to stay away from him. What happened?

He thought the investigation of her gift of shadow was a smashing success. He wanted to learn more at the earliest opportunity. The possibilities for research, for Jacob, had been sparking in his mind since she'd revealed what lay in darkness. What kind of creature was she to be able to do such a thing?

They stopped at the door to the Fulton Hotel's second ballroom, which he opened and held wide for her. She went through sideways, wouldn't even risk a casual touch. Okay, very angry.

Segue's full complement of live-in research staff, all seventeen of them including Custo and Spencer, hushed as he and Talia approached the long mahogany conference table. All but Jim and Armand, who didn't pause in their heated argument for a second.

"Gentleman . . ." Adam said to shut them up.

He pulled a chair out next to his own from the table, but

Talia moved down its length and selected one near the center.

Maybe he'd been a little too blunt in his references to fear, too direct with his questions. But, damn it, she of all people had to understand how immediate the wraith threat was.

He'd talk to her again. Later.

Adam raised his hands to address the group. "I'd like everyone to extend a warm welcome to our newest staff member, Dr. Talia O'Brien. I am personally excited and honored to have her with us. Most of you have read her dissertation—if you haven't, then please do so—and should have a good idea about what near-death experiences constitute."

Armand sat immediately forward, eyes slanting first at Jim and then at Talia. "I'd like to state for the record that I'm not into any of this voodoo-hoodoo, life-after-death crap. I am a scientist. Cold spots, indeed. The wraith question is not a metaphysical one, but a biological one. You want to kill Jac— a wraith, you find a way to alter his cells' regenerative capacity."

Jim was shaking his head. "How can Jacob regenerate when he does not feed on matter?"

Armand pressed his lips together. "That's what I hope my research will answer."

Gillian raised her pen. "Perhaps if we focus on curing the original disease that caused the transformation . . ."

"I'll tell you why he regenerates," Jim interrupted. "It's obvious. He feeds on the souls of others."

Adam let the dialogue escalate. Talia's gaze twitched back and forth between the men, her forehead tense with concentration.

"There's no such thing as a soul," Armand shot back. "You're making things up to support your pseudoresearch."

"But if we look at the origin of the disease," Gillian persisted, "perhaps we can find the virus or compound responsible for . . ."

Jim's large ears turned red. "Just how do you explain Lady Amunsdale then? You can't deny the existence of ghosts if you've seen her."

Gillian dropped her pen on the table in defeat. Whenever Jim brought the lady ghost into the argument, there was no moving him. Parapsychologists in general garnered little respect. What started as professional vindication from proving the existence of ghosts had turned into deep attachment. Jim was besotted. He'd been chasing that flash of white skirt since his first year here.

Armand shuttered his eyes. "Lady Amunsdale does not have a corporeal body for me to study. I allow that she exists, but she is out of my field of reference."

Jim sneered. "Oh, don't give me that shit—taking the easy out. What about Dr. O'Brien's near-death? Six hundred and six reported cases of leaving the corporeal body and returning back to it."

Talia sat up straighter, eyes widening.

Adam winked at her. She looked away without acknowledging him.

"What about other forms of out-of-body experiences? Ones where the body persisted, alive, while the spirit roamed?" Jim Remy bored his index finger into the table in front of him for emphasis.

Armand dramatically sighed. "I know what you're getting at. You're working your way around to the idea that because Jacob has lost his humanity, he doesn't have a soul."

Jim Remy stood. "My tests prove that Jacob is dead inside. No soul."

Jim's claim still stabbed Adam, even though the results were more than two years old. Jim's tests revealed a signature electromagnetic reading in the presence of ghosts and humans. But not wraiths. Something was definitely missing from them, and if a ghost had it, the obvious conclusion was spirit, or *soul*. Jacob's utter lack of humanity, his disregard for family connections or responsibility only proved it all the more.

Adam cleared his throat, and the room's attention swung to him. "Dr. O'Brien. You are witnessing an old but fundamental Segue debate. It all boils down to a simple, but surprisingly difficult question: what constitutes death?

"Dr. Remy postulates that something forced Jacob's soul to pass on, yet the body remains alive. On the other hand, you have Lady Amunsdale, a confirmed Segue ghost. She has no body and little awareness of the physical world, and yet maintains a distinct self. Which of them is alive? Which dead?"

The room fell silent. All looked at her expectantly.

Talia wet her lips. Her eyes roamed the table, but she addressed Armand. "Uh. Well. A person has a life . . . and a death. If you stick to the physical . . ."

Armand cocked his head impatiently.

Talia cleared her throat, placing her pen at a perfect right angle to her notebook. "Then wraiths are alive and ghosts are dead. While metaphysically, just the reverse is true."

"Haven't we just said all that?" Armand interrupted.

"Well, yes, but . . ." she stammered.

Adam sat forward in his chair. He knew her mind and loved the way she organized problems like thought puzzles, then took an obvious solution and turned it on its head. This was exactly the reason he wanted her on staff. If Armand would just cool it for a second, Adam knew she could think the debate through to a new conclusion.

"Then get on with it," Armand said with exaggerated impatience.

Talia's eyes narrowed. "I will if you'll quit interrupting me."

Adam controlled a smile. This was going to be good.

She took a deep breath. "If a person can lose their life, perhaps they can lose their death, as well."

Armand rolled his eyes. "You're as bad as Jim Remy. That's just a perversion of a romantic metaphor."

"And what is a metaphor but a new way of seeing something?" she answered back. "Isn't that what we are doing here, looking at things from different perspectives?"

"Fine. Then why would a person lose their death?"

"People have been trying to lose death forever," she argued. "Industries thrive on the desire to remain young and vital. Given the choice, most people would throw their death away and never look back."

Talia's comments were simplistic, but her idea sent a slick, cold sickness up Adam's spine. Was the answer that easy?

Adam looked around the room as realization dawned on the faces of his staff. Talia glanced at him, finally shedding her anger and replacing it with pity.

Immortality. Live forever young. Forever strong. Forever beautiful.

Dreadlocks's awful song lyric came back to him then. *Human race to crush Death first.*

Adam sat back into his chair. People who gave their lives were heroes or martyrs. What if people could give up their deaths? Was such a thing possible? And what would that make them?

Adam knew the answer was locked in a cell under Segue.

Jacob suffered from no disease or demonic possession. This was so much worse, something Adam hadn't allowed himself to consider. Jacob was a monster by choice.

Talia watched Adam's demeanor change. His gaze sharpened, face flooding with color. The curve of his jaw became more pronounced. His grip on the table whitened his knuckles. If she were touching him, she knew she'd be feeling his dark passion all over again. One overwhelming goal. To kill.

"Does it really matter if it's Jacob's choice or not?" Armand whined.

Adam knocked once, hard, on the table and strode from the room. Talia knew exactly where he was going. She'd lost her family as well, and if there were answers to be had, a betrayal to identify, she wouldn't be diverted. Adam was all about answers; he'd be heading to Jacob's cell. She was glad she didn't have to be present for the impending interview.

Custo also rose. "I think we're done for the day. Thank you all for participating. This has been"—he glanced at Talia—"very interesting." Then he rounded the table to follow Adam.

The room erupted into discussion.

Jim's strident voice cut through the din. "What may seem like superstition to you, Armand, may indeed have a scientific basis. Take the Indian Fakirs, who can control their heart rate . . ."

"Been here a week and already stirring things up."

Talia turned to the voice at her ear. Spencer.

"It was just an idea." Talia gathered her notebook and pen and sidled around her chair to leave. She wanted to think through the idea herself. Outline how she arrived at the conclusion. Diagram the implications. Find a way to help Adam.

"Touched a nerve," he said, following her. "Mind if I walk you to your office?"

She stepped back, out of reach. She'd had enough touching for one day. "Uh . . . I was actually going back to my room. I'm exhausted. My recovery is frustratingly slow going. A little later?"

His brows gathered in concern. "Then I'll walk you there."

"Oh, no. Not necessary." Didn't the man know an excuse when he heard one?

"Please. We can talk on the way." Apparently, he did.

Talia gestured him toward the door. At least Spencer effectively parted the crowd.

"Dr. O'Brien!" Jim waved his hand over the group of people.

"She'll talk to you later," Spencer called back on her behalf.

Talia kept one step behind Spencer to the elevator, but once inside, had no choice but to hear him out.

"Adam told me that you can think outside the box when he was putting your hiring before the SPCI panel. I see now what he meant." He flashed a charming grin. He'd have been more charming if he'd left her alone, though.

"I thought Segue was all Adam's."

Spencer waggled his head back and forth as if conceding a minor point. "The arrangement is more complicated than that. Adam began the institute, funds it himself, and decides on the research protocols, but he does so at the . . . sufferance of SPCI. When we discovered that Adam had captured, confined, and was studying a wraith, we almost shut him down. To make a long story short, we finally agreed on oversight, in the form of yours truly, and an active exchange of information."

Talia kept her mouth closed, waiting as the elevator number blinked from one to two to three to four. The arrangement must chafe Adam. He seemed to prefer to be in charge of things.

"It's actually in the best interests of everyone. Between you and me, SPCI is rather rigid in its approach to the wraith phenomenon. They never would have considered near-death as a line of inquiry. I have to admit that I'm occasionally swayed by the unconventional ideas that get batted around here. Just now, for example."

"Like I said, it was just an idea." Talia stepped out of the elevator and started down the hall.

"So here's my question: what would a person stand to lose if they made the choice to become a wraith?"

"Literally, their humanity." Surely he could see that. "One look at Jacob and, in spite of his appearance, there's no way to classify him as Homo sapiens. Only mythology and magic have labels appropriate for his kind. Hence, wraith."

Talia stopped outside her door. She punched in her code and made a mental note to change it immediately. She didn't like the way Spencer looked over her shoulder. The lock disengaged, and Talia opened the door.

Spencer raised a hand to stop it from shutting again. "And what is humanity, really?"

Talia frowned. She had no idea where he was going with this.

"Just playing the devil's advocate here. What is humanity? And doesn't everyone lose it eventually? Is Jim's Lady Amunsdale human?"

"I really couldn't say." Talia slipped inside. "That's his area of expertise."

"What I'm suggesting, Dr. O'Brien, is that human nature, in its very essence, is about change. No other species on this planet is aware of change. Aware of passing into and out of life to somewhere or something else. From body to spirit. Your work actually supports my conclusions—the tunnel, the bright light, moving from one state to another." His hand flipped left to right to demonstrate.

"Yes. So?"

"Perhaps becoming a wraith is no different. A passage from one state to another, with the single difference of remaining on this plane of existence."

Single difference! "You forget—they feed on their brothers and sisters."

"That's just the cycle of life. We are all predators, in our own way. We all do what it takes to sustain ourselves. Lie, cheat, steal, murder. They are no different." He flashed his lopsided grin again.

He couldn't be serious.

A weird light gleamed in his eyes. "Maybe they're better."

Talia's jaw dropped.

Spencer abruptly laughed, brought his hands up to surrender. "Hey. Just playing devil's advocate here."

"Yeah, okay." Talia closed the door in his face.

SEVEN

"OUT." The guards took one look at Adam's face and left the outer atrium to Jacob's cell.

Sudden movement on the monitor drew his attention. Jacob on his feet, running his hands through his hair to bring the lanky mop under control. Then he brought his face up to the camera while his body effected the grave and servile bow of a butler. *May I help you?* Always mocking him.

"You chose this." Adam dropped his hands on the console for support.

"I beg your pardon, sir?" Jacob inclined his head as if trying to understand what Adam implied.

Playing them both for fools. Not anymore.

"You chose to be this monster," Adam clarified, careful to enunciate each syllable. "Your condition isn't a new disease, an unanticipated consequence from using an exotic drug, or some strange possession. You *chose* this. You *want* this."

"And?" Jacob blinked rapidly in an outward show of extreme patience at Adam's stupidity.

Stupid is exactly what Adam felt. The idea that Jacob, the scion of the Thorne family, the prudent businessman and philanthropist, his fucking *big brother* would choose to become a monster had never occurred to him. The man Adam had known was brilliant, fearless, and vain in his responsibility for the legacy of the Thorne family. This devolution was beneath him.

"Why?" Adam's throat had tightened and the word came out in a broken croak.

Jacob straightened. "Don't be dense."

"You killed Mom and Dad. On purpose." Fresh pain spread across Adam's chest like blood from a mortal wound.

"Stop whining. They were going to die anyway, eventually."

"You fed on them," Adam said through clenched teeth.

"Like a babe to a mother's teat." Jacob sighed and grinned.

A hundred wonderful tortures sprang to Adam's mind, held at bay these many years only by the burden of family duty.

But now, desperate fantasies grew in Adam's mind like a dark garden of twisted flowers denied sustenance too long. Colorful creations that would trap and teach Jacob what a monster really was. Exercises in the limits of pain and loneliness. Acts that rivaled a wraith's soul feeding.

First, Adam had to know why. "You had everything handed to you. Born to wealth, the best education, a loving family, opportunities to do anything you ever dreamed, a girlfriend who loved you. Hell, you had plans, years in the making, to build Thorne Industries to dominate global markets. Why this?"

Jacob shrugged. "I got a better offer."

"What could possibly be better than what you had?" *You ungrateful son of bitch.*

"I got Forever. This—" Jacob looked around his cell, mouth pursed in distaste. "—this will pass. The world as we know it will pass, and after everything is gone, I will still be here. Then I can do anything I want, whenever I want. *That's* global power."

"Tell me how you did it."

"You know I won't."

"What if I want to join you?"

Jacob snorted. "You don't have the kind of long-term vision necessary. You're stuck in the past with Jena and Michael."

"That's Mom and Dad, to you," Adam bit out.

"See what I mean?"

Rage burned in Adam's chest, cauterizing the wound that was the loss of his parents. "I will end you. I swear it. I will find the way to undo this mockery of immortality, and I will tear you apart with my bare hands." Already his hands itched, *ached*, to enact the madness in his mind.

"Is that any way to talk to your older brother?"

Brother? How could that . . . that *creature* call himself his brother? Just because they shared the same gene pool? Adam didn't think so. Not anymore. Siblings could be disowned. All natural feeling of connection and obligation severed. Happened all the time.

Adam closed his eyes and willed his heart away from the wraith in the cell. Not his brother. He sought cold indifference. A removal of all feeling. Not his brother.

Jacob laughed. A light, gleeful little chuckle that poured gasoline on the fire of Adam's rage.

Adam choked. He had to get out of there.

He stumbled to the door, tapped numbers into the panel, and tripped out into the corridor beyond.

The guards brushed silently by, eyes askance, and resumed their watch within.

Custo leaned against the opposite wall, arms crossed, waiting.

"Why are you still here?" Adam yelled. "Why aren't you off living your own life, away from this constant nightmare? Find a woman, settle down, and have a bunch of brats."

"That bad, huh?" Custo lowered his gaze.

"Talia was right. He chose to become a wraith. Admitted it freely, as if I should have known all along. And I should have." Adam fisted and released his hands. They shook uncontrollably. He didn't know what to do with them short of wrapping them around Jacob's neck.

"Not you. It's not in your nature to think that someone close to you can be that destructive by design. You save people. It's what you do. It's what you have always done."

I was blind.

"Did you know?" Adam asked. Had Custo known all along as well?

Custo pushed off the wall and gestured toward the elevator. "No, but it doesn't matter. I'm not here for him. I'm here for you. You're the closest thing to family I've ever known. And family sticks. You taught me that every time you pulled my sorry ass out of trouble." Custo's mouth curved. "Remember that business with the boat?"

Family sticks. What the fuck was family? Adam sure as hell didn't have a clue anymore.

"I wanted to impress a girl," Custo continued. "You took the blame."

"You'd have been thrown out of school." If Custo were trying to distract him, he was doing a piss-poor job. Memory lane was not exactly where Adam wanted to be.

"That's part of why I did it, too. If I had been thrown out, maybe my family would've taken notice of me." Custo had been dumped in a boarding school at nine. No visits. No communication.

"They never realized your value."

Custo shook his head. "What I'm trying to say is that my family did take notice. My family was with me. I knew it the moment you told the cops that you stole the boat."

Adam looked over at Custo. His right arm. His friend. In every way that mattered, his brother.

The anger inside Adam cooled somewhat, abated to a few degrees above that six-year-old steady burn. It allowed him to gulp at air and smooth his expression. He could live with this trade. Hell, he had been living with it, working toward answers because of Custo's dogged support.

"Are we done being sappy yet?" Custo punched the elevator button.

"Yeah, I think so." Adam fought to bring his shakes under control. Flexed the last of the tremors from his hands.

The door slid open. Custo glanced back as he entered. "By the way, if ever there was somebody who needed to settle down with a bunch of brats, it's you."

Bring children into this world? Never.

Through the peephole in the door, Talia watched Spencer swagger back to the elevator. She had to do something. Give Adam something. He might appear calm and controlled on the surface, but she'd felt the grief and pain that roiled beneath, and how close he was to becoming overwhelmed by the bright white fury that laced his being. He couldn't go on like this for much longer.

And with Spencer spouting nonsense about how wraiths might be an evolutionary step up? No wonder Adam was sick over his brother.

The elevator pinged, Spencer stepped in, and the doors . . . finally . . . closed.

Talia eased out of her apartment, took a sharp right, and opted for the stairs. She coded herself into the stairwell and hurried down to the main level of the hotel portion. She exited by the kitchen, where the stairs terminated, and chanced the elevator—yes, empty!—to the office and laboratory subfloors.

If Adam already knew so much about her anyway, he might as well know what she'd discovered about Shadowman, her father. The research that had almost cost her life in the heat of Arizona.

None of it suggested how Shadowman could help kill Jacob and set Adam free. She didn't even know what Shadowman was. A ghost, like Adam suggested? That didn't feel right, and it didn't account for her abilities either. And why would Jacob fear a ghost?

Talia coded into her office and headed directly for her laptop.

A thought niggled in her mind: What Adam needed— though she'd never tell him, *no way never*—was that other devil, Death, the dark thing with the red eyes inside the black wind of her scream. The monster. The one who slaughtered the wraiths with a sweep of his scythe, and took Melanie down, too. Then had the perversion to—Talia shivered with the memory—to caress her cheek.

That monster could kill Jacob. Easy. Jacob should fear *him*.

She selected the file of images she'd been amassing, her research on Shadowman. CTRL A. Opened them all. She could give Adam this much at least.

They blinked one by one, layering onto the screen. As she waited, her mind turned inward, shifting the puzzle pieces of her origin around:

Jacob feared Shadowman, whom she'd met upon her momentary death, who likely had her ability to alter perception. But it was the monster who could kill him, called by her scream.

Two entities, and she was connected to both. One desired effect.

The heuristic rule of Occam's razor said the simplest theory was the best.

Why *two* entities? It made no good sense. Not unless . . .

Her stomach turned. The room suddenly warped around

her, and she clutched the table before her. It couldn't be, could it? Was her heritage so horrible? Her birthright so despicable?

Yes. Somehow she'd always known. It's why she was alone.

If she tried, she knew she could probably fit the puzzle together now. If she could summon the courage to face the truth, she could probably name Death. He was her father, Shadowman.

Adam left Custo in the elevator and headed to his office, grim anticipation redoubling in his blood. If Jacob had chosen to become a wraith, then someone must have offered him the choice. Jacob was never going to give away the identity of this individual, but perhaps the algorithms of The Collective tracking program could be modified to isolate the general location of the source.

Adam turned a corner to find Talia rapping on his door. His pulse quickened. His gaze darted up and down her body, but it was hard to get a sense of her curves when she was still wearing the shapeless clothes Patty had selected. He hoped new ones would come in soon. She was too young and pretty to be dressed like that.

"Can I help you with something?" If she was here, then maybe she wasn't angry anymore. Maybe he could have a real discussion with her. Work through her idea, see if her unique talents offered any solutions.

Talia jumped and whirled. Her hair slipped, strand by strand, from a knot at the nape of her neck. He didn't know why she bothered—the curls obviously rejected constraint.

"Sorry for startling you." Adam slowed his approach. First day on the job and she'd shaken up Segue. Of course, that's what he'd hoped. He'd wanted answers, and she'd given him one big enough to turn his world upside down.

"Do you have a minute?" She tucked a strand behind her

ear. Her eyes were strained. Sad, maybe. Or worried. Something had bothered her deeply.

"Of course. Come on in," Adam said, coding the lock. He reached around her to the lever that opened the door, his body surrounding hers for a moment. Her scent hit him, dark and sweet, an exotic fragrance more suited to her shadows than sterile Segue. The combination made him want to drop his head into her hair. Breathe deeper. His weight on the handle opened the door and she moved out of his circle and into his work space.

It took a moment for his head to clear before he followed her into his own office. *Employee*, he reminded himself. He couldn't ward off Gillian with that excuse and then pursue Talia. Besides, Talia was messed up enough as it was. She didn't need him complicating her stay here. Damn her fairy eyes.

"What can I do for you?" The door closed behind him. His gaze automatically flicked to the monitor—Jacob reposed in a corner, a small smile of satisfaction on his face, still gloating from their argument—and then back to Talia.

"First of all, I need to change the code on my apartment door," Talia said. She glanced at Jacob as well, her expression carefully circumspect, but she didn't comment. "Spencer saw me punch it in."

"You invited Spencer to your apartment?" Adam had already warned her about the implications of SPCI being aware of her abilities. She was too trusting. Next time he sparred with Spencer, he was going to make sure he kicked his ass extra hard.

In her room. Damn.

"He followed me up. Wanted to discuss my ideas about immortality and choice. He spoke as if becoming a wraith weren't such a bad thing after all. As if what they did wasn't . . . abhorrent." She frowned, a worry line forming between her brows. She, who'd seen what the wraiths were capable of and had been hunted herself, would not be able to tolerate any mind games on the subject.

"You want me to talk to him? Tell him to lay off?"

"I can fight my own battles, thanks. I just want my pass code changed."

Adam sighed. "Spencer has master codes, regardless. As do Custo and I, for security reasons. We have to be able to get inside any room in the event of an emergency."

"I don't want him or anyone else going in my room."

"Talia . . ." he argued, but his heart wasn't in it. The thought of Spencer touching her, of him making himself at home in her apartment, took all the strength out of Adam's argument. He didn't want Spencer in there either.

And Segue Security? Perhaps in this one case, a modification was called for. Something along the lines of Talia Security. "All right," he conceded. "I can disable his access to your office and apartment, but I am going to retain mine and Custo's. Nonnegotiable."

She nodded. "I can live with that. Thanks."

Adam swiveled to face his computer. Called up the security system. Indexed Talia's account. Entered his administrative override. "What do you want your new code to be?"

"Uhm. Aurora," she answered.

The word suited her. Aurora borealis. The magical northern lights. She'd look just about perfect with the colors framing her features. Brink of the world, a fairy on its doorstep.

"Thanks," she said. Request granted, he expected her to beat a hasty retreat. Instead, she chewed on her lower lip.

"Anything else?"

"Yeah. Um . . . are you okay? You seemed pretty upset at the staff meeting."

Something had happened during that meeting with Talia, too. She felt sorry for him. Nothing like a little pity to get her talking to him again. At least Jacob was good for something.

"I'm good," Adam answered. "I needed to hear what you had to say." He left it at that.

"Well—" She flashed a rueful smile. "I have something that might make up for it."

"Oh?" The woman was going to be the death of him.

"I was wondering if you have anyone covering the arts."

"Martial arts?"

Her lids dropped halfway, lips pursed. "Fine arts," she corrected.

Adam rapidly sorted his thoughts. "I know that the existence of wraiths has bled into popular consciousness. I wouldn't be surprised if people tried to make sense of what is going on through music and art. But I haven't pursued it as a research focus at Segue. Why do you ask?"

She inclined her head. "I think you may have missed something."

Adam sat forward. "How so?"

"It's what I was working on in Phoenix, before the wraith caught up with me. I was tracking down an artist. If you have a minute, I'd like to show you what I've found. I think you'll find it interesting, at the very least. I don't know if it will help with Jacob." Her gaze flicked to the screen. Like Custo and Patty, he knew she'd have understood what Jacob's choice meant to him.

"Could you come over to my office? Take a look?" She was chewing on her lip again, plumping it to ruby red. The worry was still in her eyes, so it couldn't have been Spencer that bothered her. Had to be something else. Maybe something she'd found.

Adam stood and gestured toward the exit. "Absolutely."

She used her new code to open the door, glancing out over her shoulder at him with a look of thanks, and then they stepped inside.

The room echoed with emptiness. Bare shelves lined the far wall, a couple of someone else's thick books stacked and forgotten on one shelf. The walls were plain white, scuffed here and there from equipment and storage. A dark wood conference table stood in the middle, her laptop open at one end. As far as he could see, her near-death research remained in cardboard boxes, but instead of on the table, where he had put them himself, now they were beneath, acting as a footrest.

"You know you can requisition anything you need or want for this space," Adam said, looking around for signs of her personality, her work, of someone moving in with the intent to stay. He really wanted her stay. He'd be thrilled if she'd drain Segue's account to make herself comfortable. If *he* could make her comfortable.

She beckoned him over to her laptop and hit the space bar to void the field of stars moving across the screen as she took a seat.

An image appeared, a photograph of a sculpture in a gallery setting. Adam bent low to make out a mixed-media, abstract creation, a representation of a human form writhing in agony and trapped by encircling mesh layers. Adam's gut responded to the piece, aching in sudden sympathy for the futility with which the figure fought his trap. The figure could be anyone, but Adam saw himself.

"Very powerful," he said, ignoring the way the sculpture thinned the air in his lungs. It was exactly the way Jacob made him feel. Trapped.

"Did you look at the name of the piece?"

Adam glanced down again. The image wasn't labeled in text on the screen as he expected, but if he squinted, he could just make out words on a placard on the floor in the photograph. MAN OF SHADOWS.

"That's not . . . You don't think . . ." She couldn't possibly believe that the sculpture was a rendering of *the* Shadowman.

"I do." Talia smiled. Her eyes finally lit with excitement, her darker emotion buried under the thrill of discovery. The expression set his nerves zapping. Pleasure made her positively beautiful. He had to tear his eyes away to concentrate on the screen.

"Aside from the name, how do you know?"

Talia held up a wait-for-it finger while she scrolled through the many files she had open on her screen and clicked with the other hand. Another image popped up, a black-and-white photograph, manipulated with digital illustration to create a desolate landscape, a figure similarly writhing, harried by a subtly transparent whirlwind around his body. The rendering was more surreal than the first, like a Salvador Dalí, but the effect was comparable.

His eyes flicked to the title, scrawled in pencil in the white margin beneath the image. *Shadow's Man.*

"Coincidence," Adam argued. "Believe me, I've checked out every reference to Shadowman on the Internet . . ."

Talia shook her head from side to side, eyebrows lifted.

"What?" Pressure built up in Adam's chest in a strange combination of frustration and excitement. He hated the thought that he had missed something all these years, but if there were more answers to be had this day, he'd take them gladly.

"I can show you six more, all similar. The images don't come up on an Internet search. Like you said, nothing related to Shadowman does. Somebody out there is controlling that. However, text inside images is not searchable, and in each of these cases, the titles are part of the image. You have to know the names of the artists and what to look for to find anything."

Adam grabbed and dragged a chair squealing on its wheels to sit next to Talia. "Explain it to me."

His motion had her tensing, but that couldn't be helped. The way things were going, he'd be around her a lot. She better start getting used to him now.

She sighed heavily. "It goes back to the accident I had when I was fifteen. My aunt Maggie died and, for a moment, I did, too. One minute I was in the car, the next I was surrounded by a darkness far deeper and denser than my shadows. I knew I was dying. I glimpsed this man"—Talia tapped the screen—"trapped by a dark wind. I can't describe the sensation. All I can say is that I knew instinctively he was . . ." She took a deep breath. ". . . *my father*. As you know, meeting family upon crossing is common in near-death experiences. I knew his name, Shadowman. He tried to speak, but I was already being pulled back to life. The EMTs had zapped me back."

Adam kept his composure. "Your father is Shadowman."

Talia's face whitened. He felt her searching him for a reaction.

"You are the source referenced in your dissertation," he concluded.

She nodded stiffly—attempting to cover some strong emotion—and went on. "Then my first year in college I was struck dumb when I happened into the student gallery. And there he was—Shadowman—in a sketch. The artist had no idea where he got the inspiration. Ditto for the other artists I've spoken to. The image just 'came to them.' So apparently, I'm not the only one who has seen him. Others have, too. And some have attempted to make a visual representation of him." Talia clicked through a couple of screens to demonstrate.

The similarities could not be denied. A bound male identified with shadow.

"So what are you thinking? Mass hysteria?"

"Hysteria, no." She winced. "Have you seen *Close Encounters of the Third Kind?*"

"You think Shadowman is an alien?" That was just too much.

She laughed in surprise, her expression clearing again. "No. Not that part. In the beginning of the movie, all these people with different kinds of lives envision the location where the spaceships eventually land. The mountain. Richard Dreyfuss makes a giant mud mountain in his kitchen . . ."

"I get it. You think Shadowman is trying to tell us something."

"Yes." She sat back in her own seat. "Maybe he's calling for help."

"Talia, if Shadowman is trying to contact someone, why not me? I've dedicated myself, my life, to discovering . . . What? Why are you making that face?"

She relaxed her look of skepticism. "I doubt you'd readily welcome or respond to subliminal messages. You're just not the type."

"You know my type?" This ought to be interesting.

She stuck a strand of white gold behind her ear. The lock slipped out and curled again at her temple.

"Most of the images I've been able to find are by artists. You know, people particularly attuned to inspiration. You're more of a manager. A leader. You're not"—she waved her hand in the air as if looking for just the right word—"open enough."

"Not open," he repeated, processing this. Right now he was open to a lot of interesting ideas.

"Not impulsive," she corrected, peering at her screen.

"I can be impulsive," he said. He glanced at her mouth.

He'd been pushed just about as far as any reasonable man could.

Ah, shit. Here he was going to warn Spencer off pursuing her, and he was ready—to what? Drive her away completely?

"What else have you got?" he asked to distract himself. He had to do something with his hands or he was going to touch her. He reached out, grabbed the laptop, and flicked to another image.

"No!"

But Talia was too late. A vibrant illustration filled the screen.

The graphic artist depicted a nude bombshell beauty reclining on a sumptuous divan, white-blonde curls cascading, mingling with a dark, multilayered cloak that spilled from her shoulders to the floor. Her heavy-lidded, tilted eyes regarded the viewer. She was somnambulant, sexual, and powerful. The woman's facial features were unmistakably Talia's. The provocative slope of her bare hips, the dip of her waist, the sudden swell of her breasts, branded his mind and scalded his blood.

The title was painted on the lower left in script, *Sleeping Beauty*.

Talia slammed the lid of the laptop closed.

"Umm." Her voice sounded thicker, clogged. "There . . . uh . . . may be some imagery of me out there as well. Of course, grossly exaggerating certain aspects, but still . . ."

Adam took a steadying breath to redirect the flow of his blood. "There's no reason to be embarrassed. You're a beautiful woman. But you are also part of this riddle of Shadowman, so I'm going to need to see everything you've found." He kept his gaze direct, his voice professional. It was hard, what with the fantasy woman standing right in front of him and his blood roaring south. Patty's frumpy clothes on that body were a crime.

Jaw tight with forced composure, she gave a perfunctory nod. "I'll e-mail them to you."

"I want everything you have," he repeated. She'd obviously wanted to hold some things back, and he didn't blame her. The woman had spent her life hiding what she was, and the image he'd just seen stripped every last layer away. Literally. Unfortunately, privacy was a luxury none of them could afford now.

"Of course. I'll send along my notes as well."

With a deft adjustment, Adam stood to go. To give her a little space. To give him some room to clear his head. A hard run ought to take the edge off the impact of the image, burning in his mind again.

One question, though. "The title. Why *Sleeping Beauty?*"

Talia yanked the jack out of the back of the laptop and twisted to pull the plug out of the wall. She wouldn't meet his gaze, and he didn't force her.

"A reference to my name," she said briskly. "The fairy tale was my mom's favorite. My mom had been confined to bed a lot in her life, and she said that my father 'woke her.' *Talia* comes from an older French version of the fairy tale, predating Disney."

Something clicked in Adam's mind. "Aurora."

She piled the cord on top of the laptop and gathered the mass to her chest. She moved around the table toward the door. Running away again.

"Talia," he called to her.

She stopped, but she didn't look back.

"The name suits," he said.

Eight

Redrum. Murder. The heart-stopping horror of room 217.

The phone rang, scaring Talia out of *The Shining* and into the real world. The awful, humiliating world in which Adam had by now viewed the nine renderings of herself she had found on the Internet, all of which depicted her as a seductive beauty. None remotely based in reality. Laughable. Pitiable, even. Particularly the graphic novel that had illustrated her as some kind of demon-busting dominatrix all done up in strappy, studded leather.

She wanted to crawl under a rock and die.

The phone rang again. *What if it's him?*

The sleek gray portable mocked her by ringing a third time.

She grasped the receiver. Pressed TALK. "Hello?"

"Talia. It's Adam."

Damn.

"Would you mind coming down to the kitchen? I have someone I'd like you to meet." His tone was even. Too even.

What must he think of me? She could still run away. Never look back. He had all her notes. He could carry on without her.

"Sure," she answered. "Just give me a minute." *A minute to jump to my death off my balcony.*

"Thanks."

Talia hit END. Her face was on fire. It was one thing for him to think of her as a freak. After all, considering Segue's purpose and staff, he was surrounded by them already. But it was a totally, wretchedly, different thing altogether if he thought she were a joke.

Talia went to the bathroom and splashed water on her face. She dabbed it dry with a towel and resecured her hair in a knot at the back of her head.

She dragged herself to her apartment door, forced her chin up—way up—and exited into the hall.

The elevator whirred down to the hotel's main level. The drawing rooms were evening-deep, darkness webbing the corners as night encroached on day. The layers of shadow brushed softly against her skin, coaxing her into their depths. Oh, so tempting.

She ignored them and grimly pressed forward toward the comparably blazing light at the other end of the expanse. Her heart thudded as she crossed the threshold. Patty's upper body was hidden by the door of an industrial-size refrigerator. An older man whom she'd never met dipped a tea bag in a mug at the counter. As she entered, Adam pushed off the edge where he'd been leaning, skinny-necked beer bottle in hand.

Her gaze darted to his face, met his eyes briefly, directly, and then dropped as heat burned her cheeks. She needed something to do, and quick, or she was going to embarrass herself. Again.

"Talia. Thanks for coming down. I'd like to introduce you to Dr. Philip James, our sometimes-resident philosopher. He asks the big questions. I bet the two of you will have a lot to talk about. Philip, this is Dr. Talia O'Brien."

The old man put his mug down and held out his hand. "Please call me Philip," he said.

"Talia," she answered and braced as she put her palm in his. Exhaustion predominated the connection—the old man was bone tired—and raging intellect. He squeezed rather than shook, a warm, friendly pressure that helped to calm her, though she was acutely, painfully, aware of Adam to her immediate right.

"Would you like some tea?" the older man asked, raising the steaming teapot. A mixed box of tea bags was open on the countertop.

"That would be great, thanks." She could hide behind the mug if she had to. Grip it for dear life. She took a fresh mug from the cupboard and selected a mint baggie. The smell was fragrantly clean. She inhaled to fill her head with it.

She glanced at Adam. Sure enough, his gaze was on her. She held her breath. His eyes were tired, but still had the power to see through her. Her nerves quivered as heat spread throughout her body. She wondered what emotion would dominate if she were to touch him now. Her throat went dry just thinking about it.

Slowly, he shifted his attention to his beer.

She, too, took a sip of tea, but her drink only burned her up more.

"You hungry?" Patty called from the fridge. She held up paper-wrapped packages of deli meat. "We have turkey, salami, and ham."

Talia had been hiding out in her room for the last couple of hours. She was starved. "Turkey," Talia said. "But I can make my—"

"Adam? Philip?" Patty interrupted.

"Ham," they answered in unison.

The old man settled next to Talia at the island. Adam sat across from her. At the counter, Patty created towering sandwiches in need of long deli toothpicks to hold the layers together.

"I read your dissertation," Philip said as they waited. "I was very impressed with your work. I wondered if you have pursued a cross-cultural examination of near-death experiences."

"Um. No. It wasn't in the scope of the paper, I'm afraid." Talia took another sip of her tea.

"Of course. When you have the time, I'd like to discuss your findings. See if any of the ritualistic practices I've studied conform to the norms you established in your thesis."

"Certainly . . ." Talia said. She'd have to dig into the boxes and review her notes. Something told her that the professor wasn't going to accept answers not backed by good data.

"It's good to have you back, Philip," Adam said, as Patty placed a plate in front of each of them. "It's not the same here without you questioning everyone's work."

"I'm off to my lab," Patty said, lifting her own plate and breezing to the door. "Good night, all."

"'Night," Talia said. Philip raised a hand in farewell.

Talia pretended not to see Philip as he flicked a glance in her direction and back to Adam. A question.

"She's okay," Adam answered, raising those gray eyes to hers. "In fact, she's single-handedly turned our work upside down in the space of eight hours."

"Oh?" Philip raised a bushy eyebrow at her.

"I'll brief you on it tomorrow, once I've thought through everything. I'm having trouble keeping up at the moment." Adam smiled woefully.

Philip set his mug on the island. "Well, you'll have to try, because I found something as well."

"Of course you did." Adam had lifted his own sandwich, but now he lowered it to his plate. "Let's have it. I'm going to have a sleepless night anyway, might as well have it all at once."

Talia hoped whatever Philip found had nothing to do with her. "It's getting late," she said. Better to make her escape now. She slid off the stool.

"Please stay," Adam said. "I have a feeling I'll want your perspective."

Talia felt his gaze on her, but she didn't meet it. She looked at Philip, her uneaten sandwich, the steam lifting from her cup of tea, anything but Adam.

"Perhaps she should go. My information is personal," Philip said.

"I trust her," Adam answered. His tone was light, but still managed a weight that brooked no further argument.

Talia's heart clenched. He had to be making things even—a personal revelation for a personal revelation. Tit for tat. A way to keep working together when he knew too much about her. She appreciated the gesture, but she really wanted to be in her room.

"So it's like that. Good for you," Philip said. "All right then."

Talia's head snapped up. *Like what?* She glanced over at Adam, waiting for him to correct Philip's mistaken assumption, but he didn't.

Philip ignored her distress, too, moving on. "I was in England, speaking to a modern druid elder about death rituals. He was a scholar as well, and our discussion turned theoretical. We touched on the ancient Anglo-Saxon custom of wergild, in which a person is required to pay a sum for the wrongful death of a family or clan member to prevent a blood feud."

"You think I would take money for my mom and dad? For Jacob?" Adam pushed his plate away from him without taking a bite.

"No, Adam," Philip said, crumpling a napkin in his palm. "Listen. And think. We spoke of wergild as compensation for a loss. An attempt at reestablishing a balance between two parties. And then we compared it to vengeance, a life for a life."

"That's something I understand."

Talia glanced at Adam and recalled the bloodlust that tainted him. The dark desire to put an end to Jacob that went beyond justice to murder.

Philip ignored the change. "The idea behind both concepts is that there must be an accounting, a ledger in the hearts and histories of a family. As if accepting a sum or taking a life will fill the void of the loss of the loved one."

"It can't fill the void, but it can make things even," Adam said.

"No. It does not. What you get is a deficit of two."

"Then both are at an equal loss." Adam took a deep drag on his beer.

"And how does this loss serve the memory of the loved one?"

"It doesn't," Adam said, shifting on his stool.

Talia kept her gaze carefully oblique, trying to respect his obvious discomfort with distance.

"Vengeance is selfish," Adam continued. "I've never tried to hide that."

"Ah," Philip said. "Now we get to the heart of it. Adam, here is my question for you. Would you trade your claim to vengeance to set your brother free?"

Talia watched the muscle twitch in Adam's jaw. It was a hard question, an impossible, painful question, especially after learning that Jacob had chosen his current state. Jacob had chosen to take the lives of his parents. He had reduced Adam's world to a haunted hotel with a group of mad scientists. Maybe she should say something. Change the subject.

Seen any naked pictures of me today?

"Go on," Adam said, his voice thin with strain.

Philip tilted his head. "As we spoke, this elder, he made a mistake. He did not say 'a life for a life.' He said, 'a life for a death.'"

Adam frowned. "Why can't you just say what you mean? If you have an answer, let me have it. Don't play games with me."

"I'm not playing games. This is far beyond games. I meant exactly what I said. *A life for a death*. Would you give up your life to teach Jacob how to die?"

"Is that possible, or are you philosophizing a bunch of bullshit?"

"I don't know. I hope it is possible. I have found a druid rite dedicated to death. A blood rite to the Others to end a scourge. It requires a voluntary human sacrifice. What if the rite is literal? What if a life is required to end ongoing death? It makes sense to me. It is a solution that has symmetry. The account comes into balance when you pay for a death with a life."

"I die, Jacob dies?"

"That is oversimplifying, but yes."

Adam sat back in his chair. "But there are more wraiths out there. Thousands. What about all of them?"

The old man's hands shook as he raised his mug. "I guess it would require . . ."

"People are not going to line up to die for wraiths. Hell, *I* don't want to die for a wraith, not even my brother."

"Of course not."

Adam stood abruptly; his stool tottered. "And more are being created every day. Someone or something out there is changing people, and I have to find out what. I can't let that continue."

"You asked me to find a way to end Jacob. I think I have. Something similar must have happened in the past, and a way was found to end it. It's horrible, yes. But the alternative is horrible, too."

If Adam heard him, he did not acknowledge it.

"I have to stop the source first, even if it is fueled by revenge. Then I will see to my brother." Adam paced the length of the island. Tension rolled off him in such great waves that Talia stood as well, reaching for shadows.

Philip put a hand up in reconciliation. "It does not have to be now. Live your life, and when you are ready to pass, then end it for you both at the same time."

"What if something happens to me in the meantime? A car accident? Illness?"

Philip shrugged. "I don't know."

"You don't know. Well, I don't know either. Six years and I don't know anything. How much more is that monster going to cost me?"

"Adam . . ."

"Screw it. Jacob has been trying to kill me for a while now, and it seems like he is going to get his way." Adam stalked from the kitchen, the darkness of the connecting rooms breaking around him.

Talia glanced at Philip, who had lifted his sandwich again.

He looked over at her. "Are you going to go after him or not?"

Talia startled. *Why me?* He was the one who'd dropped this bombshell on Adam. Shouldn't he be the one to make sure Adam was okay?

"Pretty girl like you ought to know what to do. Go on now." Philip took a bite of his sandwich.

Horrible old man, insinuating . . .

Talia glanced into the darkened rooms beyond the kitchen. She could see Adam perfectly. He strode through the adjoining rooms toward the double doors to the terrace. His broad shoulders were visibly tense, his gait long and fast. If she were he, she'd want to get out of here, too.

"Go on," Philip said. "I'll clean up."

Talia looked over at him. "You didn't have to . . ."

"Tell him the truth? Don't be silly. He needs the truth. Go on, now."

Talia didn't want to spend another second with the old man. She started across the dark, empty space. She was going to go back to her room and think things through. Things were getting too complicated. Out of control. Better to pull back.

She hit the button on the elevator and waited in the marble atrium, but the double doors of the terrace beckoned. A man stood on the other side, grappling with an unknown, but certainly horrible, destiny. If anyone could possibly relate, she could.

At least that's the excuse she gave herself as she coded out onto the terrace.

The night air was bursting with scent. Sharp grasses and pine dominated, but the broader fragrance of undergrowth underscored each breath. Stars glittered piteously above. Segue's paltry lights offered feeble competition. The contrast suggested another hard truth, comforting in its own way: No matter what havoc wraiths or humankind wreaked on earth, those stars would keep on shining. Everything good or evil would eventually be scorched from the earth by the inexorable domination of the universe.

"For someone with such an overdeveloped sense of self-preservation, it was damn foolish of you to come out here after me. Go to bed, Talia." Adam angled his face toward her, his expression unguarded. He probably thought the darkness would obscure the pain in his eyes, but Talia could see just fine. Too well, in fact. The man was confused and exhausted with his ongoing burden. His already busted-up soul had taken yet another beating today.

"You wouldn't hurt me," she said, stepping up beside him. She sounded more certain than she felt.

"Honestly, I don't know if that's true," he sighed. "Right now I feel just as monstrous as what is locked up beneath us."

"I'll risk it." She looked across the roll of the fields toward the mountains, willing her rapid heartbeat to peace. But standing beside him, the organ only doubled its rhythm. She babbled, "Besides, I can see better in the dark than you can. The world fairly throbs with details, color, and sensation. It's too intense for me really, so much to take in, but I'm pretty sure I have the advantage over you out here."

A corner of his mouth tugged upward, though his eyes remained dull and heavy, trained through the dark on her. "You see so much, but you can't see what I see. Only an artist could capture you."

Relief flooded her as a deep ache coiled gorgeously in her abdomen. He didn't think her a joke. After everything she'd revealed, he still desired her. The knowledge rooted her to her spot, in the path of certain danger.

Besides, she needed something, anything, to escape her own discovery today. Death was her father. No one would want her if that bitter truth became known.

She saw him move in her peripheral vision, was expecting it. A small rush of air brushed by her body just before his arms came around her waist, one shifting upward to the space between her shoulders.

He'd warned her. She'd had every opportunity to run back inside.

Instead, she tilted her head up to meet his.

His mouth came down hard. Pressed more deeply than she imagined. Raw heat coursed through her, demanding without thought or reason. Just need, his knotting with hers. Her mind fragmented. A strange, tight pressure set her blood thudding in her head.

The kiss burned, his tongue parting her lips to taste her.

He smelled good: masculine, sharp, and dark. The combination was potent, his touch, a catalyst to change her. Like a drug once tested, she knew she'd crave it for the rest of her life.

His body shifted, taking more of her weight. She reached up and wrapped her arms around his neck and shoulder so that she wouldn't fall. He was tall, all firm planes and unyielding strength, wonderfully painful in his embrace.

She gripped his shirt and arched her back so her breasts pressed more firmly against him. Felt the drum of his heart against hers, the flex of his muscle, and needed more.

He groaned low against her lips, and when she broke the kiss to gasp for air, he settled his blistering mouth into the bend of her neck.

"Oh, God," she breathed. Never in the many sleepless nights she'd spent fantasizing about a man like Adam had she imagined this.

"There is no God," he answered, voice ragged. His teeth worried her shirt at her collar to find her skin. Where his hot mouth branded, her nerves sang, her body begging *please, yes, more.*

He dragged up her shirt and thrust a hand up her bare back to twist the band of her bra around his grasp. He scorched his other palm around her hip, to the juncture of her legs, where he pinned her hard against him.

Talia squeezed her eyes shut against the pulse of shadow across the valley, against the gathering darkness that her blood and bone summoned. She reached out to him from her core.

A great wave of *want* swamped her inner senses in answer. A soul-deep hunger born of long deprivation.

But . . . not for her. Not really.

She felt a twisted self-pity ruling his actions. Loneliness, pain, and hatred combined with his considerable will to bind her to him, to use her to mute the myriad hurts in his spirit. There was nothing of her there at all, only Adam and his personal demons.

The knowledge tore at her, made her hate her gift and regret the impulse to indulge in the moment.

She twisted in his arms, pushing him away with her hands. She sought the protection of darkness. Brought a knee up to break his hold.

He grunted, but grasped her closer still, fighting the on-slaught of shadow.

She bucked harder. Grabbed his hair to pull his head back. "You're hurting me," she said.

Adam stilled, his chest heaving with effort. One, two breaths . . . she felt him collect himself. Felt his control steel around his contemptible actions and bring himself to heel, his need condensed into a tight ball of frightening, devastat-ing potency. He released her abruptly, catching hold of her arms so that she wouldn't fall to the flagstones of the terrace.

Talia wrenched herself free, stumbled back, and fell any-way.

He held out a hand to help her up.

"Stay away from me," she said. Her gaze flicked up to his face. She wished it hadn't. If the man had been burdened before, now he looked utterly tortured and ashamed.

Talia scrambled to stand, vision blurring the way his jaw clenched, the way his eyes narrowed to sharpen his own sight in the dark. To see her.

She ran to the doors, fumbled with the code, and yanked them open to get inside and away from him.

Damn him for touching her. Damn Philip for finding that rite. Damn Jacob for his horrible choice in the first place.

"I'm sorry," Adam said.

And damn her shadow-bred senses for being able to hear his whisper across the stretch of dark.

NINE

ADAM gripped the marble barrier overlooking the gardens. If Jacob had brought him to the brink of insanity, Talia was going to push him over the edge. She was supposed to be bookish—to take to her offices and use her amazing mind to develop a well-reasoned theory backed up by hundreds of pages of blindingly dense text.

Instead, she exposed Jacob's damned choice, the one that ripped Adam's family away from him again. Then, not two hours later, she revealed a strange connection some people have to Shadowman. *Her father*, of all people. Their art revealed that he was trapped somewhere, bound and unable to deal with the rising wraith threat.

And she gave him images. What images! Hadn't he been dutifully and honorably blocking visions of her naked body from his mind from the moment he cut her dripping clothes off her in Arizona? Okay, mostly blocking them.

What was the daily Segue grind when Talia looked back at him with longing, glowing in vibrant color from an artist's canvas? Naturally, he had an offer in on the piece already.

Talia. Sleeping Beauty. Aurora. She was a lightning bolt. Sudden, unpredictable, dazzling. She brilliantly illuminated in the dark, yet was capable of setting things on fire.

And then he had to be a dumb prick and maul her—hell,

he'd wanted to use her sweet body to shut Jacob and the wraith nightmare out of his mind. Now he had screwed everything up royally.

The thought broke over him in a wave of panic that muted his lust. He should go after her. Make it right.

Adam crossed the terrace and stopped abruptly to pick up her fallen hair elastic. He stretched the tight, thin band round two fingers. Brought it to his nose to inhale. Caught a fresh, wet scent. He rolled the elastic along his fingers toward his palm. In a strange way—and everything about Talia was strange—the elastic became a link, connecting him to her. The tug of it felt good.

He followed her inside. The elevator took a moment to come—probably dropping her off on her floor.

When it arrived, he entered, reached out to hit her floor button, but paused at the sight of the black elastic on his hand, pushed up to the base of his fingers.

It was such a little thing, so restrained. Made him want her more. Why now, as the wraith madness was just peaking, should he find the answers to his riddles and an incomparable, desirable woman at the same time? And in the same package?

Ah, hell. He shifted his hand down. Hit Subfloor 2, instead.

One stop at his office, then a hard, killing run until he could trust himself again.

The elevator opened at his stop. He exited and found Custo approaching from the other end of the white corridor. Probably turning in for the day.

"Custo, with me," Adam said, brushing by him on his way to Patty's lab. So what if Custo's face was haggard with exhaustion. They could both be miserable together.

Adam coded himself into Patty's lab, Custo silent at his heels. Patty had said she'd be working late tonight, and she was. She straightened up from a microscope as he approached the table.

Her eyes flicked to Custo, then back to Adam. "What's going on?"

Custo shrugged in Adam's peripheral vision. "Damned if I know."

"I need a word with both of you," Adam said. "What I say can't leave this room."

Custo leaned forward on the lab counter. Patty pushed her wheeled stool away from the scope. "Of course."

Adam scrubbed a hand over his face. *Where to start?*

"I have new information. Too much information, actually." He couldn't tell either of them about the rite that Philip had found. He didn't trust them not to try something stupid, to give their own lives for Adam, before he had an opportunity to give his for Jacob.

"Why do I have the feeling I'm not going to like it?" Patty twisted her mouth into a wry pucker.

"Because it complicates the hell out of our lives," Adam answered.

"Go on," Custo said.

Adam drew a deep breath. "Talia is at the heart of this mess with the wraiths. She, and her father, Shadowman."

"Shadowman is her father?" Patty's brows drew together.

Adam could guess her train of thought. She'd want to take a closer look at that abnormal DNA. He'd be looking over her shoulder.

"Talia thinks so, and the connection accounts for her physiological differences. When she was fifteen, she got into a car accident with her aunt, Margaret O'Brien. Her aunt died, and Talia had the near-death experience that inspired her work. She claims to have had a brief moment where she 'crossed,' saw Shadowman, and knew him instinctively for her father."

"Does she know anything else about Shadowman? Where he is?" That was Custo, straight to the point.

"*What* he is?" Patty clarified.

"No. At least, she hasn't said so, and she was opening up for once, so I didn't press the point. But she thinks he may be trying to get in touch with her."

Custo pushed up to his feet. "How so?"

"Talia has been doing her own search for Shadowman. She discovered him in art. The same figure appears in several artistic renderings—paintings, sculpture, and the like, all named for him. In each image, he is bound by some kind of force against his will. I can show you what she found."

"Maybe the images have clues where to locate him," Custo said.

Adam had poured over the images—they were all surreal, indefinite, lacking concrete details—even the face of Shadowman was indistinct.

"There's more. Talia also found artistic renderings of herself."

"Oh, dear," Patty said. "The poor girl."

"Some images"—the painting of her in the nude, for example—"merely name her. Others show her variously fighting, fleeing, or fearing anthropomorphic monsters."

"Wraiths," Custo concluded.

"Yes. And we have to assume that The Collective is aware of this as well, since they tracked her for months."

"So she's supposed to save the world from wraiths?" Custo's tone did nothing to hide his skepticism.

"We have to help her," Adam said. "We have to protect her at all costs. We have to foster her, train her, and make certain that she knows Segue has got her back. Put all our resources at her disposal."

He glanced at the band on his fingers. He'd have to keep their relationship professional. He couldn't very well protect her if he were on top of her. Or beneath her. Inside her. His mouth went dry. He slipped the elastic off his hand and pocketed it.

"One more thing," Adam began. "If anything should happen to me . . ."

Patty frowned and waved her hands abruptly. "I don't like that kind of talk."

"Too bad"—too bad for all of us. "The reality is that this fight is going to become a matter of life and death. If anything should happen to me, you both must continue to support her unconditionally. I want your agreement."

Custo's eyes narrowed, but he gave a short, curt nod.

Adam looked across the table. "Patty?"

"I support her, already. Has nothing to do with whether you're alive or not."

Patty used her sass to cope, but Adam couldn't smile. Didn't have it in him.

"Okay." Adam nodded. "That's all." Now on to that run. Fast and far so that he didn't do anything stupid. Like wander up to the fourth floor.

"Adam?" Custo raised a brow.

"What?"

"You're not telling us everything."

"And I'm not going to." Adam turned away from them and made for the door.

Talia went to the roof, the last place she thought Adam would look for her since she had never been there before herself. She thought the place would be peaceful, but it was loud, a generator whirring and rumbling to disturb the night. She thought the air would be sweet so close to the sky, but it was slightly mechanical, oily, and tinged with cigarette smoke.

"Jim says the roof's haunted. Says he can sense a definite

cold spot near the eaves where someone leaped to their death."

Talia whirled at the sound of Spencer's voice. He leaned against a gray-colored bulkhead of some kind, smoking. He tapped the tip of his cigarette with his thumb, ash raining down at his feet. Behind him, the roof angled upward in a picturesque sweep. Below them, the terrace rounded the base of the hotel so that the building appeared to be floating on a white disk suspended above the earth.

She swallowed her surprise. "Ghosts have left me alone so far. I think I'll risk it."

"I don't believe in them either." He took a long drag on his cigarette and let the smoke slither out of the side of his mouth. "Lovers' quarrel? Looks like you two had a little falling-out down there."

Talia's face heated. She reached for the door. Damn hotel left her nowhere to run.

"You know you have options, don't you?" Spencer's tone was friendly and helpful, but Talia still didn't feel she could quite trust him. She couldn't trust anyone.

"What do you mean?"

Spencer cocked his head. "I wondered if you knew. Adam's got a file on you."

The word *file* bothered her, as if she were a specimen, a case under examination. But Adam had been aboveboard with his curiosity and questions. She'd shown him personally what she could do. She'd revealed her connection to Shadowman. Even the images of herself. Any good researcher would take detailed notes, and the notes would be kept in a file. So she pushed the bothersome term away.

"Yeah, tests on your DNA, et cetera."

Talia felt the blood drain out of her face. She hadn't consented to *that*.

"But it's the video surveillance Adam has on your apartment that would bug the hell out of me."

Now she felt ill.

"You don't believe me?" Spencer's eyes glittered as he took another drag. "You sleep in a T-shirt, panties, and nothing else. And by the end of the night the sheets are all twisted up at the end of the bed so that your pretty bottom—"

"Shut up."

"At least you believe me now. Things around here are never what they seem." He stamped out the cigarette on the concrete at his feet.

"Take you, for example," Spencer continued, the volume of his voice rising as she moved away from him. "You look human and act human, but you're not."

She squeezed her arms tighter around herself. He obviously had something to say. And, all things considered, she'd rather know.

"As the SPCI liaison, I'm supposed to be privy to everything that goes on here. I gather Adam has been as secretive with you as he's been with me."

Talia's eyes prickled. Adam was sick. Twisted. He'd lived with a monster so long that he'd become one himself.

"You don't have to stay here. You have alternatives through SPCI. First of all, you're not alone. There are others out there like you, housed at alternative facilities. We don't have the frills that Segue does, and the furniture is seriously outdated, but at least you know how things stand. Your rights will be protected. Your privacy protected. It's not the best life, but it's an honest one."

Honest. What a joke. She couldn't trust anyone.

"You say the word, and you're out of here. No confrontations. Just an easy transport to the SPCI compound." Spencer waved his hands like a magician before the *poof*.

Talia's mind worked furiously. She could get out on her

own. Give herself a head start. But not Arizona or Vegas. Find a little place out in the middle of nowhere, away from the flow of people. She was sick of people.

"I'll think about it," she said.

"Nah. You've already made up your mind. You'll take the hard way."

Spencer strode toward her and stopped at her side. Too close. "Adam's right about one thing. A wraith war is coming. There is nowhere on this planet that will be safe for long. Keep that in mind."

He yanked open the door to the interior and left her alone with the night.

TEN

WE want the California." Gillian held out her hand. "The salon is waiting for us, and Talia has asked to come along. So I am afraid the Diablo won't do. We need a four-seater."

The trio of women stood in Adam's office. Talia stayed back and let the other women do the talking. She'd had a long, sleepless night of deliberating, but her choice was made. First step, a lift to town.

"There are six very nice cars in the Segue lot—what makes you think I'll lend you one of mine?" Adam's tone angled up with incredulity.

Gillian didn't back down. "Our shared joy of a luxury vehicle."

His gaze darted to Patty, who grinned in agreement with Gillian.

Talia watched the byplay with resentful interest. She didn't know what the California was, but the request clearly irritated him, which gave her less satisfaction than it should. She just wanted to get out of there. Being in the same room with Adam made her skin tight, her nerves edgy.

Adam's gaze finally hit Talia and rested there, as if he were considering something. Studying her, again. She struggled to keep her expression impassive. The Segue credit card was in her pocket, and she intended to charge everything she needed. Her escape from Adam Thorne's specimen lab would be wholly paid for by him.

"Fine," Adam said. "But keep the speed down. If you get in an accident, our good doctor won't be able to help you because she'll be busted up, too. And I'll be too busy cursing you to call for other medical intervention."

Gillian bounced on the balls of her feet. "Yeah, yeah. The key, please."

He opened a slim desk drawer to the right of his main work area, under his view screen of Jacob. Probably the same screen that had afforded him an unobstructed view of her apartment, of her bedroom. As if she were Jacob, a monster to be studied.

How could she have been so stupid?

"Are you okay?" Adam's gaze was heavy on her face, searching. He couldn't possibly care.

Talia fought to keep her emotions under control, her bile down. She nodded with a fake smile. Salon! Fun! As if she'd ever let anyone touch her, repeatedly, for any length of time.

Gillian snatched the key out of his hand, drawing Adam's attention. The ache in Talia's guts diminished slightly. She wouldn't feel better until Segue was far behind her.

"Our appointment is in twenty minutes. We better get going." Gillian skipped to the door like a teenager. Talia followed, with Patty bringing up the rear.

"Wait," Adam said. "It takes thirty-five to get there."

"Not anymore," Gillian sang, waving the key in the air and pushing out his office door.

They bypassed the parking lot off the Segue loading dock and entered an immaculate garage. Four shining cars gleamed, diagonally situated, each a luxury vehicle, though Talia would have been hard-pressed to name any one. A black sedan, slightly old-world in its shape, but modernized in its aerodynamic lines, was parked farthest from the door. Next to it, a hulking SUV with dark windows and shiny chrome. Adjacent, two sports cars vied for attention, one black, shaped low, mean, and angular. The other was bold red, modern muscle tempered with sleek restraint. A silver stallion reared on the grille under a yellow insignia.

"The Ferrari," Gillian directed. She ran on tiptoes over to the red car and ran a hand along its hood. When she opened the door, she sighed in exaggerated ecstasy. "Thank you, Talia!"

Talia brought her head up in confusion as she slipped behind the passenger seat into a narrow rear bucket.

"We owe this to you." Gillian's eyebrows lifted up-up in suggestion, a smirk curling one side of her mouth. Then she gripped the wheel with melodramatic sexual pleasure.

Patty and Gillian strapped themselves in. Talia followed suit, though she was so squished she doubted the seat belt would do anything.

"I don't get it," Talia said. Did everyone know that Adam had kissed her? Had everyone been watching? Or had he left some visible mark on her where he'd touched? The bitter truth was, she could still feel the heat of his hands on her back and butt, and other places she'd briefly hoped he'd reach.

Gillian turned the key, revved the engine, and purred suggestively.

The car felt like Adam. Power, beauty, and no fuss. Smelled like him, too, under the honey dusk of the black leather.

"Oh, honey. The way he looks at you. I've been here years hoping for that gleam in his eye. He never, *ever* would have let us take out one of his babies if you weren't coming along." Gillian's eyes twinkled. "I just took advantage of the opportunity."

"Leave her alone," Patty said, but she smiled, too.

Yes, please. Leave me alone.

Gillian eased the vehicle out of the garage and onto the Segue turnabout. When she accelerated, the engine sang. Its building momentum forced Talia's head into the seat.

Talia left Gillian and Patty in the salon, trapped in their chairs by color massaged like mud over their scalp. Gillian had shiny foils tucked into her hair as well.

"Talia. Really," Gillian begged. "Just order some decent stuff online and have the clothes overnighted." She looked like she wanted to expand on her reservations for shopping in Middleton, but with a glance at the stylist, politely kept her mouth closed.

Talia wasn't going to be here tomorrow. That was the point. She had the use of the Segue card for Middleton only. Whatever she was going to get, it had to be here, or Adam would be able to track her.

Talia smiled, thanked them both, but went to check the local shopping for herself.

She found a thrift shop, packed with knickknacks, dishes, dulling jewelry, and along the back wall, a rack of clothes. They were dingy from previous use, puckered and creased from hanging untouched on store hangers for who knows how long. Probably years. She selected clothes that looked like they'd fit, and was thrilled when she found a well-worn but sturdy backpack.

The counter had been tended when she'd entered, but empty when she finished. She piled her stuff on top and got the credit card ready for payment. Waiting, adrenaline pumping, got her mind turning. Small town like this . . .

She hesitated a second, then darted around to the other side of the register.

And there it was, in an upper drawer next to a pile of old receipt booklets, a revolver, silver along the barrel and textured black rubber on the grip. A box of ammunition labeled

.38 SPECIAL was tucked alongside. Adam did say that firearms were the best defense against wraiths. Certainly couldn't hurt.

She lifted the weapon and turned it over and around, then pocketed the box of ammo and put the gun in the waist of her pants under her shirt. Her heart beat wildly at her theft, though her two months on the run from wraiths had been filled with similar crimes.

The gun felt cold and hard on her back. Unnatural, but remembering how Custo took down the wraith in the alley in Arizona, she also felt better prepared. Talia was back on the other side of the counter by the time the cashier—a young woman—emerged from a curtained hallway, vaguely surprised that Talia was still there.

Purchases in hand, Talia headed for the busiest part of town.

The Circle K sat on the corner of I-52 and Main and seemed to connect Middleton to the rest of the world. Talia entered the gas station, its door swinging wide, bell ringing overhead. She smiled at the acne-attacked boy behind the counter flipping though a magazine in his lap.

With any luck, she could hitch a ride out of town before Patty and Gillian were done with their color. Where to? She swallowed a lump in her throat. She didn't really care as long she was far, far away from Segue and Adam.

Talia used the credit card to get cash at an ATM near the lotto stand. The machine ejected $500, the card's daily cash limit, which was way more money than she'd had the last time she ran away. She tucked the cash inside a small pouch on the front of her backpack and hit the snack aisle. She selected energy bars and, from the glass-faced refrigerators at the rear of the store, a couple bottles of water.

Items purchased and stowed, she took up a position in front of the magazines at the wide front windows. A woman in an old station wagon, toddler in a back car seat, pumped at the station marked one. A man in a red pickup with oversize tires pumped at station two. Given her options, the pickup probably would be game for a ride, and if the driver got any ideas, she could always scare the hell out of him.

Time to go.

Talia dropped the magazine, shouldered her pack, and pushed out the door. She was halfway to the pumps when a black Denali SUV slid into the lot. The tinted windows obscured her view of the interior and the glare from the overcast sky washed out the windshield, but the hair on the back of her neck tingled to attention with unprovoked anxiety.

Danger, instinct warned, her heart tripping.

Paranoid. She pushed the feeling down and continued to the truck. She made eye contact with the paunch-bellied driver, and then glanced over her shoulder when the doors of the SUV opened. She caught the smooth descent of a man moving with predatory fluidity.

Oh. No. Where to hide?

The trees along the highway beckoned and beyond that the blanket of forest covering the mountain ridges, an almost-unending shadowy canopy of refuge. So many dark spots to crawl into and wait out the threat, then creep from bush cluster to tree hollow and escape.

Adam's firm voice sounded in her head, *Find the largest concentration of people.*

But . . . she looked longingly at the trees. She even had food and water. She could last . . .

The wraiths will not risk public exposure. The force of will in Adam's words anchored her.

And she couldn't bear being hunted a second time. She knew that now.

Talia angled away from the pumps and increased the momentum of her stride to intersect with Main Street. The largest concentration of people would be the mom-and-pop diner next to the beauty salon.

She cut across the street diagonally, not looking back. Not moving too quickly. Not drawing attention. *Nothing to see here.*

She rounded the corner to the line of businesses just as Patty and Gillian pushed out of the salon some doors down.

Be natural. Be ordinary. Just one of the girls.

"You look great!" Talia called, stretching her mouth into a smile as she picked up her pace.

"Did you buy anything?" Gillian asked as Talia approached.

Wraith, Talia mouthed.

The smile dropped off Gillian's face. Patty's red lips turned down, gaze darting beyond Talia.

"Let's just stay calm," Patty said, "and get in the car."

The California screamed for attention across the street. Not too subtle. Gillian pulled out the keys and beeped the lock. From the doorway of the hardware store, on the other side of the vehicle, a man appeared. His city slacks and urban T-shirt were incongruent with the small town. He pocketed his hands nonchalantly in an unassuming stance, but his eyes were hungry, potent with menace.

The three women halted in the street, midstride. Patty gripped Talia by the elbow and pulled her back, shielding her with her body as if she were a child.

Talia allowed the protection only because her attention was drawn to the right.

The SUV swallowed the street, doors already open, two shining young men standing on the running boards at the sides, as if on a joyride. Both bounded down to block the street.

"Adam said they wouldn't risk public exposure," Gillian said.

Talia blanched with realization. She should have known. For everyone else, they wouldn't risk exposure. But if she were a real threat to them, as the images she'd found suggested, then they might risk anything. Too late now.

"Talia, go get help," Patty said in a voice far too calm for the circumstances. "Middleton didn't sign on for this. Someone needs to get help or the town will be torn apart, and the only person who can get through the wraiths is you."

If Talia wanted a way to bolt out of this mess, this was it. A neat excuse prepackaged, well reasoned, and very tempting.

"I'll drive," Gillian said. She wanted to live, too. "I'll get help. I can get through just as easily . . ."

"We can't let them have you," Patty answered, ignoring Gillian. "Think, Talia."

Talia's mind took one second to consider the option and had her decision: if she left Patty and Gillian to the soul-sucking attentions of the wraiths, she might as well cough up her own spirit, because it would be dead and useless thereafter.

Talia shook her head, *no*. She was going to stay. The choice went down her throat like a rough brick.

What she needed was something that *approximated* courage, a little bravado maybe. Then, when the opportunity to run had passed, an instinctive will to live would kick in, and she'd fight for real.

The gun pressed into her waist in cold comfort.

"I'm not going anywhere." Talia managed to keep her voice respectably steady, considering acid burned up the back of her throat. She tensed her dread-weakened knees and slipped the backpack off her shoulders to drop with a soft smack on the street.

Talia's fear intensified with her resolution, and the world shifted in front of her. Shadow. Where before the thick trees and old brick buildings were crisp and mundane, the reds and greens dusted with street dirt and time, now darkness cloaked them and softened their edges.

"What the hell . . . ?" Gillian shrieked.

"Stop, Talia," Patty said, edging her voice with authority. "We can't risk you when a war is coming, and it's going to take your whole bag of tricks to get out of here, regardless."

"War's here, Patty," Talia said. "Just ask Adam."

"Damn it, Talia, run," Patty said, spinning slowly to position herself behind her.

They stood back-to-back in the middle of the street with no fewer than three . . . Talia glanced to her left . . . make that four wraiths bearing down on them.

"I can get us in the car. You just have to hold on to me." Talia chewed her lip. "Then we'll draw them after us to Segue, where there is more help."

"How the hell do you think you can . . . ?" Gillian said, voice wavering.

"Just hold on to me," Talia said. "It's about to get *dark*."

Talia reached, gripped cold, ethereal silk, and brought down the shadows. Gillian's hand floundered in the sudden absence of senses. Talia grabbed it, attached her to Patty, and clasped Patty's hand.

The wraiths waded into her darkness, searching, racing for the car.

Talia drew the gun. The handle slipped in her slick palm. She let go of the women to clasp the weapon with both hands.

She raised the gun, hoping it was loaded, aimed at the wraith climbing over the vehicle, and fired.

The report thumped dully in her grasp. The gun expelled the bullet and the glittering missile traveled the darkness sluggishly, surreal trails warping the air in its wake.

Talia saw the miss in the bullet's trajectory and—heart

lodged in her throat—willed the silver projectile on a more accurate course.

The bullet obeyed.

Whoa . . . Talia swallowed her shock and drove the pellet between the wraith's eyes with her mind. His screech cut short as his body fell dumbly to the pavement.

Gillian's fluttering hands found the car. She opened the driver's-side door and crawled across to the passenger side. Patty didn't follow, but turned and looked blankly into the darkness.

"You first," Patty called. Her voice bent and echoed, now distant, now near, across the shadows. She blindly grabbed hold of Talia's shirt to forcibly push her into the car.

Not enough time. The three remaining wraiths descended. Lacking sight, they slinked up to the car with arms outstretched.

Talia raised the gun again and shot at close range. The wraith crumbled. Another crouched, hand braced on the concrete, preparing to strike.

She aimed again, but an arm banded around her waist. Patty, attempting to drag her into the car. Talia's balance faltered.

A wraith lashed out and caught Talia at her wrist. The pressure of his grasp made her bones ache. Her fingers prickled, then burned, and the gun dropped to the street with a distant *pat* and bounce.

Talia struggled against his hold, sitting into her hips and throwing her weight back. But he was too strong. Too immovable. She was a rag doll for his rough play.

Tears blurred her vision as she tried to pry his grip away. No good. Hopeless.

"He's got me," Talia gasped at Patty. "Go!"

But Patty stepped in front of Talia. Patty's trembling hand

found the wraith's grip. Instead of trying to pull him off, which was pointless, she traveled up his arm to his shoulder.

"Patty, they won't hurt me. They tried to take me alive before. Alive. I'll be fine," Talia said. Her eyes prickled. This was it, the end, and she knew it. Those wraiths might take her alive, but once there, things would be bad. Very bad.

Patty launched herself at the monster. Grabbed hold of his head. And kissed him on the mouth.

Talia's heart stopped in awe, tears burning down her face.

The opportunity was too much for the wraith to resist. The wraith released Talia's arm. She fell back and hit her head on the car. Was grabbed from behind and pulled inside.

"Where's Patty?" Gillian shouted, the sound distant. "I can't see a freaking thing!"

Talia could. The wraith tilted his head, opened his mouth, and fed. An agonizing wrench tore at Talia's heart—no deeper—as Patty's essence disappeared into his maw. A great spirit, beautiful in its clarity, shuddered and then doused in the monster's gullet.

"Talia!" Gillian yelled again.

Talia bled internally at the loss. She didn't deserve the gift, but she wouldn't see it sacrificed in vain. Not if she could help it. She slammed the door shut.

Gillian already had the key in the ignition, the engine idling. Talia released the parking brake, set the car in drive, and floored it.

ELEVEN

ADAM settled himself into a column of numbers, expenses generated by his staff doing fieldwork all over the world. He approved most out of hand, particularly those for comfort and keep. The work at Segue was grueling, ongoing, and increasingly dangerous as the wraith population spread and redoubled. If a suite in a hotel made research less of a burden, so be it. Money really didn't matter anymore.

His mobile phone buzzed on his desk, traveling slightly over the page with the vibration. He picked it up and hit TALK.

A woman's voice sobbed unintelligibly into the phone, threaded with panic and near hysteria. Adam's gut knotted—he recognized the identifying timbre lacing her disjointed syllables.

"Gillian?" He kept his voice calm, though his pulse leaped. "What's happened?"

"They're behind us . . . coming to Segue."

"Wraiths?" Adam hit the central alarm, alerting the staff to go to their designated meeting place and account for one another. A list of on-site personnel flicked onto his monitor. The floor trembled as the redundant security measures cut off Jacob's cell from the rest of Segue—the guards downstairs would just have to wait this out. He queued the Segue perimeter cameras. A typical midmorning on the mountain.

All quiet, the tree leaves shuffling softly. Yet their early shadows seemed menacing now. Too dark and concealing.

He never should've allowed the women to leave without an armed escort. He'd succumbed to the worst possible mental rut, a false sense of security. He'd been careful to keep Segue's function hidden from anyone outside his carefully selected team of researchers, but over time the weight of secrecy would have gained an imperative inertia of its own. Someone eventually had to slip. Had already slipped.

"We left Patty." Gillian's tone was accusatory. Blaming him? He deserved it. "They got Patty. Adam, Patty's dead."

Adam felt a wrenching snap of a heartstring, the one that tethered him to Aunt Pat, and through her to his parents, his childhood, all the what-might-have-beens. But he couldn't think of Pat now. That would be another mistake. He'd remember her later, if there were a later.

He switched the handset for a mobile earplug.

"And Talia?" His voice rasped as he hit the rifle safe attached to the wall behind him. He selected the AR-15 rifle with the drum magazine, put the strap over his shoulder, and a Glock, which he kept in his hand, ready. He grabbed extra magazines and carriers and attached them to his belt.

"Talia's fine." The accusatory tone again. "She's driving."

He glanced at the external Segue vid feeds. Rolling lawn. Trees. Narrow road leading into town. Nothing yet.

"How long until you're here?" At least they had the Ferrari and its eight-cylinder engine, if Talia could keep the car on the road.

"I don't know. We just passed the boulders."

The boulders were massive distinctive crags that marked the crest of the mountain pass on the road to Segue just before the trees closed in. Ten minutes. Less, in that car.

"Direct Talia to the rear entrance. When you reach the building, be prepared to run inside. Seat belts already off.

You understand?" Adam peeled out his door and ran down the deserted corridor to the back stairs. No elevators during lockdown.

"Oh, shit," Gillian breathed in his ear.

"What now?" Keep it calm, he reminded himself.

"Helicopter."

"Helicopter chasing you?" A cold finger of horror slid down Adam's spine. Had to be a coordinated strike. It'd been six days since Talia arrived, and The Collective had used the week to formulate an extraction strategy. He thought she'd be safe here. That they'd all be safe here. Aunt Pat . . . He'd promised them all safety.

"No. It's ahead of us, turning around. *We're going to die.*"

"Calm down, Gillian. I'll get you through this"—another false promise?—"but only if you can stay calm. Is Talia okay? Is she freaking out?"

"No. Talia is fucking ice. She left Patty—Patty!—back there with those monsters."

So that was it. Patty was gone, but trust Talia to know when to get to safety. She'd had enough practice at it. Even beaten down, the woman was a survivor.

As planned in the event of a wraith incursion, Adam found Custo in front of the door to the stairwell, similarly armed with a semiautomatic shotgun, punching in the master override that barred the staircase.

"Keep your head, Gillian," Adam commanded. "Follow my instructions. I'll be waiting for you. Stay on the line."

Custo pounded up the stairs, Adam behind him with the update. "Gillian, Talia, and Pat went into Middleton this morning. Gillian called in three minutes ago that she and Talia were being chased back to Segue by wraiths. Helicopter also in pursuit. Wraiths got Pat—"

Custo turned abruptly to look at Adam, his expression a mask of disbelief and pain.

Adam had no time for that. "Has Spencer checked in?"

"Not yet." Custo coded out the exit and pushed open the heavy steel door.

Adam ducked his head out. The telltale whirring chop of a helicopter cut the sky above Segue. He craned to get a better look. It was a combat helicopter, slim, mottled green-gray, and already lowering to drop a load of men on the west lawn. A spark of reflected light drew Adam's eyes to the trees. Someone moving in there, too. Along the road.

Blocking the road. Penning Segue in.

"Slow down, Talia!" Gillian screamed into Adam's ear. "You're going to hit them!"

"Hit them!" Adam shouted into the mouthpiece. He didn't care who, as long as Talia and Gillian got back to Segue.

The din of the helicopter drowned out the voices in Adam's ear.

"Repeat," he yelled into the phone.

The Ferrari careened out of the trees, a vivid streak of crimson against dense green. The windshield was cracked in webbed impact lines. A man gripped the hood. His body swayed and dangled as he held on to the car with his fingers. Heroes might do that in movies, but in the real world, only a wraith would have the necessary strength.

"To the building! The rear doors!" Gillian yelled in Adam's ear. He could just make out the silhouettes of the women in the front seats of the car.

Custo crouched on the landing beside him. "I can take the wraith on the hood."

"Let them get closer. Besides, we've got company from the west."

Custo pivoted suddenly and shot at an oblique angle toward the west corner of the building. Warning shots with a loud report to keep the helicopter's foot soldiers at bay.

Something about the way the men moved bothered Adam. They humped across the grass in camouflage green, armored, signaling with sharp, spare gestures. They were human. What was a human military force doing striking against Segue? There must be a terrible mistake.

"Where the hell is Spencer?" Custo growled, sighting down the barrel of his gun.

Good question. Spencer better damn well be figuring out why the army had decided to attack a civilian research facility. Someone was going to answer for this, that was for damn sure.

Pressure mounted in Adam's chest as the car neared. "Right up to the door," Adam commanded Gillian.

"They'll shoot us!"

"If they haven't shot at the car by now, they're not going to. Tell Talia to pull up to the entrance. Both of you get out of the car on the right side. Do not hesitate."

Adam raised his own gun, finger light on the trigger.

The red sports car skimmed the earth like fire on a wick, taking the turn to Segue with controlled precision. Talia, accustomed to deep terror, obviously knew that survival depended on clear thinking and decisive action. She was steady—and that's all Adam needed.

A large SUV, lumbering in comparison, cleared the tree line in pursuit, but too far back to be an immediate threat.

As the Ferrari approached the back lot, Adam aimed at the wraith gripping the hood and fired.

"What are you doing? You're going to kill us!" Gillian shrieked into the phone. Adam could now see her mouth the words he heard in his earpiece. Talia's face was white, eyes fixed unblinking on the building. *Keep it steady, sweetheart.*

Adam fired again. He zeroed in on the wraith's head, bobbing at the base of the windshield, and shot.

The wraith jerked and slid down the hood. Its legs caught under the sports car's road grip, and the wheels churned the monster behind the vehicle. The body bounced once, and then lay broken on the pavement.

The car veered briefly, recovering from the sudden lurch under the carriage, and then sped to the door.

Talia overshot the entrance. Gillian had her door open and was flinging herself toward Adam before the vehicle came to a stop. The tires left black trails on a sickening collision course with the building. Adam caught Gillian's arms and pulled her to safety as Custo at his low left discharged another volley. Talia clambered out next, sneakers, then jean-clad legs, emerging in a clumsy climb over the interior leather and out the passenger door.

Adam's heart stopped beating as the rest of Talia's body emerged, white-blonde hair shining and waving like a here-I-am flag in the wind kicked up by the idling helicopter overhead.

He grabbed her arm and yanked her into the hollow he made of his body to shelter her, and together dived for the door. They fell on the floor inside, and he hit his head on the wall with a crack he heard but didn't feel. Custo backed in behind them, gun raised, and shut and secured the door.

Gillian sobbed in a ball on the floor in the corridor, mascara running black trails down her cheeks. Talia struggled to stand, attempting to disengage herself from Adam's weight.

"Are you okay?" Adam tightened his grip on her waist and held on to her a bit longer. He'd yet to see her face, yet to see how all of this was affecting her. He struggled to kneel, his hands on her body, gripping her arms to turn her to face him, then releasing to nudge her chin up to the light.

She faced him, but her gaze stayed resolutely down. He ducked into her line of sight, to force her to see him. Her eyes were dry and clear. And desolate.

"I was going to run away," she said, her voice oddly distant. "A wraith caught me and Patty saved me. She traded herself for me. She kissed the monster on its mouth." Her gaze lowered and slid away from him. Ashamed.

Oh, sweet Jesus. Aunt Pat.

Adam's grip tightened on Talia's arms. He gave her a hard shake. "Are you done with running, hiding, and all that shit now?"

"I'm here," she said hollowly. "Tell me what to do."

Adam knew that if he asked her right then to walk out of the building and give herself up to the wraiths, she would. Any secrets she had, she'd spill. Her life wasn't hers now. It belonged to Pat, just as his belonged to his lost family.

Yet the blame wasn't all Talia's, not remotely. He should have anticipated something like this and prevented it. Hadn't he counseled Pat just last night to protect Talia? And hadn't he sent the women into town without guards to look after them? A million things he should have done, all too late.

"Move," Adam said. He took Talia by the elbow, and she followed without comment.

"Put me down," Gillian cried from behind him. Custo must have had to carry her.

Adam tapped in his code at the stairs and the four descended onto the lab floor. Frightened staff members were milling around in front of his office. Decidedly *not* where they were supposed to be. Restless anxiety riddled their mutterings and movements.

"Ah, shit," Armand said when he took in the guns and running mascara. "I knew I shouldn't have taken this damn job—"

"Don't bitch about it now," someone murmured.

"Is he out?" Jim asked. He, meaning Jacob.

"No, Jacob is secure," Adam announced to the group.

"Let's just all stay calm so that Custo and I can assess the situation and give you accurate information."

"Wraiths got Patty in Middleton," Gillian blurted. "And Talia's some kind of freak like Jacob. She let the wraiths have Patty."

Talia stood apart from the group at the wall, chin only high enough to take whatever the crowd had to dish out. Adam flicked a glance at Custo, and Custo moved to stand next to her. There was no mistaking the meaning—anyone who wanted to touch Talia would have to get through him first.

Adam rounded on Gillian. "Where were you when all this was happening? Why didn't you help? Fact is, Talia saved your life back there. When you get your head on straight, you'll be thanking her."

Gillian deteriorated into harsh sobs, and he continued, addressing the group. "We are not going to get through this if we are fighting among ourselves. We need to stay calm and work together. Armand—I need a head count. There are supposed to be seventeen on the premises today." Adam thought of Patty and corrected himself. "Sixteen."

Adam took a deep breath and focused. He had contingency plans, procedures drilled in advance. His mind reviewed the steps ahead: The goal, of course, was to get everyone to safety. Grab the survival packs, guns, and ammo. Hit the underground tunnel to emerge in the woods. Four armored all-terrain vehicles would be waiting, were always waiting. Then disperse, each in a different direction. With any luck, his people would make it to any of the six Segue substations within a five-hour driving distance. He would coordinate from there. With luck, he'd have some intelligence to work from.

"Thirteen," Armand answered. Adam did a mental

count—minus the guards with Jacob, and the absent Spencer, all were accounted for.

No time to waste—even now the forces outside could be attempting to penetrate the building. He headed to the weapons-storage room two doors down from his office and tapped his code into the pad. The door opened soundlessly.

The sight of the interior was an electric shock to Adam's body.

The room was empty, shelves bare of everything except paper and plastic debris.

His nerves burned while his mind blanked, trying to assimilate this new information. Only three people had this particular code: himself, Custo, and—

"Where's Spencer?" Adam asked, his voice barking over the nervous chattering of the group in the hall.

"We haven't seen him," Jim answered.

The sweat on Adam's back chilled, goose bumps racing across his back, up his neck, to bristle his hair.

The weapons and packs were gone. The stuff was there a week ago—Adam had checked himself on a routine security pass—but now they were gone. All gone. How could that be?

"What is it?" Custo asked, coming up to stand beside him, Talia's arm in his grip. Talia let herself be pulled along, uncomplaining.

A beat passed as his friend took in the light-washed, empty room. "Spencer."

"Had to be," Adam agreed, his voice sounding soft and strange to his own ears. "Only the three of us have the master codes."

"But why?"

"Hell if I know. But if he got to this stuff . . ." The image of the military helicopter overhead appeared in his mind.

The soldiers taking up offensive positions on the lawn. Firing at Custo.

". . . then he got to the tunnel, too," Custo finished. Their escape route was lost.

A misunderstanding? Not on this scale.

Someone in SPCI had made a decision. What it was, Adam could not fathom. What sane person—what *human being*—would work in collusion with The Collective?

Obviously, Spencer. Adam remembered that Talia had tried to warn him, and he'd dismissed her concerns. She didn't know Spencer well enough to get his twisted humor. Turns out she knew Spencer better than he.

Adam had no weapons but the ones he and Custo carried. The tunnel escape plan, coauthored by Spencer, was lost as well. The implications were staggering. Any resource Spencer was privy to was now compromised, including the safe houses.

Adam ran a hand through his hair to pinch the tension contracting at the back of his neck.

"I don't get it," Custo said, defeat dulling his eyes as he came to the same conclusions. "Why don't they just drop a bomb on us? Level the building and kill us all in one hit."

"My guess?"

Custo shrugged, as if nothing much mattered anymore.

"Talia. They're taking no chances with her life or they would have fired on the car. They want to extract her alive. They hunted her for months, lost her in Phoenix, and traced her to Segue. Hell, Spencer probably told them she was here. That was six days ago. More than enough time to clean out the supply room and mobilize an assault."

Adam glanced at Talia. This was about her. There was no point in hiding the fact.

"You should trade me for safe passage," she said. Her voice was remarkably even, curiously lacking emotion.

"No," Adam ground out. Custo shook his head, too, but his jaw was tight.

"You said it yourself," Talia insisted. "They probably won't kill me or they would have by now."

"Don't you understand?" Adam said through his teeth. "This is The Collective—they will kill us anyway. They will control you. All hope whatsoever will be lost." This should not be difficult for her, a woman of considerable intellect, to understand.

Adam had to think—to regroup. There had to be a way overlooked by Spencer. Spencer was good, but not creative. Overconfident. There were things he would have missed. The ducts, perhaps, or—

The floor buzzed beneath Adam's feet. The vibration moved over his skin with a sudden terror. He knew the source: a great machine was retracting as a safety measure released.

A distant shriek echoed through the walls of Segue.

From below. From hell.

From Jacob.

The floor shook. Talia saw the lines of Adam's face tighten, his color turn ashy, and she knew what it meant. There were monsters outside, and now a very motivated one inside. Jacob.

Adam's expression focused, as if a line of thought were developing in his mind. He abruptly turned and coded into his office. Custo followed, pulling her with him, and propped open the door with a chair but blocked the others as they crowded beyond the door. Adam dropped his rifle on the small leather sofa to his right and typed madly into his computer.

Talia glanced at the monitor to the right of Adam's desk. Jacob's guards were strung up like macabre marionettes inside the cell they once guarded. Adam switched the image immediately to view a long, empty corridor. He looked over his shoulder at her, concern in his eyes.

Not necessary. Talia's fear was still tightly packed into a knot of horror in the back of her mind. It wouldn't bother her anymore. Patty had taken care of that.

Adam returned his attention to his computer monitor. "Elevators are still locked down. Coded security measures are still active."

He stepped over to a tall cabinet on the other side of the room, jerked it open, and rummaged through long rolls of papers. He selected one, flicked off the rubber band, and unfurled it.

A strong wipe of his arm cleared the adjacent work space. Files, papers, a laptop, and assorted flotsam fell to the floor, replaced with the curling page. Detailed plans of the building in delicate blue lines filled the white space, though the shapes of the rooms and corridors were not familiar to her.

"This is a blueprint of the hotel, not Segue. Spencer and SPCI were not part of the initial renovation of the building, so I'm hoping we can all slip by them and get to the garage. There are three cars left in there, though it will be a tight fit for all of us. The access road might not be blocked."

Adam traced his finger along a set of narrow lines. "There is a God."

Apparently the green parlor had an old, concealed service passage, now covered with drywall, from which it was possible to get out the west side of the building. Then they'd cut across the terrace, climb onto the roof of the garage, enter through a vent, and pack into Adam's cars like circus clowns to make a speedy getaway.

Ridiculous. Her plan was better.

"Trading you is not an option," Adam said, as if he could read her mind. He was back at his computer, concentrating on a detailed list of files, selecting and copying those he wanted.

"It's the only way," Talia insisted. "I can see it. Everyone else can surely see it. That leaves just you. No one else has to die."

From the corridor, Armand shouted, "If the wraiths want her so bad, just give them to her. One life for twelve."

Talia caught the quick, cutting look Adam shot Custo.

Custo turned to the crowd in the doorway. "Let's move back and let the man think. We're not trading anyone to the wraiths today."

Arms spread wide, gun across his chest, Custo herded Gillian and the others down the hallway toward the stairs.

As soon as they were out of sight, Adam said, "Martyring yourself won't bring Pat back. The Collective wants you bad enough to go public before they're ready." A bar slowly made its way across the computer screen as files were downloaded. "They don't have the numbers yet to sustain a full-on war, which means they are embracing years of being hunted just to capture you. You're *that* important. If we give you up now, the wraith war will be over. They'll have won."

He turned back to the cabinet, pulled out a fire ax, and laid it next to his rifle.

He just didn't seem to understand. "Adam. Maybe in an alternate universe, I am actually helpful against the wraiths, instead of a liability. But here and now, I don't know how I could possibly stop them."

If, however, she went to The Collective, negotiated safety for the Segue staff and Adam, then maybe she could do something worthwhile with her life.

He shook his head, *no*. "We need to buy you the time to figure your role out. No matter what happens today, you find out why you are so important, and then end this."

The man was insane.

He pressed a flash drive into her hand. "You've got all my Segue files here, as well as locations of global safe houses. Actually, ignore those. Find somewhere populated, but anonymous. A big city, but don't tell me which one. You'll have access to money, resources. Names of people who will help you."

Talia tried to give it back. "I'm not taking this."

"I don't want to have to give it to you, but there's nothing left to do. No, I take that back. Just one thing left . . ." His mouth descended on hers, his hand cradling the back of her head, fingers lacing into her hair. He seared her with his regret.

She didn't want to feel this. Feel what might have been.

He shifted, kicking the desk chair out of the way to mold her body to his, showing her—cruelly—just how perfectly they would have fit together had things been different. A wild surge of his emotion overwhelmed her—too many feelings to parse individually, but all racked with guilt.

He pulled back, but the sensation of his mouth still lingered on hers.

"I'm sorry for how I did it before," he said. "I was feeling sorry for myself. Still am, but what the hell."

She gripped his arms. "What? So now I'm supposed to run away and leave you to—"

He nodded. "Yep. Far and fast."

Across their touch, his determination surged, washing out all other emotion.

"No. I've seen what the wraiths do to people."

"We all have to die someday." He grabbed her around the waist and shoved her into the corridor.

She turned to find him armed with his rifle and the ax. "But they won't feed on your 'life energy.' They feed on your soul."

Adam glanced down at her briefly in the office doorway, mouth twisting a little. "My soul's half eaten already."

"No, it's not. It's . . ." There were no words to describe what she felt in him. "I could make it so dark that we could all slip out to safety."

"I assure you that we will be using that trick of yours, but your range isn't wide enough to blind them all. To save us all. Just you." He pushed her down the hall to the rest of the Segue group. Custo already had the stairwell door open.

"And I can *do* things in the dark, too. I disabled one wraith on the street . . ." she argued as she hurried alongside Adam.

"But not the one that got Patty. We have an entire army outside those doors."

Then it was hopeless. "You're not going to fight to live at all?"

"The green parlor," Adam said to Custo, who ushered the others into the stairwell. Adam turned back to her, looked her straight in the eyes. "Talia, I am going to fight to the death. Please understand. I have to see to my brother." Dark, bloody anger coursed through him, as if the word *brother* had a death grip on his heart. "You find the thing that did this to him."

She pulled back. *No. I don't want to.*

This was not the Adam that had just kissed her. This Adam was a stranger. Unyielding, implacable. Bent on fighting a creature ten times his strength. Out of his mind.

"Promise me. You're the key. You find the source of the wraiths and you end this." They exited into the hotel's front foyer. Adam speared her with a look over his shoulder. "Promise me."

"I don't know how," she repeated. His urgency was so strong, so intent, that it overrode every other feeling.

"You find out." He shifted his grasp to hold her upper arm. "For Patty."

The name gripped her and took her objections away. "For Patty."

Talia glanced down the hallway. The group ahead had stirred the air so that dust motes spun in the flood of sunlight. Outside the percussive slices of the helicopter's propellers battered the sky.

Adam followed Custo through a series of connecting doors—her arm and shoulder would never be the same—then handed her off with a push that sent her tripping into Custo's grasp. The brief touch of Custo's skin told her he was full of urgency and ready for a good fight. Behind him, Gillian's face was pinched and red. Armand cursed. And Jim Remy was restlessly shifting.

Talia looked around. The room had no windows and was gray with shadows. She could darken a room this size completely. In Middleton, she had propelled a bullet to its target—she could do that again. Take the wraiths and soldiers out one by one. She could—

A loud crack snapped her into reality—Adam hitting the wall with the ax. His arms lifted, his shoulders bunched and tightened, and then the ax came down, splintering the wall. He reached into the black hole and pulled back with the weight of his body. A large piece of drywall came away. Armand stepped up and yanked more drywall. Others grabbed at the breach to create a big enough opening to move through.

"Adam," Jim said. "Give me a gun. I'll take up the rear."

"Custo can do that."

"You need Custo, and I want to stay here. Forever. I want to be with her." Jim shrugged. Talia knew he meant Lady Amunsdale, the ghost he'd lost track of this past week. He had to be out of his mind.

Adam hesitated, then held out his handgun to Jim. A couple magazines followed.

Thick dust rose from the hole in the wall in a great gasping cloud. Beyond it, blackness stretched. Crawly things in there.

"You first," Adam said in her direction.

Custo grimly nodded, and with a soft shove started Talia's unwilling feet moving toward the black yawn. She stepped over the boards at her feet and into a narrow, musty hallway, time-drenched with webs hanging like specters to snag at her hair and brush against her arms.

"Here." A spotlight pierced the darkness as Custo nudged her hand with a flashlight. "Move fast now. The others are waiting."

She held up her arm to shield her eyes and face, then forged ahead. The corridor was long, broken at rotting steps that she descended with Custo's support, should the wood give way. This passage must have been intended for servants, bustling unseen throughout the hotel at work or on errands.

An old door was propped at the exit, its decaying hinges broken away from the wood of the frame. The room beyond was small and dour, but light shined though a graying porthole. The group crowded into the space.

When Adam joined them, the room stilled as everyone strained to hear what was to come next. "This will put us on the western curve of the terrace. We're heading to the roof of the garage. Custo and Talia are going to go first. Then the rest of you."

He tossed a key ring to Gillian. And another to Armand. "Pack as many people as you can in the vehicles."

"Shhhhh!" Custo turned his head to listen.

The room quieted. Behind them, from the mouth of the corridor, hard footsteps sounded. Pounded. Cracked wood.

Jacob?

"Damn it," Adam said. "Go now. Custo . . ."

Everyone jammed the window, each trying to get through to safety first.

"Now or never," Jim said, sweat rolling off his forehead. He dived back into the blackness. A loud pop echoed into the room. *Pop. Pop.* A strangled scream. Then silence.

No one moved for an agonizing moment.

Then Custo elbowed Armand in the face to get through the crowd. He dragged another from the porthole and levered himself up and out smoothly.

Rough hands—Adam's—lifted Talia's hips. She ducked through the hole and fell onto Custo, who hefted her up, locked an arm around her chest, and put a gun to her head.

Her heart leaped in momentary panic, but then she understood. He didn't want to shoot her, he was sending a message.

The sun blared overhead, hot on her face, but after a moment, her vision adjusted and she caught movement on the grass below the balustrade. Guns aimed, but not firing. It was as Adam said—they wanted to take her alive.

One by one, people emerged from the portal. Old Philip hefted, purple-faced, through the hole. The lab tech, Priya, followed. They staggered in the light and slowly came to attention as weapons from the grass leveled at them like a firing squad.

Adam climbed through last, though he stopped to call over his shoulder. "Jim!"

No one answered.

Custo dragged Talia backward toward Adam. "We've got to go before they call our bluff."

Adam nodded sharply. His gaze rested on her momentarily, and then he signaled for everyone to move out. The rifles below followed them as they raced to the garage, the helicopter dipping, chin down, some distance away to head in their direction.

The group climbed a service ladder to the roof of the garage, Custo and Talia first. All they had to do was get into the garage and to the cars. There was no way anyone could know which vehicle Talia was in. Perhaps they could escape, after all.

"Oh, Adam," a voice called. The tone was light, playful, flirtatious, though masculine, and it carried across the terrace in spite of the helicopter.

Talia turned.

Jacob strolled toward them. Jim, still alive, shielded his body. Blood streaked in a vivid brushstroke up Jacob's forearm, as if he'd just wiped his mouth. Talia thought of the guards in the cell below Segue and shuddered.

"Jacob," a magnified voice from the helicopter called. "Do not attack the group."

"Why not?" Jacob called gleefully, still approaching. Jim whined in his grasp.

"The Collective commands you to halt!"

"The Collective left me to rot," Jacob said.

"Shoot him," Talia said to Custo.

Custo raised his gun, but it was too late. Jacob was hungry for one person, and one person only.

Jacob darted, throwing Jim to the side.

Adam dodged, bringing up his assault rifle. Jacob smacked it down—the volley of shots clipped the flagstones as the gun went awry. Jacob grasped the strap that secured the weapon to Adam's body, wrenching him backward.

Adam heaved, jabbed a leg back, and caught Jacob in the knee. Even Talia, from her position on the roof, could hear the crack. But Adam couldn't escape.

Custo raised his shotgun again, grim conviction on his face.

"No! You'll hit Adam."

Jacob brought Adam roughly up by the shoulders in a twisted lover's embrace.

"There's no other way." Custo focused down the barrel.

"Brother mine," Jacob said, grinning. He kissed Adam once, a teasing peck on the nose, then drew back, mouth widening, teeth extending.

Horror surged in Talia. Revulsion burst all of the floodgates she'd meticulously erected around her heart. All reservations dissolved in its wake. All care for life, and hope, and love evaporated in the anticipation of Adam's death. If the wraiths and humanity wanted a massacre, she'd bloody well give them one.

Talia gulped a painful lungful of air, hardened her resolve, and screamed.

Shadowman grips the cold staff of his scythe, its blade pitiless as death and sharp as his grief. Shadows howl and roar as they surround him like great dark beasts of wind and fury.

Over the encircling snarl, a soul cries a high song of deepest terror. It is an Old sound brought up by a child's throat in a composition of broken, dissonant notes summoning Death to a hunt.

Talia.

The scream rips through veils of Twilight and rends the bindings of his prison. Freedom. Shadow snaps at his heels, but they cannot follow him.

Through his child's scream, he is born again into the world.

Day. Sunlight breaks on the cloak at his shoulders as he emerges onto the battlefield. Neither forest nor structure obstructs his view; Death was made for war.

Talia.

A host of men train their weapons on his daughter. Deathless ones ruled by soul-gnawing hunger slink toward their human prey. And beyond the fray, over the crest of the mountain, a demon, master of this chaos.

The snake who slipped by Death and into the mortal world while he was lost to Talia's mother.

Demon! Harm my child and you will see what hell Death can wreak on Earth.

The demon opens a human mouth to laugh back at him.

TWELVE

A scream shattered the air. Adam hoped it wasn't his; if nothing else, he wanted to die like a man. He summoned his will and steeled himself for what was to come.

The high-pitched sound went on, burning through Adam's head, but rendered, thank God, from a woman's throat. His eardrums contracted. The noise, unending, reverberated through his body and shuddered his marrow.

Jacob staggered, his sick kiss stalled, his grip relaxed—

Yes! Adam ducked out of Jacob's embrace. Kicked back and connected with his chest. Adam dropped to his knees, dragging his rifle from where it had flapped uselessly at his shoulder, and pulled the trigger. The impact of the shots made a dimpled trail up Jacob's torso, pushing him off balance, driving him to collide with the edge of the terrace and plummet over the ornate railing to the ground.

Brilliant light drew Adam's eyes upward, to the top of the garage. To Talia.

He stumbled back in awe.

Her skin glowed with an ethereal inner radiance, brighter than the sun overhead, yet not painful to gaze at with bare eyes. Her hair whipped wildly around her. Her arms and fingers were outstretched with the effort to push the piercing sound out of her chest. Her soul-wrenching cry for help gripped him at his core.

"Angel," Adam said.

"I think not," Philip answered. He huddled at the wall, crossing himself. "Banshee, the herald of Death."

The blue sky around her darkened and shredded. Silken azure edges snapped in a tornado of dark wind. Black wind. Out of the howling vortex, a man clawed, ripping at the grasping shadows with angry vehemence. He gripped a sickle. No, a scythe.

"Shadowman," Adam murmured.

Death glanced down on Adam, as if he'd heard him. The cloak's hood fell to Death's broad shoulders. His eyes were tipped up, like Talia's, but pulsing with violent violet. The black sheet of his long hair gleamed against shadowy skin. His arms lifted so that the cloak winged at his sides. If ever there were an angel of death—

On the rooftop, a wraith lunged with the stupid temerity to put hands on Talia. Bad choice.

As Death straightened, he twisted. His body uncoiled with a deadly swing, connected and lifted the wraith's body as the blade cleaved. Dust flew from the sundered form. The remains fell in heaps of bone and leather. Adam's heart clutched as Shadowman rounded on Custo, frozen in place by fear or shock, but Death passed him by to sweep his blade at two more wraiths, just reaching the roof. Their heads skipped as they rolled across the flat top, to plummet like stones on the soldiers below.

Still Talia screamed. The sound was a hot wire of terror. The soldiers fired on Death, bodies shaking with the report of their guns. Probably not a good idea either.

Shadowman's scythe sliced through the air at the helicopter and cut its wraith pilot from the world. The helicopter careened into the trees with a red-black explosion that shook Segue.

"Fall back," a man shouted.

The wraiths leaped from the roof to the grass and fled across the lawn, scattering and crushing the much slower soldiers, but Shadowman followed, a phantom riding the wind in their wake. The silver blade arced in a cold, colorless rainbow, and cut the monsters down.

Wraith bodies crumbled as Shadowman threshed. Shadowman, the answer to the bloodlust that beat at Adam's temples. The sight went beyond powerful—it was fucking fun, and would have been more so if Adam himself could have wielded the weapon of their destruction. But he couldn't have everything.

Maybe he could . . .

Adam ran to the edge of the terrace. He gripped the balustrade, peering on the grass for one particular monster.

Jacob sprawled at the foundation of the building, still incapacitated, but certainly regenerating.

"Here," Adam called to Death. Death did not signify that he heard as he ranged over the grass like a giant crow.

"Shadowman," Adam shouted.

Shadowman turned sharply, cloak fanning behind him.

"You missed one." Adam gestured to Jacob. Emotion clogged his throat so that that his next words came out in a low rumble. "I beg you. Kill him."

Death slid upward as if air were water. The scattered soldiers ran for the trees. Crushed bodies of others stained the earth. Some huddled on their knees, praying or incapacitated with fear.

Adam wasn't concerned. Hell, he was elated, his heart about to burst. Shadowman only destroyed wraiths, who, for all intents and purposes, were dead already. The living he left alone.

Death spun his blade in a glittering circle, then darted downward.

All sound muted as Adam watched Death plummet toward his brother.

Plummet. And disappear.

Jacob raised a knee. Turned on his side.

Adam searched the sky. Empty. His eyes scoured the ground. Only bodies lay near Segue, some dead, and others who should be—Jacob—but were not.

"Shadowman!"

No answer.

Someone behind him wept in wheezy gulps. Gillian. The sobs were loud in the otherwise stillness of the moment.

Then Adam knew. The scream. It was gone.

Adam looked up to the rooftop of the garage. Custo knelt at the edge, holding Talia's slack form.

"Is she all right?" Adam yelled up to him. Banshee? Angel? As far as he was concerned, they were the same thing.

"Passed out," Custo called down.

"Wake her!" Adam's throat was raw. He glanced down; Jacob was even now propping himself up on one elbow.

Custo took Talia's chin. "Talia! Talia!"

Adam needed her. Now. To come so close to freedom and remain shackled to the monster . . . No. He bounded over to the ladder and climbed to the roof. He crouched by Custo, grabbed Talia by the shoulders and shook. Hard.

Six years' worth of grief, frustration, and terror filled Adam's mind. The time was now. The way was clear. She had to scream again. Jacob was going to die today if it killed Adam.

"She's done enough," Custo said.

"No," Adam bit out. "She hasn't." She'd wake all right. He drew back his arm to slap her.

Custo caught his wrist. "Adam, she's done. Get a hold of yourself."

Adam fought his grip for a moment—she had to wake!—but the reproach in his friend's eyes drained the impulse. What was he thinking?

He looked down at Talia's too-pale face, flawless skin gleaming, her hair curling wildly around her.

Adam dropped his arm and closed his eyes, breathing deeply for balance. Remembering who he was. How could he even consider touching her in violence?

Lovely, bookish Talia. Hunted, terrorized. He'd promised to protect her.

Adam shuddered and opened his eyes. If he had waited this long to kill Jacob, he could wait a little longer. He had the means now, and that was what was important.

That is, if Talia survived the day. There was no way she could make it through the vents of the garage unconscious. "We better get inside before they regroup down there. Before Jacob climbs the wall."

"You take Talia," Custo said, shifting Talia's body to Adam. "I'll manage the others."

Custo relinquished her carefully, but seemed relieved to let go of her, to let go of Death's child.

"Okay," Adam said. He wasn't afraid of her. He'd been looking, praying, for Death for so long that he welcomed the chance to cradle her close—his means to Jacob's end, his tool of vengeance, his reprieve from the burden of his family.

He took Talia in his arms. She was limp, pale, and cold. She needed care, food, and water. Responsibility settled on his shoulders like a well-worn yoke.

"No, wait," he said. "Send the others on. You go with them and leave me the Diablo. I'll follow shortly. Once you get them settled, meet me . . ."

Where? Everything was different now that they had Talia. There was no reason to hide, not when she could call on her dear old dad. Where then?

New York City, where it began. ". . . at the loft."

Adam shifted her weight over his shoulder so that he could descend the ladder. The others darted up as soon as he hit bottom. Jim stood resolute.

"Jim, get going." Adam waved Jim to the ladder and, glancing at the edge of the terrace below where Jacob lay, fingered his weapon.

"I'm staying," Jim said.

"You're alive by the narrowest of chances. Don't push your luck. There's no room in my car for three."

"I'm not leaving Lady Amunsdale."

"You haven't seen her for a week."

"We've had a banshee in residence," Jim argued with a wave at Talia.

"So we have," Adam answered. A banshee. A weapon. It was about fucking time.

"Talia!" a man's urgent voice whispered.

Talia cracked a dry eye. Jim's face filled her vision. A puff of slightly turned breath hit her face.

"Talia. You're awake."

She recoiled slightly. Blinked. Glanced around.

She was in Adam's office, lying on the modern leather love seat opposite his desk. Papers were strewn on the floor. The mess was familiar, but she couldn't place why.

Her throat was desert dry.

Jim looked furtively over his shoulder, toward Adam's open office door. He pushed a water bottle into her hand. "Drink this."

Her hand shook when she took the bottle. The fluid went down like liquid heaven.

"What happened?"

Jim leaned forward, restlessly. "You screamed, Death came. Listen, I need you to do something for me."

I screamed—? Talia remembered. She let the devil into the world. The black demon with the red eyes. Her father. She had to admit that now, to herself and to everyone. Custo had reeled away from her. The soldiers fired in fear. Adam's expression had been . . . different, *strange* as he looked up at her.

"I need you to call Lady Amunsdale." Jim's words came out in a rush. "We don't have much time. Adam will be back any second. Can you call her for me? Please call her."

"What are you talking about?" Talia shifted, but Jim was ahead of her, hoisting her complaining body into sitting position.

"You're a banshee. You have some pull with Death. Maybe you can call her, get her to come back."

"I'm a what?"

"Banshee. You know, *ahhhhhhhh.*" He raised his hands to his cheeks for emphasis. "See, there have been no sightings of Lady Amunsdale since you got here, and I . . . I just really need to see her. I want to talk to her. *For once.* Please."

"I don't understand—" Talia slid away from him.

"I brought you a book that will tell you all about it. I filched it just now from Philip's library." Jim pressed a dusty hardback into her hands. "But read it in the car, when you have time. Right now just call her. Just try. Just say . . . 'Lady Amunsdale, come out. I mean you no harm. Jim wants to talk with you.'"

He waited, a weird, desperate light in his eyes.

"It's ridiculous. I don't want to." Talia pushed the book away.

"Jim, leave her alone." Adam stood in the doorway, a pack on his back, keys in hand. His gaze hard with anger. A muscle twitched in his jaw.

Jim raised conciliatory hands. "I just wanted her to call Lady Amunsdale. Is it too much to ask to speak to her one single time in my life? I've been tracking sightings and energy readings for years. I've been waiting so long to find her. To be with her."

"We've all had to wait," Adam said. "When this war is over, I'll bring Talia back. We can try then."

"The wraith war will never be over," Jim whined. "Please. Can't you just give me a moment?"

"Come on, Talia." Adam held a hand out to her. "We've got to get going. Can you walk?"

Good question.

Adam pulled her to her feet. She didn't want to know what he thought of her since her horrific performance outside, but she needed to get away from Jim.

"Think about it, Adam," Jim said. "Lady Amunsdale could tell us things. Could tell you things like . . . like . . . what that asshole Spencer's been up to. She is a *witness*. She's been here—everywhere—all along. Make Talia call her."

Adam's expression shifted, his gaze sharpening with interest. He glanced at her. Jim had finally struck a chord.

Oh, no. She shook her head. "It's crazy."

"It couldn't hurt to try," Adam reasoned. "And it could help."

Talia backed away.

"Come on, Talia," Jim said, his hands clasped together to beg.

Talia shook her head. "It's not safe. I don't want to let that . . . that devil back into the world."

"What devil?" Adam dropped his pack on the floor.

"Uhhh—the one with the scythe? The one who killed dozens of people." A sob gathered in her throat. *Say it,* an inner voice commanded. "My father, Shadowman."

"Talia, he saved us. He'll save the world."

Adam was wrong. She stepped back again, hit the wall. "I

saw the bodies on the lawn. He's a demon. Red eyes, vicious."

Adam inclined his head. "I don't know what *you* saw, but he looked damn beautiful to me." He moved toward her. "And he seemed to have a good grasp of who was man and who was wraith. He only attacked the wraiths. It was the wraiths who killed the men down there, crushing them or using them to hide behind."

But what about . . . "I saw him cut down Melanie, in my apartment at the university. A wraith had her and . . . and Death cut right through her."

Adam shrugged. "Maybe she was dead already, I don't know. But today Shadowman only killed wraiths. He's no demon; I think he's one of the good guys."

"He's Death!" My father. Which made her, by connection, worse than she'd ever feared.

"Exactly. And I, for one, am delighted that he is on our side. Will you try to call Lady Amunsdale or not? She might have information for all of us."

"Please," Jim added.

Talia looked from one to the other, swallowing hard. Jim, pining after a phantom, and Adam, twisted and tortured by his brother. They were out of their minds, and she was well ahead of them.

A banshee. What the hell was that anyway? Nothing good.

"You want me to scream again?" Her throat was too raw. "I don't think I can."

"Maybe just call her," Jim put in. "We can try the scream after if we need to."

Right. Easy for him to say.

"The sooner you try, the sooner we can get on our way," Adam said.

She sighed—that was the most reasonable thing she'd heard since Jim had wakened her.

"Lady Amunsdale," Talia said, looking around the room. Nothing. Ridiculous.

She tried again, louder, with melodrama. "Lady Amunsdale. Please grace us with your presence."

All quiet.

Jim buried his face in his hands, his bald head reddening. Talia felt bad for her mocking tone. The man was crazy, but also desperately in love.

"You're too nice," Adam observed. "It might take more of a command to get her to come out."

Talia rolled her eyes. A command—those came all too easy to Adam. This was the last time, and she was done.

She raised her voice. "Lady Amunsdale. Come here. Now."

A pause, then a distorted voice whined.

Jim's head snapped up, eyes darting, face savage with hope.

Feminine, mourning, and unearthly, the sound circled and raised goose bumps across Talia's flesh. Adam wrapped his arm around her waist and pulled her against his body. Talia could feel his heart hammer in his chest, but whatever else he might be feeling, a sense of unassailable protection grounded her.

Jim whipped around. "Therese?"

Nothing.

Jim turned back to Talia. "Please?"

Talia didn't want to do more. She didn't want to know that she could. "Lady Amunsdale? Are you here?"

"No," the voice answered, pleading, the syllable drawn out, variably loud and soft.

Talia turned, shuddering, and buried her face against Adam's chest. This could not be happening. She didn't want any of it. Death. Demon. Shadowman. Ghost. What kind of life was this? No wonder she was such a freak. She was born to be alone and scared.

"We need to know about Spencer. Ask her, Talia," Adam murmured in her hair. "So we can go. We don't have much time."

Talia groaned. She didn't want to.

"Remember Patty," Adam said, harder.

As if struck, Talia pushed away from him, shrugged off his arms. Patty. Of course. There would be no comfort in Adam's arms, not for costing him Patty. She didn't deserve comfort anyway.

If Patty could kiss a wraith, then—Talia swallowed her apprehension. "Are you here?" she called.

"Yesssss," the voice wept.

"Therese!" Jim spun in a circle. "It's Jim. We mean you no harm."

"Show yourself," Talia said.

"I'm here," Lady Amunsdale said. But her tone made it clear that she was not present by her own will.

Talia couldn't see her, but she could feel her like a feather brushing on the edge of her awareness. She was definitely here. Or near.

Talia tugged on the shadows. The room darkened. Deepened. Grew more layered.

Hands gripped her arms from behind. That would be Adam, wanting to share her sight. To use her to see the ghost. He left her hands free, which was practical, but floundered for alternative bare skin. Her sweatshirt didn't pull up easily at the sleeves. He switched to her waist and slid his warm palms across her belly.

His urgency bled through the skin-to-skin connection, as immediate as their situation was. She shut out the rest of him—his light, his want, and especially his grief. And she shoved away—denied—how the warmth he gave her took the chill off her shadows.

Jim choked in the darkness. "Talia? Adam? I can't see a thing. Where are you?"

"Quiet," Adam answered. "Just stay where you are. Talia's looking for her."

"But—"

"Shh!"

Something glimmered. A star sparked behind a black cloud.

Talia pulled the dense shadow away and found an unhappy child. Blonde ringlets coiled around an angry face, chin tensed and dimpled with willfulness.

"Lady Amunsdale?"

The child stuck out her tongue and fled. Talia started after her, but Adam held her firm, his arm locking her against his body, hand hot on her middle.

"Order her back," he said in her ear. "You can make her come to you."

"How?" And if he knew so much, why didn't he just do it himself?

"Tell her to come, to answer what we want, and if she won't, threaten her with the alternative."

"Which is?"

"Your father."

Talia didn't like that word, *father*. She made a substitution. "I'm not calling Death for that child!"

"She's not a child. She's not even a woman. She's a ghost."

Jim whipped out a fighting arm, flailing in the darkness. "Don't you hurt her! Talia, don't you hurt her!"

Talia swallowed hard.

"Lady Amunsdale. You will come here and speak with me."

Talia reached with her mind and parted the shadows like

a curtain. The child sat on a wooden crate in a dark storeroom, legs pulled up under her dress. The smell here was dusty and old, but dry, cut out of bedrock. A place built for preserving things. Foodstuffs and spirits. The child looked over her knees with resentful eyes.

"I'm not leaving!"

"Where are we?" Talia asked. She felt Adam take hold of her again. He was planted firmly at Segue, looking across the expanse of time with her. She had the feeling that if he let go, she would float away like a ship without mooring and be lost to time and shadow. Her hands gripped his forearm at her waist.

"I've got you. We're in the hotel," Adam murmured in Talia's ear. "This is the Fulton, in the past. In her time. We're the ghosts here."

"I won't go!" The child clasped the ropes around a crate, settling in for a fight, as stubborn as Adam.

"Go where?"

"Across. Away. I won't die. You can't make me."

"I'm afraid I could." Talia was literally afraid of what she could do.

"I don't think so. The dark, mean man couldn't. He can't find me now anyway." The child was solid defiance, with a cruel, adult twist to her mouth. Something was perverted about her, as if the person that was Lady Amunsdale was gone, and all that was left was her will. Her will was to stay.

"What mean man?" Talia dreaded the answer.

"The one from the other side. The one who wants me to cross."

Death? Shadowman? Or something else? "Why can't he find you?"

"He's stuck. Trapped." The little girl grinned a too-adult smug smile of satisfaction.

Had to be Shadowman. "Trapped how?"

"I don't know."

"Tell me!" Talia's command rippled through the air.

The child's voice whined through the layers of shadow. The sound deepened, broadened, and matured to the wail of a woman, but produced from the little girl's mouth. "I don't know!"

This was too frustrating. Like squeezing water from a stone.

Adam increased his pressure on Talia's stomach briefly. Right, they had to hurry.

"Tell me about Spencer." She voiced Adam's most pressing question.

"I don't know that name." The child turned her head away, bored.

"He works here, with me. At the hotel. Have you watched him? Can you see us in our lives? Doing things?" The thought made Talia shiver. "Answer me!"

The girl gripped the rope cords as Talia's shock wave warped through her. The child's face grimaced with effort. "I can see you, but I can't see anyone else. Just you and the one that is all empty skin. His belly is like a bottle with little firefly spirits trapped inside. So many little fireflies that can't get out. I stay away from him."

Talia felt Adam go rigidly still as her own heart lurched. Poor Patty. "What happens to the spirits then?"

"Ask him yourself," the girl sang. "He's coming."

Talia looked wildly over her shoulder to the door. Adam drew a gun. "Ask her what made him."

The girl giggled. "He's coming He's coming He's coming."

"Ask her!" Adam shook her sharply.

Talia trembled. She didn't want to know, but Adam's hold was too tight. He squeezed the question out of her. "What made the Empty Skin?"

The child stretched and shimmered. Morphed. She became

a woman before Talia's eyes, her hair growing wildly, curling out of her head, each strand alive. Her dress lengthened with her body, white fabric upon lace and cotton. Stockinged feet in heeled shoes momentarily peeped out from her skirts as she settled herself into a straight-backed repose. Her chin tipped up just enough to cast her eyes down her nose at Talia.

"A demon, the Death Collector," the woman said in a rich, cultured voice, as if speaking to Talia was distasteful to her.

Did she mean Shadowman? Shadowman killed wraiths, he didn't make them. The demon must be something, someone different. Must be the source of this madness.

A loud crash sounded down the hallway.

"Damn it," Adam said in her ear. "We've got to go. Jim, we're leaving. This is your last chance."

"I'm staying," he said, backing blindly in the dark. "I'm staying with Lady Amunsdale."

"She's no lady," Talia said. "She's twisted. Insane."

The ghost sneered and patted her hair.

"Jim, I can't fight Jacob, protect Talia, and drag you. This is your last chance." Adam ducked his head out the office door, glanced both ways, and returned for Jim's answer.

"Staying," he said. "Staying forever."

"So be it." Adam shifted his gun to the hand at Talia's waist and hoisted the pack on his shoulder. "Can you keep the shadows on us until we reach the car?"

"You'll have to hold on to me to be able to see." Talia took his hand from her stomach and held it. Her heartbeat thumped hard. Fresh sweat prickled in her hairline. She licked her lips. Her skin was already salty from the pelting run from Middleton and the tear through Segue to the garage roof.

He squeezed her hand in return. "Don't worry. I won't let go."

"Wait," Jim called. "Take the book."

Talia found the thin volume on the love seat and grabbed it with her free hand.

Lady Amunsdale laughed with throaty pleasure. "The Empty Skin is coming. He's going to fill himself up with you. And I'm going to watch."

"Move," Adam said to Talia. He pulled her out into the empty corridor. Talia's shadow rolled with them in a smoky wave. She slipped once as he dragged her toward the rear stairwell.

Her head swam with dizziness while Adam punched the code into the door. He hauled her upward. From behind them, someone screamed. Jim Remy joining Lady Amunsdale, or worse.

Adam dragged her up the flight of steps and out the rear exit.

In her shadow, the midday sun was a magenta orb in the sky, the world a blur of purples. The rear lot was deserted, except for the red sports car—the one Gillian called the California. It still idled, windshield shattered, keys in the ignition. Adam paused at the open passenger door as if contemplating trading his plan for a new one. Beyond, the extra-wide opening to the garage gaped.

"Run," he decided, dragging her toward to garage. "We're taking the Diablo."

They bolted across the pavement and arrived at the remaining car. It looked as cruel as Adam's grip on her, a sleek, masculine angle, slanting in a satisfied sneer. She had to duck quite low to sit inside, but beyond that initial discomfort, the car was pure luxury.

"Buckle up," Adam ordered. Pleasure washed over his face as he turned the ignition and put the car in gear.

He hit the gas just as Jacob slapped open the rear door to Segue.

Fear thrilled up Talia's back, though she was safe in the car with Adam stoking the power of the machine. Her belly quivered as the car accelerated. They flew past Jacob. Safe. She whipped her head around to watch Jacob and Segue recede into the distance.

Jacob was gone. The open door to the California shut. The red sports car jerked into a turn and aimed down the road in pursuit, mottled glass sparkling in the sunlight.

"He's following us," Talia said.

"Damn right, he is," Adam answered with a twisted smile.

THIRTEEN

THE Diablo's engine growled at Adam's back, low and feral, then climbed to a high snarl as the sports car took on speed. The ride was smooth, the sound subtly vibrating every nerve in his body as the Lamborghini possessed the road. Like good sex, driving the car was a study in exhilarating restraint and control.

Adam glanced in his rearview mirror. The Ferrari-red California lit the road behind him, a great puff of dust lingering in the air. The car's windshield was white-webbed with impact lines—Jacob wouldn't be able to see well, enhanced wraith senses or not.

"Can you do the shadow thing again?" Adam glanced at Talia, who stared, white-faced, into the side mirror at Jacob's pursuit. "Talia!"

She jerked her attention to him. Her loose curls trembled on her shoulders and down her back. Her eyes were wide with fear, chin smudged with grime.

"Can you do the shadow thing on us and the car?"

"I don't know—"

Adam reached over, grabbed her wrist, and lacking alternatives, dragged up his shirt and planted her palm on his stomach. He needed both hands on the wheel for controlling the upcoming turns, regardless of how the combination of the car's delicious power and the woman touching him made his blood abruptly and distractingly redirect itself.

Jacob. Think of Jacob. Adam glanced in the review mirror. His brother had coaxed the vehicle to match the Diablo's speed.

The boulders approached, Adam's best chance.

"We need the shadow thing, now!"

A tidal wave of darkness rolled over him, his vision surging with layers of dream-hued gray. The green of the surrounding wood intensified into exquisite lushness. Talia's hand heated, her fingers slightly pressing into his belly with her effort. His muscles contracted with her touch.

The great, knobby slabs of the boulders seemed to widen as Adam propelled the car forward. Only at the crest of the rise was the road's metal safety railing visible on the other side, a posted sign warning of a tight turn. Not a place to speed. Not unless you had a death wish.

The boulders passed and Adam whipped into the turn, managing the drag of momentum with skillful application of brakes and gas. The back end of the car scraped the metal railing—the Diablo would need a little body work—but reclaimed the road no worse for the wear.

Adam looked at his rearview mirror: The California burned by behind him. With a screeching pop of bursting metal, the car ate empty air for fifty feet before arcing into a dive. A moment later, a squealing crash and roar of fire and smoke assured Adam that his big brother had just gone boom.

Adam groaned in disgust. "What a shame. Such a beautiful car wasted. I hope the crash hurt him like hell."

He frowned into himself—once upon a time he and Jacob had enjoyed going to the racetrack together. That was *before*. Another life. Another Jacob.

Another Adam.

At least the explosion would slow Jacob down. Years

ago, Adam had tried to get rid of Jacob with fire. Prolonged fire, like they did to witches way back when. Jacob came back afterward—blood, bone, and muscle growing grotesquely over charred remains. The process took Jacob a single afternoon, and he'd been hungry and pissed when he finished.

Talia sat up from Adam's side, and her darkness dissipated. She settled back into the far edge of her seat, putting as much distance between her and Adam as the car would allow. He brushed his shirt down to cover the sudden coldness of her absence.

Fishing his mobile phone out of his pocket, Adam dialed Spencer's number. The call went directly to voice mail, which suited him just fine. "Spencer, you son of a bitch. Next time we meet, and I pray it's soon, I'll kill you. You got that? I will kill you. You tell your superiors that I want my people, those who were based at Segue, and those who work globally, to be left alone. I want their movements unrestricted, unimpeded, and unsurveilled by SPCI or The Collective. If I or any of my people do not check in at their appointed times in their prescribed manner, information about wraith activities will be posted online and sent via both e-mail and hard copy to various sources internationally. SPCI may have elected to cooperate with The Collective, but the people of the world sure as hell haven't."

Adam ended the call. He didn't know how much his threats would help. Matters may have progressed too far to deter The Collective, regardless of any public outcry at their exposure. If SPCI was now involved, The Collective could move with that much more freedom.

By now, whoever was in command would've realized that Talia posed no threat to humans—Shadowman had only attacked the wraiths. If Adam didn't get her away, there'd be soldiers checking cars at all of the roads leading off the mountain. He and Talia would be forced into slow submission.

The tight curve of the road mellowed, and Adam pressed on the accelerator, bringing the vehicle back up over ninety.

Adam glanced at Talia. "Tell me again what Spencer said about the wraiths—when he followed you to your room."

She took in and released a breath, her brows drawing together. "He said that becoming a wraith was merely a change of state, like dying—going from body to spirit. He was arguing that their way of life, immortality in particular, might be better than the human way of life."

Spencer's argument was an old one. He and Adam had hashed it out years ago. Adam had obviously missed how committed Spencer was to that view.

"He also said that you were studying me at Segue, even had cameras on me in my apartment 24–7," Talia continued. "He said that SPCI has facilities where my rights would be protected. Where there were others like me."

The cameras. Adam had actually forgotten about those. Jim had them installed a couple years back to monitor ghost activity in the west wing. The cameras and hookups were there, but hadn't been in use for a while. Unless . . .

"Talia, I wasn't watching you in your rooms, but I'll bet Spencer was. I forgot that the hookups were there. They were installed solely to capture evidence of ghost activity. And for your information, I've been to the SPCI facilities. There are no human rights there. Wraiths are caged and experimented on with indifference. I've often been tempted to do similar studies on Jacob, but Patty tried to keep me and Segue humane."

The mention of Patty stabbed at him. Patty had been his conscience for as long as Jacob had been a wraith. Adam felt another stab, hard and sharp. Okay, okay—apparently Patty didn't actually have to be present to goad him down the right path.

"I did order additional tests when you first arrived at

Segue. I knew you were different, and I wanted to know what I was dealing with. I should have told you. Patty wanted me to, and she was right. I'm sorry."

Another jab from the memory of Patty, this one much more painful.

"As far as her death goes, I am entirely at fault," he admitted.

Talia didn't answer. Probably didn't believe him.

He elaborated. "Last night I instructed both her and Custo to protect you at all costs. That you were the key to the wraiths' destruction. When she kissed that wraith, she was doing what I asked. Her death was not your fault."

Talia shook her head. "I was going to run away again. I was on my way. If I hadn't—"

"They would have still attacked Segue. Perhaps more lives would have been lost. Patty died, but you lived to warn us, to save us."

"It's not that simple."

Adam chanced another look at Talia. Her profile was bright against the rush of green outside her window. The woman was intelligent; she wasn't going to accept simple answers for complicated problems.

"No, it's not that simple," he conceded. "But Pat never would've wanted to hurt anyone. Take the life she gave you, gave us, and be happy."

"You're not happy."

"My brother is California barbecue. I'm delighted. I'll mourn Patty when this is all over."

Adam's heart twisted. He'd mourn Aunt Pat, and Mom, and Dad. And the nurse and guard who died the first year. And the lab tech from year three. And all those who died today. But not Jacob. Never Jacob—he chose this nightmare, so he could burn.

The mountain road terminated at a four-way intersection.

Adam hit the gas; the Diablo sped through the stop, adrenaline coursing through his body like a sweet drug. Talia squealed, bracing herself on the dashboard. Cars honked at him, and he didn't blame them. The Diablo was a gorgeous piece of craftsmanship.

Adam veered around the Circle K, avoiding Middleton, and hit the highway, a straight two-lane ribbon of asphalt begging for a mad rocket engine and a man crazy (or desperate) enough to use it.

He opened the car up, and the engine sang a sustained high and beautiful note. An aria to speed. Bravo.

The Diablo hit one hundred. One thirty. Mountains rose on either side of the freeway, grasses bordering the concrete, wild with specks of yellow, blurring in his peripheral vision.

The open road stretched before him, and aside from weaving around the much slower occasional cars on the near-empty highway, Adam could think. If Talia hadn't opened her mouth to scream, all this would be over. The military intervention would have shut Segue down and carted him and his staff off to who knows where for safekeeping, or wraith food.

Unbelievable.

"Talia," he said, gripping the wheel to hold on to his anger. "I need your mind. Help me make sense of all this."

"Okay," she said, tired. Wary.

"Lady Amunsdale talked about the Empty Skin, Jacob, and the fireflies within him, which have to be the"—Adam choked, thinking of his parents—"souls of the people he's fed on."

Talia gave a tight nod.

"And we know that without your assistance, Shadowman, Death, cannot reach the wraiths. Your scream somehow frees him, calls him into the world so that he can do his thing. Kill those motherfuckers."

"Yes." She looked out the window so he couldn't see her expression. She was definitely not okay where her father was concerned.

Adam continued, "Something happened, an as-yet-unknown event, resulting in the imprisonment of Death. We've seen as much depicted in all that art you discovered. And something gave Jacob that chance to live forever."

Talia supplied the name in a low voice. "The demon. The Death Collector."

Adam glanced at her, trying to pull her gaze to him. "You know we have to go after him, right?"

No answer.

"You know there will be no end until the demon is dealt with."

Silence.

He got to the point. "Eventually, you'll have to call your father again."

She leaned her head back on the seat, her eyes closed. Shutting all of this out. Shutting him out.

He wanted her immediate assurance, but something held him back from demanding it. If he pushed her, he was certain that she'd answer in the affirmative. Do what needed to be done. But something between them would be broken. A trust, a connection, an opportunity for something good in his life. He had so few, he couldn't risk losing this one. Not this one. Not even for the war.

On the outskirts of Dickerson, signs for an outlet mall announced a mind-numbing variety of shops: Mikasa, Osh Kosh, Gap, Motherhood, Saks, and more. Fifteen miles! Ten! Five!

In other circumstances, the prospect of entering an outlet mall would've been excruciating. Not today. Adam peered at the grouping of generic buildings. White and crisp, they huddled together for maximum female shopping convenience.

He took the exit and left tire rubber on the road as he peeled into the parking lot. He bypassed the wide, flat lot and rounded the back where a semi's trailer butted up against a loading dock. He tucked the Diablo at the truck's side in a square of shadow made by the late-afternoon sun angling behind the trailer's bulk.

The world went dizzyingly still as he brought the car to a stop.

"Come on, come on," Adam said, getting out of the car and dragging his pack with him. Startled, Talia did as she was bid on her side.

Standing, he pressed his lips to the Diablo's door. When this war was over, he'd be getting himself another. Damn pity to leave the beauty here, but a much better fate than that of the California.

"Where are we going?" Talia slammed her door.

Adam leaped onto the concrete loading bay and pulled her up beside him. "We need to get to New York, but the Diablo is too conspicuous. We'll catch a ride out of here and move north."

Probably have to hot-wire a car. Damn—it'd been years since he'd tried that. Where was Custo when he needed him?

Adam tried the red metal door on the right side of the loading dock. A cigarette still smoldered on the pavement at its stoop. Obligingly, the door was unlocked. Inside, brown boxes with black letters piled three or more high crowded a storage area. Beyond that, dull beige French doors, probably leading to the floor.

Talia's weight jerked his arm. *Oh, no.* He looked back, blood rising to fight.

"Bathroom," she said, eyes pleading.

He glanced around, exhaling his anxiety. He'd totally missed the open door and shiny toilet. A sign to the right read EMPLOYEES ONLY.

"Make it quick," he said. They didn't have time for this.

Hugely sighing, Talia ran inside and shut the door.

He scrubbed a hand through his hair. If they got caught and were killed because she needed to pee . . . He spotted a row of hooks, purses dangling, on the other side of the boxes. Possibility lit in his mind.

He strode over and rummaged inside the first bag for keys. Found them. With any luck, the woman who owned the vehicle would be working until the store closed at— he craned his head to peer at the posted chart of assigned shifts—nine o'clock. No need to put his rusty hot-wiring skills to the test.

"Adam?" Talia's voice called out softly.

"Here." He stepped back around the boxes to find her outside the door. He caught Talia's elbow and gestured to the French doors. "We go straight through and out the front."

They entered in the shoe department and dashed through a maze of clothing racks and accessories. The store—Saks, according to the name printed in blocky red at one end of the large room—was large, and at least a dozen women perused the clothing. Adam pushed out the front door, crossed the street, and headed into the row of minivans, SUVs, and economy cars.

He pressed the button on the key. A silver Malibu answered with the thick snick of a lock releasing. Not a Diablo by any means, but transportation nonetheless.

Adam motioned to Talia to get in, and soon they were on the road again. He set the cruise control to seventy-two mph. When a convoy of police screamed up his ass on the road behind him, he had Talia duck her conspicuous head and pulled over to the gravelly shoulder. The police tore by, but Adam veered off at the next exit anyway. Local roads and byways, then, for as far as they could take them.

He looked over at Talia. She had her head propped in her

hand, elbow on the lip of the passenger window. "Why don't you try to get some sleep?"

"Huh," she laughed, exhausted. "I don't think I'll ever sleep again."

"Why don't you give it a try? Sit back, close your eyes, and relax. We've got a long way to go."

She lifted an argumentative brow, but hunkered down, crossing her arms over her chest.

When next he looked over, her jaw was slightly slack, lips parted, chin tilted to catch the sun on her face. Talia. Sleeping Beauty. Too bad this wasn't a fairy tale.

A blaring *honk!* shattered Talia's sleep. She clutched the seat and struggled upright, blinking at the wild contrasts of dark city and bright lights.

"Welcome back," Adam said. His beard was just beginning to show.

"Where are we?" she croaked.

"New York. You've been out cold for going on seven hours." Adam sounded amused; she felt like she'd been hit by a bus.

"What time is it?" She stretched to get the blood flowing and arched her back to ease the tightness at the base of her spine.

"About midnight." His gaze flicked down to her body, then rested on her face. "You look better. You needed the sleep. Good timing—we're about to ditch the car; then we'll go to the loft."

"The loft?"

"A hidey-hole that Custo and I share, but it's not traceable to either of us. Here we go—" He turned abruptly, the car dipping into a city parking garage.

Adam stopped the car and got out. Talia followed suit, stretching more fully when she stood.

"We need daily," Adam said to an approaching attendant.

"That'll be thirty-five per day." The young guy looked bored out of his mind.

"Yeah, okay." Adam took a purple ticket and gave him the keys.

Even past midnight, the city hummed and snapped with life. An urban rhythm bellowed from an unknown source. Cars *shhhed* in passing, brakes whined. A voice rose in conversation and then dribbled away into the sound soup. Talia inhaled deeply and caught the soft scent of night, mingling with the smells of old concrete, exhaust, and waste. Strangely, the combination was not unpleasant. She craned her head to see the tops of looming buildings. So much life packed so tightly together.

"I've never been here before," she said to Adam when she noted his amusement.

"Nowhere else like it. This way," he said, "we've got to get inside."

Right. Monsters at any moment could jump out, teeth bared, with a big, bad *boo!* and eat her up. Inside was much better.

She followed Adam as he cut diagonally across the street. Three blocks down, he stopped at a doorway. She rolled her eyes when she noticed the slim keypad at eye level. Typical Adam. They took an industrial elevator to the top floor, which opened into a wide space.

He strode inside, saying, "It's safe here. Neither of my codes would have worked if anyone had entered the building in my absence."

"Uh-huh. You own the whole building?" Of course he did.

Huge, vibrant abstract paintings dominated the walls, reaching up two stories, twisting in sinuous color. Reds, oranges, burgundy, brick, all layered in oils for dimension and drama. The furniture complemented the art with clean lines and deep, solid tones, just off black. The air was slightly stale.

To one side was a sitting area with chairs, coffee table, and sofa, arranged to catch the startling and awesome view of the city at night. The windows extended from floor to ceiling, but the scarred wood floors reminded her particularly of Adam: solid, beautiful, and worn.

Talia gazed back at the windows. "Can anyone see inside?"

"The glass goes one way. Make yourself at home; kitchen pantry should have food. I've got to check in with Custo, make sure everyone else got out okay."

She turned in the direction he gestured. She stood next to an open kitchen of stark, brushed steel, but her gaze was drawn, again, out the window.

Not hungry, no. Not while that view swallowed her. Pinprick lights blinked across a speared landscape. Raw and masculine, the city pulsed with seductive power, a power that she imagined could easily be unkind, even cruel, to strangers.

She shifted her gaze to Adam's reflection in front of her, superimposed on the city vista. He was bent over a desk, jotting something down while speaking on the phone, his voice a gruff rumble. His shirt took its shape from the lines of his muscled back. When he stood, the hard plane of his chest and broad bunch of his shoulders had heat washing over her, her pulse quickening, a spark firing in her belly.

Her gaze met his in the glass. His expression was sober and serious, eyes hot and piercing. She'd run from him twice, rejecting the turmoil under his controlled surface. Shuttering herself against the burn of his intensity. That was just dumb and weak. And she was sick of running.

They were at the brink of destruction, a precipice at the edge of the abyss; there was no going back. No time left to grasp at life. She wanted him.

He continued his call, giving short, clipped instructions,

but still his gaze was fixed on her. Holding her in place. She couldn't have broken the connection if she tried. Adam was the city, dangerous with power and his own brand of menace.

He hung up and slowly came to stand behind her. He didn't touch her, but the warmth of his breath stirred the hair at her nape. His nearness had her responding to phantom touches, her body aching to arch against him, to tilt her head and give him access to her neck. She could almost feel the scorch of his mouth, just there, again.

"Is everyone okay?" she asked instead. Her voice was too thin.

"So far so good," Adam answered, distracted as his gaze slid down the reflection of her body in the window. "Custo is getting the last of them safely settled. Then he'll join us here."

"So that's good. Everything's good," she said carefully. Her nerves buzzed, willing him to touch. To take.

"Yeah." He brought his eyes back to hers.

Adam's jaw tightened, twitched, and he stepped back. Then he stepped back again.

Talia dropped her gaze to the floor, her face heating in embarrassment.

He cleared his throat. "Have you made up your mind, Talia?"

Her brain fumbled. "What do you mean?" Was he actually asking permission to touch her this time? That would be a first.

"This war, Talia, have you thought about what it entails? Can you handle it? I need you to commit to it. You're the only weapon that we have."

A weapon. The blood in her veins was hot before, but now it scalded. "You mean that you're going to aim me at the wraiths and say, 'Scream.' Yes, I kinda got that part."

"Not just the wraiths, the demon Death Collector, with SPCI on his side."

"I said I got it." Talia's words were all edge as she turned to him. One all-consuming need had ruled Adam's life for the last six years. To kill his brother. Adam wouldn't be satisfied until Jacob was in pieces, his stinking husk rotting on the ground.

"Fine," Adam growled. "I needed to make sure you knew what you were in for. What's at stake. Why we can't do anything to screw this up."

"Your priority is the war," Talia repeated. Her needs were secondary.

"*Our* priority," he said.

"You've been more than clear. And I am not an idiot. I'm capable of comprehending the implications of our situation." The situation was simple. She was the daughter of Death, destined to live alone, die in a war she didn't understand, and never to experience life as normal people knew it.

"I never said you were an idiot," he shot back.

"Do you see any wraiths here?" Talia gestured wildly around the loft. "You said the loft is secure. Is it?" She was never to fall in love, buy a house, and start a family of her own.

His eyes narrowed. "Yes."

"And your war business is on hold for the moment?" Never to share her deepest secrets or desires.

His face darkened at her sarcasm. "For the moment."

"No other life-and-death situations to tend to?" Never to know passion and be fulfilled.

"Not at present." He clipped his words with visible anger.

"Fine." Talia stalked across the room, closing the distance between them. It was past time she took what *she* wanted.

His reach was longer. He crushed her against his body as her arms circled his neck. She slid one hand up to grip his hair by the roots. His breath was warm on her face before he possessed her lips, his beard a gorgeous rough scrub against her skin.

Raw desire clouded her senses, his mixing with hers in an ominous collision that could only result in a violent storm. Whatever else he felt, or darkness he harbored, she didn't care.

His mouth finally dropped to her neck. His chin scraped there, too, and his teeth nipped at her skin down to her collarbones, coaxing her nerves to spark with hot, dangerous pops.

His hands were everywhere. One bound her to him at her waist. The other roamed over her ass, pressing into the junction of her legs, and lifted her weight with his hand *there*. His touch burned, a hungry fire licking up her core, melting her. He must have felt the heat of her arousal, because he growled again. And he wanted her just as badly—the proof of it pressed into her belly.

Talia dropped her hand to the rounded, hard muscle of his arm, reveling in the ease with which he assumed her weight. He backed them to the window and pressed her against its smooth, cold surface. Her hand slapped at the cold glass at her sides, desperate for a grip, but found none. She had only Adam to keep her from falling as they hovered at the edge of night.

"Last chance to run," he murmured in her ear. He set her on her feet, but pinned her body against the glass, his weight a delicious pressure that radiated pleasure. She couldn't get away if she wanted to.

And she didn't want to. She needed to feel this. She wanted one mystery of life revealed at the brink of death. Wanted him to change her, burn her, sear all thought from her mind with pain and pleasure. *Wanted*.

She dropped her head to his chest. He smelled spicy, dark, but good. Her fingers fluttered under his shirt where his skin was just slightly damp to the touch, each rise in his six-pack well-defined. Touching him had her nerves crying to feel more, quivering in anticipation.

The shadows in the deepest corners of the room stirred, whipped by the exquisite, demanding sensations coursing through her. She couldn't help it, and hoped he wouldn't notice. She couldn't stop now.

Her fingertips explored his heated skin, working his shirt up until she felt the separation of his pecs. He groaned, voice rumbling against her, and released her long enough to yank the T-shirt over his head, then pulled hers off in an extension of the same movement. He pushed her bra over her breasts so that it banded high across her chest, her nipples peaked. Then he pulled her body to him again.

The ecstatic synergy of skin on skin went through Talia like a bolt of lightning, a branding shock that stripped her control and stole the breath from her lungs.

She sensed his hunger grow fiercer, sharper, more determined. One goal ruled his actions. And she shared it. *Yes. Now. Everything.*

The darkness of the city throbbed behind her, roiling in a threatening storm of shadow. She searched for restraint—*please!*—but Adam eased her pants off her hips, fragmenting her ability to hold the seethe at bay. Her heart pounded, lungs labored, as Adam dropped his own pants and boxers and kicked them behind him. He stripped off her underwear, revealing her entirely, and lifted her weight again, pressing her into the glass.

She spread her arms wide on the clear, cold surface to block the imminent, encroaching darkness, to hold it back, shaking with effort.

"For crissakes, Talia," Adam rumbled at her neck. "Let it come. I'm not afraid of the dark."

He found her breast with his hot palm, a thumb flicking

over her nipple, and then he pushed. Her weight and his thrust shred her innocence and the last of her control.

The black storm of the city flooded the room. Its undeniable pulse of power and vitality fired her nerves. The acuity of her senses redoubled, but she squeezed her eyes shut. She didn't want to see with her death-bred eyes, she only wanted to feel the brilliant, molten heat of Adam inside her. He worked his hips in a single deep stroke and she split with pleasure. Her body contracted in exquisite near-pain and she wrapped herself around him, a shock wave rippling out from her core.

"Talia," he breathed. He shifted his hips back slightly, and then forcefully reseated himself inside her.

Talia's breath caught and she tightened against his assault. He drove into her again, touched her deep enough to stir the shadows into a frenzy around their joined bodies. She clutched him as he made every last dormant nerve in her body wake, aware and reaching for fulfillment. And then he delivered with a primitive growl, stretching her to the limit and shocking her again with intense ecstasy that rippled out from him and through her in an explosion of fierce bliss.

Adam panted against her, his head resting on the glass above her shoulder. His emotions were shredded, a near blackout of the worries that followed him. Now a strange peace dominated.

Her own storm mellowed into eddies of shadow.

Talia cracked her eyes to see him. To see how handsome he looked with his inner demons silenced. Her dark vision pierced the surface of his skin and bone, the mortal layers of his body. She found that she embraced a column of light and condensed will, undeniable and beautiful beyond imagination. She regarded the pale gleam of her arms wrapped around his shoulders.

Different. She looked different from Adam.

She'd always known that she was unlike anyone else, but she had never considered that she was actually made of different stuff.

Talia went as cold as her shadows.

How could she be so connected and yet alone at the same time?

Adam chuckled, planting a hand on the glass and pushing his bulk up to gaze at her face. "If we live through tomorrow, I'll make sure next time is better. You're so damn sexy, I just couldn't think. I should have been slower, more careful. Did I hurt you?"

A sob gathered in her throat, but she shook her head. *No.*

He slid out and lifted her to cradle in his arms. She huddled against him, hiding from the knowledge that they could never really be together. She was too different, too alien, too strange to ever really belong to him.

He brought her through a doorway and into a masculine bathroom of sleek grays and set her on her feet. He reached into a recessed room of smoky green, set with multiple jets, and turned on the nozzle. The space was large enough for two, and when steam began to fog the mirror he pulled her inside with him. He soaped up a washcloth and had just put the sudsy softness to her shoulder when an electronic warble reached them.

Adam paused, midstroke. The phone rang again. "Damn it, Talia, I have to get it. I'm sorry."

Yeah, she was sorry, too.

FOURTEEN

Y ES?" Adam said, phone gripped between ear and shoulder as he secured the towel around his waist. Shower drops ran down his back and chest in chilling rivulets—but he welcomed the cold against his overheated skin. Behind him, the shower softly hissed in the bathroom as Talia finished cleaning up. In a perfect world, he'd be in there with her, wet skin on wet skin, taking his time with her now that the bite of his desire had mellowed slightly.

"Staff from Segue is secure," Custo reported. "I have them all waiting for instructions in various inconspicuous locations. That is, all but Gillian, who opted to take her chances on her own."

"Excellent. Where are they and how long can they last?" Adam walked to the modern desk situated in an alcove off the kitchen, grabbed a pad of paper, and took the lid off a pen with his teeth. As Custo ran down a list of locations, Adam jotted notes. Seemed like everyone could hold out for a couple days before they'd have to move again. By that time, he hoped this would all be over, one way or another.

The shower cut off. Adam imagined Talia stepping out of the steam, eyes big and beautiful in her thin face. Her sweet, pale curves would be rosy and fragrant, hair slicked sinuously down the slope of her spine to reach the twin dimples at the base of her back where her hips flared and her ass deliciously rounded.

His gaze shot to the scatter of their clothes in front of the big windows.

"Just a sec," Adam said to Custo—he muted the phone, strode down the short hall, and knocked on the bathroom door. "Talia, the bedroom will have some clean things to wear. Take whatever you like. Take whatever works for you."

He waited in silence for her to answer. "Talia?"

"Okay, thanks." Her voice was moderate, but her tone was slightly off.

Ah, hell. Adam rested his forehead against the door. This was not the way it was supposed to go. He'd managed not to touch her for nearly a week, had only slipped that one time—okay, twice—to kiss her. And who could blame him? She was brilliant and gorgeous. Some things were just inevitable. He wanted her. He'd known that truth back in that stinking alley in Arizona, holding her overheated body. The way she fit the curve of his arm. How he could just rest his chin on the top of her head. Her soft voice whispering a warning. She made him aware of what living could be without this war on his head. Yeah, he was good and screwed.

"Adam?" Custo's voice brought Adam's attention back to the call.

Adam unmuted the phone. "I'm here."

He stalked back to the desk and his laptop. He scraped a chair back and sat at the desk, forcing his concentration into the monitor.

Work. Focus. Jacob.

The thought of Jacob snaked around Adam's neck and tightened in a noose, cutting off the flow of blood from his heart to his head. Jacob, who started this nightmare. Jacob, who killed Mom and Dad. Jacob, who very badly needed to die. After that, maybe Adam could get his own life, but not until then.

"So when I get there do we move our base of operations to the New York office?" At least Custo had his head on straight.

"No," Adam answered. He touched the monitor screen and selected the tab that revealed his remote connections to the Segue offices around the world. The hub at the New York office had timed out, as had the one in San Francisco and Atlanta.

"Our U.S. satellite offices' systems are down," Adam informed him. "What happened in West Virginia most likely happened here, too. If anyone survived, they are in hiding. Any intel stored at those facilities is compromised. No point in going there now and risking our own exposure."

How could he have forgotten, even for a moment, the people who labored on his behalf? He'd handpicked each staff member of the New York branch—the thought that they were dead or worse made him ache with frustration. Twenty-six employees, all dedicated to his cause, lost or worse. They depended on him to keep them safe. And what was he doing? Screwing their only hope of survival.

Idiotic. Especially when he was so close to the end.

All he needed was one well-placed, well-timed scream. Nothing short of witnessing the swift strike of Shadowman's curved blade cutting down an army of wraiths would ease the grip of anger on him.

"I thought The Collective was just after Talia. You think they decided to take out all of Segue?"

"Yes." Adam understood The Collective's strategy. To achieve their ends, destroying Segue was the smart thing to do—limiting Adam's resources, scattering his personnel, and confusing his strategy by changing The Collective's MO. As matters stood, the Segue staff, Adam and Talia included, had been reduced to underground renegades in a matter of hours.

But as long as Adam had that scream, he could win the war. Victory and vengeance were as easy as one breath of air.

"Why? Why risk that kind of exposure?"

"Talia is the only thing they want. She's the only one who can make a difference."

"I still don't understand. Why don't the wraiths just kill her and be done with it?"

"Good question." Why not just silence the voice that can call Death? There had to be a damn good reason or things would have played out differently in West Virginia. They wanted her for something.

A soft sound behind Adam had his head whipping around.

Talia padded into the room on bare feet. She wore an oversize black T-shirt, braless judging by the twin tips peaking the front, and baggy gray sweatpants she'd rolled up to her ankles. His socks covered her slender feet, which he found both adorable and intimate. She shoved her feet back into her shoes. Two months on the run had obviously taught her a thing or two about being ready at all times. Habits die hard.

She fished the flash drive Adam had given her back at Segue out of her pants pocket and collected the discarded clothes on the floor. He caught her glancing at him from beneath the cover of her wet hair, but she shifted her gaze away again when she met his eyes, pretending to ignore his conversation with Custo. The woman wouldn't win any Oscars.

"When you get here we will assess our available resources and locate the demon's base of operations." Then move in fast and strike.

Talia passed him again and found the stacked laundry/

dryer unit behind a folding closet door in the hall to run a load. She returned to the room and rummaged in his backpack. After finding a book—where had that come from?—she set herself up on the sofa to read.

"How do you plan to do that with the New York office out of commission?"

"I have other sources." Ghosts. Talia could call on the ghosts tied to New York and have them locate the demon for him. Witnesses everywhere, and they had to answer to her. Damn, it was almost too easy.

"I know all your sources," Custo argued.

"Not these ones. Trust me. How long will it be 'til you get here?" Adam checked his watch. 2:23 A.M.

"Hour and a half, two hours, maybe."

"I'll be ready." Adam ended the call and glanced at Talia.

No need to interrupt her reading just yet. She seemed engrossed, and well, he had no idea what to say to her anyway. *We made a mistake* warred with *We have just enough time for another good go.* Experience told him both approaches were very wrong.

Adam discarded both, electing instead to keep his mouth shut like a coward for the time being. He went to the bedroom, dressed, and then returned to the desk. He worked on his simulation, adding the unexpected support of SPCI to The Collective's already worrisome resources. The projections the program generated made him sweat. In an abundance of numbers divided by geographic and industry-specific percentages, the computer was certain there was no hope.

He looked at Talia and knew different.

Still, he didn't like putting a woman in harm's way if he could help it. He'd have to be very certain of Talia's safety.

She sat on the sofa facing the sprawl of the darkened city beyond the window, feet tucked under her, nose in a book. Her hair had partly dried in the time he'd been working, slowly brightening and coiling into loose curls over her shoulders. She'd scarcely lifted her nose since sitting down.

Book must be damn fascinating reading, because she hadn't so much as glanced his way.

Better to do damage control now, before Custo arrived.

Adam stood and, twisting, cracked the strain out of his back and neck. As gritty as his eyes were, his body hummed as he took a seat opposite Talia.

"What're you reading?" he asked in lieu of *Are you okay?*

Talia snapped the book shut and let it rest on her thighs. Lucky book.

"Jim gave it to me right before he asked me to call Lady Amunsdale. It's a sort of encyclopedia of mythical figures, including an entry on banshees."

Adam leaned forward in his chair. He caught the bright smell of shampoo and soap, still fresh on her skin. The sweet scent was probably thicker at her neck, just behind her ear, and darker still between her legs. He sat back again, scrubbing his scalp with his hands to get the flow of blood back up to where he needed it most. "What does it say?"

"Not surprisingly, the word *banshee* is Irish. The *ban* part means woman. And the *shee* part refers to fairy mounds, or the Otherworld."

Talia's tone conveyed an academic distance from the information she related, as if learning about her birthright were an intellectual exercise and not the personal discovery she'd been searching for all her life. Her act didn't fool him. Adam knew that birthrights were a bitch—either you shouldered the burden until you passed it along to someone else, most often your children, or you were crushed beneath the weight of it. If Adam's burden sat heavy, hers must be near intolerable about now.

She continued in her dry tone. "A banshee's cry precedes death. Heralds death, in fact, which is in keeping with how it worked for me and Shadowman. One point of difference, however, is that banshees are associated with royal Irish families, which I am not." She pressed her lips together, closed the cover, and tossed the book aside.

"Your mother was Irish. Perhaps her people can be traced back to royalty. Perhaps you're a fairy princess." Of course she was. He'd known it all along.

"Can I abdicate?" she laughed harshly, eyes finally watering. She blinked rapidly to clear them.

"Not just yet," Adam answered. "I need you."

Talia went so still that he reviewed his last words in his mind. *I need you.* What kind of a thing to say was that? It begged a follow-up question—needed her for what? Weapon or lover?

He cleared his voice, dodged the deeper question, and went for the obvious. "I think that becoming a wraith severs a person's connection to Death. Your scream reinstitutes it."

Talia shook her head. "I'm sure I screamed as a kid. Temper tantrums, roller-coaster rides, scary movies. Shadowman didn't appear then."

"I don't think you were in the presence of a wraith, of death. I'll bet you were surrounded by life."

Her chin quivered. "I screamed when I got in that car wreck with Aunt Maggie. I saw Shadowman, my father, then. I have spent a long time wondering why I lived while everyone I've loved died."

The reason seemed obvious, but Adam voiced it. "You had something important to do with your life. It wasn't your time."

"So what now? You take me to Times Square and I let it rip?" She laughed bitterly.

Reading the naked pain in her eyes, Adam filled with regret—not for the sex, not anymore—but for everything else. Everything that she'd endured, and yet she remained bright, intelligent, and strong. The woman was remark-able. She'd handled her burdens far better than he had handled his.

There was no way to spin what had happened between them. He owed her the truth.

She must have seen the shift in his eyes because she reached for her book again, opening it to a random page and tensing her forehead in deep concentration. "There are actually some very interesting folktales recorded here . . ."

"Talia." When she didn't lift her head, Adam grabbed the book and dropped it on the floor. Her hands, now empty and open, trembled. He filled them with his own and gripped.

"Talia, listen to me. In another world, another time, we could have been something to each other. But it's impossible now—I know you understand that. I should've never allowed it to go as far as it has. I'm so sorry . . ."

Her head snapped up, eyes flashing. "I'm not. I'm the child of Death, and this war is probably going to kill us both. I'm not sorry for one minute of it that I choose to live. I know what I am now, and I've got a general idea of what I am supposed to do. I could've, *should've*, been living all along."

He stroked his thumbs across her palms—she was silky soft, warm. It would be so easy to run his hands up her smooth arm, to gather her onto his lap and follow the softness of her skin to warmer places on her body. To use sex to forget everything. If Custo weren't going to be here any minute, he just might have.

He forced himself to cease stroking her. "We've got a tough road ahead of us, and I don't want to confuse the situation."

She pulled her hands free. "Don't patronize me. I'm not confused. It's not so very difficult what I have to do."

Talia stood and walked to the windows overlooking the sharp lights of the city.

"I didn't mean it that way." He followed her, gaze meeting hers in the night-darkened glass. And just like that they were back to where they started an hour before. His body remembered and stirred against his will.

"It's fine. I'm fine. I'll do what needs to be done. I've been searching my whole life for a reason I'm so different. Now I have it. Ending the wraith war is the reason I was born." In the reflection, her face was composed. Too composed. Stony.

Adam dropped his gaze to the floor. If he continued to look at her, he was going to do something that messed with their heads even more.

But she was right. She had something to do. Jacob was still out there. He and his maker had to die.

Adam raised his head. "Custo's going to be here soon. I've got to get some things together, inventory the supplies we have here."

Talia watched Adam retreat into a back room, presumably to check supplies, but more likely to get away from her. The distance between them was both a relief and a disappointment. If the conversation had gone another way, and it could have if she'd let it, there would be no distance between them right now at all. None whatsoever. Her core contracted at his absence, fisting with an ache in her abdomen that echoed in her heart.

This could have all been different.

Another world, another time, he'd said. That was just the problem. Even if they managed to live through the next twenty-four hours, they were literally from different worlds. The hard truth was that death and life were incongruous. Those who attempted to meld the two either ended up wraiths—everlasting life, or ghosts—everlasting death. She was the daughter of Death. Adam was bursting with life. Incongruous. Incompatible.

Maybe Aunt Maggie had fed her one too many fairy stories as a kid. Tales of magic and kisses and wishes. Of happily-ever-afters and obstacles surmounted by love. Aunt Maggie had been a die-hard romantic, but maybe the emphasis had been because she knew something about how Talia was conceived. What must her mother have told Aunt Maggs about her father? Talia had asked, many times, but had never received a straight answer. In the light of her newfound knowledge, Aunt Maggie's fairy tales did not seem so misplaced.

The book Jim had given her had suggested something else, something that she couldn't yet voice to Adam. The faery were a breed apart—they were old, diminished spirits of the earth, shut out from heaven, and consigned for eternity to the Otherworld except for occasional trespasses into mortality. Her instincts told her that there would be no world but this one that Adam and she could share, and no time but *now* in which to share it.

At least she could give him her scream and with it, she hoped, peace.

The washer buzzed the end of its cycle and Talia tore her eyes away from the city to throw the clothes into the dryer.

She turned toward the corridor, spied the book on the sofa, and thought to tuck it away in case Adam decided to investigate further. The last thing she needed now was—

A crash behind her had her bringing her arms up to protect her head.

After her initial cringe, she whirled back toward the window to find a hole the size of an apple radiating white cracks up the glass. Beyond the hole, the fresh black of New York City night. An odd metallic burning smell hit her senses. Before she could identify the source, another impact sent something whizzing by her side to lodge in the sofa. Shards scattered the floor.

Her heart beat wildly, breath coming in shuddering draws

as she turned to run down to the hallway. Smoke rose in her path, smelling sharply chemical and rankly . . . *wrong*. Wrong to a degree that superseded the normal world. She knew it with every freakish cell in her body.

She attempted to breathe through clenched teeth. The stench made her mouth taste sour. Her eyes teared profusely. She swiped at them with her palms and wrists.

A third crash brought her to her knees, huddling in the middle of a rising cloud. Her body screamed for air. She chanced a breath and choked on the fire that seared her nose and charred her lungs.

She covered her mouth and nose with the hem of her T-shirt and tried a breath. Her throat burned.

"Talia!" Adam's voice was a thick roar.

"Here!" The word was a rasp. Stars floated in the periphery of her vision. *More air!* her body cried. Reflex took over and she drew in a shallow gasp. Pain.

An arm came around her, dragged her up. Adam. She knew the hard lines of his body, the curve of his arm, the warmth his body exuded. Together they moved through space, though in which direction, she had no idea until Adam kicked open a door and blinded her with light.

A storage room. Boxes open. Guns. His supposed inventory work.

She tried a little air in a series of thin pants to move oxygen into her blood and to clear her vision. Her throat and lungs felt raw.

Adam slammed the door shut and powered through the room to the other end. He tapped a keypad. The concealed door slid open to reveal a tight room, smaller than a closet, just big enough for two.

"Can you stand?" Adam's voice was low, gruff, angry, a perfect match to the feelings she sensed in him.

She nodded, though she really didn't know the answer.

Her breathing became long, broken wheezes that left her light-headed. She put a hand to her chest, but it neither helped her move air nor stopped the pain.

He took her hand and pulled her in, hitting the second of two unmarked buttons. The urgency that poured through his touch spurred hers. Get away. Get away fast.

Talia's stomach hit her throat at the sudden drop. An elevator. A bullet to the bottom.

"Are you okay?" Adam gripped her chin and turned her head to face to his. His expression was controlled, but his emotions a mix of concern and horror. What she felt from him kept her on her feet; she wouldn't add to his worry if she could help it. With his free hand he lifted each of her lids in turn to look at her eyeballs, and then moved a raised finger in an arc before her eyes to track the response of her eyes.

"Yes." Her answer exhaled in a harsh burr, several octaves below her normal tone. And it hurt.

"Damn it." Adam's face was flushed, though white around the mouth with tension. "You look like hell. Had to be some kind of chemical weapon in aerosol form. Poison gas, maybe."

And mixed with something worse. Otherworldly worse. But Talia didn't voice it.

". . . okay." She meant to say *I'm okay*, but the first word was lost on uncooperative vocal cords. It was a lie, and Adam had to know it was a lie. What she meant was that she would keep going until she fell over. He'd find her medical attention. Immediate medical attention, preferably.

The elevator came to an abrupt stop and challenged the lock she had on her weak knees. Adam pushed her behind him, protecting her body with his, then drawing his gun, touched a button. The door slid open.

The darkness beyond was mellowed by soft light, its source unknown. It took a couple of her weak breaths for a wet, fetid stench to hit her. She pressed her face into Adam's shoulder.

They could be in only one place. The sewer. A mangy rat darted past the elevator door.

"We've got to move. Got to find somewhere safe." Adam sounded like he was talking to himself. He stepped out into a tunnel, looking each way as if weighing his options, debating between the two stretches of stinking tunnel.

It was strange to see Adam at a loss. Adam, who had a contingency for everything. Adam and his redundant securities. Not that she blamed him—no one could think of every unforeseen need. He'd done so much already by taking the whole of the wraith war onto his shoulders.

"Ah, hell," he said, dragging her to the left. "The loft should have been safe. Should have been secure. It's not affiliated with Segue, but they found us anyway. How'd they find us?"

Talia knew he wasn't really asking her. Her job was to keep breathing, and she poured her concentration into that effort. It was the only way to help him.

"If they find us again, Talia, you run and hide. Got that? You run and hide. You do your dark thing and get to safety. I'll try to hold them off as long as possible."

He took some of her weight by circling his left arm under her shoulders. The dank length of darkness was slick with wet—the kind of dampness that never dried. It clung to the walls and soaked the debris at their feet made of disintegrating newspaper and unrecognizable trash. Only the bright white plastic of a fast-food cup seemed impervious to the sludge.

He stopped at a rusted metal ladder bolted to the concrete wall, manhole disk above, and peered at it intently.

"What about—" Talia began in a croak. She meant *What about Custo?* who was to meet them at the loft. Had he turned traitor like Spencer and led to the attack or was he walking unsuspecting into the hands of their attackers?

Adam turned quickly to her. "Shhh. Don't talk. You need to rest your voice. You need to heal. You won't be safe until you heal. No one will be safe until you heal."

In a rush of horror Talia understood. Her scream, their great defense against the wraiths, had been silenced.

Fifteen

Oh, shit. Which way? Indecision crushed Adam's shoulders. It bowed his head with its incredible, immediate weight. He gripped the cold, wet metal of the ladder in frustration. Each stinking breath in this rotting tunnel cost them time they did not have.

He glanced at Talia—her face was gray, chest heaving as air rattled in her lungs. She'd needed him, and he fucked up. Again. Every time he fucked up, people died.

Case in point: The Collective had not challenged Segue and he'd been lured into a false sense of safety. He may have gotten his people out of the West Virginia research facility, but the satellite offices were unresponsive, his people most likely dead. His fault. And he'd stupidly thought the New York loft was secure, yet it was attacked, and Talia, the only weapon they had against the wraith war, was hurt. His fault.

Now it all came down to an either-or decision. Up to the surface or stay in the tunnel. So simple.

But he had no idea.

Talia needed medical attention, which could only be found on the surface, but then again, *no* medical attention was better than capture and final defeat.

Ah, hell—what should he do?

"Pssst."

Adam spun, swiftly drawing and pointing his gun in the direction of the sound.

He'd taken too long. They'd been found.

His heart pounded as he anticipated an attack. Soldiers most likely—wraiths would have overpowered him by now. He strained his eyes and aimed down the barrel. Murky darkness swallowed the tunnel. He couldn't see shit.

Talia's hand on his arm startled him. He darted a glance at her and she shook her head. *No. Don't shoot.*

He peered back into the darkness. Whatever was down there didn't alarm Talia, but he wasn't about to make another mistake. His grip on his gun tightened.

Talia squeezed his wrist, her hand warming with pressure. The shadows around him shifted, differentiated like overlapping thunderheads on a moonless night. The stench grew thicker, smells separating into distinct pools of foulness, each with its own fetid personality. Drops of water pinged clear notes in a strange wind chime of wetness.

And in the depths of the tunnel, a white face became visible.

A ghost.

No. A young girl, eyes outlined and dramatically shadowed in black. She had to be—what? Sixteen? Seventeen?

What the hell was she doing down here?

Adam almost started toward her—she might know a safe, sheltered way out of this hellhole. Somewhere they could hide.

But he pulled back. He wouldn't make another mistake and get that young girl killed. He couldn't possibly trade a hope of safety for a child's life. He drew the line there.

Up the ladder, then.

He turned his back on the girl and heaved himself up a rung. He'd have to dislodge the manhole before helping Talia up the ladder. The motion pulled her hand from his wrist. The blackness flattened. The smells stirred back together in a rank soup.

A soft splash had him looking down again as Talia moved beyond the ladder toward the girl.

"No. Talia!"

But she was already a couple yards away. Another step, and she disappeared into the darkness.

Damn it. "Talia!" His harsh whisper echoed.

No answer. He had no choice but to follow and hope that they didn't get that kid hurt or worse.

Three long strides and he found her. She wasn't that hard to track what with her wheezing and smothered coughs.

Closing the distance, Adam could finally see the young girl clearly for himself. Dressed in a witchy getup, she was gothed out with black hair shot through with streaks of scarlet. Her skin was pearl white and though smooth, somewhat older than he had first suspected. Midtwenties, maybe.

"You the faery?" The girl lifted a multipierced eyebrow.

Adam startled. *Faery? How the hell could she possibly know—?*

In his peripheral vision, he saw Talia nod the affirmative.

"'Course you are or you wouldn't be skulking around this shit hole. This way." The girl cocked her head, turned, and headed down the sewer tunnel.

Talia took his elbow and pulled him after her. When they'd caught up, Adam leaned forward, keeping his voice low, and said, "Who are you? Where are we going?"

The goth girl canted her head over her shoulder. "I'm Zoe, and I'm taking you to Abigail."

That made everything much clearer.

Adam tried again. "How did you know we'd be down here? And who's Abigail?"

The girl smiled wickedly back at him as she walked. "Abigail is my sister, and I knew you'd be down here because she told me where to find you."

Adam wanted to shake her. Her answers only begat more questions, and she was enjoying this. "How did Abigail know where find us?"

"She saw you." Zoe didn't even look as she drawled her answer.

Adam could come to only one conclusion: they'd been spotted. Where? "How?"

He hadn't realized he'd voiced his last question until the girl answered, "That one I don't know. You'll just have to ask her."

They trod the length of the sewer, breath and footsteps too loud, echoing off the walls and creating phantoms of sound and movement along the corridor. Adam felt Talia's weight grow heavy on his arm.

"How much farther? This woman needs medical attention."

"Abigail's got a doctor for you. She saw that, too."

Abigail better damn well have some answers.

When Talia stumbled, Adam caught her before she hit the sewer water. She groaned as he lifted her into his arms. He'd have liked to sling her over a shoulder so that he could have at least one arm free to aim and shoot, but he didn't trust the pressure on her diaphragm. Cursing, he shoved his gun in his belt and opted to cradle her, baby-style, though it was damn frustrating that her body protected him more than he could protect her.

The tunnel came to a crossroads of refuse, and Zoe took the left path toward a buzzing bass din accented by a high whine—somebody's idea of music.

She stopped at a metal ladder directly under the noise.

"This one," she said, though Adam had to read the words on her lips to understand her.

The girl climbed, and Adam wondered briefly if he would have to sling Talia over his shoulder after all, but Talia struggled against him and reached for the bars herself, scaling the ladder one rung ahead of him. When she neared the top, several arms reached down to lift her out of the hole as if they expected her.

Adam cleared the hole and found himself in a dark alleyway, damp concrete buildings jutting several stories high on either side of him. A group of people carried Talia into the back entrance of the nearest one. A wave of distorted electronica poured from the door.

He leaped out of the manhole and followed, fingers itching to draw his gun again, but cautious reason overruled the impulse.

Wait and see.

He entered into the back of what appeared to be a club, a heavy metal door thumping closed behind him. The smell of stale cigarette smoke clung to the doorway and pervaded the air of the interior. The walls were painted black, as was the concrete floor, and papered with layers of bright, cheap flyers, which lent the underriding gloom of the place a decidedly happy spin.

Likewise the music was bottomed by a murky bass beat and overlain with melodic guitar effects that would've been downright perky if the tone hadn't been subtly dissonant. A woman's voice crooned the melody with ethereal, if synthetic, perfection.

A group of decidedly counterculture people clustered around an open door to the left, some swathed in black, like Zoe, their club attire selected for mood and show, rather than dancing. One wore a variation of the goth getup, sexed up with a corset and fishnet stockings, while another paid homage to piercing, including a rather tribal stretching of his earlobes around metal rings in addition to the series of studs he wore across his eyebrows and in his lip.

Like the music, their expressions were contradictory, evoking a strange combination of nihilism and concern about Talia's condition.

Adam craned around the group, glimpsed Talia's telltale white-blonde hair in the noir hole of what must have been a dressing room, and pushed his way through the crowd.

A transparent oxygen mask was in place over Talia's mouth and nose, and a young woman in jeans and a T-shirt crouched at Talia's back with a stethoscope. How she hoped to hear anything in this squealing noise was beyond him. The doctor attached a white clip to Talia's finger; the clip connected to a digital reading, probably for pulse and blood oxygen levels.

Adam searched Talia's eyes for signs of distress, though her skin was pinking nicely. "Are you okay?"

Her eyes wrinkled at the outer edges in answer, an attempt at a smile, and she raised a thumbs-up.

The tension in Adam's neck and shoulders eased somewhat.

Adam addressed the doctor. "Is she going to be okay?" He hadn't meant his voice to sound so demanding, so stern. He knew a little gratitude was in order.

The woman's gaze shifted from Talia to Adam. "Give me a minute, yeah?"

Adam stepped back—patience was not one of his strong suits. "What about this Abigail? Where is she?"

"I'll take you," a voice piped up from behind him.

Adam turned. Zoe, again.

"I'm not leaving Talia. Bring Abigail here."

Zoe raised a thin eyebrow. "What—you think we're going to hurt her?"

"You might not, but the people who did this to her might be behind us." At the very least, they had to have discovered the concealed elevator by now and its route to the sewer. This building was not that far away from his loft.

Zoe waved away the concern. "Nah. Abigail would have seen it."

"Who is she? Has she got the sewer wired or something?"

Zoe snorted. "She's got the whole world wired. Come with me and meet her yourself."

Adam looked down at Talia. He couldn't just leave her here.

Talia lifted a hand and waved him away. When still he hesitated, she shoo-shooed him again. "Oh, go on." Her voice rasped into a cough.

"Please," the doctor added, her eyes rolling.

Damn it. Adam leaned down to Talia's ear. "Stay alert. Be ready to use the dark." And because she managed to retain a hint of sweetness in her hair after the foul crawl in the sewer, he dropped a kiss on her jawline.

Zoe led him down the hall to a staircase. The landing, vibrating slightly with the music below, lengthened with rooms off to each side. They took the second to the right and straight on until they reached a starry curtain, which Zoe pulled aside.

In a rocking chair sat a dried-up old crone of a woman in a tentlike, flowery housedress, presumably Abigail, though far too old to be Zoe's sister. Her eyeballs were covered with a dark, brackish film that did not clear when she blinked. Her hair was stringy gray. The room smelled sharp and stale, like illness.

Adam glanced around. Sickbed, sink, stacks of books— lusty romance novels from the look of their covers—and on the bed, an open package of store-bought chocolate chip cookies, which made his stomach rumble. But there were no surveillance systems in this room; the tech center had to be somewhere else in the building.

"You're cuter than I thought." Abigail's voice was clear, young, even, at odds with her appearance.

Which made Adam look a little closer. "Who are you? How did you know where to find us?"

"I'm Abigail. And I knew where to find you because I saw you there."

Now Adam could see the family resemblance; she spoke in cryptic taunts like her "sister." He had no patience for this. He needed to collect Talia and get to safety.

"Oh, take a cookie and sit down. You're safe enough here."

Adam hesitated, then perched on the corner of the foot of the bed. He forced his voice to controlled courtesy. "Thank you for your help and for the medical assistance you're providing my—" What was Talia to him anyway? Employee? Lover? "—friend. If you knew where to find me, you may have some idea of the circumstances that brought us there. So I would very much appreciate it if you or your sister would be more forthcoming with answers."

Abigail pressed her lips together in a grimace of disapproval. "Life's short; you should try and have a little more fun."

Adam chuckled with bitter irony. "Not possible at the moment."

"Then quit being so dense. I could see you in the tunnel because I have the Sight. My Eye has been drawn to you for a while now—" Her mouth quirked up to one side. "By the way, that was some very nice work earlier. Up against the window like that. Very nice." She fanned herself with her hand.

Adam frowned, his mood black, but she continued, "Don't begrudge me a little vicarious pleasure—I'm thirty-three years old, and what my Eye has shown me has turned me into an old woman."

Adam swallowed thickly. "Can you see the future?"

"I see many futures."

"Many?"

"As many futures as there are choices."

"Do I defeat the Death Collector in any of them?"

"No."

A wave of helplessness rolled over him. So all this was pointless. The Collective was going to win after all. He couldn't breathe. He braced his hands on his knees as a devastating roar filled his head.

Abigail clucked with her tongue. "Look at you. So arrogant. So self-important. You've gone and cast yourself as the hero. Do you really think this war is about you?"

Adam's head snapped up.

"Now I've finally got your attention. The demon does not die at your hands. I see only one ending for you, the same ending everyone in this world must face."

Death. The knowledge took a painful, disappointed moment for him to process, but deep down he'd always known that he would not survive this war. He thought of Talia, Death's daughter, and the pain mellowed. If she were anything like Death, the end of his life couldn't be all that bad. He warmed slightly inside at the memory of her soft darkness sweeping over him. Not that bad at all.

But what about the rest of the world? The wraith war? "Does anyone else defeat the demon?"

"Perhaps."

"Who?" But he already knew the answer.

Abigail's eyes wrinkled with her smile. "Clap if you believe in faeries."

Shadowman. "Then Talia's voice must heal so that she can call Death."

"Let me be clear," Abigail said. "My Sight does not permit me to see the fae. Not the one you call Shadowman—"

Adam's breath caught at the depth of Abigail's knowledge. Someone had had the answers to his riddles all along.

"—nor the woman downstairs. The lives of the fae are not their own, their destinies are bound, existence predetermined by the function they were born to fulfill, and so I cannot see the paths before them. My Sight can only see those of the mortal world. You and me and Zoe and the poor man whose body hosts the demon. I cannot see the demon himself."

Adam's heart stalled. He leaned forward, elbows on his knees. "What do you mean 'the poor man whose body hosts the demon'?"

"A demon has only as much power as a mortal gives him. This poor soul gave the demon his free will in exchange for . . ."

"Power," Adam finished.

Abigail's mouth made a disappointed moue. "No. Power is your weakness. You like to be in control, the one making decisions. The man who hosts the demon was tormented by fear. He was afraid to live, afraid to die, afraid of people. He wanted to live without that fear. To have peace."

Adam was disgusted. All this because of fear. Unbelievable.

Abigail lifted an eyebrow. "Do you know what it is to be afraid? Truly, deeply afraid?"

"Of course." *Everyone is afraid. But trade yourself to a demon because of it? No.*

She chuckled, mocking him.

"I've been afraid," he said again. "Have you seen my brother? I've stared down his gullet as he prepared to suck the life out of me. It was fucking terrifying." The memory alone had his heart accelerating, his stomach tightening. Yeah, he'd known fear.

Abigail seemed unimpressed. "There's worse."

Adam couldn't possibly conceive of worse and pressing the issue was irrelevant anyway. He returned to his original question: "Can I kill the host, and therefore the demon?"

"Like a happy, convenient loophole in the sticky problem of the demon's immortality?"

"Yes. Exactly," he said, though he didn't like the sarcastic tone she'd used to restate his question.

"You'd kill the man, but not the demon. Sooner or later— probably sooner—the demon would simply find another host."

"So we're back to the beginning: Talia must scream to call her father, and then Shadowman will finish this." Adam rose. If there were no new answers to be found here, he had to get Talia moving before anyone caught up. He rose.

Abigail shrugged her shoulders. "That's one way to do it," she mumbled. She hunkered down into her chair and didn't elaborate.

Adam wasn't biting. He'd had enough of her games. "Can you tell me where to find the demon?"

"You thinking of joining The Collective?"

Irritation tightened the muscles across Adam's scalp. He'd had just about enough of this. He bit back his desired response and said, "No. I need to know where to find him so that I can get Talia into position safely."

"I think you underestimate her."

"Can you tell me or not?"

She sighed a world of exhaustion. "I see water. I see the Styx."

"Are you being needlessly cryptic again?" Spouting about ancient Greek mythology when he needed a modern address.

"I'm being literal," she bit back. "The Styx is a ship, just an aptly named ship. Buy a ticket on the Styx and you buy a ticket to the underworld."

"Can you see anything else? Anything that will help me or Talia?"

"No, that's all—" Abigail broke off, her gaze shifting past Adam's shoulder.

He turned and found Talia, framed by the field of stars on the curtain dividing the room.

"Welcome," Abigail said behind him. "I've been waiting a long time for you."

Talia gazed at the old woman in the chair. Light touched strands of gray hair, turning them to silver. Her skin was crumpled, sagging flesh. And there was something . . . odd about her that went beyond the dark glaze that covered the woman's eyes.

Adam took Talia's shoulders and searched her face. "You're okay, then?"

"I'm—" Talia's already thin voice broke. She delicately cleared her voice so the burn in her chest wouldn't flare up. She tried again, keeping her words whisper soft, though the sound still came out stilting and rough. "I'm fine. Amalia, the doctor, says I was very lucky. I need to take it easy, rest, and after a while I will be back to normal."

Normal. Not likely. The Earth-made component of the gas might've been slowly wearing off, but the Otherworldly part slicked her throat and lungs like malevolent oil. Neither water nor hacking coughs cleared it.

"This just confirms my suspicions," Adam said. "If they wanted to kill you, they've had ample opportunity. They want you alive. The gas was meant to incapacitate us long enough for them to get to you. Did she say how long it would take for you to recover your voice?"

"I dunno—" Talia shrugged. The vibration of her vocal cords made her throat ache. Breathing through both her nose and her mouth seared. And that dark stuff coated, suffocated, and made her lungs scream for undiluted air. But she wasn't about to burden Adam with the last part. The man was burdened enough.

"You shouldn't speak." His hands tightened on her shoulders as his jaw flexed in frustration. He dropped his forehead to touch hers, to rest there, mind to mind. His concern filtered into her consciousness. "Okay. We need to find a safe place to wait out your recovery. Somewhere solitary and inconspicuous. In the meantime, we can plan."

Talia nodded shallowly, not wanting to jar their moment of intimacy. She really wanted to walk into the circle of his arms and curl against his chest, but his words from the loft, "another world, another time," kept her back. She knew that Adam cared about her, but his priorities were unchanged: war first. That truth burned more deeply than the chemical gases she'd inhaled, though he was right. She was born to end this war.

"You can stay here for a while," Abigail said. "It's safe. I don't see a future where The Collective searches the building." ·

Huh? Talia replayed the old woman's words in her mind. It made no sense.

"What—" *does she mean?* Talia meant to ask, glancing up at Adam as her throat flared with pain and eroded her words.

Adam broke contact and turned. "This is Abigail, and she can see the future. Or lots of futures, depending on what people decide to do."

"Can she—" *see mine?* Talia brought her hand to her chest.

Adam shook his head. *No.* "She can't see faery futures."

But . . . Talia made a cutting motion with her hand down the front of her body, symbolically halving herself.

"I know," Adam answered. "You're half human. Abigail says she still can't see your future. Apparently, your father's blood runs a little thicker than your mother's."

Can she see yours? Talia gestured to Adam.

"Bits and pieces," he answered, looking away.

Which "bits and pieces"? Talia wanted to shake him.

Talia's gaze flew to Abigail, who merely raised an amused brow.

If the woman could see Adam's future, she had to be able to glimpse something of Talia's as well. Adam had to be there when she screamed, when Shadowman ended the war. And after? What happened after? Did Adam's future include her?

"You can stay here for the time being. We've prepared a room for you down the hallway. You'll get used to the noise from downstairs. When you've rested and"—Abigail twitched her nose—"cleaned up, it would be nice of you to come downstairs and make an appearance."

"I don't think it would be a good idea to show up in a public place," he said. "I don't want to tempt fate by allowing a club full of people to see us."

Talia agreed with him.

"But they're all here for you." Abigail looked directly at Talia as she spoke. The force of her statement had Talia stepping back.

"What—" *do you mean?* Apprehension escalated wildly in Talia's body, tension flexing the small and large muscles of her aching diaphragm.

"This is no club," Abigail explained. "This is a celebration. A Death Fete. We gather to celebrate you, Banshee, and your father, Shadowman. We have long recognized that the demon who calls himself the Death Collector is chaos in the making, a disease that threatens the world. The death-less creatures that have roamed New York's streets finally have the attention of a faery who can do something about them. We celebrate because an end is in sight. We've waited many years for this day."

Talia brought her hands to her heating cheeks. "I— I—" Everyone was waiting for her? Face a roomful of people who knew what she was? Who her father was?

Adam's arm circled Talia's waist as he spoke. "If you know so much, *see* so much, why didn't you seek out me or Talia before?" His voice was even, but Talia felt the anger he concealed. "You could have stamped out the threat before so much damage was done. So many lives lost."

"We could have, but my Sight revealed that route held no victory. The only way we could defeat the demon was if *you* found Talia." A smile played about Abigail's mouth.

"Why?" Adam lashed.

Talia could guess. She caught the dart of Abigail's eyes seeking hers. Abigail held her gaze a fraction of a second, but more than enough time to read Talia's expression, then sit back with a sense of smug satisfaction. Abigail knew.

Old Talia could never have faced a single wraith, much less the leader of them. But she was different now. The months running from the wraiths, each moment in that burning alley in Arizona, her respite at Segue, the understanding she'd found in Adam—all of it had changed her. Allowed her to function through her fear. To seek answers in spite of her terror. To accept herself and her dark gift. And, remembering Patty's sacrifice, learn to embrace her fear for something bigger, more important than herself.

Now, if need be, she could scream in the face of an immortal demon.

Apparently Abigail *could* read faery futures after all.

Adam opened his mouth to ask again, but was cut short when Abigail gasped. Her eyelids flickered as her head fell against the back of the rocking chair. She moaned loud and low.

Adam looked to Zoe. "What's the matter with her?"

"Another vision," Zoe answered.

If possible, Abigail seemed to grow even older before Talia's eyes.

Curious, Talia reached for shadow. The layered veils slipped around her shoulders as her senses sharpened. She didn't fight the darkness, but let the boundary to the Otherworld flow freely around her. This was, after all, what she was born to do.

"I see a man," Abigail wailed.

Talia observed Adam as he crouched at Abigail's chair to catch the clues her vision divulged. Shadows circled him, gathering and rolling off his broad shoulders like a thunderstorm.

"A man searching . . ." Abigail repeated.

But Abigail was different. Wisps of smoky blackness filtered *through* her body, collecting in her eyes, sharing space with her spirit.

The woman should be stark raving mad. Perhaps she was, a little.

In the penumbra of Abigail's shadows, Talia caught a glimpse of her vision.

Yes, the face and body of a man appeared, and he was searching, entering the bottom floor of the building that Adam had once thought safe, but had turned out to be a trap.

A trap.

"Who is it?" Adam asked.

"Custo," Talia answered. And he was walking right into it.

SIXTEEN

I⊤'s Custo," Talia repeated as she peered into the dense haze of shadow seething around Abigail. Then the image slid away.

"He was supposed to meet me at the loft." Adam's voice was thick with controlled emotion.

Talia looked wildly around at the overlapping waves of darkness, trying to recapture the slippery vision of Custo. She let her eyes relax, inhaled the seductive dark wisps that she'd kept at bay all her life, and let them fill her.

Potential futures sparked into existence in her vision, proliferating until there were as many glimmers of "might be" as there were stars in a clear night sky. She noticed how each discrete decision affected another, and another, until choices formed constellations of possibility that had no reference to probability. It was difficult to isolate one person. One event. To index one segment of time. At last she caught a sliver of Custo, a flash of his fair eyes.

Her heartbeat accelerated as she strained to make out his location and what he was doing, but she could only see shimmers of motion and the occasional delayed reflection of his environment. The glint of steel. A wash of vertical concrete. The glitter of the rising sun beyond a tall, wide window, now punctured with fist-size holes.

Talia let the shadows slide on her skin, caressing her face

and stroking her body. If she didn't fight them, if she allowed the strands to insinuate themselves around her limbs, hug her curves and wrap her in darkness, then her sight grew clearer.

Her vision doubled, then tripled. Another Custo approached the loft's building and surveyed the coded pad at the door. Yet another Custo followed at his heels, taking the sidewalk at a jog. One cut across the street on a diagonal. Another walked to the crosswalk at the corner, just as a car circled the building, Custo in the driver's seat.

"I don't get it. Which one is him? Which one is real?" Talia looked to Abigail for clarification.

"None of them is real until he acts," Abigail answered. "These are just possibilities. And you are only seeing the versions of him that go to this building. There are probably many others who elected not to come. To opt out of this fight."

"No," Adam said with conviction. "There are no other versions of Custo. He is a man of his word. Custo will meet me at the loft."

Adam was right. Each and every one of the Custos she saw, in spite of their small differences in approach, concentrated on the coded panel at the building.

"But he won't go in," Adam continued, as if he could direct Custo by will alone. "Our escape will have rotated the entry codes. He'll know something is wrong. If he's smart, he'll walk away."

Talia saw the many Custos' expressions change as, indeed, his initial code was rejected. One Custo swore. Another raked his hands through his hair. Another stepped back onto the sidewalk to peer up the height of the building, then approached the keypad again.

All of the Custos entered the building.

Talia's eyes teared, her breath coming faster. She had always liked Custo. He'd always seemed solid, direct, and real.

Adam groaned in frustration. "Damn it. No."

"He's a good friend," Abigail said.

"He's an idiot," Adam roared back. The pain in his voice reverberated through Talia.

Every Custo drew his gun. All but one took the stairs; the other went with the elevator. Firearm raised, Custo entered the loft apartment.

A blur of movement obscured what happened next, but Talia caught the moment when Custo's head jerked back, as if struck. She witnessed the sudden curl of his body around a belly-planted kick. She shuddered as he fell, spitting blood.

"What?" Adam asked. "What? What's happening?"

Talia shoved away the shadows and retched, trying to get them out from inside her body, her mind. The coating of Otherworldly ick grasped at her throat as she heaved for air. The effort knocked her off balance and burned her from her core out, but Adam steadied her, drawing her against him.

A tremor of relief washed through her body—she'd wanted, needed, to be in Adam's arms for a while. She just had no idea how to get there.

"Are you all right?" Adam spoke low, words short with tension.

Talia's lungs were screaming, but she nodded a mute *yes* against his ribs. A faint tinge of sewer still clung to him, but underneath the smell was all Adam.

"Will you be okay here for a while?" He backed them both to the door of the room.

She shook her head. *No.* She knew he was thinking. No way on earth was he going without her.

"Talia, these people seem fine. If they meant us any harm, they would have done something by now. And I'll be back as soon as I can. I can't stay. You have to understand, I can't just stay and let Custo die."

Talia did understand. He was being condescending again. Taking over. She wasn't asking him to babysit her. If he could just get over his macho I-have-to-save-the-world routine, then he would know she understood. Her "no" had nothing to do with staying with these people.

He was going after Custo. She was going with him. She cocked her head to tell him so.

"Don't look at me that way, Talia. You just said that the doctor wants you to take it easy," he argued. "You need to heal. Besides, I'll probably be walking into an ambush. I won't be able to protect you."

She pointed to herself, and then pointed to him. *I'll protect you. Duh.*

His eyes narrowed. "You can't scream. How can you protect me?"

Talia laid a hand on his chest, just under the U between his collarbones where she could feel the soft echo of his heartbeat, and pulled the shadows around them.

Adam knocked her hand away and the shadows snapped back. "No. The risk is too great."

He may as well have slapped her. She gritted her teeth and glared at him from her darkness. Idiot man. She was going, whether he liked it or not.

Abigail laughed. "Poor Adam. Probably thought he'd found a woman who would follow his lead, do everything he said. Got a banshee instead. I need one of them big windows for you two to work it out against. Zoe, do we have a big window somewhere? Adam's particularly good with windows. Maybe he could convince her that way."

Talia's face heated, but she ignored Abigail, stubbornly crossing her arms and blocking the door.

Adam looked back at Abigail. "Can you quit mocking me for a minute and help me convince her to stay?"

Abigail shrugged. "Why would I waste my time doing that when I know very well that she goes with you?"

Talia controlled a smug smile.

"She—? What—?" Adam stammered. Then he turned to Talia. "Oh, hell. Come on."

Zoe followed them down the stairs, shouting over the rising whine of a mournful melody as they neared the main floor of the building. "You can take my car if you want."

"Good," Adam said as he looked over his shoulder, beyond Talia. He didn't want to attempt a reverse trek through the sewer, nor did he feel comfortable with an open stroll up the five blocks from his current location to the loft's building, especially with Talia's distinctive looks.

Zoe passed off the keys and directed them up the alley. Adam regarded Talia as they sprinted toward it. "You'll do what I say, when I say it, or I'm not going anywhere. Got it?"

"Yes, sir," she croaked.

This was a bad idea, taking her back to a building infested with either wraiths or SPCI operatives, or both. She was supposed to heal so that she could call her father and end the war. It was beyond irresponsible of him to allow her to come on a fool's errand.

As a realist, he knew he might lose Custo, his surrogate brother. He couldn't lose Talia as well. Yet, he couldn't very well risk her following after he'd left.

Zoe's car was a beat-up blue hatchback Accord circa the midnineties. Adam ran around to the driver's side and crouched to get into the car, his knees hitting the steering wheel. Talia was seated and belted before he managed to fold himself into a position in which he could drive.

The car smelled like burned plastic in spite of the scented cartoon character dangly thing hanging from the rearview mirror. Random papers and debris littered the backseat. At least the car had a manual transmission.

Fiercely missing his Diablo, Adam slammed the Accord into first gear and accelerated down the alley at a crap seven mph.

The car brayed when he floored the gas, but got him up to twenty by the mouth of the alley. He'd buy Zoe another car if he killed this one. Hell, he'd buy her another car if he survived the day.

Traffic was thickening with the start of the morning rush. A fleet of taxis jockeyed for position, blocking the intersection. Adam took the car onto the sidewalk with an ear-bracing scrape of the undercarriage, maneuvered around the cars to the angry shouts of their drivers, and ran the light to turn onto his building's street.

"There," Talia said, startling him. He hit the brakes.

"What?" The street had no pedestrians, only a line of parked cars.

"The red sedan. It's what Custo was driving." The red sedan was illegally parked directly across the street from Adam's building. Adam pulled up alongside, stopping the Accord in the middle of the street, and hopped out.

"Get out," Adam barked. He met her at the tail end of the car, grabbed her hand, and pulled her across the street. With his right hand, he drew his gun.

"We have to assume that whoever attacked the loft knows we're here. They'd be watching the street. They'll be waiting."

Talia nodded. Her face was ash white. Scared, but not shaking. Not retreating into her shadows. She'd come a long way from that alley in Arizona.

"This is your last chance, Talia. You could make it back to that club. They'll hide you. You could be safe there." Why had he trusted Abigail's word anyway? Just because she seemed to know everything didn't mean she actually did.

Talia shook her head once, sharply. *No.*

He raised his hand to the keypad, but a suffocating pressure built in his chest. He turned to her, grabbing her shoulders and abandoning all dignity to plead, "Please, go back. I can't let you in there. Not even for Custo. I just can't. I won't deliver you into their hands. Will you go back to the club? Will you go back *for me*?"

"I'm going inside that building for you," she said in a jagged whisper, but whether it was because of emotion or her injury, he couldn't tell.

"Damn it, Talia. I should never have had sex with you. I told you that we couldn't have a 'you and me' right now." He released her abruptly, shoving her away from the door. "Don't lose the war because of some sentimental attachment you have formed in a stressful situation."

Talia stepped forward again. Her black eyes glinted dangerously. "I choose my own battles, not you. Don't make me try to find a way inside on my own. It will only cost Custo time."

She waved him back to the keypad.

Damn it. Abigail was right: Talia was determined to follow. He should've tied her down somewhere. Too late now. Too late for everything now.

He coded inside. The small lobby was empty. "Stairs or elevator?"

"Elevator's faster," Talia answered.

Fine. He sheltered her body as he punched the pad at the elevator. The metal door slid open.

Empty.

Talia stepped around him and entered. "I think we should do this Dark." She lifted an eyebrow waiting for his response.

He stepped inside beside her, lacing his fingers through hers, and pulled her against the side wall. "Dark sounds good."

Shadows caressed him, feathering lightly across his body like an extension of Talia. His perspective altered, senses sharpening as the physical world deepened and became more distinct, hyperaware of the environment. Of Talia's slender, warm hand in his.

The steel box had them to the top of the building in five seconds.

Adam gripped her hand. "Here we go."

The elevator door slid open, and Talia sent a churning wave of darkness tumbling into the room. The flood of shadow poured out from her and filled the great room of the loft, skating across the floors and climbing the walls until the space was thick with the watery veils that separated the mundane world from the Otherworld in a wash of obscurity.

Armored men knelt in assault position, aiming toward the elevator as shadow-blindness overcame them. They were clothed in bulky black, as if *that* color could hide anything from her, and they wore gas masks. Behind the men were two wraiths moving around the perimeter of the room with the slow, predatory fluidity of a mudslide.

Talia sniffed the air. A faint trace of the sickly chemical tang still lingered. There was too much at stake for her to succumb to that again.

The loft needed air.

Talia reached for the window with the fingers of her shadows, tracing the splintered cracks in the glass from the earlier impacts. She insinuated darkness into the thick panes with a gentle, but building, insistent pressure. With a hiss, a crack darted, gashing through the window. The heavy glass buckled and slid to crash partly on the loft's floors and partly on the sidewalk many stories below. But Talia let no sunlight penetrate the loft as fresh air replaced poisoned.

"Whoa," Adam murmured, gaze slanting down at her. Was that respect in his eyes?

He tugged her hand, pulled her toward the kitchen, and brought them both to their knees behind the kitchen counter. He silently slid open a drawer and selected a knife, which he tucked into his belt. He pulled out a second, a short utility knife, and held it out to her.

No. She shook her head. She could protect him, but she wouldn't kill anyone.

He pressed the blade into her hand. "You asked to come," he reminded her. "Now take the damn knife and use it, if necessary."

Her fingers closed around the wooden grip. She had no handy place to stow it—the elastic waistband of Adam's sweatpants was too loose on her waist.

Adam ducked his head to hers and murmured, "Can you see Custo?"

She shook her head. *No.* But she could see a spray of blood on the wall in keeping with Adam's stark, abstract paintings. An aggressive red splatter on white evoking Jackson Pollock.

Custo was here, and he had met with violence.

"The bedroom, most likely," he said through gritted teeth.

But he didn't move. Resolute anguish swept across the connection of their hands.

Talia understood why. If they both crept to the bedroom, the shadows would lift in the great room, allowing the men and wraiths to corner them. But Adam wouldn't leave her alone to keep the place cloaked in shadow either, not in a room of guns and wraiths. His first priority was the war, so he had to protect her before saving his friend.

"You just have to trust me," Talia whispered. She wasn't afraid. Hiding was what she did best.

He shot her a tormented look.

Talia squeezed his hand, wishing he could feel her emotions for once. She resorted to words. "I hid in shadow for months without detection, I can handle a few minutes while you get Custo."

"But—"

"No time for 'buts.' I'll hold these men here, in the dark. I'm not afraid—this is my territory. I'll be safe. Trust me to handle myself."

Adam hesitated, indecision mixing with his worry.

"Go on." She released her hold on his hand and waited for him to do the same.

Urgent focus surged within him. He pulled her close to stroke her face, a soft caress across the plane of her cheek, and murmured, "I'll be right back."

Adam touched the right angles of the refrigerator and moved around the side to the alcove where his work station was located. The foot of the desk indicated that he'd reached the turn to the hallway, but the chair was missing. He crawled through the space until the shadows weakened and he could see the outline of his hand on the floor.

He stood, gun in hand, and approached the diluted line of vertical light at the bedroom door.

The door swung open, a female wraith bolting from the room in an eerie glide.

Adam shot her in the head and kicked her body back inside, where the shadows were thinner yet, Talia's reach weakening. The wraith hit the edge at the end of the bed awkwardly and thunked to the floor to regenerate while stinking up the place.

"Hello, Adam."

Spencer stood in the center of the room, outfitted in black gear like his team and aiming a gun his way. His stance blocked Adam's view of a person bound to a chair behind him.

Alive. Please be alive.

Adam braced and kept a throttle hold on his thumping

heart, sweat burning through his skin with the effort, as he shifted to the side to get a better look.

Custo sat in the office chair, hands bound to the armrests, feet bound to the legs of the chair, one ankle cruelly skewed. His head lolled forward, blood staining his shirt and the lap of his pants. The faint acrid smell of urine made Adam grit his teeth.

Hold on, Custo. Stay alive.

He sighted down the barrel at Spencer's head, shifting from foot to foot in anticipation of the sweet satisfaction of pulling the trigger. Spencer was going to die, had to die. Right now. "Why? You son of a bitch. Why?"

Spencer kept his gun steady. "I was sure he knew where you were, he always does. But this is much easier. Him bringing you and the girl to me. Really very convenient."

"How could you do this?"

Shrugging, Spencer answered, "I had to get your location somehow. Got to hand it to Custo; he didn't give. But there's no fighting The Collective."

"I've found a way," Adam said. *She's just outside the door.*

"It's too late. The world has changed. The wraith population tops ten thousand, headed by an immortal demon. Cooperation is in our best interests. The wraith revolution is over. The Collective won."

The hell it did. Adam's finger tightened on the trigger.

"But I'll, uh, throw you a bone if you let me out of here," Spencer said with a flash of his teeth.

"You're not leaving this room alive." *Hold on, Custo.*

"Really?" Spencer asked. "I can show you how to end a wraith without a scream. It's actually very simple. Your perspective at Segue has been so myopic that you couldn't see it for yourself."

Adam thought of Talia. Her small, fragile frame struggling

for air. He couldn't imagine her fighting a demon. Couldn't imagine her slack body if she died trying.

"What is it?"

"Wraiths can't tolerate death."

"What the hell does that mean?" *Can't tolerate death.*

Spencer glanced meaningfully at Custo, slumped in his chair. His rounded shoulders were too still.

No! It couldn't be. Not Custo.

A life for a death. Philip's druid rite, his theory of symmetry in which a person gives up their life to teach a monster to die. That wraith wasn't worth Custo. His only friend. His brother in every way that mattered.

"Out," Adam said. He had to get to Custo. Save Custo.

Spencer's eyes glittered in satisfaction. Adam kept his gun trained on him as Spencer eased out the door.

"I'll be just outside when you're done," Spencer said. Him, his SPCI team, and a couple wraiths. All that, and still Spencer would die when Adam was finished here. His banshee easily trumped Spencer's backup.

Adam rushed to Custo and gently felt his blood-slick neck for a pulse as his own clamored wildly. He couldn't find it.

No, wait. The vein at Custo's neck trembled. The pulse was there, just thready. Weak.

Hang on. Hang on.

Adam knelt on the floor beside the chair, forced his trembling hands to gentleness to raise Custo's chin. His face was a nightmare of brutality, even softened by Talia's shadows. His eyes were red-ringed, his nose askew, his jaw oddly hanging. "Oh, God. Custo, I'm sorry."

Not that Custo could hear him. He was well beyond that.

Adam swallowed bile as a rage of helplessness filled him, vision blurring with water. Custo couldn't die like this, tied to a chair. Adam took the knife out of his belt and severed the cords that bound his friend, so very careful not to nick Custo's skin.

Custo's body sagged forward when Adam freed his arms.

"Easy now," Adam said, shouldering the weight. Warm wetness seeped through his shirt, Custo's blood flowing freely. Adam brought him to the bed. There was nowhere else to take him. No help he could get to save him.

He was too late, again.

Adam's arms shook as he laid out his friend. He couldn't hold Custo's hand as he died, because his fingers were cruelly twisted, broken. He took Custo's wrist instead to wait out the fading heartbeats.

One beat.

Custo as the poor kid with no family, new to Shelby Boys' School, rumpled and rearing to fight.

A second beat.

Custo, showing no fear when first confronted by the horror of Jacob. Working side by side to contain the monster. Helping found Segue instead of living his own life. Custo should've had his own life. A woman. A family. Of all things, Custo should've had a family of his own.

The darkness of the room thickened.

No third beat touched Adam's fingers. A smothered sob wracked him as a warm fleeting presence brushed by— *Custo!*—which Adam knew was only palpable in Talia's half-light.

A depression formed, tendrils of curling darkness reaching out as if whipped by an unseen wind.

Adam slowly rose next to the bed and peered inside the layers of shadow for a trace of Custo's passing. The loss hollowed him, scraped out his heart, stealing the breath and words he so desperately needed to say good-bye and thank you and I am so fucking sorry.

But there was only darkness. Darkness and Shadowman.

Shadowman stood trapped within a vortex of intense, swirling shadow. The wind slowed and died, coming to rest in a rippling cloak about his body. Shadowman twitched his cloak aside, and Adam perceived a gleaming light beckoning within the deep like a bright promise.

A glow moved within and across the darkness. Custo. Gone. Adam felt like a limb had been severed from his body. Something vital missing, yet the ghost-pain of it remained to haunt him.

The wind picked up, binding Shadowman again.

But the rod of Death's scythe was long. He whipped out the curved blade, speared the wraith's just-stirring body, and dragged her out of the world. The "fireflies" within the wraith floated free into forever, the consumed souls released at last to the hereafter.

As darkness swallowed Shadowman again, he brought up his bloodthirsty gaze and met Adam's.

Adam understood. Spencer was right. The answer was so simple. No one else Adam loved need fear The Collective.

Yes, Talia could free Death with her scream. But anyone else could, too. They just had to die to do it.

Cold will hardened in Adam as he stepped away from Custo's broken body. This wasn't good-bye. No. Now he planned to follow Custo's lead. If Custo could give his life to protect his friend, to screw Spencer, to kill a wraith, Adam could, too.

But there was no way Adam would spend his life for his selfish brother Jacob. No, if he were going to court Death, it would be for the demon himself.

SEVENTEEN

TALIA watched as the soldiers moved stealthily into the center of the room, fanning out to search the dark while that coward and traitor Spencer lounged on the wall next to the bedroom, giving orders from his headset.

Where was Adam? Why was he taking so long? One more minute and she'd go in after him herself.

One soldier's trajectory headed perilously toward the open air of the window. With his senses muted, he wasn't aware of his danger, even as his boots crushed glass underfoot.

Talia retracted her shadows slightly from the sharp drop of the loft's broken window. If the man fell to his death, it would not be because of her.

The man stepped out of the shadows into sunlight. The sudden deluge of stimuli and imminent danger had him flailing for balance. But he recouped, shuffled forward, and peered cautiously over the edge. He took up position there, as if Talia and Adam planned to escape that way. Not likely.

The wraiths, one a bald, thickset male, and the other, a tall and lithe female with the graceful poise of a ballerina, slinked across the room.

"Been lucky all my life," the male wraith muttered. "I deal with a demon, and my luck dries up. I pull the short straws every time now."

Demon.

The female held out her hands to feel her way across the dark. Her fingers fluttered across the shoulders of a soldier twice her weight. She found his mask and used it to lift his body out of her way

The soldier thrashed and screamed, though his cries sounded smothered in the darkness.

"Oh, I'm not going to eat you," the female wraith sneered and dropped the man to the floor. "Treaty won't allow it."

Treaty. Spencer. Custo.

The female's hand found the long wall that led uninterrupted to the hallway. She was headed to the bedroom.

Not going to happen.

Talia gripped her knife, drew her arm back, and threw the blade across the shadowy room.

Talia couldn't aim to save her life, but that didn't matter in shadow. The knife sailed through the air at an awkward spin, and would've probably dinged the female wraith on the shoulder with its shaft, but Talia corrected its course with an upward shift and twist of shadow and drove the blade into the wraith's left eye.

The female wraith screeched as she hit the wall and then slid soundlessly to the floor, grabbing at Spencer as she collapsed. They fell in a lovers' sprawl of twining limbs. His labored breath broke the silence of the room. Pushing up, he crawled off her corpse, trapped on one side by a wall, and on the other by the sofa. He was almost clear when the wraith grabbed his ankle.

Regenerating was hungry work. The wraith pulled the blade out of her face, flicking white tissue on Spencer's black clothes, and brought him to her gaping mouth. He got a shot off. Hit her in the shoulder. Ineffectual. The wraith, like the sun, was rising and she was hungry for breakfast. Spencer screamed high, like a girl, as the wraith sealed her kiss. His body jerked once and then lapsed into a slack sack of skin.

Talia felt Spencer blink out, and she shuddered at the waste. So stupid. What other end had he imagined for himself? This was the only one fitting.

With Spencer now a used heap on the floor, the wraith resumed her progress toward the bedroom. She was at the threshold when she suddenly reared back, clumsy in fear. Heedless of obstacles she scrambled through the great room, slid on glass, and plunged backward out the window.

Adam. Talia crawled toward the bedroom door just as he exited. She scrambled to meet him near the alcove, took one of his hands, sticky with blood—*his?*—and pushed her shadows at him. The pungent tang of the blood clung to him like a corpse, and she controlled a gag by switching to breathing through her mouth.

Adam's gaze focused on her with the resurgence of her shadows. He'd aged ten years in the last five minutes. His eyes were clouded with an emotion, but she couldn't name the feeling that flowed from him and into her—something dark, tinged with grief and pain, but strangely settled and resolute. She didn't trust it, found herself preferring his anger. This new sensation made her ache as if she were dying a little inside. Whatever he found in that room must have been very bad.

"I'm sorry," she whispered. Her words were woefully inadequate, but she couldn't think of anything better to say.

Adam's expression hardened as he glanced around the room, taking stock of the soldiers spreading slowly in blind stealth, and the remaining wraith.

Adam's gaze finally rested on Spencer. His lips curled into a sick smile before he dismissed the sight altogether. Spencer was scum; he didn't deserve to be mourned.

"We'll take the stairs," he said.

Yesterday Patty, and now Custo. Adam's losses just kept piling up. His strain was showing—he had every right to break and should have, a long time ago.

Emotion squeezed Talia's heart. She had to say something more. She had to let him know that he was not alone.

"Adam, I—"

"Not now." His grip on her hand tightened painfully; the rest of his body went very still.

She swallowed the rest of her words.

Not now. She understood. He couldn't take comfort with Custo's blood on his hands.

"The stairs," she repeated.

He seemed to relax slightly, gave a short nod, and then guided her in a crouching walk through the kitchen. He maneuvered past the elevator to an adjacent nondescript door. The door hissed when opened, leading to a stairwell.

A soldier on the other side of the door backed against the stairwell wall, raising his weapon.

Adam shifted and kicked the man head over heels down the flight of stairs. They stepped over his body, rushing downward, trying to keep ahead of the remaining soldiers within the loft. Talia strained to hear footsteps, but none followed. She figured they had a few things to deal with what with Spencer dead and all. Several minutes of quiet, panicked descent later, they exited the rear of the building, Talia trying to smother her gasps of air.

Adam grasped her hand to keep her close, alert for signs of pursuit. He was too quiet, too calm, the roar within him utterly silenced. Solemn resolution dominated now. Stripped of all his resources and everyone he trusted, he still tried to hold the world together with his bloody bare hands. Adam Thorne was the strongest—no, the best man she'd ever known. She understood why Custo gave his life for him, because she knew she'd do the same. Adam could take anything he wanted from her, her breath, her body. He already had her heart.

At the end of a short, clean alley, a car waited, Zoe sitting at the wheel. Had to be Abigail at work again. A cop shouted *stop!* just before they pulled away, but Zoe didn't even bat an eye. She must have known he wouldn't follow. She took one nonsensical turn in a backward-moving direction, but redirected toward the club on the next block.

Once inside, Adam parted the motley crowd with a sweep of his arm. "Where's that doctor?"

"Here." Amalia shouldered through.

"She can't stop shaking. Her color's not good. And her skin's gone clammy," Adam said.

"I'm fine," Talia argued, but her weak, raspy voice contradicted her. The suffocating coating had not thinned at all.

He strong-armed her back into the little dark room and planted her in a chair. "You don't look fine."

"Neither do you," Talia said.

"When did you last eat?" Amalia asked as she fit an oxygen mask over Talia's face.

Her question stopped Talia short. Adam, too, from the look of his confused expression. Food hadn't been high on their list of priorities.

"Maybe twenty-four hours," Talia admitted. Adam grudgingly nodded confirmation.

"Slept?" the medic prodded.

"I slept in the car," Talia said. She pointed to Adam. "He never sleeps."

"You inhaled poison gas," Amalia said. "I specifically ordered you to rest." She looked over at Adam. "And you look like hell. Is that your blood or someone else's?"

Adam's expression tightened with grief.

"Someone else's," Talia answered for him.

"I'll order some food," Zoe offered, retreating out of the commotion.

Adam turned to Talia. That too-calm look was in his eyes; it had her stomach clenching and her soul screaming *no! no! no!*

Proving her suspicions correct, he shifted his gaze away the moment hers met his. "If you're all right, I need to make some calls."

Calls. Right.

"Abigail said we could stay here," he continued. "Try to get some sleep. You need to rest to heal."

Sleep. Impossible.

"I won't be long."

Then why won't you really look at me?

But she couldn't ask him in front of all these people. Not with his pain so raw. And she couldn't hold on to him while she was tethered to the oxygen. She didn't even know if she had the right. So she had to let him go. She just hoped he didn't do anything monumentally brave or stupid. At least, not without her.

Outside the room, Adam begged a black tee off the back of a guy with a silver shaft piercing the cartilage between his nostrils. As he shrugged into the shirt, Zoe descended the stairs, opening her mouth as if she were going to impart some more of Abigail's wisdom.

"Leave me alone, Zoe. And tell Abigail to stay out of my business, too."

He didn't wait for an answer but headed back out the building and down the alley on foot, food and sleep be damned. He had to get out of there, away from Talia's damn faery eyes. Her lost, hurt look. She saw too much.

Patty gone. Custo gone.

He wouldn't, couldn't, tolerate Talia's death on his hands,

too. No way on earth would he allow her within screaming distance of the demon. Not now, not ever. Not even if she could save the world. It wasn't happening. Not while he still breathed.

He punched a number in his mobile phone, one he knew but had never allowed himself to use. The line rang once before Jack picked up.

Jackson Flatt traded in some very illegal exotic weapons and paraphernalia. He was a first-come, first-serve kind of operator, who made no connection between the weapons he sold and the innocent lives lost because of them. Over the years, Adam had had some *special needs,* but never, under any circumstances, would he have done business with Jack.

Times had changed.

"It's Adam Thorne."

"Adam Thorne." Jack stretched the vowels of Adam's name for pleasure. "To what do I owe the honor of your call? You slumming?"

Adam controlled the impulse to end the call and bit back a retort. "I need something. Can you hook me up, or what?"

"Why don't you ask your go-to boy, Spencer?"

"Spencer's dead and I am no longer affiliated with SPCI," Adam answered.

"Hm." Jack paused on the other line, processing this new information. "Welcome to the dark side. What do you need?"

"L-pills." Just saying the words made Adam's neck sweat.

"Have anything to do with your wanted face on the news?"

News. Damn. If he was on the news, then so was Talia. Even if he managed to pull this off, her life was going to be completely messed up.

"Indirectly," Adam answered.

"You going to be able to pay with all the heat you got coming down on you?"

"Always."

"Then, yeah. I can probably hook you up. I know a guy. Correction, I know the widow of a guy who might have what you're looking for. You get my meaning?"

Jack wasn't exactly subtle. L-pills or lethal pills were designed for quick and effective suicide. Ingestion of potassium cyanide would precipitate brain death within minutes and heart failure shortly thereafter.

"How fast can you get them to me?"

"Say an hour. Maybe two. Grand Central. Buy a paper to kill time, and I'll find you." The line went dead.

Adam didn't know how much Jack wanted for the pills, and he didn't care. A thousand. A hundred thousand. A million. Really didn't matter.

Adam bought a newspaper, but he didn't read it. He snagged a laptop from an unsuspecting college student at the station and worked, the paper propped up at his side. In a couple of hours, he had Talia's security planned, instructions for her to leave the country detailed on a file on his flash drive.

When Jack dropped onto the bench at his side, three hours later, the second floor of the station was teeming with busy, colorful, vibrant people oblivious to the imminent crisis.

Adam shut down the laptop, slipping the flash drive into his pocket, as Jack sized him up with an undisguised once-over. "What are you on? Coke? Acid? Something more exotic?"

"I'm high on life," Adam said in bitter irony. "Do you have what I need or what?"

"This shit will kill you." Jack lifted a crumpled brown paper lunch bag.

"That's the point. What do you care anyway?"

"I don't," Jack said. "I just don't get why you'd want it. The fucking world's turning upside down. Some seriously scary shit on the street lately. My business has doubled, but the guys coming in to pick up their stuff are looking over their shoulders like the boogeyman's behind them. And now Adam-fucking-Thorne gets off his high horse to place an order for L-pills. Shit. Makes me want to retire early and move to a nice tropical island somewhere."

"How much do you want?" Adam took the bag, fumbled inside for a vial of pills. He was too tired to illuminate Jack on The Collective.

"It's free. I saw a news clip of you beating the shit out of a monster in Arizona before the station replaced it with pretty pictures of you and your lady friend like some kind of conspiracy cover-up. Don't know why they bothered. It's all over the Internet anyway. Can you tell me what the fuck that thing was?"

"Wraith." Just saying the word doubled his heart rate, adrenaline flowing to fuel this last push. Just a few more hours and it would all be over. He could sleep forever, then.

"Are there more than one of those monsters?"

Adam nodded, standing. "Lots more."

"Fuck."

No kidding. Adam rose, opened the bag, and pocketed the pills. Without looking back, he headed toward the exit, leaving Jack to contemplate the future.

As for his own, all the things he had left to do in his life could be numbered on one hand. He had to get back to the club, give Talia the flash drive, somehow get out without her following, find the *Styx*, and open the way for Shadowman to kill the demon via the little pill. Pretty straightforward.

He took a cab back to the club, AMARANTH, according to the abused sign above the main door, but entered through the rear. The place was quiet, which had Adam's heart accelerating. Where was the music?

Adam kicked open the dressing room door. Empty.

A kid dressed in jeans and a tee, almost normal-looking

in spite of the tattoos crawling up his neck, shouldered some equipment through the back entrance.

Adam stopped him. "What's going on here? Why's it so quiet?"

The kid scowled. "Everyone's getting ready for the fete. I'm trying to figure out how to work the stupid fog machine. Zoe says Abigail sees fog, so I gotta figure out how to get the stupid fog machine to work in the next hour, or I won't have time to get ready."

The kid was going round in circles. Adam cut him off. "And Talia?"

"Lady Shadow?"

Uh, okay . . . Adam nodded.

"Upstairs, asleep. Zoe says not to disturb her."

Asleep. The perfect opportunity—leave her a note and the flash drive with everything that she needed to know to survive and then get out while she was still sleeping.

"Thanks." Adam headed for the stairs.

"Hey!" the kid called after him.

Adam paused, looking over.

The kid shifted his weight, as if nervous. "You her man?"

Adam's mood darkened. What a question. Her man?

He'd certainly dedicated his life to Talia's cause, even before she knew what she was meant to do. The network of resources he'd established had therefore been set up for *her* purposes, *her* ends. The lives that had been sacrificed had been lost to protect *her*, so that she could end the wraith war. And all this was done freely.

That's not what the kid meant, though. Not the way he held his breath waiting for Adam's answer. The kid was speaking literally and not a little hopefully. As if he might just have a shot with a faery princess. Poor kid.

Maybe Abigail had been blabbing about the window again. Adam's body stirred at the memory. The way he'd buried himself in Talia as they hovered over the city, her impossibly perfect, silky skin under his hands. Her heat squeezing him, her shadows filling the room. The glimmer of a beauty, hers, recognized not by his mundane senses, but by something deeper. Maybe his soul, if he still had one. He thought of the pills in his pocket, the fact that he'd trade his life to make sure hers was safe, that strange beauty untouched.

"Yeah," Adam answered. In every way possible, he was her man.

"Oh." The kid sighed heavily. "Okay, then."

Adam left the kid with his dashed dreams and headed up the stairs.

The narrow hallway at the landing had doors off to each side, but Adam bet the one with the handwritten DO NOT DISTURB!!! sign was Talia's. The three exclamation marks screamed Zoe.

He let himself quietly inside, shutting the door behind him, turned, and stopped in dumb shock.

The scene from the painting *Sleeping Beauty* shimmered in reality before his eyes. The artist had to have been a visionary like Abigail, but with the talent and technique to capture the sight on canvas.

Talia reclined on an old-fashioned divan. She wore a black satin robe, deeply parted to the thigh, a long, slender leg revealed to the hip. Her white-gold hair tumbled over the red velvet cushion on which she rested, fat curls gleaming. Her face was peaceful, lips parted just slightly.

Talia. Sleeping Beauty.

To match the painting perfectly, that robe needed to be parted, her body revealed entirely. Her eyes needed to be open, though still slumberous. And she needed to be looking at him with desire.

The thing to do, of course, would be to kiss her. To wake her like a princess in a fairy tale. To set the fantasy in motion.

But Adam couldn't. There was no time left for fantasies and dreams. All the happily-ever-afters of the world were bankrupt.

He crossed soundlessly to a side table, took the flash drive out of his pocket, and placed it on top of a pad of paper. He paused over the note, but had no idea what to say. There were no words for how he felt. All of the ones that came to mind seemed too short, or too simple, or too overused to capture the knot in his chest.

For Talia~ It's everything I have. Adam

The note was crap, but it'd have to do.

He straightened, brought his gaze back one more time to look at her, and took a deep breath to inhale the moment. To hold it within him where he was going.

Her eyes fluttered and opened, sleepy and sensual.

Adam froze, rooted to his spot.

He caught the moment consciousness flickered into her gaze. Awareness of her surroundings and awareness of him. And with it, damned desire. Desire was the last thing he needed, but the only thing he wanted.

Heat roared into his exhausted body; the room swayed slightly in his vision.

She slipped a finger into the knot at her waist and released the satin tie. The robe parted and completed the image from the painting.

Eighteen

The blur of sleep cleared from Talia's eyes, but the dream remained.

Adam. Back.

Grizzled with stubble, stinking with exhaustion, gaze hooded, wary, and troubled—the weight of the war bearing down on him as he gazed at her.

But back.

Now: how to keep him here?

Talia brought a hand to her robe and pulled the tie apart. Gravity slid one side of the robe off her body; the other she brushed aside herself. Her heartbeat went from sluggish to surging, her nerves from idle to quivering and edgy. The exposure of her skin to the cool air of the room sent a wave of goose bumps racing up her legs, over her stomach, to peak at her breasts.

Adam groaned as he gazed at her, the sound wrenching from his gut, soul deep.

Talia's throat ached with a soul-sound of her own, but she held it back. What she felt would probably come out as babbling nonsense anyway—worry running over stones of reproach, a deluge of fear seeking the solid banks of his strong arms, liquid desire flowing too fast toward a fall she'd never survive alone.

But how could she say any of that when she needed to

remain silent to heal? She'd heal, then scream as if his life depended on it. No, she'd scream *because* his life depended on it.

Frustration clogged her heart as Adam stared at her—he looked half dead already. He was her center of gravity, her solid ground, the bedrock of this world, yet he swayed on his feet.

The man needed sleep, not sex. Maybe this wasn't such a good idea after all. Talia sat up, uncertain.

What little willpower Adam had disintegrated with the upward shift of Talia's bare body. Her breasts rounded, her legs parted slightly—a tantalizing triangle of darkness forming as her feet came to rest on the floor, her robe fanning out behind her, her hair a mess of curls over her shoulders. His sleeping beauty, now wide-awake.

His mouth went dry as his body betrayed his better judgment, hunger superseding willpower. *There's no getting out of here unseen now,* his blood rumbled, escaping from jagged cliffs of his higher reason in a chaotic, mindless avalanche of craving.

He should leave. Use any pretense to buy a few hours. Leaving was the smart thing to do. The *right* thing to do. Talia didn't need to be any more tangled up than he'd already made her. And neither did he.

But he fell to his knees with the downward force of his exhaustion and want, bracing his hands on each side of her. He gripped the cushioned bench with all his strength, fighting himself and trapping her at the same time. Chest heaving with effort, he dropped his head on her lap, her skin soft and cool against his hot cheek.

The knots in his neck released as another part of him tightened unbearably. Touching Talia was yet another mistake. His mistakes just kept piling up around him, stone on stone. So many things he should've done differently, should have figured out long ago. Resting his head on Talia's lap had to be among the most boneheaded, because how could he be so close and not taste her?

He slid his hands along her sleek outer thighs until he came to the tight curve of her ass. He took hold, filling his palms with her, and pulled her to the edge of the seat. Her hands dropped to his head, fingers lacing his hair, sending a lightning bolt of desire through his system, washing him in wild fire.

He buried his face briefly in the hollow of her hips, just above the waves of her curls—she'd showered and smelled sweet, like spring rain. She'd be damp there, too.

"Just no fighting this," he said against her skin, mouth searing a trail up her belly to her breast.

"Then don't," she whispered back, aching to feel his body on her, skin to skin.

Talia gripped the shoulders of his T-shirt and pulled it off him, his hands and arms lifting momentarily from his business of simultaneously removing his pants.

In one heat-slick movement, he was inside her.

Sudden shadow flooded out of Talia's pleasure, seething between them like dark steam born of water and fire. For once she didn't fight her instinctive response. She let the dark fill the room as Adam filled her, body and soul.

A wave of his lust burned her senses, a need so thick and insistent that her body arched in response. She wrapped her legs around him and drew him closer to her, to give him everything she was to slake his thirst.

He'd needed her like this before. That first kiss they'd shared at Segue had been ruled by it, and she'd run away. Now, she didn't close herself off or pull away. He drove into her to obliterate himself, his cares, his worries, and she answered with her own need. Adam, only Adam could she trust to see her like this, her faery and human halves utterly undone. At last.

Adam pressed Talia back onto the cushions, covered her body with his, and submerged himself in her darkness with a kiss. His teeth grazed her bottom lip. His tongue tasted her mouth, her neck, her breast. The tight bliss of their connected bodies permitted no thought, no argument. Just him and her, rocking on waves of fire.

She was glowing again—her shadows revealed her as much as they concealed her—impossibly beautiful, magical, and a woman just the same. His woman.

He slid a hand around her hip, reaching deeply between her legs to open her more fully, and drove into her again. And again. The carnal friction was like a match on flint. They ignited.

Talia sensed it coming like a flash on the horizon, a transformative explosion that altered her perception forever. Adam's layers of self-recrimination, regrets, and grief became transparent, and Talia perceived the reason behind Adam's unfaltering will.

It was her. He'd do anything for her.

When Adam got out of the shower, Talia was gone. He dressed quickly in black jeans and a long-sleeve tee he'd picked up at a used clothing store outside Grand Central. Time to get going.

His mind was clear, his purpose defined. He hadn't felt this centered in a long time. Bone tired, yes, but strangely better prepared for having woken Talia.

Talia.

He retrieved the flash drive and note and put them back on the side table, where she would see it. Her future was as secure as he could make it.

Exiting the room, he stuffed the vial of L-pills deeper in his pocket. He peeked into Abigail's room as he passed her open door, but she wasn't there. At the bottom of the stairs, he grabbed a kid with jet hair, accented with candy purple streaks.

"Where's Talia?" Adam demanded.

The dressing room door opened and Zoe emerged. She held a tuxedo jacket out to him by the collar.

"Just in time," she said. "But then again, I knew you would be."

"I can't. I've got to go out for a little while." He pushed past Zoe to have a last word with Talia.

Talia turned at his entrance. All follow-up questions, all his plans, disintegrated as Adam's heart arrested.

Her hair was a wild spill of white, curling gold over pale, bare shoulders. A black corset cinched her already trim waist to near nothing and did things to her breasts that made him want to drag her back up the stairs again. The long black skirt she wore seemed simple until she angled to check herself nervously in the mirror, and he got a peek at a Victorian bustle in the back. His fingers itched to get under the material and rediscover the satiny texture of the ass it concealed. The pointy toes of her shoes peeking out from the hem were slightly witchy, but all sex.

Talia brought a hand to her narrowed waist. "I shouldn't have let Zoe talk me into this. She told me that it was appropriate, but I should change. It's clearly not me."

Adam's mouth went dry. "—lovely." He swallowed deeply and tried again. "You look lovely."

"She fought me over the hair, but I won," Zoe said, coming at him again with the damn jacket.

"I like her hair down, too," Adam murmured. Her ponytails had all but driven him crazy at Segue.

Talia blushed, color flooding over the delicious curves of her cleavage and up to her cheeks. His blood went in a decidedly different direction.

Talia looked regal, every bit the faery princess, but not the kind from mainstream childhood fairy tales. Not even close. Talia was the realization of *his* fantasies, his darkest dreams. The ones that begged for the Little Death over and over, but with a woman who challenged him mind, body, and soul. She'd done all that, and in that order. If such a thing as soul mates existed, Talia was his. He knew that now.

His appraisal made her black eyes sparkle with pleasure. The sight made him ache somewhere inside not touched by blood or nerves. The intangible part of him that would always be hers.

"Whatever it is can wait." Zoe's raised eyebrows and pointed expression conveyed a secret knowledge and heavy threat. The brat obviously knew what he was about and would tattle if he didn't go along with her. Zoe nudged him with the jacket, and he took it with a meaningful look of his own.

Zoe stuck out her tongue and turned her back on him. "Talia, put on the gloves already."

Talia lifted a black satin glove, bunched the extended sleeve, and slid her right hand in the sheath, fingers wiggling as they found their places at the end. She pulled the fabric up her white arm, over her elbow.

The sight was both bliss and torture. He wanted to be there when the gloves came back off. Scratch that, he wanted to peel them off himself.

"Breathe, Adam," Zoe laughed. "And put on the jacket before we all grow old."

He shrugged into the tuxedo jacket as Talia drew the other glove up her left arm.

He didn't have time for this. He needed to talk to Talia alone, and then be on his way—

"It's a little snug, but you'll do," Zoe said. "Now stop ogling each other and come on."

Zoe led them down a narrow hallway on the first floor and around to a paint-peeling door that ostensibly led into the heart of the club.

"Wait ten seconds, then follow me in," Zoe directed. She cracked the door and slipped inside.

Alone with Talia.

The vial of pills was heavy in his pocket, separating them forever.

Adam waited a beat, choosing from the million things he wanted, needed, to say to her, but settled for the one loudest in his mind.

"I hope we're getting married," he said.

Talia let out a strangled squeak. Her expression was priceless—and here he'd thought anything could be bought for the right amount.

Her wide eyes tensed with incredulity. And then a touch of hurt. "Don't make bad jokes," she answered back.

"I'm not joking, Talia. The club's got a psychic in residence. It's got to be pretty obvious to Abigail what I want for my future." *If I were to have a future, that is.*

"It's not a wedding. They just want me to make a grand appearance." Her gorgeous eyes filled. She bit her bottom lip to cherry red.

So, of course, he had to kiss her.

He brushed his mouth softly over hers once, because he wanted the touch to be romantic, but his blood ignited as soon as her mouth parted and he drowned himself in her. His hands slid up the bones of the corset, holding on to her for dear life as she fisted her own hands in his hair to keep him close to her. The kiss fell apart, her lips grazing his chin as his skimmed her forehead, as they gripped each other, straining to be closer.

Dimly, he became aware that she was shaking. No, that was him.

He straightened for a little manly composure. "Shall we go in, my lady?" He offered his elbow.

Her eyes were a mess of tears. She dabbed at them with her gloved fingers and took his arm.

She raised her chin regally and answered, "Let's."

Talia took Adam's lifted elbow and he opened the scarred door to the club's main room.

They entered a court of the underworld.

The club was a concrete hole, just under street level. The low ceiling enhanced the impression of being buried underground.

As the door settled shut behind them, the gathering hushed and parted, revealing a wide, amaranth-red floor runner that glowed against the three-dimensional black on black of the interior. The symbolism was not lost on Talia, who'd been submerged in near-death research for half her life: amaranth signified immortality.

The runner terminated at a raised dais, the club's stage, where an ornately carved black Oriental chair waited. To one side sat Abigail, in a wheelchair, her body more shrunken than ever, her eyes a roil of shadow. To the other side stood Zoe, puffed up with importance.

Talia's stomach knotted and she froze on the threshold of the room.

Oh, please, no. The chair waited for her.

Adam started forward, and she had no choice but to follow. Either that or bolt back out the door, and since she wasn't letting the secretive man out of her sight again, she forced herself to move up the aisle.

The murmuring assembly to either side of her was in their funeral best, fashions ranging from modern Victorian to urban vampire. The women radiated powerful sexuality in corsets of leather and vinyl, some baring midriffs, fishnets, tattoos twisting with wicked thorns, beautiful and severe. Among them, one wore black tulle fashioned in a punky tutu, others in skintight leather pants, or peep show–short skirts. The men wore black pants, jeans, or combat fatigues, and some in elegant long leather coats that grazed the black floor to the effect of the wearer rising out of shadow. The coifs were black or electric with color, the styles varying from jagged-chic to glossy sheets. Makeup accentuated man and woman alike, some effeminate while others were fatalistically disturbing.

As soon as Talia reached the dais and turned, Zoe spoke. "For some time now we've all been aware of a growing threat. A demon has escaped into our world. He calls himself the Death Collector, because that is what he does, collect deaths. In so doing, he creates monsters of men. They can't die, but feed on people to keep themselves from devolving into ravening animals. Abigail's been promising an end will come. Well, the end is here."

Talia watched as Zoe's gaze slipped briefly to Adam. What were they up to?

"May I present to you a princess of the fae, daughter of Lord Death, Talia O'Brien. Talia, if you'd like to say something."

Wha—? Talia looked with alarm at Zoe. There were no secrets here.

Adam cleared his throat. "Talia is recovering from an injury at present and can't speak. But I would like to say thank you for your hospitality. For all the help you've given over the past day or so. As for the monsters out there, the wraiths, we have a plan and are doing everything that we can to stop their spread."

The gathering applauded.

Talia watched Adam turn to Zoe. "Can we have some music? Something slow. I'd like to dance with Talia."

Zoe nodded, looked thoughtful for a moment, then stepped to the side to whisper into the ear of someone just offstage.

Adam took Talia's hand and led her to the dance floor. Her breath quickened as the crowd parted. The gathering circled as Adam led her to the center of the space.

"A little bit of shadow, please," Adam asked her loud enough for everyone to hear. "No more hiding. Show them how you glow."

His words, coupled with the warmth in his eyes, did, indeed, light something in her. She bid the shadows to fall lightly on the room as the deep thrum of a bass guitar, beating like a heartbeat, signaled the start of their song.

Adam's arms went around her. Everything was going to be okay. The way they fit together so perfectly it just *had* to be. No demon or monster could triumph against anything so wonderful. Not when she'd finally found the answers she needed. The connection she needed.

The melody line of the slow song skipped over the rhythm, keening of haunting love. Adam stroked a hand up her back to rest on the skin at her shoulder, his fingers in her hair, his body moving slowly with hers.

"I'm going to have to take off for a while," he murmured.

Talia held her breath, her heart contracting with the falsehood she sensed in him. She had half a mind to confront him with it. But what would he think of her? Would he pull away at last?

"I've just got to do some legwork, and then I will be back," he said, his tone placating as if he knew she'd object.

"Can't you wait until this is over? I can come with you," Talia whispered. *Please let me come with you.*

"I have to speak with some informants. They're cagey. They won't talk to me with anyone else there."

Another lie. So be it.

Talia raised her chin and confronted him with her last secret. "You might as well know . . . I can feel what you feel. Another one of my freakish gifts."

His brows came together, but he didn't release her.

She continued, "You're lying to me. I know it. My whole body is screaming *lie*. Ever since we went after Custo, you've been different. Closed off."

"You feel what I feel." Adam grazed her forehead with his lips. "That makes sense. I knew you could see through me, I just didn't stop to think why."

"I should have told you—"

"Shhh. It's too late for regrets. What am I feeling now?"

Talia swallowed hard, let him turn her on the dance floor. "Grief."

"Custo—" Adam started. Talia felt him take a deep breath against her body. "Custo shouldn't have died like that. Tortured and broken."

Talia leaned back to look Adam in his eyes. "His death was not your fault."

Adam glanced away. "He was at my place, following my instructions, fighting my war. I may not have taken his life, but I sure as hell put him in the line of fire."

"He was fighting *my* war," Talia said. She could not explain the weight of responsibility she felt over Custo's death. If she'd just mastered her differences sooner, perhaps both he and Patty would still be alive.

"The world's war, then," Adam said. "The point is, he's gone. I'll get past it, but not until the demon is destroyed. In the meantime, I've got to work. There are some things I have to do alone. Set in motion. Later, you can help me scout out a new place for your convalescence. Somewhere with a little more privacy."

Another lie, but carried with such sweet love that she had to let it go.

The side of his mouth lifted in a kind of half smile. She'd have to settle for that, though she didn't like it.

"Now will you just dance with me?" Adam pulled her close again, not waiting for her answer.

Talia wound her arms around him tightly to keep him as close to her as she could, while she could. The melody soared higher to its climax, as if with hope, but the words were about loss. About sundered love.

What did Zoe know about the future to select such a song for her first dance with Adam?

"I'll be back in a couple of hours," Adam murmured, feathering a kiss across her lips. He led her from the floor.

Talia caught his surreptitious glance at Zoe when they returned to the chair at Abigail's side.

Zoe obviously knew plenty, and if Talia had to drown her in shadows to get some answers, she was going to do it. Adam was going nowhere without her.

NINETEEN

ADAM emerged from the dark fete into a muggy New York City night. Above him, a blocky road of glittery sky led through a concrete and glass corridor. The urban smells of stale exhaust, dank gutters, and a life mix of alcohol, food, and metal layered the city's vital, industrious air. He breathed deeply, taking it all in.

He was glad he was going to end the war at night. Night, like death, was the conclusion of one thing and the beginning of another. Night cast the world in shadow, and therefore, night was Talia's time. He headed for the deepest falls of darkness to be close to her as he headed toward death.

Adam kept to the alley and zigzagged through the laundry of an adjacent building north of Amaranth to cut across to Fourteenth Street.

No point in trying to track the ship Abigail called the *Styx*. Adam didn't trust his sources anymore, and instinct told him that he could accelerate a meeting with the Death Collector if he went through personal channels.

As he walked, he dialed his parents' number, the number to the picture-perfect family home in the Hamptons where the nightmare began.

Jacob's intervention.

Punching the combination of numbers released the

memory in the box again. Sounds, images, smells escaped to the surface of his consciousness: Jacob's distended jaw widening. His inhuman teeth. Dad's tumbled malt whiskey, its peaty smell permeating his study. Jacob's effortless clutch and sick kiss. Mom's piercing scream—Adam could still hear it in the back of his mind.

Never in the six intervening years did he think it would end like this.

The phone warbled at his ear. If there were a God in heaven, Jacob would pick up.

Jacob picked up. "Thorne," he said.

Rage skimmed cold and clammy over Adam's skin. How that monster could still use the family name—

Didn't matter. Not anymore. He calmed himself with a controlled breath.

"Hello, Jacob," Adam said. It was some comfort that he could still guess Jacob's movements. Jacob would've needed a place to stay after his escape from Segue. The family compound had everything he required, including the satisfaction of rubbing Adam's face in the painful dissolution of the Thorne family legacy.

Silence on Jacob's end, then, "It's only a matter of time before we find you and your . . . harpy."

Adam bit back a retort and stuck with his plan. He'd rehearsed several tacks in his mind; this seemed the best way to go.

"Well, you can consider me found," he said. "I need to speak with the demon. Talia wants to cut a deal. I'm acting as her intermediary."

Jacob grunted. "Whatever she has to say, you can say to me. I'll get him the message."

"No can do. I have to speak with him directly. In person. Nonnegotiable."

"Come now," Jacob said. "You've been fighting The Col-

lective for years. Caged me all that time. I doubt very much
that you would capitulate now."

Exactly so. This kind of change of heart would require a
tremendous inducement.

"Talia's pregnant," Adam said. He wished it were true, too.
Something of her, something of him to leave behind. A little hope for the future.

"Not likely," Jacob drawled. "Even if she did screw your
pathetic, mortal self, it would be way too soon to tell."

"Talia's half fae," Adam explained. "The rules of mortality don't apply to her. She says she can sense a spark of life
within her when she's in shadow. She bled some after the
attack on my loft and it scared her. We're willing to cut a
deal, the specifics of which I'll save for the demon."

"I don't believe you."

"You don't need to. Just contact the demon and ask him
what he wants to do. You've got my mobile number." Adam
ended the call. No more arguments. No going back.

Adam jogged down a row of cars parked along the street.
He'd need something without an alarm system, easy to hot-
wire.

He stopped short at a rusty piece of shit, window cracked
for summer ventilation and begging to be stolen. Too easy.
Adam stuck his fingers in the partition and forced the glass
down just enough to reach his arm over and open the button lock. He sat in the driver's seat and took the screwdriver
from his rear pocket that he'd lifted from the stash of random tools near the DJ station at the club.

His mobile phone rang as he inserted the screwdriver into
the ignition and turned it like a key. The car started right up.

Adam answered, "Thorne," same as his brother.

"He'll see you," Jacob said without preamble.

Good. "Where do you want me to meet you?"

"Come on up to the house. We'll take a stroll down memory

lane." Jacob's tone was upbeat with sarcasm. This time Jacob hung up on him.

It had been six years since Adam drove the two and a half hours of summer traffic to Southampton. At that time the gridlock was extremely tedious—he'd had better things to do than answer his mother's summons for some trouble over Jacob. What trouble could Jacob, businessman extraordinaire and favored son of the Thorne legacy, possibly have? No trouble was too difficult for Jacob's ambition and ego to surmount.

It was ego and ambition that was the problem.

But now the drive went quickly, traffic at night was thin and fast, speeding Adam's way out of the city and into oblivion. The greenery of Sunrise Highway blurred on the edge of his vision as time melted the distance to a reunion with his brother.

No, not his brother. His brother was dead.

Suddenly Adam was on Gin Road, the narrow lane of tall walls and hedges behind which New York elite lived during the summer season. Neither he nor his brother would be going to any of the formal parties anymore.

The gate to Thorne House parted before Adam could buzz his arrival, and he started down the gravel drive that led to the beachfront compound. The main house was lit up, every room ablaze so that the sweeping lines of the white summer home gleamed against the deep sky.

The message was clear: No shadows welcome here. Only Life.

Jacob was right to be suspicious.

Before Adam parked the car in the wide circular drive, he took the vial of L-pills from his pants and popped one into his mouth to hold in the pocket of his gum line. The rubber coating would protect him until the moment he was introduced to the demon. Then a quick grind between his back molars. Death would be uncomfortable, but relatively quick.

Adam's heart leaped once, a last-ditch complaint against its planned demise, but he thought of Talia. He wouldn't have her bleeding and ruined like Custo. Not when there was something he could do about it.

Adam got out of the car and started toward the front door of the house.

Déjà vu. Six years. Full circle. Home.

Mom and Dad wanted an intervention. Well, Adam was about to intervene.

Four steps led to the elegant front door. That was Mom— elegant and formal, even on vacation. Adam gripped the handle and opened the door, each movement an echo of the memory of the last time he was here.

No. *This* was the last time, Adam reminded himself.

The entryway was white. Clean. Graceful. A chandelier sparkled overhead like suspended drops of magical rain over a round marble table, where Mom would've had a bowlful of colorful flowers to break up the coldness of the space. And beyond, the living room, the panoramic windows of the night-black ocean brightened by the lit series of decks that led to the sand. Everything in its place. So much of Mom here.

And Jacob, the new Lord and Master of the Thorne family summer home, where was he?

"In here," Jacob called.

Dad's study, where Jacob had killed him.

Adam walked the long hallway to the French doors of Dad's private space, his refuge of "work" when Mom's friends were over.

Steeling himself, Adam pushed open the door.

Jacob sat, straight-backed, behind Dad's desk, as if he thought he belonged there. Adam's vision went red. If he had carried a weapon, he might have used it.

Instead, he fisted his hands, his knuckles aching with the

pressure. Talia. He didn't fight for Mom and Dad anymore. They were gone, lost to the past. Talia was the future.

Jacob wore a gray pin-striped vest, white shirt, and tie—Adam had called him *The Banker* long before any of this happened. Jacob threw a pen onto the papers spread about on the desk and relaxed into Dad's leather chair.

"I'm just going over Thorne finances. By my rough accounting, you've spent nearly fifty million in six years." Jacob mimicked Dad's tone, the one he'd used whenever Adam had exceeded his allowance and drew on his company account for whatever lark he was up to that week.

"Closer to a hundred, I should think. I tapped the overseas accounts," Adam said. His current pursuit was far from a lark.

Jacob sneered with distaste. "What a waste. And now you want to play house with that little whore?"

A cold wave of rage rolled over Adam. His voice was rough, almost broken when he spoke. "Talia is not a whore."

"Well she spread her legs for you, and her mother spread her legs for Death." Jacob smirked at having finally hit a nerve. He laced his fingers across his stomach and rested his elbows on the armrests of Dad's chair.

Adam's tongue touched the little pill in his mouth. A bite, a grind, and Death himself could answer Jacob's taunt. But his brother was no longer his responsibility. Talia was.

With effort, Adam let the insult to her go. It'd be unwise to let the argument escalate. There was a good chance Jacob would lose his grip on whatever vestiges of civility lurked in his monster mind and turn wraith. Much better to keep him on track.

"Will the demon be joining us here?"

Jacob stood and pulled down his vest as he walked around Dad's desk.

A flicker of movement and Adam reeled backward, his body slamming against the built-in bookshelf to the right of the door. Pain knifed through his jaw. He blinked hard against the spots swimming in his vision and focused again on his brother.

Jacob seemingly remained stationary, adjusting a cuff link on his sleeve with too-nimble fingers. The cuff was dotted with red. "You've stained my shirt. Now I'll have to change."

So fast. Too fast. Must have just fed.

The pill was still hard in Adam's mouth. He shoved it aside with his tongue and spat blood. Straightening, he said, "The demon—"

Another flicker of movement and pain exploded behind his eyes. The room swam. Adam's back connected with the edge of a piece of furniture, which broke with a resounding crack. Thick, wet heat trailed out of his nose and smeared across his cheek as he landed facedown on the rug.

"Disgusting, Adam. Bleeding like an animal." Jacob planted a foot on the center of Adam's back, along his spine, bearing down so that Adam's nerves radiated SOS signals in hot electrical currents outward from the point of contact.

"How I'd love to break you in half," Jacob said, voice on edge.

"You're the animal. You've just fed and you're still out of control," Adam gasped.

The pressure intensified.

"Sitting behind my father's desk as if you were still a human being," Adam continued, the rug rough on his jaw. Muscles contracted over his scalp as his spine bowed.

"My father, too." Jacob dug in and pain roared through the long muscles of Adam's back.

"No, the demon's your father. Your keeper. You answer to him."

"And why not? He gave me immortality. What is Thorne money to the power of time?"

"My father gave you immortality, too. It's called a soul."

"Dad was weak. The demon is not." The pressure abruptly disappeared.

Adam fought the gorge in his throat as he pushed himself up to his knees. "Is there a meeting or not?"

Jacob shrugged. "Yes. Yes. He wants to see you. But he permits no death near him, so you'll have to lose the little pill you've got in your mouth."

Adam flushed, then chilled. He touched the pill with his tongue again.

"Did I mention that the demon can see the future?" Jacob laughed.

The Sight.

"He saw this coming." Jacob nudged Adam's shoulder with the toe of his shoe. "Even had me come here to wait for you. You're that predictable."

Adam was certain that Zoe knew full well what he intended to do. If he were destined to fail, why didn't they stop him? He might have made a different decision.

"I'm going to need that little pill, and then we can go meet with the Death Collector," Jacob said.

Crush it now and end Jacob? A week ago, Adam wouldn't have thought twice. Even now, the temptation was sticky sweet, muting the pain that throbbed in his face and back. Oh, how he'd love to see Jacob's expression when Death struck him down.

Jacob's mouth tricked up. "I know you won't use it on me, Brother. Not even for Mom and Dad."

Abigail had to have seen a chance. Crazy old bat had to have seen this eventuality.

Adam spat the pill onto the rug and raised his face to Jacob. Voice thick with sarcasm, he said, "Okay, then. Take me to your master."

Jacob rolled his eyes, then lashed out an arm. Connected. The world shuddered dark.

* * *

"If I could just take a deep breath, maybe I wouldn't feel so light-headed." Talia made a show of reaching over her shoulder for the ties lacing her snugly into the corset. The rasp in her voice made her lie that much more convincing.

"Sure," Zoe said. "I guess I should've thought about that, what with your injury and all. I'm sorry."

Talia walked into the dressing room and waited until Zoe closed the door behind her. The club's pumping music rounded into muted thumps and whines.

The click of the lock made Talia's pulse jump with satisfaction.

Now for a little information.

Zoe stepped deeper into the room and Talia pulled shadows down. Layered darkness surged into the room and all sense of mortality was blotted out entirely.

"Talia?" Zoe's voice was thin in the dark.

Talia took Zoe's hand, shared her senses with her, just as Zoe's fear coursed across their connection. No wonder people needed to be ushered across the divide of death. Humanity would be utterly lost without the fae.

Zoe's gaze found her and focused. Her eyes were wide with alarm. "What's going on?"

"I wanted to have a private chat with you," Talia said softly, careful of her voice. "Just you and me, with absolutely no interruptions."

Zoe swallowed audibly. "What about?"

"Adam."

"Uh . . . What about him?"

"Where is he?"

Zoe's eyes flicked to the right, preparing to lie. "I don't know. Didn't he tell you?"

"No, he didn't." Damn him. "But I know you know."

Zoe fidgeted with her feet, but met Talia's gaze. "I have no idea. Honestly."

Honestly? Even now Zoe's emotions communicated her duplicity.

"You're lying. You know where he went."

"I don't. Now let me go—you're scaring me." Zoe pulled her hand out of Talia's grasp.

Talia knew the dark would swallow her, deafen her, choke her with its absolute vacuum of stimuli. She let the horror of that isolation settle in for a moment.

When Zoe began to shake, Talia touched her shoulder lightly and leaned into her ear. "I'm a banshee. I'm supposed to be fucking terrifying."

"Let me out of here right now." Zoe's heart had to be beating furiously. The surrounding shadows trembled with her. Her terror swept across the fluid veils.

Talia was unaffected. The little brat was going to spill if Talia had to make her pee her pants in fright to do so. "Tell me where Adam went."

"I don't know." Zoe shrugged definitively. Her eyes shined with tears, reflective like mirrors in the magic of darkness.

Talia kept her voice whisper low. "Then we're at an impasse. We'll just have to stay right here until we can come to some kind of agreement." How to speed this up? Her turn to lie. "However, you should probably know that it may not be good for you to remain in my shadows for any length of time. These are the shadows of death and will by nature have an adverse effect on your longevity."

Zoe rolled her eyes, batting away the wetness. "Abigail says I live to old age."

Talia's laugh burned in her throat. "Abigail can't see the fae. There's no way she could see this coming."

"You wouldn't hurt me." Zoe crossed her arms over her chest.

"But I am hurting you. Right now. How bad it gets is up to you."

She released Zoe's shoulder and stepped back, allowing the screaming nothingness to inundate her again. Talia whipped the veils to quicken her thinking process, to goad her fear into real panic.

Zoe's chest hitched as her breathing became irregular. Her heart beat frantically as black eyeliner ran down her cheeks and her trembles turned into full-bodied shakes.

Stupid kid. All dressed up to welcome Death. Truth was, she didn't welcome death any more than anyone else.

As if in agreement, Zoe spoke, "He went to the *Styx*. To destroy the demon Death Collector."

Shock washed Talia's skin with ice. She dropped her shadows abruptly and the veils hissed back out of existence.

"He went where?" It was her turn to be horrified. "How did he plan to accomplish that? I thought only I could call Shadowman!"

"Adam found a way." Zoe stepped back, her hand reaching for the doorknob.

Talia lifted the shadows again, flung out a hand, and held the door closed with a wave of darkness. "What way did he find?"

"Uh . . . I . . ." Zoe didn't finish her answer, and Talia didn't want her to. The implications were already spinning. Back at Segue, Philip had spoken of a way. An ancient death rite. To usher an immortal monster out of the world, someone had to sacrifice their life. A life to balance out death. Adam had fought the idea then. But now, he couldn't possibly intend to— He did.

Over her dead body.

Talia grabbed at the back of her skirt. When the clasp wouldn't come undone, she yanked hard on the fabric at the waistline, ripping it. The skirt puddled at her feet. The slip followed. She didn't have time to wrestle with the corset, not when Adam could be facing the demon at any moment.

"There was no stopping him, Talia." Zoe's words tumbled out in a rush. "Abigail said he was going to go, no matter what. He wouldn't listen to her when she said he couldn't win against the Death Collector. She couldn't stop him."

"Maybe *she* couldn't," Talia snapped back, throat aching, "but *I* could have."

Damn Abigail and Zoe to hell. How hard would it possibly have been to lock him in a room for a couple of days? How hard would it be to counter his decision with one of their own? Change the future.

"We acted in your best interests. Me and Abigail *and* Adam. What will be, will be. You need to heal. If his way doesn't work, then your scream is the only thing that can save us. You can be safe here."

"You'll tell me exactly where he is and how to get there, or I swear I will kill you myself." With no other clothes available, Talia yanked on the skinny black leggings Zoe had worn before the party. Talia shoved her feet into Zoe's discarded combat boots.

Zoe's gaze hardened. "I can't tell you that."

"Can't or won't?" Talia's voice rasped. No way to scream. Frustration at her weakness had her snapping the laces as she tightened them.

"Won't. When you're healed, then—"

"By the time I'm healed, Adam will be dead." Talia stood. "And why should I care about saving the world if Adam isn't in it?"

Talia ignored Zoe's stricken face, took her roughly by the arm and made for the rear exit, dragging her out into the night.

"There's no stopping him," Zoe said.

"There's no stopping me either," Talia said. "Where do I go?"

When Zoe hesitated, Talia gripped harder and shook. "Where, damn it?" Her voice broke and she had to work for air.

"The ferry waits at the Seventy-ninth Street Boat Basin."

"Ferry to where?"

"The *Styx*. It's a boat, the Death Collector's lair."

Talia gathered shadow as she pulled Zoe down the slim lane of the alley to its junction at the street. Not a busy street, by any means. Dirty, littered, undoubtedly dangerous. Gang tags decorated a boarded building on the corner. A few blocks up, cars chased each other through a busy intersection. They could get a cab there.

The combination of anger and shadow gave Talia the strength to haul Zoe's sniveling ass down the three blocks to the intersection. She'd have preferred to have left the girl back at the club, where she'd be safe, but who knew what important tidbits she'd left out? Talia didn't trust the girl for a second.

For that matter, she didn't trust Adam either.

Stupid man. What did he think he was doing? Going off and leaving her with a bunch of freaky babysitters. She'd kill him when she found him, if he weren't already dead. And if he were dead, she'd call his sorry ghost back from Beyond and kill him all over again. Stupid, *arrogant* man.

When Talia reached the corner, she held her free hand up in the air while Zoe sulked.

"The Death Collector will kill you," Zoe said. Her expression was partly mutinous, partly imploring. "I won't be party to your death. You can't make me go."

"Oh, you're going all right." A taxi pulled up to the curb. Talia opened the door and pushed her inside. Roughly.

"Where to?" the taxi driver asked.

"Seventy-ninth Street Boat Basin," Zoe muttered.

The cabbie shook his head. "No, ladies. They haven't caught the Riverside Park murderer yet. I'm not taking you there."

Zoe mouthed the word *wraith* with a look of triumph. "The park borders the dock," she explained. "Someone or something in the park is preying on stupid people who venture there. It's all but deserted now."

Talia ignored the implied insult. "Sir, I'm going straight to the dock. I promise I won't linger in the park. I'll be safe."

The man shrugged and pulled away from the curb into traffic.

Zoe sneered over her shoulder at Talia. "I don't know what you think you're going to do. How can you possibly help Adam now? All you'll accomplish is to ruin the world's chance at destroying the Death Collector."

Talia smiled. "Not so. If Adam fails, and if I fail, then there is a world full of people who can give it a try themselves, sacrifice themselves to kill the demon." Her voice grated painfully over the words, probably ruining all the healing she'd done that day. But her words did the trick.

Zoe went white.

"That's right. Anyone, even you, can teach the Death Collector to die. You can lecture me all you want when you're prepared to face him yourself. Until then, shut up and let me think."

Okay. So the scream was gone. She still had her shadows. She couldn't kill the demon, but maybe she could rescue Adam's sorry—but mighty fine—ass. He rescued her, once upon a time. In that alley in Arizona, he'd pitted himself, weaponless, against a wraith and they'd come out alive. She could do the same for him now. Damn him.

The taxi traveled down West Seventy-ninth, dipped under an overpass rumbling with traffic, and turned into a wide circular drive surrounded by trees, presumably the lethal Riverside Park. The black ribbon of the Hudson River glimmered beyond, the city lights twinkling on the water. Its smell infiltrated the cab, yeasty and rotten.

Goose bumps spread up Talia's back and across her scalp.

"Stop here," Zoe said. She gestured to a break in the concrete barrier. "Down the steps. Keep to the sidewalk. You'll want the *Charon*—it's moored at the dock on the far right. The *deserted* one, you know, as in deserted because everyone knows to stay away. The ferryman will take you to the *Styx*, but please don't make me go. I've seen what the wraiths do. I want to live."

"If you've left anything out . . ." Talia began hoarsely.

"I haven't. Go on and die now, if you want, just leave me here."

"Fine." Talia got out and slammed the door.

"Lady?" The driver asked, leaning out his window. "You sure?"

"I'm sure."

Talia didn't look back as the taxi pulled away. She followed the concrete road to the steps, and then jogged down those to the center of the lower level of the concrete circle. A deserted café was dark and shuttered. The place echoed with silence.

Though deep in her shadowy cloak, Talia's heart hammered as she traveled down the sidewalk and across the jog path. The gate to the pier was open, as if the ferryman were expecting her.

Something knocked against the planking with a lonely, hollow sound. Exactly the sound her heart was making in its own mooring.

At the end of a walkway, a man stood, leaning on a staff. She couldn't make out much about him, but by the hunch of his shoulders, he seemed very old.

Talia released her cloaking veils as she approached.

He blinked up at her sudden appearance, but didn't stop chewing on the gristle of his white-bearded chin. His face was weathered and wrinkled like a brown paper sack. The faded plaid shirt he wore was far too warm for the summer night.

"Hello," she said.

He chewed.

Talia frowned. "I need to get to the *Styx*. I was told you could take me."

The old man chewed his whiskers again. "It'll cost you."

Damn it. "I don't have any money with me, but I will come back tomorrow and pay you whatever you ask. I promise."

The old man grunted. "I'll take you to the *Styx* for a lock of that gold faery hair."

The man seemed out of myth himself; Talia was not surprised that he could name her origins.

"A lock of hair?"

He nodded and gestured to a boat with an open-air seating area in the back. The interior was dirty, with a crust and smear of brownish red covering the rear seat. Probably blood.

Talia's stomach rolled with nausea. "Okay."

The old man pulled a pocketknife out of his pants pocket. He held the wood handle, glossy with age and handling, and flicked open a blade. He reached up and cut a curl from the mass on Talia's shoulder.

"Done," he said, sniffing at the curl. "Climb aboard."

Talia scrambled down into the boat, sat at the edge of the malodorous filth, and held on for dear life.

The old man went to a grimy control panel and started the engine roaring. He angled out of the slip, away from the hum of the city, and into the lurching dark waters of the river.

No going back now.

TWENTY

THE *Charon* left the glittering banks of the Hudson behind. Talia tensed her body against the deep vibration of its engine and the choppy bounce of its progress on the water. Her nerves already had her stomach roiling. She couldn't afford the extra encouragement of the boat's movement. At least the speed of their passage brushed away the onboard smell of decay and whipped her hair in a sweet wind of revitalizing water spray.

They angled into dark waters spotted by the gleam of other boats, small and large. In spite of the considerable haze of the city's light pollution, the sky above was brilliantly starcrusted, as if heaven had finally brought its attention to the goings-on of Earth.

Faster, faster, Talia urged.

The shoreline fell behind. All hope of safety dimmed as the lights grew smaller. They traveled into an ocean of rippling darkness, as if toward the end of the world. She sought no refuge now, no hiding place from monsters or herself. All that was in her past. Running away was not an option, not when everything that mattered—good and bad—lay in front of her.

And suddenly, hell loomed on the deep.

The *Styx* was a great upside-down anvil of a war cruiser, its deck blazing with the kind of light that drew misguided moths. The armored vessel hulked under the starlight, a product of industry and war, fitted and braced against nature.

Talia's heart stuttered at the sight. No doubt the *Styx* had long seen the *Charon's* approach. The demon Death Collector had to know someone was coming—another person ready to trade their humanity for immortality.

The old man brought the boat alongside the great ship with a wrenching scrape and idled near a narrow ladder. He turned, the pallor of his skin sickly yellowed in the ship's light.

"The *Styx*." He cocked his head at the wall of gray steel.

Talia's nausea peaked as the wind died and the *Charon* rocked. She clenched her teeth against throwing up and gripped the side of the boat as mute terror blanked her mind.

"You want me to take you back?" The old man didn't look like he cared much either way.

Talia shook her head slightly, so as not to be sick.

She could do this. Only yesterday her shadows had protected her and Adam during the failed attempt to save Custo's life. And in shadow, she could manipulate objects with her mind. The combination of abilities would get her to Adam and then get them both to safety. She wasn't asking for more than that. The destruction of the demon who called himself the Death Collector could wait for another time.

Right now was for Adam.

Her fear transmuted into an electric clarity that ran in a bristling current, just under her skin.

Talia stood, gathering shadow from the night. The cold, veils of darkness hung off her shoulders in billowing layers, at the ready. She pulled them more tightly around her to mask her boarding as she took hold of the ladder.

The rungs were chilly and wet on her hands.

A wraith—a woman with the slender face of an angel—

leaned down the ladder to look for the demon's newest supplicant.

Talia waited, heart pounding. Below, the *Charon* pulled away, leaving her one choice. Up.

"Must have chickened out," the wraith called to the others and ducked out of sight.

Talia continued her climb, and near the top she glanced about the deck. To one side, a raised helipad hosted a faster mode of transportation to and from the ship. Handy. Wraiths clustered nearby. Ten, twelve, their attention directed on a pair that were sparring. The cracking blows they landed each other would have killed any normal person.

With this distraction, Talia crawled on deck.

Across a flat gray expanse was a narrow doorway, rectangular with rounded edges, leading to the interior of a bulky metal structure.

She forced herself to breathe more slowly, her heart to ease its frantic pace. Freaking out would help no one. She'd start with inside rooms and work through the ship. Check every corner, carefully and methodically.

Buried in shadows, Talia kept to the edge of the deck as she moved toward the door. She insinuated herself along the natural shades of dark and light that fell in the sharp lines of the ship's construction.

She glanced at the *Charon*, now a spark in the distance.

A deep-toned click and snap on deck brought Talia's head back around.

The door was open, a figure just emerging.

A single glimpse of dense blackness, and time ground to a halt. The Earth stopped spinning on its axis. The ocean stilled and the stars winked out.

All of Talia's senses were overridden by a roar of static in her ears.

The thing that crossed the threshold was *Wrong*. He might call himself the Death Collector, might style himself as a giver of immortal youth, but Talia's mind and soul rang with the more apt term, *demon*.

Had it not been for her grip on the side of the ship, Talia would have fallen to the deck in revulsion.

The demon was a snaking horror of black absence fitted in a sinuous twist around the body of a man. His human host. Deep in shadow, Talia could see the slick offal of the demon penetrating the host to his core. Whoever the man might've been was gone, his identity destroyed. Now his body, used and broken, shared his life with a terrible intelligence in writhing misery. Expression vacant, jaw slack, the man moved as if in a long nightmare, looking only for an end. Whatever end that might be was clearly beyond his caring.

The thought that Adam faced that horror stripped Talia of all hope that he might still be alive. The wraith soul-suckers were bothersome insects compared to the genocidal seethe of the demon. The only being powerful enough to destroy that *thing*, that condensation of defiling chaos, was Shadowman. Shadowman could be demon enough himself if need be. He and he alone could cut the demon out of the world.

A sudden pressure welled up inside her.

Scream. Now. Right now. Pour every drop of fae blood into one piercing sound. More instinct than impulse, the need was sharp and urgent.

Talia stifled a groan of abject frustration. Her throat ached to call her father, yet screaming was impossible with the constant suffocation that choked her. A wasted effort. Tears streamed down her face at her impotence.

She swallowed the gorge of sound with a shudder. Today was for Adam, but she would be back. She would open her mouth and shred the sky. The demon would know Death.

The wraiths on deck stopped their rough play and stood

in a thrall of attention, regarding the demon snake and his human host.

The host cleared the threshold and held the door to allow three snarling dogs to join him. Like great, rabid wolves, the dogs' ears were pinned back, heads lowered. Their golden eyes peered in her direction.

No, not in her direction. They looked directly at her.

Talia stopped breathing and pressed her body into the metal wall at the edge of the ship as her heart gulped for oxygen.

The host's face contracted into a half smile while the rest of his expression remained sallow and dumb, as if the demon had pulled a marionette string at the edge of the man's sagging mouth.

"Banshee," the host said. His voice grated as the demon puppeted him. "These are my hellhounds. They were bred in shadows far darker than yours. Shall I loose them to fetch you or will you come out and talk to me yourself?"

The dogs slavered in anticipation, wicked yellow teeth bared.

Talia's heart clamored with alarm. Shadow had always been her refuge.

"Banshee. Though I have forever, I find I am impatient at present." The host's gaze slid to her. "I punish sneaking and subterfuge. Yours is the second attempt on my life tonight, and I guarantee that the other is regretting his actions now. I grow weary of being distracted from my work. Come out. Now."

The second attempt on his life? Had to be Adam.

And if Adam "regretted" anything, he had to be alive to do so.

Alive. Talia clung to that as she released the shadow at her shoulders.

"Ah. There you are." The black coil of demon turned his

host's head. "Welcome, Banshee. You needn't have boarded my ship like a diseased rat. The invitation has always been open for you."

Talia remembered how months ago the wraiths had come to collect her for a "date" with their master. She'd discovered her scream too late to save Melanie.

Whatever the demon wanted with her— *No, thank you.*

"I'd—" Talia's hoarse voice broke. She tried again. "I'd rather die than become one of those things." She flicked a glance at the gathered wraiths. One sneered back at her and worked his lower jaw in a threat, as if he could accommodate her declaration.

"No. No. That hungry life is not for you," the host said. In his human eyes, a glimmer of surprise, contradicting the assurance of his demon-puppeted speech.

Perhaps the man was still in there after all.

"If you were to become a wraith," he continued, "you could not bear me a child."

Talia froze, midbreath. Her gaze shifted from the host to the demon and back again.

Bear him a what?

"Don't look so shocked," the host said. "If Death can get a child on a mortal woman, then surely I can get one on a Twilight half-breed. Our union will greatly accelerate the plans I have already put in motion with the wraiths, ensuring my success. The trifold combination of mortal, Twilight, and demon blood in one being will destroy the boundary between the mortal world and Twilight forever. No Death. And without Death, the heavens will fall as well, and I will reign over the ensuing chaos."

Talia's already tight stomach turned and she retched on the deck.

The host inclined his head. "Granted, our intercourse

will not be pleasurable for you, nor will the pregnancy. But I think the delivery will be worst."

Talia swallowed to clear her mouth. "No. Never."

She'd jump over the side first. Drown. There was no way she'd allow the demon to touch her. Not that way. Not any way.

The host's lips pulled into a smile while his eyes wandered, at odds.

"We'll see," the host said. "How about we discuss the matter with your sweetheart? He claimed you were pregnant already, but that isn't so, is it?"

Sweetheart. Yes, Adam was that, but also so much more. He was her Reason. He was her model of courage, of strength, of endurance. It would be pure joy to give *him* a child.

Talia's eyes prickled with unshed tears. That future was all but lost.

"Jacob's been playing with him for a while now." The host worked up another false smile. "I should check on his progress. If I know Jacob, the upstart Adam Thorne should be all but broken."

Talia raised her chin. The demon might know Jacob, but he obviously didn't know Adam. Every cell of her body ached for what Adam must be suffering, but she had complete faith that the light of his soul was as bright as ever.

"You disagree?" The demon tried to inject mirth into the host's tone, but he still sounded lifeless and sour.

Talia remained silent. She didn't want to goad him to hurt Adam any more than he already had.

"Why don't we go see, shall we? Let's see how your Adam fares." The host's head jerked toward the group of wraiths. "Martin, bring our lady banshee along. I'm finally about to be entertained."

* * *

"Blink once for yes, and twice for yes-right-now." Jacob's laugh puffed fetid air on Adam's face.

Adam closed his eyes, shutting out the small, windowless utility room and his brother's contorted expression. Adam tightly sealed his eyes so there could be no confusion: *Never. Ever. Would he become a wraith.*

He would have answered a definitive and resounding NO, but his mouth was taped shut. He'd have flipped Jacob the bird, but his hands were taped behind his back and had long since gone numb.

"How much do you want to bet you will?" Jacob sounded happy. Delighted even. The tables had been turned, and he was enjoying every minute of it.

Adam kept his eyes closed and assessed his situation. There was no getting out of here alive. Not only was he bound to a chair like Custo had been, but he was pinned to the chair by a knife in his side. The blade pierced the flesh at his side and was rammed into the wooded backrest. Hurt like bloody hell.

But maybe . . . just maybe . . . if he pulled hard and fast against the blade, he'd hit something vital and bleed out quickly. Maybe he could bring on Shadowman yet.

Something clicked—the latch of the door—and a rush of rotten air circulated through his holding cell.

A wave of dank hopelessness swamped Adam. He could name the source of the feeling: the demon and his host were back. The demon's dogs whined in the corridor.

Adam gritted his teeth in a show of pain to cover his inner determination. Providence had just handed him the opportunity of a lifetime. Just a few more moments to let the demon get all the way inside the room and Adam would throw his weight to the side to drag the blade into his belly. He prayed the knife was razor sharp.

Ready, set, g—

A woman sobbed, low and hoarse.

Adam froze, his thundering heart clutching hard. He opened his eyes.

The demon snake and his host entered, grin jacked up while his eyes wildly tracked around the room. Behind him, Talia was grasped in the unforgiving hands of a wraith.

The sight was a sucker punch to Adam's soul.

Talia. How? Had to be a trick.

Talia swayed forward with a choked cry, but the wraith brought her roughly back.

Not a trick. She was really there.

Adam's myriad hurts vanished beneath a storm-surge of terror. The threat of Jacob's kiss was nothing to this. In fact, nothing Jacob could do to his person scared him anymore.

Abigail had warned him that he hadn't yet known true fear. He should have listened when he had the chance. True fear has nothing to do with what might happen to you, however painful or vile that might be. True fear is all about what might happen to someone you love.

The host canted his head toward Jacob. "I told you I don't tolerate weapons aboard my ship."

Jacob huffed and pulled the knife out of Adam's side with a searing twist. "He's tied to the chair. He can't do anything."

With the knife gone, the chance was lost. Panic shuddered Adam, but a glance at Talia's white face, and he brought himself sharply under control. The only thing he had left under his power was himself. Giving in to fear would not help anything. He had to hold it together for her. Stay with her to the end.

"Are you arguing with me?" The snaking black demon flexed its menace on the host's body.

Jacob ducked his head in sudden obedience. "Of course not."

The host gestured, sharp and perfunctory. Jacob handed the blade to the other wraith, who released Talia and left the room. The door shut with a devastating click.

Talia dropped to the floor at Adam's knees, her hands fluttering at his side where the blade had pierced him. Blood now seeped through his shirt, but not enough for a mortal injury; Jacob had chosen the spot too well.

Jacob grabbed a fistful of Talia's hair to haul her upright again. She whimpered as her shoulders followed the oblique angle of her body.

Adam strained against his bonds, growling.

"Let her be," the host said. "This will go more quickly if they have a moment together."

Talia fell back onto Adam's lap. Adam ached to pull her into his arms, to cover her body with his so she could be safe. No torture was more painful than Talia, weeping on his lap.

Finally she brought her shining upturned eyes to his.

Adam's gaze fixed on hers with a million questions. Why was she here? Why wasn't she hiding in shadow? She could do things in shadow. Escape. Save herself.

Of course she understood him. Of all the people on this earth, Talia was the only one who could really understand him.

"I couldn't let you do it alone," she said, her voice rasping with effort. "You should have waited for me."

I couldn't risk losing you.

"You should have trusted me." Talia worked her fingers on the tape on his face.

I had to protect you. The harsh reality was that he couldn't protect her. He'd tried everything, and still had fallen short.

"You can't just run off to save the world whenever you want. I need you," she said. The tape burned as she stripped it off.

"I love you," Adam said. He needed those to be the first words out of his mouth. Something right amid so much wrong. "I had to do *something*."

"You still can," the host interrupted.

Adam brought his gaze up to the demon and his host. The host lifted a hand to Talia's hair and wound a blonde curl around his finger.

The demon. Touching Talia.

"You've been a thorn in my side—" The host paused expectantly.

Adam got the joke, but he wasn't about to laugh for a demon.

"—for some time now. I would take great satisfaction, and make significant progress in my plans, were you to join my army of wraiths."

Dread pooled within Adam. He could see where this was going.

The host's gaze darted back and forth between him and Talia, expressive and emoting. It seemed the man, independent of the demon, had taken an interest in the proposal that the demon used his human lips to form.

"If you accept my offer of immortality, I will give the banshee the gift of time. I will allow her off my ship. Give her a day to run and hide before I hunt for her again."

Adam didn't want to hear the "or."

"Or, I will rape her now, before your eyes, and get my child on her."

Talia clamped her hands over Adam's ears, but too late. He'd already heard.

"No no no no no," she croaked. "Don't listen to him. Don't even think about it."

Tears streaked black makeup down the face he loved. Even with all that goth gunk, she was beautiful. So much magic in such a small package.

Adam had seen what had been done to Custo. Saw how his friend had been wrenched to death. He knew he couldn't watch Talia be defiled before his eyes and not do something about it. The mere thought of her desecration sent excruciating pain searing through his veins.

With a painful snap, something broke inside Adam. Something vital, essential to life. Something that connected him to Talia, Segue, and his lost family. Something that set him apart from everything he loved. The demon had just effortlessly named the price of his soul.

"No no no no no." Talia sobbed against his shoulder, seeking comfort he couldn't, wouldn't, give.

Adam strained his head away from her. He couldn't bear her frantic touch, the sound of hurt in her voice. If anyone could weaken his resolve, she could, and it would take every ounce of will he possessed to do this last thing.

The host's head cocked in an affectation of thinking. "Actually, my plan would be best served by fucking her now. Jacob could hold her down, if necessary. As much as you and your Segue have been a constant irritation—"

"—I'll do it," Adam interrupted, though he knew the demon was now playing with him for sport. "I'll become a wraith."

"No." Talia's voice was a sob-clogged whisper. Shadows shuddered with her surge of horror and dread. She took Adam's head in her hands to make him face her again. To look into his eyes and compel a different answer out of him. She was already on her knees. Now she used her position to beg. *Please, anything but a wraith.* She could not imagine a worse fate for him than to become the thing he'd dedicated his life to destroy. She refused to be the means of his undoing.

Adam kept his chin firmly to the side, the muscles in his jaw flexing with effort, his gaze refusing to meet hers.

"Don't do this, Adam," she rasped. "Take it back. You can still make a different choice. They'll find me anyway. The demon has hellhounds that can see in shadow. I can't evade them. You'd be doing this for nothing."

The door opened behind her. Talia could hear the dogs whine. For a moment, she thought the beasts would be brought in to demonstrate her point, but instead the host said, "I'll need my cup," to someone outside the small room.

"Adam, why won't you listen to me? Please, listen to me!" For all her efforts, her voice was a harsh whisper; she could barely hear herself.

The door opened again—Talia whipped her head around to see what awful thing was next—and the cup was handed in. An old-fashioned goblet of sorts.

The host held it while the demon snake belched black tar to the brim. Talia could smell its sulfurous reek paces away. Something about the stuff echoed the tar coating her throat.

"You'll need to drink this," the host said to Adam, lifting the cup as if to toast.

Oh please God no.

But he obviously didn't care. For whatever stupid, cosmic reason, neither God nor Shadowman was going to help her. Talia glanced at Adam's inscrutable expression. She was in this nightmare alone.

Well, they couldn't have him.

Talia stood in front of Adam's chair and faced the demon, her feet braced for maximum stability. *Over her dead body.* She hoped the demon would take her challenge literally.

The only way the demon was going to get through her with his revolting brew was if he killed her. Which would be just groovy, because then Shadowman would come and cut his disgusting, slimy black hide to pieces.

"I've made my choice, Talia," Adam said behind her. "Now get out of the way."

Adam's tone made the small room drop thirty degrees, and bitter goose bumps raced across Talia's skin. She braced against the cold. She could be stubborn, too.

The host smirked awkwardly at her, though the man's eyes were wide with acute horror and sadness. Talia found it ironic that the human half of that demon-host marriage should empathize with her situation, especially since his choice was the first to give the demon power.

Well, if that coward wanted forgiveness, he'd have to look elsewhere.

The host's gaze seemed to read her answer, because it dulled again, the man retreating back into the shadows of his mind. Still choosing the easy way.

She wouldn't.

"I'm not moving," Talia said. The room darkened, shadows stirring with her inner turmoil as if a gale circled the room.

Jacob stepped toward her, but the host raised his hand to stop him.

"Release Adam," the host said to Jacob. "Let him deal with her. He has to take the cup himself anyway. The banshee will settle when he becomes a wraith."

Not likely.

Jacob moved around Adam's chair. Talia heard the tape at Adam's hands rip.

Adam stood, his arms dropping to his sides, fingers flexing to restore circulation. His expression was closed and grim.

"You'll see her safely back to New York?" Adam asked over her head.

"I will," the host answered. "Safe and sound. As a creature of Twilight, I cannot break my word."

This was not happening. This could not be happening.

"Don't do this." Talia clutched at Adam's sweat-dampened shirt. He smelled stale and stressed, but still so good. So

Adam. She planted her hands on his chest to hold him physically back.

He gripped her shoulders—would this be the last time he'd hold her?—and finally met her gaze.

"Talia," he said, voice gravelly, "you are an expert at running and hiding. I've left you everything I have to help you. I need you to take this chance; I'm going to give it to you regardless. I need you to run. I need you to heal. Then you track this bastard down and scream."

"Please, if you love me, don't do this," she begged. She hated the determination in his voice. Adam was impossible to stay from a decided course of action. Tears blurred her vision in frustration.

"Look at me, Talia," Adam commanded. "Look at me!"

She startled painfully. His shout felt like he'd struck her.

"Then I need you to track *me* down," he said. "I need you to scream for me. Will you do that, Talia? Will you scream for me?"

A sob of anguish broke out of her. "No." But what she was refusing she couldn't name. "No" to his choice. "No" to running. "No" to this whole goddamned nightmare. Couldn't he see that the only answer to give was "No"?

Adam's grip on her shoulders tightened just enough to move her out of his way.

She dived into his side and threw her arms around his waist to drag him down with her weight. He stumbled slightly, then regained his balance.

She pulled on shadow to blank Adam's vision. She coaxed the veils into a frenzy to bar him from reaching the demon. She summoned her will to push him back with her mind.

If the demon wanted to sic his dogs on her, so be it. She could fight wraiths. She could fight the demon and his hellhounds. And she'd damn well fight Adam if she had to.

The demon could not have him.

Adam struggled against her, his will against hers. He pried his arms away, his grip biting into her flesh.

"See how easy it is," the host observed lightly, presumably to Jacob. "She's been here perhaps ten minutes and he's broken. Watch how they fight each other."

Jacob snickered in agreement.

Blind fury rose in Talia, the likes of which she'd never felt in her life. The room darkened deeper than pitch. Her hair lifted and whipped around her as the veils layered shadow upon shadow.

She drew a deep breath of outrage and grief, and screamed.

It was a broken, pitiful noise that set a fire in her lungs.

The host laughed outright.

She tried again, pushing all the life and love she had into one sound, an extended gasp of pain and sorrow.

Still, nothing. Goddamn nothing.

"Stop this, Talia," Adam lashed. "You're only doing more damage to yourself."

The room churned with her storm of shadows, but still he managed to move forward, carrying her with him a full step toward the demon and his hateful cup.

Sobbing, she leaned into Adam's body with her shoulder, her arms reaching beyond him for something to hold on to. Reaching for something to give her leverage against his greater strength. Reaching for *anything* that would delay his insanity.

Cold steel met her palm. A frigid rod or shaft of this ship's pipes. Her fingers wrapped around it.

Power flooded up her arm and through her body in primeval recognition.

Not a shaft of pipe, then. The shaft of her father's scythe, handed father to daughter across their native shadow. Her fae inheritance, the legacy of Death.

A dark glee of demon bloodlust suffused Talia's half-breed

senses. She pushed Adam firmly back, once and for all, and turned to face the demon, the crescent moon of the scythe's blade circling over her head as a vane signals a change in the weather.

The wind was finally blowing her way.

TWENTY-ONE

ADAM stumbled back at Talia's astonishingly hard shove. The room disappeared. Without her touch, he swam in a sea of mute darkness, his sense of direction upended.

Damn stubborn woman. Couldn't she understand that this was the only way?

And damn if her newfound strength didn't make him love her even more. As if that were possible. If she could stand between him and the demon, daring the Death Collector to do his worst, then she could survive on her own. She could run, heal, and then find her way to a scream that would end this nightmare. Perhaps they'd all wake to a bright morning where anything was possible.

First, he had to get her off this ship. It didn't matter in the least what her safety cost.

"Talia!"

The darkness broke suddenly. Talia reeled back into Adam's arms, a vicious dog scraping at her corset to get to her throat.

Adam hit the beast in the head with his fist. It yowled and broke away, as the other two snarling hellhounds rounded Talia's side.

A glint of elongated steel struck down like a flash of lighting, and the first dog dissolved into a dense cloud of black smoke. The other dogs jumped to retreat in a braced crouch, ears pinned and teeth bared.

"Call off your dogs!" Adam glanced at the door.

The demon and his host were gone, the door to the cell swinging ajar. The goblet full of demon vomit rolled on the floor on its side, smearing the goo in a half circle at the threshold. Adam darted a glance to Jacob, whose face had lost all of its previous mirth. He, like the dogs, was braced to fight or flee, his eyes trained on Talia, his body twitching to anticipate her next move.

Talia.

Adam's gaze traveled up the staff of the lowered weapon to Talia's grip. He swallowed hard and looked her in the face.

Her already pale skin was shining alabaster, her eyes churning with deep shadow and rimmed with smudged makeup that accentuated her fae bone structure. Off her shoulders her white hair lifted, crackling with energy as a cloak of translucent veils fell, rippling layer upon layer, to hazy nothing at its edges. Her corset was deeply scored, but no red soaked through. Her bosom heaved as she lifted the scythe again.

Banshee. Beauty. And, well, badass. He always knew she had it in her.

Talia lifted the staff and brought the scythe down again in a glittering arc. The hellhounds danced out of reach, growling deep in their throats and barking dire threats.

Where she'd gotten the weapon, Adam could only guess. It was way past time that the Other side helped them out. But he wasn't complaining, not if the scythe belonged to who he thought it belonged. No—with a fae weapon in the hands of a fae fighter, Adam wasn't complaining at all. He could work with this. Elated relief, or blood loss, made him near giddy.

Except Talia's position was too open, unguarded. Adam grabbed the chair by its back and heaved it up as Jacob darted forward to seize the advantage. A chair leg went through Jacob's eye socket and cracked his skull. Jacob fell back against the far wall in a slump.

The movement was a sharp stab in Adam's gut where Jacob had used him as a pincushion. Adam pressed a hand to the wound. Blood seeped through his closed fingers.

Damn it. Wraiths moved too fast, and the ship had to be chock-full of them.

He'd been soft at Segue about self-defense. No longer. He was going to have to teach Talia to watch her sight lines. If they got out of here alive, his woman was in for some serious instruction. Basic self-defense would not be enough. She'd need combat training. And he'd have to find a specialist who worked with blades, a swordsman of sorts, most likely. His banshee would need the best.

"Spread your grip on the shaft," Adam commanded, keeping his gaze fixed on Jacob and the hellhounds. "You'll have better control. And don't lock your knees. Stay on the balls of your feet."

The hellhounds leaned into a round of ferocious barking, the echo bouncing in a clamor off the room's metal walls.

Jacob stirred across the room. Damn it. Wraiths healed too fast, too.

The scythe flashed as Talia suddenly lunged. The hellhounds' shouts were cut into sharp squeaks as they lifted into dark, sulfurous smoke.

The blade arced up again and Talia paced forward, as if she could read Adam's mind.

Go. Go. Go. His heart thumped hard, pounding in time with his internal chant.

The blade swept down in a deep threshing movement.

Talia took Jacob where he lay in a heap on the room's floor, his head rolling to a light tap against the wall. His body gasped and settled as if he'd already been long dead. The smell confirmed it.

And just like that Adam's promise was fulfilled. An old tightness in his chest, one that had robbed him of air for six years too long, released. The rush that followed made his eyes water with slightly euphoric realization: He'd seen to his brother, what was left of him anyway. And now he was free. Adam didn't know how he could ever thank Talia enough, but he would try. Over and over again, as necessary.

Talia turned. "Are you okay?"

The wrinkle between her brows told him she was worried. She bit her bottom lip to deep red. If they got off this ship alive, he'd start thanking her by kissing that lip first. The one that took all the punishment for her nerves.

"Never better." Bleeding from his belly in a ship full of wraiths, captained by the demon Death Collector, and it was the absolute truth.

Her teeth scraped her lip again as she smiled back at him.

Yeah, that bottom lip had to be first, and then maybe the delightful dip of her cleavage. Those goths were definitely onto something with their corsets.

"Let's go finish this, then," Talia said, her humor fading from her face. She gripped her staff with one hand and held out her other to him.

As Adam took hold, he felt her pull on the shadows between the mortal world and the Other beyond the veils, the passage called death. Dark magic infused her until every cell gleamed potent in the shifting gloom. Never had she straddled that boundary more completely than she did now.

He stepped to the door and carefully checked the narrow gray corridor. It was broken by connecting doors, but otherwise empty.

"Watch your step," he said, gesturing to the demon vomit.

Now he wanted to stay as far away from the stuff as he could. He'd have to thank her for that, too. Deeply and repeatedly.

They moved down the hallway. The rhythmic pounding of feet from elsewhere filtered to their position, but they met no resistance. A steep stair—almost a ladder—led to the deck above. Talia ascended first, leaving him in pitch blackness. He climbed up after. A cool hand on his face brought the ship back into focus.

Adam held her in the shadowed cabin, arms around her cinched waist, considering their next move.

"If the demon is smart, he'll have positioned the wraiths to the sides of the door, to pick us off as soon as we try to exit. The ship probably has a communication center. I'd radio for help, but I've no one left to call. I'm afraid it's just you and me." It was hard to believe—all the resources he'd labored to amass were either destroyed or scattered.

Adam felt Talia's body shake as she chuckled.

"I'm not afraid anymore," she whispered. "I say we go through the door. My father's scythe has a long reach. Longer than I thought possible. It'll be enough."

"You sure?"

"Yep." Talia's touch trailed out of the embrace to find his hand once again. She squeezed, ready.

Talia braced as Adam shifted to unlatch the door and kick it open; then she blew a storm of darkness onto the deck. Beyond, the deafening *chop-chop* of a helicopter signaled the Death Collector's escape route, but the gusting air was nothing to the gale of her shadow.

Adam loosed her hand, so she could grip her scythe firmly. She wasn't about to leave him in the dark, so she pushed the veils away until the world lay in turbulent gray.

A wraith darted inside the cabin door and was cut in half

for his stupidity. The blade cleaved with only the slightest resistance, enough to gain her the satisfaction of the kill without slowing her. A second wraith scurried back as she and Adam emerged onto the deck. Dozens more crowded the open-air surface.

All of them backed away from her. It was a heady sensation—the hunted finally becoming the hunter. And while the scythe was too large for her frame, the humming energy that charged her senses felt just right.

Beyond the press of wraiths, the demon and his host were just climbing the stairs of the helipad. In only moments, they would be safely inside and take to the sky. The scythe's reach was long, but not that long.

Talia's fae senses screamed the time was now. She drove into the crowd of wraiths, swinging. Adam swore coarsely behind her, but she pressed forward.

She brought down the blade and caught a wraith at the knees. The strike was enough to collapse the rest of him, mouth gaping as he was sundered from life.

"Your left!" Adam's tone was deep and angry.

Talia whirled. Two wraiths charged her, both baring inhuman teeth. She panicked. Adam blurred in her side vision, kicking one in the belly. She swung at the other, and he fell; then she pivoted to swipe at the first. She cut his monstrous gape right off his face.

Adam's arm came roughly around her waist as he pulled her suddenly back. The blade sliced through the air, caught a third wraith at his shoulder, and sent him spinning into death.

Chest heaving, Talia darted a glance right and left, looking for the next to attack. But the wraiths were backing away.

"They're jumping ship," Adam said into her ear.

Talia's gaze flew to the edge where, indeed, a wraith leaped over the side. It made sense: The wraiths might drown, but they couldn't die. Talia wouldn't be able to reach them beneath the waves without drowning herself, and she was after hooking a much bigger fish.

"To me!" the host called. He hadn't moved from the top step of the helipad.

The demon's call went unacknowledged as his army deserted him. That made sense, too: Anyone who chose the monstrous existence of a wraith was fundamentally selfish to begin with. They wouldn't stay to fight for the demon if it cost them their lives, the very thing they had traded their humanity to sustain.

Talia stalked across the clearing deck to the stairs. The helicopter was ready; why wasn't the demon and his host aboard, safe?

She looked closely for signs of subterfuge.

The host was corpse pale, expression lined with stress.

"Kill us quick, before it takes me completely," the man said, gasping in a human voice. His white-knuckled grip on the railing trembled as the demon snake poured itself into his ear. The host's jaundiced face contracted into a rictus of pain, his eyes wide-open, sightless, and horrified. Thick tar coated the inside of his mouth and bled from his nose.

Talia understood. The host, lesson learned, was making one last choice. Withstand the demon's rape of his body, wait for the scythe, and be freed.

"Half-breed . . ." the demon said, voice pitched to a feral growl, in command of the host's mouth again.

Sharp, sweet power rose within her as Talia raised the scythe.

". . . whore's get . . ." The host, overcome, lost his battle and released the railing to scramble, crawling, toward the waiting helicopter.

The power ached beautifully in her muscles and tingled

to her fingertips. Fantasies of death played in her mind. Her blood roared to stain the ship's deck with a smear of demon.

She stalked the demon-host abomination, Adam at her back. There was no way the demon could escape. No place to hide and no time.

Talia gathered the force of her scream, and channeled it into a great, slashing swing.

The blade sang through the air and cut the abomination in half. Talia trembled on the edge of rapture with the thrill of the kill.

The man whimpered into death as the demon split, its sinuous form condensing into a dark tongue of shadow before losing all cohesion, just like his hellhounds.

Dead.

For a moment, Talia couldn't breathe. She didn't want to anyway near the dispersing black gases.

Then the cloud of demon reek convulsed.

Talia jumped back and bumped into Adam. His strong arm circled her waist protectively.

Out of the stagnant black cloud, a dusky hand whipped out, midair. The hand jerked just as suddenly back into oblivion. Before Talia could take another breath, the arm again clawed through the center of darkest shadow, as if fighting against an unseen force.

Talia's heart seized. Another demon? Her hands tightened on the shaft of the scythe. She could do this. Her muscles coiled to strike, waiting for the moment the being emerged.

"Be ready," Adam murmured. She felt his body tense at her back.

She pulled on shadow, the source of her power. Pulled hard until the scythe glowed overhead amid layers of darkness. Pulled until . . . the being himself emerged out of his wild prison and into the world.

Talia shook with shock and recognition.

The being fell to the deck in a cascade of seething shadow-cloak and gleaming long black hair. When he straightened, his tilted eyes coming to rest on her, there could be no doubt whatsoever. Death was her father.

They regarded each other for a long moment, the intent of his gaze rippling the surrounding veils.

Talia raised her chin, heart hammering, and returned his scrutiny.

Her father had a face like a dark angel, ageless with cruel compassion. His body appeared strong and healthy, though shadows of death circled—the very same shadows that twined about her. His stillness had grace, yet she knew his strike was brutally fast, the results a mess of pain and hurt.

No wonder people stayed away from her.

"You have your mother's face," he said at last. His voice was dark velvet, brushing over her like a caress.

Talia's heart leaped with emotion. She had no words.

But Adam did. "Is it over?"

Shadowman's gaze slid to Adam, leaving her bereft. "Chaos is back where it belongs."

Her father inclined his head again to her. The tide of shadows lapped strongly at her body, as if to draw her into its sea. Through its dense waves she could feel the solid press of Adam's body, and deeper to the core of his emotion.

"How did this happen in the first place?" Adam's tone was hard, demanding. The pain of his loss was so acute, Talia wondered that he didn't shake his fist in Death's face. She thought of her own mother, taken at her birth, Aunt Maggie, Melanie, Patty, Custo. Death everywhere.

Shadowman canted his head, but not in contrition. "I parted the veils between life and death when I had no call to do so. Chaos escaped and took root in the mortal world."

"You—? Why?" Adam's voice was coarse with strain.

"I loved a woman."

"Was it worth it?" Adam mocked Death.

Shadowman's gaze shifted to Adam again. "Is Talia worth it?"

Adam's body went rigid behind her, anger—and something else—surging within him.

Talia felt herself grow old with a hideous knowledge that blotted everything else out. Shadowman and her mother—the fairy tale—ending in a scourge.

"All those people died because of me?" Her broken whisper carried clearly across the veils. The scythe clattered to the deck. If Adam weren't behind her, she might have fallen with it.

"Did you kill them?" Death's pretty face was impassive.

"No, but—"

Shadowman raised a hand. "Then, no. The demon escaped to the world because of *me*. I should have been the one to face him, but I was bound by my own transgression."

"All those lives lost because . . ." Talia couldn't finish the sentence. She swallowed the words. How could Adam love her now? How could he love her when the same act that brought her into the world destroyed his family?

Talia straightened slightly, pulling her weight from Adam's body with a step forward so that she couldn't feel him anymore. Shadow succored her.

"The demon's children made their own choices. Not even chaos could compel them to join him without their consent. Their actions are theirs and theirs alone."

"And the ones they fed on?" There was no mistaking the bitterness in Adam's voice.

"Crossed. They are where they belong."

"And the wraiths that got away?" Adam shot back.

"Must be sundered as well, the souls within them freed."

Talia drew the shadows more tightly around her, willing its chill folds to freeze the aching part of her into numbness.

"Are you ready, then?" Shadowman asked her. Of course, he noticed her separation from Adam and interpreted it correctly.

Adam reached for her and met only shadow. "What do you mean?"

"I mean to take my daughter home."

The darkness broke into vibrant colors the likes of which Talia had only seen in snatches of dreams, and yet, their hues were familiar. Music filled the air, drowning out the noise on deck. She heard a song at once sweet and sorrowful, sung in a round unending.

"What? You can't have her." Adam may as well have been shouting at the wind.

"For your unparalleled aid," Shadowman continued, "I grant you the immortality that these others sought, but without their sharp hunger."

"You mean without Talia," Adam corrected. "No. You hear me. NO."

"Talia is fae, and as such, belongs in Shadow."

"She is half fae, half mortal, and *all* mine."

Talia turned at Adam's declaration. From her dark vantage she regarded him. Adam was distinctly different than she—in shadow that fact was very clear. He was clay, animated by the internal core of his will. And just then his will burned bright enough to force her fae eyes to squint. Bright enough to quell the shadow around her. Bright enough to find and grip her hand.

Through their crossed palms a current of energy flowed—an anchor, a lifeline, a connection that did not discriminate between fae and mortal. She was his and he was hers.

And he wasn't letting her go.

The intensity of his vow made clear that he didn't hold

her accountable for the hurts to his family. On the contrary, Talia understood his deep trust, a soul recognition, that superseded what they'd endured. It was more than enough.

"Whatever moments you hope to steal now, your union cannot last." Shadowman's voice carried the weight of personal experience. "The time will come when Talia must bide in Twilight and you must pass beyond."

Adam pulled her into his embrace and locked his arms around her. He was flesh and bone and fragile mortality, but she never felt safer in her life.

"You breached a barrier once; when the time comes, you watch us do it," Adam said.

"I am Death, and I know it cannot be done."

"I am alive, and I know it can. We'll find the way."

"I will go when he goes," Talia said, "*where* he goes."

Shadowman's gaze rested on Talia, sadly. He stooped like a lonely old man to lift his scythe. It seemed heavy in his hand's grasp. "Call, and I will come."

A twist of shadow and her father was gone. The welcome of Twilight evaporated into glittery black ocean spray as the deck of the ship rocked with the roaring rhythm of the helicopter's propellers.

She'd see her father again, probably soon. The demon might be dead, but thousands of wraiths still skulked the earth. Her work, and his, remained unfinished.

"You know I'm not done with all this," she said to Adam's chest. And probably would never be done.

"Then neither am I," he answered.

Adam's embrace transformed from possessive to . . . possession. He buried his face in the curve of her neck, while he fitted himself intimately to her. Relief, determination, hope, and love coursed out of him. So much, and with shattering intensity. She could feel like this forever.

But they were on a stinking boat, and he was hurt and

bleeding. The wind from the helicopter's propellers was making wild with her hair.

Talia pulled against his hold to lift his shirt and examine the wound. The raw pucker of flesh was oozing blood. The fighting must have hurt terribly. She needed something to bind it with, to stop the flow until they could find help.

"Take off your shirt," she said. It was already wet and sticky with blood, but it would have to do.

His gaze didn't leave her as he peeled it off, disregarding how the movement made his side bleed more. He was pale and panting, but the look in his eyes warmed her to her bones. She ripped down one of the side seams of the shirt to make a bandage. Then ripped again to make two long, semisodden strips.

"Do you have a preference?" Adam said. His rough knuckles brushed her cheek softly, and she caught a hint of gathering intent within him.

She glanced up from her work. His left cheekbone was swelling. "For what?"

"Our trip. The one I promised you. Anywhere in the world. You name it." Poor man could barely form a sentence and was already planning the next thing.

Talia would have rolled her eyes, but she could feel how serious he was. "Somewhere restful," she answered. *Somewhere you can heal.*

"Not too restful."

She knotted the fabric over his belly, which tensed, muscles firming as his arms went around her again. "Somewhere quiet."

He kissed her, deep and dark, too short for satisfaction, but just enough to prove again where she belonged. "Don't worry about it," he said. "I'll handle everything."

The abused man had half his weight on her shoulders, but

she wasn't going to point it out. His mouth skimmed along her jawline.

"I don't suppose you know how to fly a helicopter?" Talia asked the sky as Adam dipped to her neck. Her throat was suddenly feeling much, much better.

"Yeah." He found her earlobe.

"And do you have a good idea where we can find medical assistance?" A hand rounded her breast, doubling her heart rate.

He grunted.

"It's just that, though I am agreeable to your . . . uh . . . present course of action . . ." His other hand slid over her ass.

"We should pursue a . . . uh . . . strategy of doctor first, life-affirming acts later."

He pulled back, swaying on his feet. "Promise?"

Talia looked him in the eyes. "Promise."

EPILOGUE

SHADOWMAN stands in a darkened room at the bedside of a grandfather. The air is sweet with tobacco. Except for a clock's tick, the house is still, soft snow falling outside the window to insulate the home from sound. Down the hall, a woman sleeps in the hollow of her husband's body. Farther still, a nursery. In one house, three generations. Soon to be two.

The old man's heart flutters. The veil thins for his cross. Such is the way of the three worlds: each belongs in its place, Earth, Shadow, and Heaven.

It is a folly of pain to disregard the boundary. Shadowman lives this truth, as will his daughter. Time is a miser to the fae, and the penalty for stealing is great.

The heart stills. The veil parts.

A family in this house. The glimmering tie that binds them together heart by heart cannot be severed, not even with his fell blade, not even by the great distance from this house to the shores of Heaven. Though the patriarch will cross, he will still be tethered to the generations. And thus is so, a chain through time, forged by love.

Love.

Kathleen. Talia. And Talia's strong, misguided man, Adam. He dares to scorn the laws that govern the borders between the worlds. So stubborn. So ignorant. So mortal. Talia has chosen a dreamer.

They will learn.

Love is not a magic the fae can wield. Love will not obey a fae heart.

Except perhaps, that once when Talia reached across Shadow and found the weapon best suited to her need. That once, love prevailed.

The staff of the scythe chills in Shadowman's hand. A great soul lifts out of the old man's body. Shadowman turns to guide him through the fae forest of Twilight. The old man lingers, his attention drawn on the slumbering forms in the rooms beyond.

"They're so beautiful," the old man says, his ageless eyes shining with awe.

"Yes." But Shadowman is thinking of Talia and Kathleen.

"I will see them again." Conviction underscores the man's words and the soul-string at his heart glows.

Yes. Shadowman borrows the old man's confidence.

If Talia can breach Twilight for Adam, perhaps Death can breach Heaven, too.

The old man steps into the slender boat. "I am ready."

Through the dark forest and across the water. A thought brings Shadowman to the shores of Heaven. He has made this journey times without number. The isle is encircled by a shimmering wall of light. Its rippling, translucent colors burn away his cloak of veils and buffet his naked skin. It has always been so.

The old man steps out of the boat. "Thank you," he says, but his gaze is drawn to Heaven, waves of rapture leaving a trail of golden light as he approaches the wall. He lifts a hand to touch the surface. A step, a spark, and he is drawn within. From one home, to another.

On the other side—*what?* Kathleen.

Dark winds lift Shadowman off the waters that lap the shoreline.

"Kathleen," he calls, his voice a groan.

There is magic in names. Can she hear him?

"Kathleen," he calls again, louder.

Behind him, the denizens of Twilight murmur.

"KATHLEEN," he cries. His anguish batters the shining wall, shifting the starstruck colors from rose and lapis to deep purple and bloody magenta, but it remains inviolable.

Shadowman drops his scythe in the waters. He'll scream forever, if need be, until the day the walls tumble into the ocean.

"Hey, you."

Shadowman's attention whips to the top of the wall some distance down the shoreline to his left. An angel is perched on the edge—fair hair, fair-eyed, skin a soft café. A recent crossing.

"Trade you," Custo says.

Shadowman has no words.

"You want in or don't you? Heaven's no place for me, and I'm not hanging around until they figure it out." The angel glances over his shoulder.

The murmurs of Twilight grow louder, sharper, but Shadowman pays them no mind. Not anymore. They've already done their worst.

"I do," Shadowman says.

Custo flashes a grin. "Meet me at the wall."

Shadowman sets foot on the sandy shore, each grain a diamond white sparkle. He peers into the wall of colors and a face appears. Custo's. Custo raises a hand, and Shadowman mirrors him. They reach for each other across the brink. A touch, a spark . . .

Kathleen, I come.

Go deeper into the Otherworld . . .

SHADOW FALL
by
ERIN KELLISON

(Available July 27, 2010)

Heaven's gate cracked open.

Without a backward glance, Custo set off at a run across the beach, then dived into the channel. Something sinuous grazed his leg as he reached Shadowman's slender gray boat.

The shadow of a large creature—not a fish—broke the surface nearby. A mermaid, if he had to put a name to it, with greenish skin that went blue over defined cheekbones, forming the features of a water goddess. Her hair twisted in thick, serpentine pieces like Medusa's, and her black eyes blinked rapidly, regarding him. She lay on her back so that the water lapped her full, tight breasts.

Oh, sweet beauty. His mind clouded, Adam and Segue and Earth receding from Custo's consciousness. Adam would understand . . .

The mermaid smiled and teased one of her nipples.

A wave of desire flowed over him, painfully gathering at his groin. His sudden need washed away everything except the mermaid's glorious undulating body. His gaze roved over her slick form, looking for a place to plug himself in and drown in ecstasy. Now that would be a good death!

A tremendous bellow snapped his attention again to the great wall. Shadowman's low-pitched shout of rage shook the sandy shores of Heaven like an earthquake, the grains settling into fine, tiered ripples.

Uh oh.

The water rose with Shadowman's anger, the boat perching precariously on a wave as the water retracted away from the forest's shore with a great sucking sound.

The mermaid screeched and bared pointy piranha teeth before diving into the choppy waves.

Custo reared back—not the kind of kiss he'd been looking for.

A tsunami was building, the waters swelling beneath the boat. Custo looked for an oar. Nothing. An oar wouldn't save him anyway. He sat in the boat's bottom and gripped the sides.

With a sudden rush, the boat was propelled toward the Shadowlands. He sailed through the air like a spear until the water hit the tree line and he lost his hold, tossed into the grip of an oak. He clung to the branches as the water tumbled beneath him. The boat careened away, shattered nearby, and showered him with the splinters of Shadowman's bitter disappointment.

Custo shook his head clear, the mermaid's seduction receding with the water. She had utterly enslaved his mind, subsuming his purpose to her will. If her power over him was any indication, the Shadowlands was one seriously dangerous place.

Mortality had to be on the other side of the forest, didn't it? Through the deep trees and a bright crossing, Earth would just have to accommodate this no-name bastard again. Then Segue and the message for Adam. After that, he had no idea.

The damp sent a chill running over his body, which he ignored as he moved deeper into the forest. There was no path, only shadow layered with black trunks, illuminated by a soft glow that had no discernable source. A woodsy smell predominated, not that he could ever guess the variety of the tree, nor care to. The rich earth below was layered with dead growth and overrun with rambling tree roots.

He was much better suited to civilization. Give him a fight in an alley any day over a walk in the woods.

He stretched his mind again, but that sense had grown dumb in the forest. He couldn't tell what was ahead or behind, not for sure. But there had to be a way to get back. The Segue Institute had documented ghosts. Segue was simply going to have to find room for one more haunt.

A small creature skittered through the trees, something like a rabbit. It stopped on its haunches and craned its head to regard him with too-human eyes. Strange. The animal perked up its head, as if sensing danger, and bounded off again.

Custo listened as well, but he heard only the shift and sigh of the trees. An occasional crack. An eerie whine.

No. Not a whine. Sad, slow violins.

He turned around, his gaze searching the trees. Ahead, a scrap of white light glowed, partially obscured by black trunks. The light dimmed and then grew again.

He moved forward to investigate and discovered a clearing surrounded by wicked, wintry trees. In the center of the clearing, a woman danced. She was made of light, her figure slight, long and waifish, her skin pale and glistening. Her dark hair was pulled into a knot at the back of her head, like a fairy or a ballerina. Likewise, she floated on tiptoe and defied gravity with the stretch and arch of her body. The haunting music was part of her, yet it scored him.

More faerie magic? He didn't care.

She kept her eyes downcast for the most part, so terribly sad, but when she raised her face to twirl, shining like hope, he knew he would never be the same.

She had to be his. He knew it with every broken fiber of his being.

Dorchester Publishing is proud to present

⊰ PUBLISHER'S PLEDGE ⊱

We GUARANTEE this book!

We are so confident that you will enjoy this book that we are offering a 100% money-back guarantee.

If you are not satisfied with this novel, Dorchester Publishing Company, Inc. will refund your money! Simply return the book for a full refund.

To be eligible, the book must be returned by 8/29/2010, along with a copy of the receipt, your address, and a brief explanation of why you are returning the book, to the address listed below.

We will send you a check for the purchase price and sales tax of the book within 4-6 weeks.

Publishers Pledge Reads
Dorchester Publishing Company
11 West Avenue, Ste 103
Wayne, PA 19087

Offer ends 8/29/2010.